ALSO BY MEG M. ROBINSON

A FURY'S HEART

IMMORTAL LOVE BOOK 2

MEG M. ROBINSON

ARCANE CROW PUBLISHING

CHAPTER I

Night had fallen hours ago and brought with it a soft chill in the air. Two men sat in a clearing in the woods of northern Washington, but the trees did little to shield them from the cold breeze that gently flowed over them. Nor did the branches above them block the light from the moon that had been full only a week before.

The men didn't notice the chill, or not much in any case. They were too busy complaining about the task which brought them to this remote part of the state.

"With as often as something actually comes through these portals, you'd think they'd only send one person to suffer the watch," the taller of the two, David, said, as he looked over the worn cards in his hand. He'd been babysitting portals for a century and had gone through quite a few decks of cards in that time. They could only be shuffled so many times before they simply fell apart.

"Yeah, but think of how fucking boring it'd be to be out here for hours by yourself," Lamar pointed out with a smirk. "I bid five," he added as an afterthought.

"Call." Poker was the only way they could really entertain themselves as they kept watch. It had its downsides, playing with only two people, but the other alternatives they'd tried had been worse. Dice were all too easy to lose in the dark, and that was if they had a decent place to roll them. The same went for essentially any other type of game. Playing on their phones was a way to pass the time, but it did tend to destroy night vision. Not to mention the electronics didn't do well in the elements, and having a dry, comfortable watch was a rarity. And anything else tended to be too much of a distraction, which they couldn't allow. Their job, however tedious, was too important.

The Venatoribus Noctu had to ensure no demons escaped to Earth, which was why Lamar and David were currently killing time at an hour to midnight when they'd rather be doing anything else.

Lamar smirked and laid his cards on the fallen log that rested between them and served as a makeshift table. "Queen high straight," he said proudly. When David cursed, proving his hand couldn't beat that, he grinned. "So, how much do you owe me now?"

"That makes twelve thousand tonight," David grumbled. "Damn good thing we never play for actual money."

"Nah. You win plenty. We're probably about even," Lamar said as he gathered up the cards to shuffle for a new hand. While the cards moved neatly in his expert hands, he glanced out into the center of the clearing. "You ever wish that one of these watches wouldn't be a dud?"

David followed his gaze and shrugged. "Sometimes. Especially when the damn things stay open for hours. Though just because something comes through doesn't mean it'll do much to distract us. Didn't one of the guys say they saw a freaking bunny hop through one? Okay, so it was pink, but still, just a rabbit."

"Yeah, that's a good point," Lamar said with a sigh. "Maybe we'll get lucky and this one will just be a quick open and close thing so we can be home by midnight," Lamar added hopefully.

His companion snorted. "Like we'd get so lucky? Personally, I'm just hoping that it doesn't start raining while we're out here. Remember that time about thirty years ago when a portal decided to open right in the middle of a record rainfall and we damn near had to wait in a boat?"

"I'd tried to forget," Lamar said blandly before he started to deal another game of five-card draw, whistling as he did.

Off to the side, there was a light shimmer in the air, accompanied by the faintest tingle of magic as the portal opened.

Used to it and positive nothing would happen, they didn't do more than give it a quick glance. Lamar had to do a double-take though, when he caught movement out of the corner of his eye. His second look had the cards slipping from his fingers.

In all the years they'd watched portals, they'd seen something come out of one precisely twice, and one of them had only released a single, minor demon, easily dispatched. The other had taken a little more effort, but still not much. So to have anything come through was unexpected.

A figure wearing a hooded cloaked ran out of the portal and stopped abruptly when it saw the two witches sitting there, shocked. "Run!" it shouted, the voice decidedly feminine and extremely urgent. She wasted no time in taking her own advice and darted to the left and into the woods before Lamar had time to do more than stand.

She'd only just disappeared into the blackness when more figures came through the portal. Lamar mentally cursed when half a dozen demons arrived, all armed, all pissed.

"Trouble at the portal! Demons!" Lamar mentally shouted across the hundreds of miles that separated him from Marco, the head of the Venatoribus Noctu.

The demons looked eager for a fight the moment they saw the two Hunters, but it was Lamar who began it. He quickly gathered his magic and threw a fireball at the group as he tried to run for cover. Though it hit, and he heard the hard sound of a body hitting the ground, he knew they were still outnumbered.

Why hadn't the seers foreseen this?

David wasn't as lucky. He got off a shot of pale blue magic, but didn't even have time to get to his feet before one of the demons relieved him of his head with a single stroke of a wicked looking sword.

"Kill the other one quickly," snapped one of the demons. He got a snarl of protest in response, but the other demons didn't seem inclined to chance angering him. Two of them came at Lamar, circling around him from opposite sides. Not willing to go down without a fight, he shoved a hand full of power at the one to his right, knocking the hulking, green-skinned figure back several feet and onto his back. Shifting, he blasted the other figure over and over again with flames before he realized they weren't affecting the demon. That could only mean one thing—it was a fire demon.

Before he could switch tactics, the demon reached him and picked him up as though he were a toy. The demon slammed him against the tree until Lamar's eyes slipped closed and his body went limp. Only then was he dropped, where he landed hard on his side. The green-skinned demon recovered and added a sharp kick to the fallen man's ribs before they turned back to their leader.

Thinking both their opponents dead, the demons searched the clearing until they found the tracks the woman had left. They rushed off in search of the prey that had momentarily eluded them.

But the Arcane were tougher than that, especially those who spent their life fighting demons. Struggling to remain conscious, though his head pounded and blood poured down his face, Lamar reached out to Marco again. *"David...dead..."* It was all he managed before blackness took him.

The leader of the Hunters appeared only moments later, a knife already in his hand, the other held ready for a less physical battle. He looked prepared for either one. Not just ready, but *greedy* for it. One of his men had been killed, another severely injured, and he was pissed.

Marco was a tall man at six four, and a lifetime of honing himself to withstand the rigors of combat—both mystical and physical—had left him with a muscular body that performed precisely as he wanted it to. Though he'd never been in any type of army—unless the Hunters were included—he sported a military cut for his black hair. He had eyes that could be a warm chocolate color when he was relaxed, but angry as he was, they were a cold color that was nearly as dark as his hair.

Those eyes quickly took in the scene. The fallen demon, the state of David's body, the badly injured Lamar.

Marco gave himself only a second to register it. He couldn't take time to dwell on David's death, or to mourn. That would come later. For now, he had to ensure there weren't further casualties. He knelt by Lamar, and with his limited knowledge of healing, he took care of enough of the injuries to stabilize the witch and help him regain consciousness. Regret that the man would be in pain took a back seat to the fact that they had little time to waste. If demons powerful enough to do this to two trained Hunters were on the loose, then there was no telling how many they'd hurt if they weren't found immediately.

Lamar came to with a groan of pain and struggled to open his eyes.

"Don't try to talk. Think to me what happened," Marco said gently, his big, scarred hands carefully wiping blood from the smaller man's face.

Even communicating telepathically, Lamar's voice was thin, but it was enough.

"One came through first. A woman. Told us to run. She did, before six more came through. Got one. Sure I got one. Then they...they killed David." His eyes squeezed shut, but not before a single tear escaped at the thought of his oldest friend, now laying dead only feet from where he lay. *"They got me, and left."* He sighed. *"Tired now..."*

"I know. I've already called in others, and a healer. We'll take care of you, Lamar. You just rest," Marco murmured, even as Lamar's body went limp as he slipped back into unconsciousness. For now, it was probably a blessing.

He rose when he felt others teleport in. All gentleness was gone when he turned toward them.

Six men and two women stood before him, all exceptionally well trained. Most were witches, though one of the men was a water elemental, another a vampire. They were all equally deadly. He saw the same rage he felt move over their faces as they saw the body of their fallen comrade.

"You and you, stay here. Wait for the healer and take care of Lamar. The rest of you, come with me." He followed the tracks in the dirt to the edge of the clearing, his steps long and full of purpose. "We have demons to kill," he said quietly.

Samara ran as fast as her legs could carry her because she ran for her life. She knew the demons weren't far behind her. She was probably only a minute or two ahead of them, possibly three, if the witches at the portal had put up a good fight. Her next step faltered as remorse lanced through her. Those men didn't deserve to die, not just for being in the wrong place at the wrong time. Maybe they had taken her advice and run, though she doubted it. If only she'd been able to help them...But she needed to put distance between her and the portal. It was vital.

Luckily, she knew the demons who followed her didn't have a true tracker with them, and that might just save her, even if it didn't help the witches any.

She glanced upward and saw that the moon, despite being more than half full, was now hidden by clouds. That gave her more options.

Fingers worked open the clasp of her cloak and she shed it without pausing, letting it flutter to the ground behind her. A shift of her shoulders freed her wings from the prison of her body. Normally, they hid magically within her back so she looked like any other person, but now the large wings spread outward, black feathers gleaming almost purple in the faint moonlight. They swept downward, the powerful stroke propelling her into the air. She didn't fly high, but skimmed the treetops so she wouldn't be easily seen from below. Or above, for that matter. And now she would leave no tracks and she could move much more swiftly than she ever could on foot.

Miles passed quickly beneath her before she started getting tired. At home, there wasn't often the opportunity for her to stretch her wings, and they already ached at being used so well. She glanced below her, but saw no signs of pursuit, either witch or demon, and let out a shaky breath at the reprieve. Perhaps she could take just a few minutes to rest her wings.

After another mile, she spotted a small cabin, mostly hidden by the tops of the trees. She carefully circled down and landed in what passed for a yard in front of it. It looked cozy, and it was obvious that someone lived here, because it was in good repair.

Cautious, she tucked her wings in against her body, but didn't put them away in case she needed to make a quick escape. She crept toward the cabin and peeked inside the window, but she saw no one. She circled around, glancing in the other windows, but still saw no sign that anyone was inside. When she returned to the front of the house, she checked the door and almost shouted with relief when she found it unlocked. She could have broken in, but that would leave a sign someone had been here, and she wanted to leave as little behind as possible.

Years of vigilance had her easing the door open and stepping silently inside. After all, just because she hadn't seen anyone, that didn't mean no one was here. She closed the door, then stood absolutely still, paying attention to all her senses for any sign of life. When she sensed nothing, her shoulders sagged with relief. She let her wings hide within her body once more and moved around the house.

Hopefully, the demons chasing her had gone in another direction, especially if they'd found her cloak, so it was probably safe for her to rest here for a little while.

She didn't bother to try to find a light of any sort as her night vision was sufficient to allow her to see clearly. It did not, however, explain the purpose of some of the odd things she found. There were several box-like contraptions, some small, some big, that she didn't dare open, though they all had handles on them. She came to a deep basin of metal and frowned at it before she absently gave the knob above it a curious poke with a finger. When water started running, she was surprised for a moment before she bent her head to greedily drink the cool liquid. It soothed her parched throat and partially helped to fill a belly that had been empty for more than a day. When she was done, she fiddled with the knob again until the water stopped flowing, pleased that she'd figured it out.

Searching the cabinets rewarded her with a loaf of bread, though the wrapping that surrounded it baffled her. She drew one of her knives and cut through it to get to the soft food inside. Once the knife was sheathed, she pulled out a slice and started to eat as she wandered through the rest of the cabin.

So much of what she saw was alien, and unlike the sink, she didn't have any idea what they were for. Nor did it really matter, either. She wouldn't be here long enough to need to decipher their uses. But it was an intriguing dwelling and nothing like she was used to. She liked it.

When she came across the bedroom and saw the large, heavy bed covered with a thick comforter, her fatigue rushed up, threatening to consume her. She'd been running for so long, even before she'd found the portal.

The bread was laid on the table beside the bed and immediately forgotten as she climbed onto the giving mattress. She'd just rest for a minute. Just a minute, then she'd leave and put some more distance between herself and the ones hunting her.

She curled up on her side, savoring the softness of the pillow beneath her head. She sighed once, and by the time the sound ended, she was asleep.

CHAPTER 2

Wade was exhausted. The rogue shifter he'd been tracking had certainly not wanted to be found and had led Wade on a merry chase through seven states. But Wade took pride in always finding his quarry, so the job was done and the world was a little safer without the feral, homicidal bear in the world.

All he wanted now was an hour long shower and at least twelve hours in bed.

When he pulled up to his cabin, his weary mind thought it was the most beautiful thing he'd ever seen. Even playing treasure hunter with Julian a few months back hadn't left him this tired, and he'd nearly died then. His movements were slow as he climbed out of his SUV, limbs too leaden to move with any speed. Yet when he heard someone approaching, quickly, from the woods, he surprised himself by whirling and dropping into a crouch while simultaneously drawing one of his knives. He wouldn't have thought he could move like that in his current state, but decades of conditioning his body had him reacting before he had time to even think.

He was further surprised when he recognized one of the people emerging from the woods. "Marco?" he called as he straightened.

"What the hell are you doing here this late? And with friends?" he asked, fatigue making his voice more growl than anything else.

"Hunting demons," Marco answered before looking to the three Hunters with him. "Had a portal open about an hour away by foot, and seven demons came through. Six left the site." He turned back to Wade. "Have you seen anything?"

Wade shook his head. "Haven't seen a damn thing." He frowned. "What about the men guarding the portal?" If seven had come through but only six left it, then that meant there had been a fight.

Marco's mouth thinned and he curtly shook his head. "David's dead. Lamar will be okay. Physically, at least."

"Damn. I really liked David," Wade murmured. "I haven't seen anything," he repeated, "but if I do, you can be damn sure that I'll let you know. And keep me in the loop? I just got back from dealing with a bounty and desperately need sleep, but in the morning I'll join in the hunt if you haven't found them all. David was a good man."

"He was. And I'd appreciate it. You're the best tracker we've got." The corner of his mouth twitched. "Now, if I could just convince you to make it full time."

"Not a chance in hell, but you keep dreaming. Happy hunting."

"Thanks." Marco nodded to the other Hunters before they slipped back into the woods to continue their search.

Wade ran a hand through his hair. Demons in the area? This wasn't good. Rarely did that part of his life hit this close to home, and he found that he really didn't like it. Part of him wanted to join Marco now, but he knew that he'd be all but useless until he got some sleep. And it only took a single sluggish reaction to end even the most skilled fighter.

He sighed and continued inside, only to pause, caught by indecision. He knew he needed a shower, desperately. When he could smell himself, it was bad. On the other hand, he wasn't sure he could stand up long enough for a shower. *Fuck it,* he thought, *there's no one around to smell me, anyway.*

Decision made, he stripped off his shirt as he started for the bedroom. A scent caught his attention just before he reached the doorway and stopped him dead in his tracks. It was a woman. A woman with an extremely alluring scent. His face tipped upward and he drew in a deep breath, savoring the aroma. He'd smelled women before, of course, and several had smelled delicious. But never had the scent of one ever sent a bolt of pure lust straight through him and caused his body to harden in a rush like this, especially when he was so tired that he shouldn't have been able to get aroused.

He was so hard he hurt.

The reaction was strong enough that it momentarily slipped his mind that there shouldn't be any women in his cabin, much less in his bedroom. No matter how much he desperately wanted her to be in his bed, sight unseen.

He frowned when he came back to reality and he stomped into his bedroom to confront his mystery guest. Except when he got there, she was curled up on her side, sleeping in his bed. Not the way he wanted her there, but now he fought between annoyance and arousal at his intruder.

At his best guess, she was half a foot shorter than his own six-two, and she took care of every inch of it. There was some softness to her, but it looked like most of it had been honed away by exercise. That softness extended to her face, which looked peaceful in sleep. Her skin was fair, and he didn't see a single freckle or line. A thick, dark braid was draped over her shoulder, gleaming in the shaft of light that came in through the window. It looked black, but he supposed it could be brown, and that braid was long enough to reach halfway down her back, at the very least.

His gaze lingered on her lips, full and kissable, and wished she were awake so he could see what color her eyes were.

Her clothing did nothing to help ease his internal struggle. The black leather pants she wore molded to each and every curve until they disappeared into her knee-high boots. Also leather, of course. He had a weakness for a woman in leather. The deep red halter top she wore was equally as distracting. With the position she was in, her breasts were thrust upward, their swells visible, while her belly was bare. Images flashed through his head, of tasting that exposed flesh, and he had to bite back a groan.

Silently, he admitted that the sheer sensual beauty of the woman had allayed most of his irritation at having his very own Goldilocks. At least until he realized that the seductive fragrance wasn't all he was getting from this woman. Unlike most people, even unlike most shifters, he could smell more than the usual scents. He could 'smell' magic, especially strong magic, and the woman in his bed reeked of it. Worse, she reeked of dark power. A power he was all too familiar with.

Demon.

He growled, quietly, but the sound woke her instantly.

Her eyes opened and fixed on him, and part of him cursed that he couldn't tell what color they were, just that they were dark.

For a minute they stared at each other, neither moving, hardly even breathing. Time seemed to just stop while they watched each other, studied each other.

Samara felt a pang of relief to not see one of the demons standing just a few feet from her. That relief shifted to something else as she took in the man in front of her.

His tall frame was muscled, that was much was clear. His shoulders were broad, his stomach was flat, his chest strong. Both were tattooed, as were his arms, enough that it looked like an intricate shirt rather than warm skin. Muscles corded in those arms and chest as he clenched his fists—no doubt in reaction to her presence, she thought.

Her gaze lowered and she saw that his legs were just as strong, and...

Oh my...

All thoughts flew out of her head for a moment as she caught sight of the bulge in his pants. She'd never paid much attention to such things before, never had the time or inclination to worry about sex, but now? Now she had to fight to look upward as warmth pooled between her legs.

But while his body was heart-stopping, his face was just as distracting. His hair was light blonde and came to his chin, but it showed signs of having had fingers threaded through it recently. His skin was tanned and he clearly hadn't shaved in a day or two. The stubble matched the rugged features of his face and gave him a dangerous appearance. A dangerous, delicious appearance. The fact that his gray-green eyes were narrowed and his whole bearing screamed predator only added to that.

Apparently, she had a weakness for dangerous men.

Outside, an owl hooted and broke the fragile truce.

He growled and stalked toward the bed, his intentions clear. No matter how turned on he was, he wasn't going to act on that need, but on a more violent urge.

Samara rolled off the bed away from him and landed lightly on her feet. She considered grabbing her knives, but she really didn't want to kill this magnificent man. And there was no doubt in her mind that she could kill him, no matter his strength. She'd fought worse than him and lived to tell about it.

He only gave her a second for that thought before he jumped over the bed at her, swinging out with one large, scarred fist. She leaned back and twisted to the side so quickly that surprise flashed in his eyes. The surprise disappeared when she grabbed him and used his momentum to throw him forward so he crashed into the wall. The sound of the impact was so loud she was surprised the wall didn't collapse.

He was on his feet only a moment later, and angrier than he had been just a few seconds ago. The flash of yellow in his eyes gave her pause. Eyes like that, coupled with the growl...he was likely one of the wolf shifters. They were often formidable opponents, more feral than not and exceptionally strong. Still, he didn't worry her.

He lunged forward after just a heartbeat and the fight was on.

They traded punches and kicks, though to his frustration she blocked most of his, while several of hers slipped through. And with enough force that he was going to feel them in the morning. He wasn't one to underestimate a fighter just because it was a woman, but this demon surpassed all of his expectations. So when his fist finally connected with her jaw and her head snapped back, he felt a thrill of triumph. The sight of her split lip immediately after, however, made him feel a surge of guilt that he shoved down. He would *not* feel guilty about punching a demon. Especially not one who'd broken into his house.

She wiped the back of her hand over her bloody mouth, then had the audacity to *grin* at him. The sight of it not only surprised him, but unexpectedly turned him on even more. Because of that, his next punch went awry. Later, he would tell himself it was that error that caused the rest.

The demon caught his wrist and slipped behind him, pulling his arm against his back. Once there, she hooked a foot around his ankle and pulled hard, causing him to fall onto his face. She followed him down, twisting his arm upward and using her body weight to help pin him beneath her.

Her lips were close to his ear when she spoke, her voice low, smooth. Husky. The fact that he found it appealing as well enraged him. The last person he wanted to lust after was a demon.

"I'm not your enemy, wolf. I don't mean you any harm."

He bucked beneath her, growling dangerously, and she leaned more heavily against him. "I mean it. I didn't come here to hurt you. I don't *want* to hurt you. To prove it, I'm going to let you up now, and I'm going to trust that you're not going to attack me. Okay?" She waited a moment, but there was no response, just the heaving of his chest as he panted angrily.

Slowly, she eased back, but kept his arm pinned until she could get to her feet. The moment she was upright, she let go of his arm and stepped back.

She'd only taken a single step when his hand shot out and grabbed her ankle. He pulled sharply and spilled her onto her back. Not trusting her, he twisted around and punched her hard in the jaw the second she was down. To his relief, the hit did what he intended; it knocked her out. He hadn't been sure it would work, given how resilient she seemed.

Body protesting with the movement, he got to his feet with more speed than grace and left the room, returning with a coil of rope. Moving quickly, he tied her wrists together, then tied that rope to the heavy post of his bed. He wasn't sure how long she'd remain unconscious, but he didn't want her to be free when she came to.

A hand rubbed over his ribs. She was surprisingly tough, especially given her beauty. If that was her trying not to hurt him, he didn't want to fight her when she was playing for keeps.

He sighed as he looked down at her still form. It really was too bad she was a demon.

CHAPTER 3

W ade turned the light on to get a better look at his houseguest. He had just frisked her and taken two lethal looking knives before the woman came to and she surprised him once again.

He expected struggling and cursing, expected her to try to escape. Instead, she shifted until she realized she was bound, then went still and looked at him as he stood.

Though he'd known her eyes were dark, he hadn't expected them to be black. Not entirely, only the irises, but they were truly black, with nothing to differentiate the iris from the pupil. He expected to be repelled by the sight, but on her it was just another thing that was attractive.

Her head cocked and she grinned. "This really wasn't necessary," she told him, her voice still husky.

Not a product of the fight, but her actual voice? he wondered. *Interesting.*

"Considering that you're a demon and you were in my bed, I'd say it's absolutely necessary," Wade drawled as he folded his arms over his chest and leaned against the door frame. "But if you'd prefer the alternative—which is to kill you now—I'm more than happy to oblige."

"I could have killed you, wolf, but I didn't," she pointed out. "For that matter, I have no interest in killing you, unless I have to in order to protect myself."

He snorted. "You could have tried," he corrected, though secretly he thought she might be right. She had beaten him easily, and without using any weapons. "But want to tell me what you were doing sleeping in my bed? I'm a wolf, not a bear, and your hair sure as hell isn't gold."

She looked completely baffled by that. "Of course you're a wolf. And what does the color of my hair have to do with anything?"

He shook his head and waved a hand to dismiss the subject. "Never mind. What are you doing here?"

The demon hesitated a moment before she shrugged. "I was running from a group of demons who want to catch me and take me back to their evil master." There was another pause before she added flatly, "My evil master."

He scoffed. "Right. And why would you do that? I thought you demons stuck together. Especially if you serve the same demon."

"Not all the time," she said and shook her head. "Not all demons are evil, wolf, and not all demons like being forced to serve that cause. I'm one of them. Unfortunately, the demon who ruled over me is one who revels in evil and has evil plans. I will not serve him anymore," she said, her voice strong, fierce, and it made him consider her words a little more carefully.

The man in him wanted to end this demon now, before she could kill him. The wolf somehow thought she was no threat and wanted to see her in his bed. Now. He tried not to listen to the wolf, not about her.

"Right," he said dryly. "Who is this demon? Who are *you*, for that matter?"

"I'm Samara, though you can call me Sam. And he…he is Bellar, the Lord of Evil Things."

"Okay Sam. So why run here to Earth? We're not exactly demon-friendly here," he said. "We tend to kill your kind."

"No, you're not," she agreed easily. "But Bellar wants Earth. And unless he's stopped, he *will* get it."

"Oh, and you're here to stop him?" he asked sarcastically.

Her simple, "Yes," almost had him smiling. Almost.

"You realize we have some very impressive people here who can kill demons, right?" he asked instead.

"It won't be that easy, wolf." She wrinkled her nose, which he found oddly cute. "Can I have your name? It feels odd to keep calling you wolf," she grumbled.

Part of him really, really didn't want this demon having his name, but he said, "Wade. And I'll be right back. If you want me to trust that you don't mean me harm, then be here when I get back."

She sighed and nodded, so he stepped out of the room and pulled out his phone. Before he dialed, he glanced over to Sam, then stepped out of the cabin for a bit more privacy. He had no idea how good her hearing was and wanted privacy for this call.

The voice that answered was slurred with sleep, and a quick calculation of time zones had him wincing guiltily. "'lo?"

"Julian, sorry about the time. I forgot that it would be early for you," Wade said apologetically.

"Mmm. 'Sokay. What's wrong?" the witch asked as he struggled to wake up a little more. It was just five in the morning in England, and he wasn't a light sleeper.

"Need your demonologist expertise."

Julian sat up, and when his wife sleepily asked who it was, he just murmured Wade's name and ran a hand down her arm. "Be right back, sweetheart." There was a rustling that told Wade Julian was getting out of bed. Probably leaving the room so Paige could go back to sleep. "What do you need?"

"You ever heard of a demon named Bellar?" He almost stopped there, and frowned at himself. There wasn't any need to hold back, not from Julian. "Or Samara?"

"Not sure. Give me second." It was more like a minute before he was awake enough to process the names. "Yes. On Bellar, at least. I don't know that I've heard of Samara, but I can definitely do some checking."

"That's fine. We can start with Bellar. What do you know?"

"He's bloody old. Some say he's older than the gods, but there's no real way of knowing how accurate that is. And he's also one of the worst demons I've heard of," Julian admitted as he made his way to his workshop. He had an extensive library, which included a listing of a great many demons. He was the man the Venatoribus Noctu called when they needed information on demons. He was the man *everyone* called, for that matter.

"Worse than Gurnov?" Wade asked, having heard about that particular demon just last year.

"Yes and no."

Wade growled lightly. "Useful answer there, bud."

Julian chuckled. "You just got me out of bed, remember? But actually, my answer is accurate if I'm remembering right, and I am. His methods are different from Gurnov's. Less bodily harm and more... turning people to the dark side."

His wife's love of movies was starting to get to him, Wade thought with a smile.

"What do you mean? Brain-washing?"

"Not exactly," Julian hedged. "Or that's not how it sounds, anyway. It sounds more like seducing people into believing that evil is a good thing."

"Is that why he's called the Lord of Evil Things?" Wade asked with a frown.

"Lord of Evil Things? Where'd you hear that?"

He glanced back to the cabin. "Doesn't matter. Is that why?"

"One moment."

Wade heard Julian flipping through pages and took the moment to peek in the window at his captive. Samara was right where he'd left her, and the ropes looked intact. She didn't look too happy, but that didn't bother him at the moment.

"No, that's not where he got his moniker," Julian said. "Says here that he's able to directly influence evil beings. Maybe even control them. We're not exactly sure on which since he's never been to Earth. But if that's true, and given who it says his consort is, he'd be a pretty damn formidable enemy. Wade...you haven't run into Bellar, have you?" he asked, his voice full of worry.

"No, never met the guy. His name came up when I was dealing with a demon earlier." Wade wasn't sure why he didn't tell Julian more about Samara. "Who's his consort?"

"Have you ever heard of Lilith?"

Wade frowned as the name tickled a memory, but he couldn't quite bring the information out. "Sounds familiar."

"Legend says she was the first woman created, and was to be the wife of the first man. She refused and wreaked havoc over the earth, giving birth to all manner of monsters and demons until the gods banished her to another dimension. When they did, she was transformed into a demon, which only made her more dangerous. More powerful."

"I remember that story. She was marked, wasn't she? On her hands or something?"

"Her palms, yes. If she really is Bellar's consort, then we don't want them anywhere near earth. The two of them could do a hell of a lot of damage individually, but together? They'd be nearly unstoppable."

"I hear ya. I gotta go, but give me a call back if you find anything about Samara?"

"I will, but Wade? You're going to have to explain what's going on soon," Julian told him.

"Count on it."

He hung up, but before he could even take a step toward the cabin, he heard Samara yell, "Wolf!"

There was no fear, but the urgency in her voice had him breaking into a run. When he reached the bedroom, he mentally cursed. Marco was back. Worse, he was in Wade's bedroom, a look of utter hatred on his face as he lifted a sword. There was no doubt that his intention was to lop Samara's head off. The fact that she hadn't attacked Marco, or even tried to free herself, made him believe her intentions a little more. Someone who wanted them all dead wouldn't have risked her life like that.

"Marco! Stop!" he yelled as he raced to get there before the sword fell. He caught the witch's wrist just in time to prevent it from cutting into Sam's skin.

"What the hell, Wade? You're protecting a demon?" Marco roared, outraged. His body twisted, his free hand coming up in a punch.

Wade couldn't avoid it, so he turned and took it on the shoulder. Pain shot down his arm. "Dammit, Marco! Just listen to me!" he growled, shoving both hands against Marco's chest with enough force to knock the big man back a few steps. "Listen!" he snapped.

It was obvious Marco wanted nothing more than to kill Sam, who had been perfectly silent aside from calling for Wade. But he stopped, his fist clenched tightly around the hilt of his sword. "This better be good, Wade," he snarled.

"She's got information, Marco. On another demon," he said quickly. "I just talked to Julian and this other demon is a really bad dude, with an equally bad consort." He thought he heard a sound from Samara at that, but couldn't risk even a glance back at her to check. "If she can help us stop a worse demon, isn't that worth letting her live?"

It galled part of him to be defending a demon. More, to be arguing for a demon's life, but there was a need in him that wouldn't let him do otherwise.

Marco wasn't convinced. "What demon? What consort?"

"Bellar and Lilith."

Marco's eyes narrowed and he leaned to one side so he could glance at Samara. It was clear he recognized the names. "So we get all the information she has, then kill her. There's no reason to keep her alive," he said with disgust. "There's no such thing as a good demon."

"Marco…"

Samara spoke up then, though her voice was quiet. "He wants vengeance, Wade. And he's earned it. He has every right to hate me and all those like me." Her dark eyes lifted to meet Marco's surprised ones. "If killing me will give you some measure of peace, if it will fulfill your need for retribution, then I will not stop you. But please, let me tell you what I know first."

Those soft words shocked both men, but not as much as the sincerity in them. Even Marco lost some of the intense rage that had gripped him at the sight of the demon.

"What sort of demon are you to offer me that?" Marco demanded. Never had a demon acted like this one, and he worried that it was a trick of some sort. It had to be. No demon would offer to sacrifice themselves to satisfy another's lust for revenge.

"A demon of vengeance," Samara answered in that same quiet tone. "I can feel your need for it, and the reason for it. It is justified."

Marco was shocked once again. "You're a Fury?"

She nodded and Wade noticed that Marco no longer gripped his sword quite so tightly. "Someone wanna fill me in?" he asked.

"A Fury is....not the normal sort of demon. I didn't think they truly existed," he admitted. "I won't say they're *good*, because they're still demons, but...vengeance is their god," Marco explained.

"So?"

"*Just* vengeance, Wade. Eye for an eye, tooth for a tooth, that sort of thing," he clarified, looking at Samara in a new light. The hatred inside him still burned to eliminate all demons, but this one had him thinking. "They'll do anything to right a wrong, in equal measure."

"And wanting justice for the death of a family is just," Samara said with a nod before she leaned her head back so it rested against the bed and her throat was bared.

Wade couldn't process all this. Marco didn't sound like he wanted to kill a demon, and a demon was offering her life to ease someone's pain? What the hell had happened to the world? "What the fuck?" he demanded. "Did we just step into an alternate universe and no one told me?"

They both ignored him while Sam accepted death and Marco contemplated giving it to her.

"If you're a Fury, where are your wings?" Marco demanded.

Samara leaned as far as she could away from the bed and freed her wings with a sigh of relief. Keeping them contained within her body wasn't always comfortable, but most often, it was necessary. She stretched them out and looked not at Marco, but at Wade.

Both men were astounded. While Wade had seen people who could fly, either by shapeshifting or using air magics, he'd never seen anyone with wings in human form. He found himself wanting to touch them and instead shoved his hands in his pockets.

Metal slid over leather when Marco sheathed his sword. "I will not kill you today, demon. Give Wade the information that you have. But if I find out this is a trick, or if you step one foot out of line, I *will* kill you."

Sam willed her wings into her body once more and leaned back. "Understood."

"And she's *your* responsibility, Wade. She escapes, she kills anyone, it's on your head, and I'll take it just as I'll take hers," he warned.

Wade frowned. When had his life gotten so damn complicated? He was caretaker to a demon now? To a Fury? "Fine," he bit off. "And what are you even doing here?"

"We found footsteps that circled back to your cabin. Just one set, so I came alone and sent the rest of the team ahead to try to find the others." He looked to Samara. "I was a little late." He frowned. "You were the first one out, weren't you? The one who told my men to run?"

"I was. They listened then?"

"No. One is dead."

Samara closed her eyes and once again Marco wondered if it was all a trick. "I'm very sorry about the men. I hoped they'd listen to me."

Marco didn't respond to that. "Call me if you learn anything useful," he told Wade, before disappearing.

CHAPTER 4

Almost a quarter of an hour went by without either of them speaking. Wade was still tired, but the sheer exhaustion had burned off in the rush of adrenaline. He knew it would fade soon enough, and he still had quite a bit to do before he got horizontal. Like figure out what in the hell he was going to do with his demonic prisoner.

"You said you came here to stop Bellar. How? And what is he planning?" he finally asked as he leaned against the wall.

"By the next full moon, he'll be able to escape his dimension and come to Earth. Once he does, he'll start to conquer it, even if he has to do it one person at a time. He's patient, and he's sly. If he has to slowly build up his army in order to achieve his goals, he will. If he has to kill half the people here to do it, he'll do that instead," Samara told him, and her voice was weary now, no longer strong and confident.

For some reason, that bothered him.

"Do you know where he'll escape?"

She shook her head. "I only know the approximate when, not the where," she admitted. "Portals aren't exactly something easily predicted."

"And how do you know all this?" he asked suspiciously. For all he knew, she was just preparing a trap for him or the Venatoribus Noctu. Marco was right. He shouldn't trust her just because she appeared to do good deeds. Maybe she was telepathic and knew that Marco wouldn't kill her if she'd offered to let him. Demons were tricky, after all.

"A seer told me, just as she told me when and where a portal was opening tonight that I could use to escape to Earth. But seeing the future isn't an exact science. Seers can't just pick and choose what they see, or how much they see."

That was true enough, but instinct told him that she wasn't telling him the whole truth. Before he could press, she continued.

"I can't stay here, Wade. His minions will be coming for me. The other demons who came through the portal."

Wade shrugged. "Marco's men will take care of them. This is what they do, after all."

She didn't look so certain. "Even if those demons are eliminated, more will come. And they'll be able to find me. I don't want to be within their reach when they start looking."

He scowled. "How?"

She leaned forward as far as she could and shook her head so her braid fell to one side. "This."

He pushed away from the wall he'd been leaning against so he could look. On the back of her neck were arcane symbols, inked into her skin in a vaguely circular shape, but it wasn't an ordinary tattoo. Even in the dim light, he could see that there was a faint shimmer to the ink, one that could only be caused by magic. "A tattoo?"

"It lets him track me, no matter what dimension I'm in. Worse, it prevents me from harming him, directly or indirectly." Her mouth tightened. "And it cannot be removed."

"How do you know? Seems like it could just be cut off or something." Which would be exceedingly painful, but possible. Most of the people he knew would rather deal with the pain than with having a tracking device embedded in their skin. "There are always ways to get rid of unwanted ink."

When she straightened, he saw she was smirking, but there was no actual humor to it. "No, it can't," she said confidently. "Do you think I haven't tried?" She shook her head. "It's invulnerable to blade or flame. Acid doesn't work, either. Nor does magic. I've tried for years to get this thing off my neck, but as far as I can tell, the only way to get rid of it is to get rid of him. Even then, it might stay there forever and just be useless after he's gone."

Unbidden came an image of Sam trying to slice the tattoo off herself, and he cringed inwardly. "Oh."

"They'll be here no later than morning, I'm sure."

"Then what is it that you plan to do if you knew you'd be constantly chased and couldn't hurt him yourself?"

"It depends on what's available to me, but I only have two options. I can find a way to keep him from coming through a portal, any portal, which is less a solution and more a way of delaying the inevitable. Or I can find a way to kill him. That's actually why I came to Earth."

"How so?"

"I need to find a particular book, one made of stone. The seer saw it and told me that it will lead me to a weapon that can kill him. We're not sure I'll be able to wield it, not with the tattoo, but I'm not the only one who wants him dead."

"A stone book? That's...only possibly helpful."

"I know, but it's all I have, and I'd rather find a way to kill him than just delay him."

"Understandable." He couldn't think of any books like that himself, but he knew people, including Julian, who excelled at research who might be able to point him in the right direction. "Well, nothing we can do tonight, though, right? And you said we've got until morning?"

"Most likely, yes. It would take time for him to realize the first group failed and send another. And that's assuming that the first group either lost my trail or were found by your friend's people."

"Then let's get some sleep while we can, and in the morning, before they get here, we'll take off. And I want to know the rest of what you're not telling me."

Sam smiled faintly. "What I'm not telling you could take years to share." She paused. "Am I to sleep here on the floor? Bound?"

He grimaced. "No, I guess not. Though if you kill me in my sleep, I'm going to be seriously pissed."

"I told you before, I don't want to hurt you, wolf. The only one I want to hurt is Bellar. And those who follow him willingly," she said with such sincerity that he actually believed her.

"Well, before you sleep on anything of mine, and I don't care if it's just the couch, you need to get clean." She didn't smell bad, but up close, he could see the dirt and blood staining her skin and clothes. She may not have attacked the Hunters, but she'd been in a fight with someone besides him.

Color crept up her cheeks. "I'd love to get clean, so that won't be a problem."

He sighed and cut the rope around her hands. "I'm still keeping your knives," he told her as she started to rub her wrists. "Bathroom's that way," he said, pointing with one of them.

"Thank you," she told him formally as she stood. Her legs were stiff, but she was so happy to not be bound that she said nothing. Her stomach growled lightly as she left the room, but sleep was a much more pressing matter than food. In the morning, after they'd left, then she'd talk to Wade about finding something to eat.

She took her hair out of the braid before she stripped out of her clothes, leaving them in a pile on the floor. It was only then that she realized she recognized nothing in the bathroom other than the sink, but she couldn't very well bathe in that. Stumped, she started poking around the room to see if she could figure it out.

Once the door shut behind her, Wade ran his hand through his hair, wondering just what in the hell he was going to do. The last hour had been so fucked up, in so many ways. He was lusting after a demon, and one he was supposed to babysit so they could kill a worse demon. Not to mention that in just a few hours they'd most likely be getting a visit from another group of demons.

What happened to the life where he just spent his days tracking people and things down? Things were simple that way, even if he occasionally took time off to help a friend with a treasure hunt.

The bathroom door opened and when he turned to see what she wanted, his jaw dropped.

She was naked. And she was the sexiest woman he'd seen in all of his three centuries.

Her hair was unbound and fell in waves around her from the braid. It was thick enough that it almost hid her breasts, which were lush and tipped with coral nipples that were already tight little peaks from the cool air. Her belly was flat, her hips just full enough to give a man something to grab hold of. Legs that were long and toned made him envision them wrapped around his hips as he pounded into her.

She had the body of both a warrior and a seductress. The combination had his cock throbbing with need as he stared hungrily. For a moment, he was tempted to go to her, press her against the wall, and ease the ache he'd been feeling since he first scented her.

He realized she was speaking and had to clear his throat before he could speak, but even then his voice was a rough growl. "What?"

She didn't seem to realize anything was off, but stood there as casually as if she were fully clothed. "There's no bathtub. How do you bathe?" she asked.

He frowned. There wasn't a tub, no, but there was a shower stall. True, it was bigger than most since he was a big guy, but a shower was still a shower. "You use the shower." She looked confused and it clicked that she was from another dimension. One that, apparently, didn't have things like showers. "I'll show you."

"Thank you."

To his delight, she turned and walked back into the bathroom, giving him a look at the most perfect ass he'd ever encountered. Before he followed, he took a moment to adjust the erection that had appeared the moment he'd seen her nude. Not that adjusting it helped much. It still ached. That only got worse when he stood beside her to show her how to turn the water on and off and adjust the temperature. She brushed against his arm as she reached out to try it herself, and he gritted his teeth. This woman, this *demon*, was entirely too enticing.

He put some distance between them so she couldn't touch him again. "Soap and shampoo are there. Use whatever you want," he told her before he escaped. If he hadn't, he knew he would have done something unwise, like joining her and seeing if she was so relaxed when they were both naked.

To distract himself so he wouldn't picture that luscious body bared and wet, he called Julian back.

"I didn't wake you up this time, did I?" he asked.

"No, I'm still trying to find something on Samara. None of the books I've been through so far have any mention of her."

"She's a Fury, if that helps."

He heard Julian's surprise when he said, "She is?"

"Mmhmm. She convinced Marco of it, anyway. Even offered to let him kill her, since his need for vengeance was just or something like that. Which was really fucking weird."

"That...sounds like the information we have on Furies, I just didn't think it was accurate."

"Consider it verified."

"Duly noted, but you're saying that she's there?"

"Yeah. In my custody, because she may or may not be willing to help us kill Bellar. Who, she said, is planning to come to Earth and conquer it by the next full moon. She even says she's here to find something that can kill him."

Julian let out a curse, which oddly made Wade smile. He never knew what language Julian was going to curse in. He thought it might be Arabic this time, but he wasn't sure.

"I'll focus on him, then. But be careful, Wade. Fury or not, she's still a demon, and they can't be trusted," Julian warned.

"So you don't think that a demon can ever not be evil?"

Silence.

"Anything is possible, I guess, but I've never heard of a single demon being anything but bad. And if you end up dead because you thought one selfless act meant she was good, I'm going to be pissed."

Wade chuckled. "Noted. Let me know if you find out anything I need to know, okay?"

"I will. Be careful."

CHAPTER 5

Samara couldn't sleep. Oh, she'd dozed a bit in the last few hours, but true sleep eluded her.

After her shower—and what a wonderful thing a shower was!—she'd been given one of Wade's shirts since hers was coated in dirt and blood, then she'd gone to bed. He'd taken the couch, though he hadn't looked too happy about it. Her best guess was that he gave her the bedroom since it didn't have a door leading outside and had only a small window, so she couldn't escape. Not that she intended to, but she could understand his reasoning. In his position, she'd probably have done the same.

Her mind drifted back to his reaction when she'd come out of the bathroom naked. She thought nothing of nudity. She had the same parts as every other woman—wings not included, of course—so it had seemed silly to get dressed just to find out how to work the shower. And where she was from, nudity was as commonplace as clothing. But he'd acted absolute stunned.

She wasn't going to lie. His reaction, baffling though it was, had felt...good. She normally ignored her more womanly attributes, and often bound her breasts when she was able since they tended to get in the way, but for the first time she'd been pleased to have them.

What would a kiss from him be like?

Sighing, she flopped over onto her back. No sense in wondering about that. He didn't like demons and she had a job to do here. She didn't have time to remember that she was a woman.

Still—

A small weight landed on her stomach, with just enough force to make her oof softly. Before she could even think about defending herself, the thing that was resting on her stomach stilled enough for her to recognize it. It was Keen!

As an imp, Keen was only about two feet tall with a round little belly. His skin was dark gray, thick, and leathery, as were his bat-like wings. But while she found him adorable, he clearly portrayed some demonic features—a pair of small horns on his head, fangs just a little too long to be cute, and claws. Each of his fingers was tipped in razor-sharp claws, and the top point of his wings had them as well.

Small he might be, but he could be dangerous, too. Just not to her.

"Keen!" she cried happily, sitting up and gathering him in her arms.

Normally, he'd welcome such affection from her, but now he squirmed in her arms and screeched wordlessly.

"What is it?"

"They coming!" he told her in his child-like English and made her blood run cold.

Wade had heard her cry and appeared at the doorway.

"Demons are coming!" she told him as she scrambled out of bed. Keen tumbled off her and landed on the bed, face first.

She yanked her pants on and was reaching for her boots when Wade noticed Keen, who had gotten to his feet. He growled and started for the imp, only to get shoved back by Sam after she stepped between them. Keen peeked out from around her and hissed at Wade, baring his fangs.

"He is *not* a threat. He's warned me." She shoved her boot on and glanced up at him. "Did you hear me, wolf? They're coming. Here. Now," she told him angrily. "You can thank Keen later."

It took some effort for Wade not to attack the clearly inhuman creature, but he took her words seriously. "How long?"

The front door crashed open and Sam sighed. "Now," she said wearily. "Can I have my knives back?"

She saw the reluctance in his face, but he nodded. Unfortunately, they weren't on him. "Table by the couch, if you can get to it."

They moved to the doorway, though Wade pushed her behind him as much as he was able. The action almost made Samara laugh, but nothing else about the situation was the least bit funny.

There were five demons in his living room. They spread out loosely, and each one of them looked lethal, though their appearances all vastly differed. One had gray skin, another a large set of horns, the third looked perfectly human, and one was furred. But the one who really worried Wade was about his height, bald, with horns and red skin. The most disturbing part of him were his silver eyes.

It was that one who spoke while looking at Samara. Wade expected his voice to be harsh, unpleasant, but it was surprisingly smooth and not quite as deep as he would have thought it would be.

"You need to come with us, Samara."

She snorted. "There's as little chance of that as you sprouting a full head of hair, Tornuth," she told him with a sneer.

His eyes narrowed and Wade wondered why she was baiting him. Clearly they had a history, but now he was curious what that history was.

"You *will* come with us. If you do, your father has told me he will forgive your act of treason. You'll be welcomed home again."

Samara fought a wince, but didn't allow herself to even glance at Wade. She could feel the added tension radiating from him, which was bad enough. She really wished she'd have been able to kill them before they came through the portal, but there had been more of them on the other side.

Her knives were on the little table beside the couch, just as Wade had said. She had to stop this. She had to stop it now. There were five of them, yes, but she was beyond skilled at killing. Her father had made her his assassin for centuries, so she had plenty of practice.

Before Wade could realize what she intended, she ran forward, surprising all six men—and probably Keen, too. One of the demons tried to stop her, but she dropped into a somersault that carried her just past him and to her knives. Her hand slapped down onto a familiar hilt, and she picked it up and flung it in one movement. It sunk deep into the chest of the one who'd tried to stop her.

His face radiated shock as he stared at the hilt, then started to sway. As he fell, there was a stillness from everyone else that lasted no longer than the space of two heartbeats. Then everyone was moving all at once. Everyone but Wade.

The other knife was grabbed as she leapt to her feet, but she was quickly rushed by three of the four remaining demons. Tornuth hung back, watching. Of all the demons here, he knew best just how talented a killer she was.

Wade watched, too, but he was more staring in awe. He knew she was a good fighter since she took him down so easily, but this? She was magnificent when she wasn't holding back. It was almost enough to make him forget what the leader had said about her father. Almost.

The three demons fought to get a hit in on the Fury as she ducked, twisted, and spun with amazing grace and speed around them. He'd never seen someone move like that before. And she wasn't solely on the defensive either. Those knives of hers slashed out, slicing deeply into the demons, though he knew that none of them was a killing blow. Yet.

When he realized that he was just standing there watching a bunch of demons in his house, he scowled and mentally cursed himself before he dove into the fray.

While he didn't think he could match Samara's speed, he had her in strength and grabbed the gray demon from behind and slung him across the room with enough force that he nearly went completely through the heavy wooden wall.

Sam took advantage of the distraction it caused, ducking below the arm of the horned demon as he tried to claw her so she could plunge her knife deep into his chest.

The remaining demon went after Wade just as Tornuth stepped forward. "Enough, woman! You will suffer less if you concede now!"

"Fuck you, Tornuth. I won't be anyone's lap dog, and I'll die before I go back there," Samara growled at him.

"You will not get that opportunity. You will serve as you are meant to. You cannot escape, even in death."

Wade managed to get behind the last demon, arm around his throat in a choke hold. He kept the pressure on while he watched Samara and

Tornuth. He was sure he was missing something in their exchange, but kept quiet.

Samara smiled and slowly shook her head. "No, Tornuth. I won't. I'm done serving. I'm done being his pet assassin. And you're finished, too, you're just too stupid to realize it yet."

Both of her knives were protruding from bodies, but she stood tall, proud, and confident, making no move to reclaim them, even though Tornuth had more than half a foot and a hundred pounds on her. To face him unarmed was suicide, no matter how skilled she was.

When the demon in his hold went limp and Wade no longer felt a pulse, he let the body drop. He'd just taken a step toward Tornuth when the demon's eyes went wide with fear, but Tornuth wasn't looking at him. He was staring at Sam.

"No!" he screamed, backing up quickly. "Stop! You can't do this, Samara! He swore you wouldn't be able to do this!"

Wade glanced at Samara, but she hadn't moved, and seemed to just be smiling at her enemy. But he noticed that there was a grimness to her smile, a tightness around her eyes. She wasn't as pleased as she looked at first glance, but there was power radiating from her. What kind, he didn't know, just that it was strong.

Tornuth backed himself right up against a wall and started to shake his head emphatically until the movement slowed, then stilled. He slid down the wall, his body relaxing, and Wade was confused to note that his eyes were going unfocused, like he wasn't really seeing them anymore.

"What's going on?" he asked, but there wasn't even a flicker from Sam to show that she heard him.

Tornuth started to giggle then, a high-pitched sound that was out of place for anyone but a child. His fingers plucked at the hem of his shirt before trying to absently pick apart the seam. "Angry. Very angry. The bad angel is gonna be angry," he mumbled. "If he's angry, I won't get any sweets." His eyes widened. "I'll hide! I'll hide in a hole, far, far down, until the ugly ones find me. Maybe they'll have sweets."

"Sam? What the hell is going on?" Wade demanded.

He saw the look of regret on her face before she closed her eyes, trying to shut out the absurd ramblings. "He won't try to attack again," she said softly.

"Why not? What'd you do to him?"

The demon he'd thrown against the wall started to stir and Wade snarled, stomping over. One quick jerk of the demon's head ended his moans of pain. Turning back, he asked, "Samara?"

"You heard that I was a Fury, Wade," Sam told him, bending to retrieve her knives and wipe them off on the demon's shirts.

"Yeah? So? Greek mythology isn't exactly my strong suit," he snapped. "I'm doing good to even know it's Greek."

She sighed and looked up at him, still crouched. "It isn't mine either. But Furies, true demons of vengeance, can inflict punishment on those guilty of wrongdoing. Including madness."

Wade looked back at Tornuth, who was still mumbling and trying to take his shirt apart with his fingers. "He's insane?"

"Yes."

That was almost scarier than her fighting skills. "Is it permanent?"

"Yes."

Keen peeked out of the bedroom, and, seeing that the coast was clear, flew over to land beside Samara. He laid his head on her knee, patting her leg comfortingly. "Had to," he told her.

She smiled fondly at the imp, though it was weak. "I know."

Wade scowled, unhappy with having such a creature here. To distract himself, he asked, "What did he mean about your father? Who's your father?" He thought he knew, but he wanted to hear her confirm it. He could find out about the creature in a minute.

Even the faint smile faded and she wouldn't meet his gaze. "Someone I never want to see again. It doesn't matter," she answered quietly.

"I think it does," he argued. "Your father is Bellar, isn't he?" When she didn't answer, he asked more forcefully, "Isn't he?"

"Yes! That bastard is my father! But what does it matter?" she yelled as she straightened. "I'm still going to kill him! I don't care what I have to do, he is going to die."

"What does it matter?" he repeated, astounded that she could ask that. "Your father is this major demon who wants to take over the world and you ask how it matters?"

Keen took offense at the way Wade was talking to Samara and hissed, flying at him and raking him with his claws. They bit into Wade's shoulder and he snarled, one hand lifted to strike the imp.

"Don't!" Samara cried, grabbing Keen out of the air and half turning to shield him with her body. "He was just protecting me, Wade. He's my friend."

"You're friends with a...a...what *is* that thing?"

"*He*," she emphasized the word, "is an imp. And yes, I'm friends with him. His name is Keen," she told him, still hugging the tiny demon. "He's my companion, and my one friend at home. Besides, he has a useful skill."

Wade doubted that anything so small could be useful, and it showed on his face. "What's that?"

"He can slide between dimensions as easily as we walk through doors. Which means he can give me information on what's going on back there, and take messages to the seer if need be."

Despite himself, Wade was impressed. He had thought that, aside from a few gods, travel between dimensions was nearly impossible without portals. "I take it you're going to want him to come with us, then?"

"I do."

Wade sighed. "Fine. Get cleaned up. We're leaving in fifteen minutes."

Samara glanced down at herself and grimaced. "Do you have another shirt I could use?" The one she was wearing was spattered with blood.

Wordlessly, he stalked into his bedroom and returned to throw one to her.

She set Keen down and turned her back on them as she changed. While she was doing that, Wade grabbed a duffel bag, shoving clothes and supplies into it. Afterward, he called Marco and told him about the dead demons—and Tornuth—in his living room. Marco was a whiz at disposing of dead demons.

It was just under the quarter hour he'd given her when they stepped outside and he walked to his SUV. He'd already put the bag in the back seat and had his door open when he realized she was still on the porch. "What is it now?" he asked impatiently.

"What is that?"

"It's a car. I'll explain later. For now, just get in." To help expedite things, he went around and opened her door for her. Unfortunately, he also had to explain the seat belt, but minutes later he was pulling out.

He glanced over to her and saw that Keen was curled up in her lap like a puppy and fast asleep.

CHAPTER 6

It was nearly noon before either of them spoke again.

Keen was still in Samara's lap, but now he was awake, holding onto the door and peering curiously out the window, as was Sam. It was clear that neither of them had seen half of what they were driving past, and they were fascinated.

Tired of the silence, Wade asked, "Where'd you learn to fight like that?"

"Hmm?" Samara drew her gaze away from the window. She'd been so absorbed in the differences of this new world that she hadn't registered his words.

"Where'd you learn to fight like that?" he repeated.

"Here and there," she answered with a shrug. "Mostly, I've just done a lot of practicing and training."

He frowned. "I can't imagine the practice it would take. I've had a couple centuries and you..." No, he wasn't going to admit out loud to her that she kicked his ass. "Those demons probably had a lot of practice too, and you killed them pretty quickly," he said instead.

She smirked. "Tornuth and the others are lazy." She paused, then corrected herself. "Okay, Tornuth isn't actually lazy, but his men are.

Were. They got lazy. There was no need for them to be better fighters, so they didn't bother to hone their skills. I did."

Wade wasn't entirely certain he wanted to know, but he asked, "How long have you been...honing?"

Her brow furrowed a little as she thought. "Roughly? About two thousand years, I think. Give or take a decade. Years aren't quite the same there."

He boggled. Two *thousand* years? No wonder she could have wiped the floor with him. Not only that, but her age was nothing to scoff at either. True, he'd briefly met the god Hephaestus, who had to be ancient. And sure, demons were known to be immortal, but it still wasn't common to meet anyone older than a thousand years. But here was a woman who was a confirmed two millennia old.

His lack of response made Samara frown a little harder. "Does that displease you for some reason?"

"No, just wasn't expecting that answer," he admitted. Then, to change the subject, "Who is Tornuth anyway?"

"My father's right hand. He doesn't really do a whole lot since my father doesn't really trust anyone completely, or delegate anything important, but he's got a small measure of power, which he enjoys." There was a lengthy pause. "Or did."

"No, I don't imagine he'll be enjoying much anymore," Wade agreed. Thinking of the newly insane demon, he remembered the sight of Samara's face afterward. "Did it bother you?"

"Did what bother me?"

"Taking his sanity."

She shrugged and looked back out the window. "Yes and no. I don't regret doing it, because he's evil and would have killed you and Keen and taken me home in chains. But I never inflict madness on someone lightly, no matter what you think of me. Besides, I can only do it when someone is truly deserving of it. I couldn't do it to you, for example."

For some reason, he believed her, which filled him with relief. True, he wasn't entirely sane, not with his chosen profession, but he never wanted to experience true insanity.

They fell silent again and drove until the sun had set. He took a lot of back roads and stopped only to put gas in the tank and grab some fast food. But by nightfall, he was tired and his muscles had tightened up after being in the car for thirteen hours. Demons coming after them or not, he needed a break from the car, not to mention an actual destination.

He pulled off at a motel and got them a room for the night. After they were settled, and while Sam was taking a shower—she really seemed to love showers—he ordered Chinese. No way was he going out again. And he sure as hell wasn't getting back in the SUV until morning unless he absolutely had to.

When she didn't emerge from the bathroom naked again, he was both relieved and disappointed. It was the latter that irritated him. He may not be as hard core in hating demons as Marco was, but he still wasn't fond of them.

That irritation continued through the arrival of the food and until he told her that he was going to sleep. He suggested she do the same.

Though she gave him an odd look, she agreed, and was asleep a good hour before he managed to follow.

A few hours later, he was awakened by odd noises. He lay in the dark for a minute until he realized that the sounds were coming from

Samara. They almost sounded like moans, and not the sort he'd prefer to be hearing from her. It sounded like she was in pain or scared.

He rolled onto his side and tried to ignore it until she started to thrash in the bed.

Her imp was up and started to shove at her shoulder in an attempt to wake her, but wasn't having any luck.

Wade growled and threw back the covers to move to her bed. He moved Keen to the side—more gently than he intended, as the creature still made him uneasy—and took Sam by the shoulders, giving her a firm shake. "Sam! Samara, wake up! It's just a nightmare."

She whimpered in protest and tried to pull away from him, but he didn't let up until her eyes opened.

He was struck by how eerie her eyes looked in the darkness. Never before had she really looked as demonic as she did right now, even when her wings were out. But still, he kind of liked it.

He forced those thoughts away and straightened. "You were having a nightmare," he told her, voice curt.

She shook her head. "Not nightmares, not exactly," she told him, voice quiet and a little breathless.

"Sure sounded like a nightmare," he told her dryly.

A shoulder jerked in a shrug before she got up and moved to the sink, splashing cold water on her face. Once she was a little more steady, she rested both hands on the counter, leaning into it. She could see him in the mirror and took in his stiff posture and unhappy expression. "If we're all up, do you want to go ahead and leave?"

"May as well." His eyes narrowed. "But just how long do you expect me to run, Samara? If they can track you, it's just a waiting game. You'll never be able to stop. And they don't want me, just you," he said, more cruelly than was normal for him. But his attraction to her was annoying him, and he was taking it out on her. It wasn't something he meant to do, but he couldn't help it.

He struck his mark, too. She flinched visibly before she turned away. He felt an unbidden surge of respect for the proud way she stood, chin lifted.

"Tell me, wolf. Based on what you know of my father, do you really think he's sending all these demons to reclaim me out of some sort of fatherly affection? Do you think he'd waste so many demons on a daughter who had no purpose, even if it was just to punish that daughter for running away?"

He hadn't thought of it like that.

Wade frowned and slowly shook his head. "No...So why does he want you back so badly?"

It was clear that she didn't really want to tell him, but she didn't hesitate. "I can amplify the powers and abilities of others. He wants me to boost his, so when he gets to Earth he'll be unstoppable," she said flatly.

Oh. Not good. Not good at all.

"Okay, new plan. Keep you out of his hands."

"Yes. And if it looks like he's going to get me, I want you to make me a promise."

His eyes narrowed. "What sort of promise?" he asked suspiciously.

She glanced over her shoulder at him, her eyes meeting his. "Kill me."

The words were spoken bluntly, with no uncertainty. Her eyes were equally as flat and he could tell she meant it. If it was a choice between being taken to her father or death, she chose death. He didn't know if he'd make the same choice, so he couldn't simply agree.

"Why?"

Her lips curved, but there was nothing but resignation in her expression. "Because I'd rather die than be forced to take part in destroying your world, or any other."

For several long minutes, he studied her and warred with her request. It wasn't in him to kill without just cause, regardless of whether it was self-defense or because it was someone who needed killing, which meant his initial reaction was to tell her no. Except...not only was she a demon, but her death could, potentially, save the Earth. He didn't have a choice.

"Okay," he finally told her, voice gruff.

Her shoulders slumped at his acceptance, which made him think she'd doubted he'd agree. "Thank you."

"Don't thank me," he almost growled. "Let's go." He sat down to pull his boots on, watching her as she did the same. In minutes, they were back in the car and on the road.

"Tell me more about this stone book," he told her.

"I don't know much more than I've already told you," she admitted. "The book itself isn't the way to kill him, but the seer is positive that it'll lead to a weapon that can," she answered without looking at him.

"But you won't be able to use it."

"Probably not, no. I've tried over the years to get around the mark, but nothing I do works. I can't physically strike him, I can't use negative magic on him, and I can't even lead him into a trap that I've set. My hand just turns away so I miss him or my magic fails entirely. He put a hell of a lot of work into that tattoo, and it works better than he could have hoped."

"Then who do you plan on giving this weapon to? A weapon does no good unless it's used. And why do we need a special weapon, anyway?"

"First, I can't guarantee we do need a special weapon, but I do know he's several times my age and extremely powerful. I wouldn't be surprised if even decapitation wouldn't kill him at this point. I'd rather do more than needed than not enough." She sighed and shook her head. "As for the rest...I'm well aware that a weapon does no good if not used," she said dryly. "I also didn't come here with anyone in mind to use it. Back home, most everyone is loyal to him, either out of fear or because they agree with him. I was hoping to find someone here who would be willing to take it and use it, even without a guarantee that it'd work. Because I can't promise that it will. The seer is sure, but she's not absolutely certain."

Minutes passed in silence before Wade spoke. "You're positive about his plans for Earth?"

"There is no doubt in my mind," she confirmed as she lifted Keen to her chest, cuddling him while he laid his head on her shoulder.

Wade sighed. Getting in the middle of a fight between demons wasn't a smart idea. Normally they'd just kill each other, but the odds were stacked in Bellar's favor. Except Bellar intended to come to his home and turn them all into slaves or corpses, and he couldn't allow that. He could likely pass the job onto Marco, but Marco didn't trust Samara, and Wade wasn't sure how well it would work. The same could be said for anyone else he knew who had a grudge against demons and the training to fight them. Which only left...

"I'll do it."

Sam's head turned quickly enough that she almost smacked herself in the face with her braid. "What?"

"I said I'll do it," he repeated in a low growl. "You think I want him taking over Earth? And I can't think of anyone else dumb enough to do it. Besides, I'm already with you, so it won't take any time to find someone else, which leaves more time to find this book."

"Thank you, Wade. Sincerely. Bellar absolutely must be stopped, for all our sakes," she told him, her eyes bright with appreciation. "I'll do everything I can to help you, I swear it."

"You'd better," he grumbled. "Is there anyone else I need to be worried about, though? Another guy like Tornuth or an ally of Bellar's who might try and stop us?"

She hesitated for a moment. "Specifically? No. Except for his legions of demons, of course."

His eyes narrowed. He could all but smell the deception. As he tried to figure out what she was hiding, he remembered something Julian said. "What about Lilith?"

Sam stiffened and turned her attention to the trees alongside the road. "What about her?"

"She's his consort, right? Raised hell here on Earth, gave birth to all sorts of monsters, got banished, and turned into a demon? Shouldn't I need to worry about her?"

"No. You don't," she told him in a clipped voice.

"And why is that? Shit, is she your mom?"

"And I'm not a monster," she answered coldly. "Not all stories about people are true, and even if they began as fact, years tend to twist things until they're unrecognizable."

Wade scrubbed a hand over his face. This was getting more and more complicated. "Look, I understand feeling loyalty to your parents...usually, and I'm happy that you don't feel loyalty to Bellar, but if she's that dangerous, shouldn't we—"

"Stop right there," she said, twisting to face him. "We are *not* harming my mother," she said, her tone dangerous. "Who do you think sent me here? Who do you think told me about the book? About the weapon? Who do you think sent Keen to watch over me? If there is one person in Olarid who wants Bellar dead more than I do, it's my mother. She's been through all manners of hell that you can't even imagine, and I'm not going to let her be killed just because her name is associated with an evil bastard that she absolutely loathes and has since the moment she met him."

He glanced at her angry face. "You're really saying the stories aren't true?"

"Have you never known history to be twisted by the victors until it's almost unrecognizable to the truth? They won. Of course they're going to skew things to make themselves look good." She shook her head. "No, if she's guilty of anything, she's only guilty of saying no, and I can't see how that should be a crime in any dimension. And we're done talking about this. She's innocent and not to be hurt. That's final, and I will kill anyone who tries to hurt her."

He couldn't deny she was passionate in her argument, and he sensed that she meant, and believed, every single word she spoke. In her eyes, Lilith wasn't the monster that history had portrayed her as. But she was also looking at her mother through the eyes of a child, so he wasn't sure how accurate her opinion was. He was, however, too smart to press about it right now.

"Understood," he said as he continued driving.

CHAPTER 7

Wade drove on autopilot. His mind was too absorbed with all that had happened the last thirty-six hours. And with the woman currently dozing in the passenger seat.

He needed to talk to Julian and Marco soon, to figure out what to do about Bellar. Knowing the when—mostly—was good, but not knowing where was a problem. Then there was the small problem how to kill him if he did show up, assuming he was really as difficult to kill as Samara had suggested. But maybe one of them had heard about this stone book, which would be a step in the right direction.

But would Bellar show up without Samara there to amplify his powers? Probably. He sounded arrogant enough to believe he could succeed just with himself and his army. Arrogant enough, Wade hoped, that he would do something foolish. It only took one mistake to bring down even the mightiest prey.

But none of that would matter, not unless Sam and Wade could manage to keep ahead of the demons Bellar was sending—because Wade had no doubt that there were already more on the way. They were most likely hitting every portal they could find. He just hoped that they continued to come in small enough numbers that they could be dealt with.

He snuck a glance at Samara and nearly smiled. Then again, she could probably handle a small army by herself. It really was too bad she was a demon. She was fierce and proud and brave...and sexy as hell. The imp was a little off-putting, but anything demonic tended to be that way. So why wasn't he put off by her?

"Samara?" he asked quietly. Keen cracked open an eye sleepily to look at him, but Sam didn't stir, so Wade pulled out his phone.

He dialed Julian first, knowing he'd take everything better than Marco would. He might be more useful, too, at least for the time being.

"Good. You're still alive," was how Julian answered the phone.

Wade's lips twitched. "For now," he agreed quietly.

"Why are you whispering?"

"We're in the car and Sam's asleep."

There was a lengthy pause. "You've progressed to nicknames?"

He fought the urge to snarl at the phone but couldn't prevent his fingers from tightening on it. "Do you want to hear what's going on, or do you want to piss me off?"

"Actually, I'd like to do both, but business can come first."

"Gee, thanks," Wade said sarcastically. "After Marco left, we tried to get a little bit of sleep, but Bellar put a tracking tattoo on Samara."

"Bloody hell. They didn't catch you in your sleep, did they?"

"Close," he admitted. "She...ah...has a friend—an imp, actually—who showed up just in time to wake us up and warn us."

Julian was doubtful. "I don't know how I feel about an imp—they're a type of demon, as far as I know—but the fact that it warned you..."

"Yeah, that's about how I feel about it, too," he admitted, gaze slanting toward Keen, who was watching him with one eye barely cracked open. "Turned out they were there to take Samara to her father...who just so happens to be Bellar."

Again he heard Julian's multi-lingual cursing, but this time it failed to amuse him. "Are you certain?"

"She admitted it, finally. Bellar and Lilith are her parents. And he wants her back, bad. Found out a little while ago that she can amplify powers, which he wants to make use of."

Julian's head started to throb and he rubbed at his temple. "So we can't let him get his hands on her."

"Bingo. We'd basically be signing our death warrant, it sounds like."

"Can we just kill her? It would solve part of the problem. He'd be easier to take down without the extra boost."

The wolf in Wade tried to surface with a snarl, and the sound trickled out of his lips. Never mind that he'd agreed to doing just that as a last resort.

Julian heard it. "I take it you don't like that idea," he drawled.

Drawing himself back in, Wade said, "We might need her. For information." He ignored Julian's snort. "She knows Bellar. We don't. She could be useful. And she's got a line on a potential weapon that could kill him."

"Lie to yourself all you like, Wade, but don't lie to me. Or do I need to repay you for all that advice you shoved down my throat when I was struggling with my relationship with Paige?"

Oh, Julian was enjoying himself. A lot. Wade wanted to punch him.

"No," he snapped. "I'll take care of it. I just wanted to let you know what was going on. We need to figure out where he's going to come through, and how to kill him when he does. And we only have until the next full moon, in a little more than two weeks."

"I hate deadlines," Julian muttered.

"So do I. So help me beat this one. Sam was sent here to find a stone book. Don't ask for more details because I don't have them. A seer—" He wasn't going to mention Lilith and deal with *that* argument— "said that this book tells how to get a weapon of some sort. The seer thinks it'll help kill Bellar."

"A stone book? You don't mess around when you go for vague clues, do you?"

"Like the clues we got last year from Red were any clearer?" Wade asked blandly.

"Touché. I actually think I've heard of one, though. It might not be the same one, but...give me a second."

"Sure."

He heard Julian typing for a minute before the Englishman came back on the line. "Where are you at right now?"

"Middle of Montana at the moment."

"Then there's one not too far from you, actually—about half a day, I think—but it could be problematic to get to, unless you want to turn cat burglar."

"Dammit. I don't want to break into a museum, Julian."

"It isn't in a museum. It's in the home of a collector. A rich collector, I might add. He fancies himself an archaeologist, though mostly he pays actual archaeologists—shady ones—to find artifacts for him. This one was found in the southern part of Mexico, but so far the language is undecipherable. Not anything local, as far as anyone could tell. Doesn't even seem to be related to the local cultures. I'll text you his address. Maybe you can get in to see it without breaking in. No reason to commit a crime unless you have to."

Wade's gaze slid over to Sam. "Other than a rich guy with delusions, you have any information on what kind of guy he is?"

"I'm sure I can dig some up. What are you thinking?"

"A lot of guys like that tend to either have huge egos or really like impressing the ladies. Usually both."

"Ego isn't too hard to play to, but impressing the ladies? Are you telling me you find that demon of yours attractive, Wade?" Julian asked, humor dripping from his words.

"She's not—" He cut himself off, worried the loud words might have woken Sam, but she just made a small sound, shifted, and settled again. More quietly, "She's not mine, but anyone who's into women would find her attractive. Be impossible not to."

"Mmhmm. Whatever you say, mate. And it looks like this guy is very big on both the ladies and stroking his ego, judging by the pictures I found. So between you and the attractive demon, you should be able to convince him to let you see the book."

"That makes it easier, then. If we decide it's the right one, then we'll see about buying it. Or stealing it if we have to. Though I'd be happy just taking some pictures and sending them to you. Only person who might know more languages than you is Suni, and I think you know older languages."

"It's possible, and I'll be more than happy to translate if I can. Just keep me in the loop either way, okay?"

"Deal. Now send me that text and go give Red a hug for me."

"I will, but I'm kissing her for me."

Wade hung up on a laugh.

A few minutes later, Samara woke. Wade tried to ignore the skin revealed when she slowly stretched and kept his eyes fixed—mostly—on the road.

"Feel better?" he asked.

She yawned then nodded. "Much. I could still use a full night's sleep at some point, but it helped."

"You need a few before I ask you some questions?"

She shook her head. "No, I'm good. What do you want to know?"

He hesitated. There was a lot he was curious about, but some of what he wanted to know would no doubt piss her off if he addressed it wrong. "You mentioned Olarid. Is that the dimension you come from?"

"It is," she said slowly.

"Tell me about it? I've never been to another dimension. I know they exist, and they're all different, but I've never really studied up on them. Never had a reason to before, but I figure knowing where he came from might help us fight Bellar."

For a minute she looked at him like she was expecting some sort of trap, but then she started to talk. "At first, it looks like a paradise. The weather is almost always sunny, and when it rains, it's a light rain that soaks the earth and makes the plants grow, so everything is lush and green. There are tons of flowers and everything seems so alive and perfect. Just looking at it, you would think you could live anywhere in the dimension and just pluck food from the trees. There are lots of animals, too, in all sorts of shapes, sizes and colors." She shook her head. "But it's *not* a paradise. It's *not* perfect. Damn near everything there is dangerous. The most beautiful flowers are poisonous, some plants are carnivorous, and every single animal that calls Olarid home will do its best to kill you. Most of them are really good at it, too, whether they look deadly or not. Even the demons there don't like to stay too long outside of stone walls. It's always a gamble to see whether demon or animal will come out on top in a fight to see who eats who."

"You said the demons there. Does that mean there are other people, too? Or is it just animals and demons?"

She grimaced. "No, it's not just demons, but demons are the only ones who are even remotely free. And I say remotely because most are more on the lines of indentured servants, if not worse."

"What do you mean? Who else is there?"

"I imagine it's about as varied as it is here. There are humans, elementals, shapeshifters, witches...And of course imps. We even have some people that are from dimensions other than Earth. Bellar doesn't really discriminate there. Though most of the ones there have never actually seen their home dimension."

"Wait, are you saying...they're slaves?"

She winced at the outrage in his voice and nodded. "They are. Even Keen was considered a slave."

Wade glanced at the imp, which is the only reason why his anger fizzled before it could reach the boiling point. "You don't treat him like one."

"No, I don't, because he isn't a slave to me. He's my friend. And before you ask, no, I don't condone slavery. No one should own another person, regardless of what they are."

"I guess the rest of the demons don't agree with that?"

"I know of a few who do, and I'm sure there are others, but most hide that opinion because Bellar terrifies them and he enjoys having slaves. In his mind, everyone should worship him and do everything for him. If he has to lift a finger, it had better be because he chose to."

"What about in other parts of the dimension?"

Sam frowned and shook her head. "What do you mean?"

"Away from your fa—Bellar. Do other places on Olarid agree with him on slavery?"

"Ah. Wade, you don't understand. There *is* no place on Olarid that isn't controlled by my father. He is the ultimate ruler of the entire dimension," she said sadly.

Shit. That meant Bellar was probably more dangerous than he'd expected. "How does he control all those demons? Surely there have been demons who thought they should rule in his place."

"Sure. There used to be attempts to overthrow him every few decades, but he's the Lord of Evil Things."

"So? What's a title have to do with it?" He asked. Julian had given him an answer, sure, but even he had admitted to not knowing what was truth or rumor.

Sam sighed. "I thought you knew about demons."

"I do," he muttered.

"Titles like that aren't just chosen, wolf. They mean something. They point to the main powers a demon is known for. So when I say that he's a lord of evil things, I mean that he rules over evil things. As in, he can control them."

"Fuck." So that was confirmed, then. An army who can't argue with the bad guy? That was really not good. They needed to separate Bellar from anyone evil when they went to kill him. He frowned. "Wait, but he had to tattoo you to keep you from attacking him."

She arched a brow at him. "Yes, yes he did," she said dryly. "And why do you think that is?" she asked, bitterness coating each syllable.

He didn't say anything, because the enormity of what it meant had just hit him. If he believed her—and he did, despite everything—then Bellar hadn't been able to control her because she wasn't evil. And if she wasn't evil, then she'd been sorely misjudged based solely on *what* she was rather than *who* she was. But the realization made something ease within him. Some of the guilt he'd been harboring for being attracted to her lessened. Maybe she was still a demon, but maybe she wasn't bad.

"I'm sorry," he told her, and he meant it.

He expected her to gloat or drive the point home, as so many would have, but she just gave a single regal nod. "It's okay. We should figure out where the book is and focus on that."

"I've got an address on one. We'll see if it's the right one when we get there, but Sam?"

"Hmm?"

"We're probably going to have to suck up to the person who owns it in order to get a look at it."

She frowned then sighed. "Whatever it takes. If only that were the worst we'd have to suffer to get this job done."

"Seriously," he mumbled. "We should be there in another hour. There might be some problems though, even if we get in to see it without a problem. No one's been able to translate it so far. But we can take photos and send them to some of my linguist friends and see if they can come up with something."

"That sounds great, so long as we can get something to eat afterward. But what's a photos?"

Wade chuckled and spent the rest of the drive explaining the wonders of modern technology to an ancient demon.

CHAPTER 8

T he house Wade's GPS led him to looked pretty much how he expected it to look; large, wealthy, a little gaudy, and a lot ostentatious. He was glad he'd decided to make a stop before they headed to the estate, getting new clothes for both himself and Sam so they looked less like what they were and more like academics. He hated them, and resolved to change as soon as they were done here.

They stopped at the gate and Samara goggled at the house. "You said just one man lives here?"

He made a noise of agreement and nodded. "Probably with a dozen or so servants, but yeah."

"It seems..."

"Ridiculous? Stupid? Egotistical?"

She nodded. "Yes."

He grinned at her. "Well, let's see if Mr. Ridiculous will let us in." He rolled down the window and hit the call button on the intercom.

"Mr. Delaney's residence."

"I'm Wade Mooreton. I'm a historian here with my—" What to call Sam? "—assistant, Samantha Cunningham." While fake names had been discussed, and Wade had thought it would be funny for him to use Julian's last name, he couldn't figure out why in the hell he'd stuck his last name on Sam. It was too late to change that now. "We were hoping we might have a word with Mr. Delaney about one of the artifacts in his collection."

"One moment, sir."

It wasn't even two minutes later when the man's voice returned. "Mr. Delaney can give you twenty minutes. Pull down the drive and park by the fountain. You'll be met at the front door."

"Thank you." When the gate started to open, he gave Sam another grin and put the car in gear. "And we're in."

When they rang the doorbell a few minutes later, it was answered by a silver-haired man in a black suit. When he spoke, Wade recognized the smooth, cultured voice as the same one from the intercom. "Follow me please, sir, madam."

The inside of the house was just like the outside, only more so. Sam had to fight not to let her jaw drop at all the artifacts on display in glass cases and horrible but expensive paintings hanging on the walls. Worse, everything was cream and gold, with enough of the latter to almost hurt her eyes.

They were shown into a study which housed even more relics of the past, each secured behind thick glass, each identified with a brass plaque. The man who waited for them was dressed in an expensive suit, and a quick glance at Scott Delaney's well-manicured hands told Wade that he'd never been at a dig site in his life. Still, he put on his best professional smile, and after a small nudge to Sam, she did the same.

"Mr. Delaney, I want to thank you for seeing us on such short notice. We were in the area doing research and I realized that you were close. I do apologize for the intrusion, however," Wade said, pouring on the charm as he offered his hand to the other man.

It was accepted, and where Wade's hands were rough, Scott's were as smooth and pampered as they look. "It's quite all right. I'm always happy to support those interested in history. I'm very proud of my collection, and the bits of that history that I've been able to contribute to others."

Smug little asshole, Wade thought, though his smile never faltered. "As you should be. It's quite the collection you have. I can't say I've seen anything of this quality outside of museums."

"Thank you. I didn't catch which particular piece you're interested in, however," he said, his gaze sliding to the silent Samara.

Wade didn't miss how Scott's eyes never went higher than Sam's breasts, and he quickly released the other man's hand before he crushed it. "It's a book, actually. A stone book. I was told that you had one in your possession, though translation was proving difficult. While not trained linguists, my assistant and I do enjoy attempting to decipher ancient texts."

"Ahh, the crown of my collection. It is quite an intriguing piece of work. I'm afraid it's not on display, but if you'll come with me, I'll be happy to show it to you." He led them through another door and into what looked more like a lab or clean room. Metal boxes, each with a lock, lined the walls and made Wade think of safety deposit boxes. In the center of the room was another table, one with lights hanging over it, no doubt for studying the artifacts. Or showing them off, more likely. If this man actually studied any of the artifacts in his collection, Wade would kiss Keen.

Scott went to one of the drawers and unlocked it with a key and his fingerprint. He took a cloth-wrapped bundle out and carried it to the table where he unwrapped it, showing the book. It was thinner than Wade had expected, and he counted five pieces of stone, each only a quarter inch thick. They were bound together with leather strips, though they looked new to Wade's eyes. Three sets of white gloves were taken out next, with two pairs offered to Sam and Wade. "I know it's stone, but I'd still rather not take any chances with the oils on your skin. I'm sure you understand."

"Of course," Sam said with a smile as she slid the gloves into place.

Just hearing her talk increased Scott's interest in her, and while Wade wanted to rip him apart, he forced himself to let Sam distract the man for a minute.

"Would you mind if I took some pictures? I doubt you would want to let something this precious out of your sight, even for a translation," Wade said as his gaze skimmed over the front of the book. It only took a glance for him to mentally curse. He could see why it hadn't been deciphered yet. None of the words looked even the least bit familiar. Hell, the letters didn't match up with any alphabet he knew, though he was a novice at those sorts of things. He tracked people down, he didn't do this kind of research.

"No, no, pictures are all right, just don't use any flash and be careful when you turn the pages. Because of how thin they are, even a short fall could break them," Scott said as he stepped closer to Sam, enough that his body brushed hers. "And what is your name?" he asked, fawning over her.

Wade gritted his teeth and made himself tune out the flirting. Sam wasn't his. Nor had she shown any interest in him. More than that, they had a job to do and she could certainly handle a sleazy human if he got inappropriate. Though he knew that she probably wouldn't have a chance to handle it if Wade got there first. And he would. He wouldn't be able to help himself.

He took his phone out and took several pictures of the first page before he carefully turned the stone over. Each of the ten pages of the book had multiple pictures taken so he could ensure that every symbol was captured. Once done, he closed the book and turned to Sam. "Do you want to take a look at it now, or are you okay with seeing the pictures later?"

She carefully extracted her hand from Scott, who looked openly disappointed at the lack of contact. "I'll take a peek now and just study the pictures later," she said as she moved closer to the book.

Wade and Scott both watched her as she studied the first page of the book for a minute, then two, before she turned back to them and smiled. "I think I'll be okay with the pictures now. I just wanted to be able to say that I'd actually looked at the book up close. Thank you so much for giving us this opportunity, Mr. Delaney."

Scott puffed up and looked like he was about to try touching her again. "Please, call me Scott."

"Scott then. But I'm sure you're busy, so we won't keep you any longer."

"Very true," Wade agreed. "We'd hate to stand in the way of your next big archaeological find. Good luck."

Disappointed, Scott nodded and led them out of the clean room. "Jackson will show you out," he said with a wave toward the door. "But please, do come again if you have *anything* you want to see," he pointedly told Samara, but she only smiled and left the study.

When they were back in the SUV, Sam grimaced while Keen climbed out of the back seat and into her lap. "That man was creepier than some demons I know. I feel dirty."

"I know, and I'm sorry for that. But we shouldn't need to steal the book now. I got pictures of everything."

"We wouldn't need to steal it, anyway."

He cocked his head as he started back down the driveway. "What do you mean?"

"It's not the right book."

"How do you know that? I didn't recognize any of the letters, and you only looked at the first page."

Sam frowned. "You really didn't understand any of it?" When he just arched a brow, she went on. "The book that we're looking for is apparently all about how to get the weapon. That? Was...um...was not about a weapon," she said, gaze averting from his and fixing on something outside the window.

Wade was intrigued. "No? And what was it about then?" he pressed.

Seconds ticked by and he thought she'd ignore the question, but finally she said, "Sex. It was a manual on sex."

"And you say you could read it? Well now, I might just need to get you to translate the whole thing for me," he said with a wicked grin as he started the car.

"Are you saying you need a manual on how to have sex?" she asked dryly, though her dark gaze was amused.

He chuckled. "I walked right into that one, didn't I? No, I don't need a manual, but I'm always happy to learn a new trick or two," he told her with a wink. "What do you say we call Julian and then grab something to eat?"

"Julian's the friend who's doing research for you?"

"He is."

"Then I'm okay with every part of that plan."

"Good, because I'm starving."

"You're sure it wasn't the book?"

Wade had put Julian on speakerphone, so it was Samara who answered.

"I'm positive. It only mentioned one weapon, and it wasn't one that I'd like to go into battle with."

"What? What weapon?"

Wade laughed. "Think Kama Sutra, Julian."

"Oh. No, I guess it wouldn't help in a battle with a demon, would it?"

"Not unless you were fighting an incubus. Have you gotten any new hits?"

"I didn't, but Paige did."

"Good on Red. I always knew she was a smart girl, even if she decided she liked kissing you more than me," Wade joked.

Joke or not, Sam's eyes narrowed. Keen, sensing her mood, leaned over and bit Wade's arm.

Wade jerked his arm away and glared at the imp. "Ow! What the hell?" Fortunately, while it had hurt, the imp's fangs hadn't broken skin.

Sam quickly drew Keen back and cuddled him to his chest. "That wasn't nice, Keen," she murmured to the imp.

"What was that?" Julian asked.

"The imp bit me. That's gotta stop, Sam. I'm not kidding."

Samara shrugged. "Maybe it does, but you do know he can understand you, right? You've heard him speak."

"Yeah, yeah. Fine. Stop biting me. I'm helping Sam out, which is why I'm tolerating an imp."

Keen hissed at Wade before hiding behind Sam's body.

Julian sighed. "Can we get back on track?"

"Yes, please," Sam replied.

"The Smithsonian has a stone book in its collection. It's at the American Indian Museum. If you have to steal it, it'll be damn difficult, so I'm hoping that you'll be able to read this one, too."

"It's likely. I know quite a few languages."

"You do? How many do you know?" Julian asked, his interest piqued.

"Julian? Not now, okay? You can nerd out later. Reading the book is going to be problematic even if she knows the language. You have to turn pages to read books," Wade pointed out.

"Not this one. Apparently it's two sheets of stone, or that's all they found, and it's displayed open, as far as we can tell. So unless the really important information is on the front or back, you're golden."

"Oh, well, that's not so bad then. I'll let you know what we find after we take a look."

"All right. Stay safe."

"Will do."

He disconnected the call and glared at Keen. "Seriously, what's up with the biting?"

"You hurt her," came the muffled reply.

"What? No, I didn't. I was just sitting here. I didn't even touch her!"

"You hurt her," Keen repeated.

Sam shook her head. "No, he didn't hurt me. I'm okay. And we're going to go get some food, okay? I'll bring you back something." Keen turned large, sad eyes up to her. "I can't take you in with me. They don't have imps here, so someone would try to hurt you. Probably a lot of someones."

"I promise we'll bring food, okay?" Wade added.

Keen gave a heavy sigh and climbed into the back seat and underneath the blanket Wade had put there just for the imp to hide beneath.

They climbed out of the SUV and Sam stared at the diner with apprehension. "You won't let me do something stupid, right?"

"Nah. And it's just a diner. Nothing fancy. You just look at the menu and tell the waitress what you want, then she brings it to you. Not really anything you can screw up."

"Yes, but I don't really know about the food here other than the cheeseburgers you've bought me," she pointed out as they started inside.

"I can order for you if you like."

Relief blossomed through her. "Yes, please."

They sat in a booth near the back, away from the other customers, though there weren't many at four in the afternoon.

"I'll have a deluxe burger, fries, and a sweet tea. The lady will have the meatloaf, mashed potatoes, and a chocolate milkshake," he told the waitress when she came by, then grinned at Sam. "You're going to love the milkshake if they don't have chocolate back home."

"I've never heard of it," she confirmed. "How long will it take us to get to this museum?"

"We're going to have to fly. Driving would take about two days, and we don't really have the time to waste."

Her eyes lit up. "Fly? You can fly?"

He glanced around to make sure no one was close, then shook his head. "Not like that. It's a machine, sort of like the car, but it's bigger, has wings, and a more powerful engine. I take it you like to fly, though?"

She nodded. "I love it. I just don't get to do enough of it to suit me."

"Well, maybe that'll change after Bellar's gone."

She smiled faintly. "Maybe. It would be nice."

"How strong are your wings?"

"Ah...pretty strong? I mean, they can carry me for quite a few miles before I get tired, and I could go further if I had more chances to exercise them. Why?"

He gave a short laugh and shook his head. "Nothing. I was just curious." No way was he going to tell her he was wondering what it would be like to fly with her. It seemed too personal a thing, not to mention the logistics of how she'd have to hold on to him to carry him. Then again, the thought of her wrapped around him...

That thought was interrupted when the waitress brought the food and set it in front of them. Sam was hesitant as she started eating, but after a few bites it was obvious she approved of his selections.

"This is so much better than the cheeseburgers," she told him, nearly on a moan, after she got her first sip of the shake.

Unfortunately, the sound of that moan went straight to his crotch. He shifted in his seat and gave her a strained smile. "I thought you'd enjoy it. Now eat up. We've got a plane to catch." And a wolf to distract.

CHAPTER 9

After they left the diner, Wade called and arranged for a private plane owned by the Venatoribus Noctu. They always had an Arcane as a pilot, so there wouldn't be many questions asked, especially since the pilot was going to be warned about the demon and imp traveling with Wade. Marco wasn't thrilled, but he knew that dealing with Samara and Keen was definitely the lesser evil. Especially after Wade spent ten minutes convincing him that Sam was actually helping.

On their way to the private airfield, they stopped and got a few things at the store. Sam needed some more clothes, and they got a notebook so she'd be able to write down anything she was able to translate from the book. He also got her a prepaid phone, programmed his number in, and showed her how to use it. He didn't think they'd be separated, but just in case, he didn't want her to be completely alone on Earth. More, he wanted to be able to find her if Bellar's demons got a hold of her.

Sam was excited about the thought of flying, even if she'd be using artificial means instead of her wings. "Do you think it'd be okay if I brought my wings out on the plane? I feel better when they're not hidden," she asked as she got out of the car carrying Keen. "They get kind of itchy when they're hidden for too long."

"Don't see why not. I'll just warn the pilot first, so he doesn't freak if he comes back and sees them," Wade said, grabbing the bags from the cargo area.

"That seems reasonable." She started to follow him to the plane, only to watch him falter and give a grunt of pain. It only took her a second to realize that there was an arrow now sticking out of his leg. She gently tossed Keen upward, which gave him time to unfurl his wings so he could fly toward the relative safety of the plane.

Almost a dozen demons were headed their way, one of them carrying a crossbow, which he worked on reloading as they moved.

"Shit! How'd they find us? We were on the move," she said as she helped Wade to his feet. When she saw him shift his weight off his injured leg, a hint of dread curled in her belly.

"Do you know any of them? Better, do you think we can take all of them?" Wade asked, pulling a knife.

"I don't know. We could take some of them, but they're mostly strangers, so I don't know how well trained they are," she admitted, though it galled her. But Wade was already wounded and she wasn't going to risk him. "Get to the plane, make sure it's ready to fly. I'll hold them off for a minute."

He bristled at the thought of leaving her to such odds, but he'd seen her in action. If anyone could give the pilot time to get ready to take off, it was her. On impulse, he grabbed her braid and yanked her to him, giving her a hard, hot kiss. Only the approaching demons kept it from being anything more than that. "Don't take any stupid chances," he told her before half-running, half-limping to the plane. "Get the engines going, now!" he yelled.

The kiss startled her and stirred her up more than she would have liked, but she had a job to do and couldn't dwell on it right now. Once they were safely in the air, she could ponder on what it meant.

Wade had returned her knives to Sam, and she drew them now as she faced off against the approaching demons. She heard the sound of the engine start behind her and smiled. It was a feral, dangerous smile that had the demons slowing on their approach. "You all know who I am," she called to them as she adopted a deceptively relaxed pose. "You know *what* I am. Are you sure you really want to fight me? At the very least, some of you won't be leaving this spot." She shrugged with feigned nonchalance. "Not with your heads attached, in any case."

One of the demons stopped outright. In Olarid, Samara did have a reputation for being ferocious and merciless. Not cruel, no, but when she was ordered to kill, or deemed it necessary to right a wrong, she gave no quarter.

And she never, ever failed.

"Come and get me boys," she murmured, fingers tightening briefly on the hilts of her knives. The demon she judged as the leader of this group broke off from the others, rushing at her.

His first attack was obvious as he swung out at her with an axe that probably weighed as much as she did. She ducked under it and slashed at his hamstring with her knife, slicing through it. He let out a yell and went down as his leg gave out on him. The demon tried to roll to put some distance between him and Sam, but she was on him before he could move, stabbing the back of his neck with her other knife, neatly killing him.

Knife still embedded in his body, her own body still in a crouch, she looked up at the other demons, who hadn't moved. No longer did she smile, but stared at them with death in her eyes. "Who wants to be next?"

"Sam! It's time to go!" came Wade's yell from behind her.

Slowly, Sam stood, drawing her knife out of the demon's neck. No one else was willing to risk a fight with her one on one, so they moved en masse toward her. Though it galled, she turned and ran for the plane. One of the demons was as fast as she was though, and she could nearly feel his breath on her back of her neck. Before she could turn to take care of him, she heard the whisper of a blade moving through the air, then the sound of a body hitting the ground and somersaulting with the impact.

She leapt into the plane and Wade slammed the door closed behind her. "Go!" he yelled to the pilot.

The sound of the engines increased and Sam felt the plane start to move, gaining more and more speed. She hurried to the window and watched as the demons tried to figure out how to get onto the plane. One by one, they were left behind as the plane taxied up the runway, then started to lift off the ground. Finally, the last one fell, but not until they had risen to fifty feet.

Wade had his phone out again, sending a text to Marco so the corpses could be cleaned off the runway before humans found them. It was bad enough they'd been there at all, but if a human got a hold of a visibly inhuman body...It didn't bear thinking about.

Safe now, Sam slumped into the seat closest to her. Keen spoke so rapidly she couldn't follow it as he flew to her and wrapped his small arms around her neck. She comforted him with a pat between his wings. "That...was unexpected."

"Maybe we'll lose them since we're going to the other side of the country now," Wade suggested as he lowered himself into the seat opposite her.

"Damn. You were shot," she remembered. After gently dislodging Keen, she knelt in front of Wade. She used one of her knives to cut open his jeans so she could get a better look at the injury. "It's not too bad. It doesn't look like it hit bone, just muscle, though it'll be a pain to walk on for a few days unless you have a healer."

"I do, but she's not anywhere close to where we're going," Wade said, voice strained. "I need to get the bolt out."

"I'll do it. Do you know if there are any bandages on this thing?"

"Probably. It's owned by a Hunter, and that's a high-risk job."

"Where?"

"Bathroom, most likely, back that way," he pointed.

"I'll be right back. Don't touch the arrow."

He gave her a lazy salute. "Yes ma'am."

She hurried into the bathroom and found the bandages, along with a bottle marked rubbing alcohol. She didn't know why anyone would rub alcohol, but she knew that alcohol cleansed wounds, so grabbed it along with a couple of towels.

Upon returning to Wade, she sat on the floor in front of him. "You ready for this?"

"If I say no, is that really going to change anything?" he asked with a faint smirk.

"No." Not wanting to give him time to think, Sam snapped the head of the arrow off and set it aside. She grabbed the fletching firmly in one hand and braced the other against his leg. A quick glance at Wade's face told her he was as prepared as he was going to get, and she pulled the shaft of the arrow out as quickly as she could. He let out a sharp hiss of pain as his hands tightened on the arm rests, his knuckles white with the pressure.

"That never gets any better," he said, teeth clenched.

"And it's about to get worse. I assume this is for cleaning injuries?" she asked, holding up the bottle.

"Fuck. Yes, it is, but I want some real alcohol before you dump that on my leg."

She could understand that. "Where?"

He pointed to a cabinet and she got up, surprised to find several dozen bottles inside. "Grab the whiskey," he suggested. She found one labeled whiskey and brought it back to him. He opened the bottle and took several deep swallows before he nodded at her. "Do it."

She held the towel beneath his leg before she dumped a generous quantity of the alcohol over the hole where the arrow used to be. He made a strangled noise at the sharp sting of it while every muscle in his body tightened. Not yet done, she poured some more on the other towel and started to clean the blood off his leg.

"I'm sorry you were hurt helping me," she said quietly.

He frowned down at her. Every time she acted...human...it surprised him. "Not your fault. It was my choice to help."

"Maybe so, but I'm still sorry."

He shrugged. "Apology accepted, but it's still not your fault. And you did keep the demons busy long enough for us to get the plane ready, so I think you more than made up for it."

After she'd cleaned and bandaged his leg, she put the alcohol and towels away, though she left him with the whiskey. She retook the seat across from him and noted that Keen had already fallen asleep in the next chair over.

Minutes passed as the plane climbed higher into the blue and Wade took several more swallows of the whiskey.

Though she was worried about his leg, her mind kept going back to the instant before they'd separated on the tarmac. "Why did you kiss me?"

Wade cocked his head. "Why do you think?"

"If I knew, do you think I'd be asking?" she grumbled.

Looser now that the alcohol was in his system, he gave her a lazy grin. "You might. Women do strange things sometimes. But to be fair, so do men. Remind me to tell you about Julian and Red sometime."

There's that name again. The woman he wanted to kiss him. Sam narrowed her eyes at him. "Who is this Red person?" she asked coolly.

"Julian's wife. Met her a year or so ago when she was his apprentice. Man, I really had to work to get Julian to make a move on her," he said, shaking his head.

Now she was confused. "So you're not interested in her?"

"Red?" He laughed, a deep, happy sound. "Hell no. She's like the little sister I never knew I wanted. Being interested in her would just be...wrong."

"Oh." She did her best to ignore the quick thrill that shot through her. "So, why did you kiss me?"

Wade took another drink without taking his eyes off her. "You really don't know, do you?" he mused.

"I really don't."

He lazily swirled the whiskey around in the bottle and studied her. "You're sexy as hell, Samara. Beautiful, dangerous, smart...It's a potent combination. On top of that, you were about to face off with a dozen demons in order to give us time to escape. Seemed like the least I could do, for both of us. Especially since those odds? They weren't in your favor."

"So it was...what, a good luck kiss?"

"Partly, yes. But I shouldn't have done it. Don't get me wrong, I wanted to, but I shouldn't have. Especially not now. We've got a job to do, don't we?"

Sam slowly nodded. "We do, yes. Distractions would be...unwise."

"Probably, yes." His head tilted. "You wanted to let your wings out, didn't you?"

That perked her up and served as a safer distraction. "I did. Are you saying I can?"

"Absolutely."

She was happy now that she'd worn the halter she'd just purchased out of the store. While she did occasionally wear shirts with backs, she preferred clothing that allowed her to release her wings if needed. She leaned forward and freed her wings with a low sigh of relief and pleasure. It really was uncomfortable keeping her wings put away for so long.

"They're beautiful," Wade murmured, watching as she flexed them, stretched them.

No one had ever complimented her wings before, which accounted for the faint blush that rose to her cheeks. "Thank you."

"Can I touch them?"

He had to be drunk, she knew, for him to ask for such a thing. A kiss when he thought she might die was one thing, but this? He'd avoided any sort of personal contact with her since their fight that first night. She should say no, since his sober self wouldn't be so happy, but she found herself nodding. "Okay," she said quietly.

He pushed himself out of his seat and half sat, half dropped down into the empty one beside her. He almost landed on one of her wings, but she said nothing, just watched him. Fingers brushed along the top ridge of her wing, light as a breath and more gentle than Sam had known he could be. "Soft…They're almost purple, aren't they? Or green. Just like a crow's feathers." Still, she didn't speak, even when his hand ran down the length of her wing, then carefully up, until his fingers brushed against her back.

Sam needed space before she did something unwise, because having him petting her wing felt entirely too good. She got to her feet. "I think you should get some rest. Let your leg heal before we get to the museum."

His hand dropped, but he wasn't sober enough to completely hide his disappointment. "Maybe. Wake me when we're about to land, okay?"

"Sure. Want some help?"

"No, I got it." He pushed himself upright and hobbled to the back of the plane, where a bed waited. He paused and glanced back to Sam, saw she was breathing a little harder than before. "Sam?" He waited until she looked back at him. "I'm not sorry for kissing you. Or for touching you." When she ducked her head, he smiled and slipped into the small bedroom and climbed onto the bed. Within seconds, he was asleep.

Sam sank back down into her seat and tucked her wings around her body like a cocoon.

She may be the better fighter, but Sam had no doubt that Wade was much more dangerous. To her, at least.

CHAPTER 10

"Wade? Wake up. The pilot says that we're going to land in a few minutes."

Someone was shaking his shoulder, and he really wished they'd stop. Every movement jostled his head, which pounded in reaction and made him groan softly. Had he gotten drunk? He didn't usually drink enough to get more than a buzz, and definitely not when he was on a job. For that matter, normally he didn't get hangovers, thanks to how quickly shifters healed.

Healed. A job.

Samara.

He jerked upright but immediately regretted it, since his head felt like it was going to explode. "Shit," he whispered.

"Hey, easy. You were hurt, remember?" Sam soothed.

"No. My head," he groaned, holding it in both his hands.

For a second she looked concerned, then understanding lit in her eyes. "Oh. From the liquor. I'm sorry, just move slowly. We're going to land in a few minutes," she said quietly.

"Yeah, moving slowly is good. Give me a few, will you?"

"Sure. Call if you need me," Sam said with a nod, slipping out of the bedroom and closing the door quietly behind her.

"I need a pocket Suni," he muttered, wishing he had the healer here right now. In lieu of her, he carefully got out of bed and found some aspirin in the bathroom. He was tempted to take a shower to see if that would help, but didn't want to waste the time.

It wasn't until he went to leave the bedroom to join Sam that he remembered what he'd done before he'd laid down. Talking about kissing Sam, touching—stroking—her wings. What the hell had he been thinking? No, a better question was what the hell was in that whiskey? He could usually hold his liquor better than that.

He wasn't a coward, so didn't hide in the bathroom, but rejoined Sam a moment before the plane touched down on the runway. With his hangover, he was jostled a little, but managed to remain on his feet with only a light touch to the back of a chair.

"Oh good, you're up. How are you feeling?" Sam asked, looking him over, her gaze lingering on the hole in his jeans where she'd cut them open hours before.

"Like shit, but I'm good enough to go wander around a museum. Though...you know Keen's going to have to stay here, right? We can't take him around people, and there are always a ton of people at the Smithsonian."

She looked at the imp, still snoozing, and now that Wade was focused on him, he could hear tiny snores. "Will he be okay here with the pilot?"

He nodded carefully. "Should be, but let me go check. In the meantime, put your wings away and get ready to head out? There should be a car waiting for us."

"Sure."

By the time he got back from convincing the pilot that Keen was harmless—which took some doing—Sam was ready to go. She'd woken the imp to explain that he had to stay here and, though he had pouted, he'd also agreed to behave. After Wade checked his bandage and changed into a fresh pair of pants, they left the plane and got into the vehicle outside. To Wade's relief, a driver wasn't waiting with it.

An hour later, they were inside the Smithsonian. Where Sam had been overwhelmed and a little horrified by the sight of Scott's museum-like home, now she was in awe at the exhibits they passed. It was all she could do to avoid stopping and staring at several of them. "This is amazing. Do your people have lots of these museums?"

"Quite a few, yeah, devoted to all sorts of things. Art, science, history, and a bunch of random weirdness. I'm pretty sure every country on Earth has multiple museums, though not all are as big as the Smithsonian." He inclined his head toward the left. "I think the book should be this way," he said, resting a hand on her back to guide her through the crowd.

"After this is all done, if I'm still alive, I think I'd like to visit more of these museums," she told him in a hushed voice.

His lips twitched as he ignored the idea that she might not live through this. "I think that could be arranged."

Sam pointed to a display and quickened her pace. "Look, I think that's it."

Trapped beneath glass lay two pieces of rectangular stone, bound together by a leather thong. This leather didn't look new, but neither was Wade sure it was as old as the carvings likely were. On the stones were symbols etched centuries before, but like the last book, it was nothing but gibberish to Wade. They looked sort of like hieroglyphics, but weren't quite right.

"Shit. Please tell me you can read that," he whispered as he snapped a few pictures.

She frowned and leaned closer to the glass until her nose was nearly touching it. "Technically, yes...sort of."

"What do you mean, sort of?"

"Well...you know how when children are starting to write, their words or sentences might not make much sense?"

"Yeah..."

"This is kind of like that. Most of the symbols are written incorrectly, and they don't actually make any sense." She lightly tapped the glass. "Like this right here says 'Water broke calf death honor.' None of the other sentences are any better."

"Are you kidding me? That's worse than kids learning to write," Wade said, frowning. It didn't make any sense. Even if it hadn't been the writer's native language, it should have been at least a little more coherent. Rudimentary, perhaps, but coherent. In fact, he could only think of two reasons for the text being so chaotic. One, the author had gone insane and the supposedly random words had made sense to him at the time. Or...

"I think this is a fake," he murmured to Sam.

Frowning, she cocked her head. "Fake? What do you mean? A fake what?"

Wade started to give her an incredulous look before he remembered—again—that she wasn't from around here. He drew her away from the book and into a quiet corner. "Around here, people will fake historical artifacts. Sometimes they just want to be famous for discovering it, but most of the time it comes down to money. People—like Scott Delaney—will pay a lot of money for stuff like ancient stone books or weapons or whatever. So some people will create a book or ring and do what they can to make it *look* much older than it is."

Her eyes narrowed as they flicked back to the display. "So someone might have taken two stones they just found and carved random words so they could sell it? And this is allowed?"

He chuckled and shook his head. "No, it's not. But some people are very good at what they do, so it might take a long time until it's discovered that they sold a fake."

Nodding slowly, she turned back to him. "Should we tell the leaders of this museum?"

"No," he replied instantly. "For one, they might not believe us. It's a language that isn't known to the humans, so they could argue that it's just undecipherable. Or they could demand to know how we're so sure. Either way, it's not worth the time we'd spend. Especially not when we're on a deadline."

"This world is so wonderful in some ways, and so confusing in others," Sam decided.

"It can be. But c'mon. Let's make sure they don't have any other stone books. If we're lucky, they just happen to have two and the other one is the right one."

Though it was obvious she wasn't counting on it, she nodded. They went through every public room in the museum but didn't find another book, stone or otherwise.

Wade had known that it wouldn't be easy to find the correct book, but if they didn't get a break soon, it would be too late.

They left the museum and grabbed some food before returning to the car. While Sam started eating, Wade called Julian and put him on speakerphone.

"It wasn't the right book."

Julian sighed. "What was this one about?"

"Nothing," Sam chimed in.

"Nothing? It was blank?" he asked, sounding shocked.

"No, it wasn't blank. It was a fake."

"In the Smithsonian?" Julian said skeptically. "How do you know?"

Since Sam's mouth was full, Wade answered. "She could read it and it was literal gibberish. One of the lines was something about water breaking a calf's honor. Said the symbols weren't quite right, either."

There was a lengthy pause before Julian chuckled. "They're going to hate that if they can ever figure it out."

"I'm glad you're so amused, because it means we don't have the right book. And before you asked, yes, we checked to make sure there wasn't another book."

All traces of humor died. "One moment. Let me check something. And did you get any pictures, by any chance?"

"I did."

"Send them to me."

Wade did, but it wasn't until several minutes later that Julian spoke again. "That's not the original."

Sam stopped eating and frowned at the phone. "It's not?"

"No. It's close. The dimensions look to be the same, and the overall style of the words is the same, but there are definitely some inconsistencies between the original photographs and the ones you sent." He made a low sound. "I wonder how they didn't notice it if I did," he murmured, more to himself than the people he was speaking with.

Sam and Wade exchanged looks, with the former looking baffled, the latter annoyed. "So where the hell is the original?" Wade demanded.

"I've been looking into it for all of five minutes, so how would I know?" Julian shot back. "Let me call you back." Before Wade could protest, he hung up.

A little growl trickled out of Wade's mouth.

"Maybe he'll get us the location of the real book," Sam suggested as she picked at her fries.

"I hope so. I can be patient when I need to be, but we're running out of time." Despite that, it was another thirty minutes until Julian called back.

"Tell me you didn't hang up on me for nothing," Wade snapped.

"I didn't. I spoke to a friend at the Smithsonian. She's one of us, so I could skip a lot of the small talk and red tape."

"What'd she say?"

"The book has been there for two months, but it's only been on display for two weeks. There was a lot of interest in it just prior to it being put on display, and a few people were allowed to view it when it was still being documented and cleaned. And you're never going to guess who one of them was."

"Who?" Sam asked.

"Scott Delaney."

"That motherfucker!" Wade exploded. "I knew he was a sleazy sack of shit, but now I want to rip him apart," he growled.

"Calm down," Sam murmured. "Your eyes are yellow." There weren't a lot of people around, but it only took one to notice something weird.

Wade closed his eyes and took several deep breaths until he could speak normally. "Did she say anything about his visit?"

"She seemed to have much the same opinion of him that you do," Julian answered. "She didn't trust him, knew his reputation, but apparently he donates to the museum often enough that the ones in charge decided to give him a sneak peek at the book."

"Is this the first time he's done that?" Sam asked.

"No, and she's going to be checking on the authenticity of every artifact he might have come into contact with."

"But we need to fly back to his house and get this other book," Wade said, shaking his head. "Which is going to be tricky because he does have some impressive security in his vault. Needs a fingerprint and a key."

"I'm sure you'll figure something out, but if you need help, just let me know. You know I can be there in an instant if necessary."

"I know. I'll call you."

"Good luck."

Wade hung up the phone and rubbed his temples. "Okay, so we have to go back to South Dakota. We can figure out a plan on the plane," he told her as he started back to the plane.

"Can we not just force him to show up the book?" Sam asked.

"It might come to that, yes, but that plan has problems, too. It's doubtful he'd send the cops after us since it's stolen property, but he could have hired thugs."

"Could they really be worse than demons?"

His lips curved. "No," he allowed. "Still, let's save that for plan B."

Though he couldn't argue that the thought of beating the slimy man did have its appeal.

The drive to the plane was uneventful, and no demons met them at the tarmac this time. They spent the flight discussing the best way to get the book, or at least get a hold of it long enough for Sam to get the location of the weapon. Assuming this one was the right book.

Wade was going to be pissed if it wasn't.

They considered, then rejected, the idea of going back in the way they had the first time. While Scott might let them in just for a chance to seduce Sam, he wasn't likely to respond well to them accusing him of having a stolen artifact. That would just result in him trying to kick them out.

The idea of breaking in was turned down, too, since they had no idea where it might be and couldn't bypass the biometric locks. Wade knew some who could, of course, but it would take too much time to fill them in and get them here.

Then Sam came up with an idea Wade absolutely detested.

"What if I go in alone?"

"No," he said, flat and with zero hesitation.

She wasn't put off by his quick answer and just shook her head. "Let me finish. If I go in alone, he'll think I'm vulnerable or willing to be seduced. He's human, so he has no idea that someone like me can even exist. It won't cross his mind that I could kill him before he could lay a finger on me."

"No," Wade repeated, but Samara kept talking as though she hadn't heard him.

"I tell him how intrigued I was by his book, how I love things like that, and really play it up. You said he has an ego and loves to impress women. Don't you think he'd show me the other book just to try to get me into bed?"

The problem was...she was right. Men like Scott cared about nothing but themselves. He would absolutely show off if he thought it meant he'd get a beautiful woman like Sam in the sack. Except Wade hated the thought of her having to pretend to be some brainless woman. And he really hated the idea that Scott might have to touch her.

He also wasn't enough of a chauvinist to tell her she couldn't decide for herself. It didn't mean he wasn't going to try to talk her into getting the book some other way.

"I do," he began slowly, "but I also know that you're unaccustomed to technology. If something went wrong and you ended up locked in the house, you might not be able to escape. Hell, depending on his setup, I might not be able to get in to help, either."

She was quiet for a moment, and he hoped she was truly considering his words. "That is a fair point," she allowed after several minutes, "but this is still our best chance." She arched a brow. "Unless you'd rather storm in there and try to force him to show us to the book and hope that we don't end up slaughtering everyone at his house. Which, I might point out, is a bad idea because we have no idea if this book is the right book."

Wade wanted to curse. He also wanted to punch someone, because she had a point. While he wouldn't mind beating the hell out of Scott, he didn't want to kill anyone. "Fine. But if we're doing it your way, I'm going to make sure you know what you're getting into, and we're doing it right. I know full well that you could annihilate Scott if he tried anything you didn't like, but we're not taking any unnecessary risks." A sentence which felt weird to say, since he normally loved taking risks, but that was when it was his life on the line.

"Of course," she agreed easily as her lips curved. "Teach me what I need to know."

Sighing, he pulled out his computer and spent the remainder of the flight explaining modern security features to a Fury while an imp dozed in her lap.

CHAPTER 11

J ust before they landed, Samara changed into a pair of the jeans Wade had bought her and the red halter top. She'd wanted to put her leather pants back on, since they were so familiar and comfortable, but Wade had thought it might be difficult to pull off her academic ruse while wearing them. It didn't make much sense to her, and she wasn't sure how the clothing she did wear said academic, but he was the one who lived here and knew the culture, so she conceded.

Wade had also wanted to drive her, but had admitted that Scott wouldn't act the same if he was there, even if he stayed in the car. Instead, he hired someone to drive her to the Delaney estate, though he promised he would be close by and would have his phone on and ready in case she needed him.

It was kind of sweet, even though she had no doubt that she wouldn't need anyone's help to deal with some humans.

The car drove up to the gate and she followed Wade's instructions, pushing the button of the box. When the same man as before asked what she needed, she smiled. "It's Samantha Cunningham," she said, using the same fake name Wade had used. "I was here yesterday, and was hoping that Mr. Delaney would have a few minutes for me."

"One moment." He took so little time that Sam had to wonder if the man had been given instructions to allow her inside if she'd returned. "Please proceed to the fountain as before."

"Thank you."

When the gate swung open, the woman in the front drove to the fountain, stopped, and twisted in her seat. "You want me to wait for you?" she asked, her face full of concern.

Sam smiled and shook her head. "No need. Thank you," she told the woman before she stepped out of the car and up to the front door. Before she rang the bell, she ran her fingers through her hair, hair which was unbound for this. She wasn't going to give the man any reasons to think rather than react, not when the fate of an entire dimension was to be decided.

The butler once again opened the door and motioned her inside. "Mr. Delaney is in the parlor. This way." He led her to the same room as before, and like before, Scott was waiting for her. Instead of the suit, he was now wearing a pair of black slacks and a charcoal sweater, and he looked very pleased to see her.

A slight nod dismissed the butler, who silently slipped out and closed the door behind him. "Samantha," Scott purred as he strode across the room to her, taking her hands in his. "This is a wonderful surprise. I wasn't expecting to see you again."

"Then I have to thank you for seeing me," Sam told him, smiling and letting him keep hold of her hands. "I hope I'm not interrupting anything."

"No, no. Of course not. What brings you back to my home?" he asked, thumbs stroking the backs of her hands.

She let her smile go sheepish. "It's kind of embarrassing. The man I was with before, he's my boss, and he's kind of...demanding. He wants what he wants, when he wants it. So even though I would have loved to get a better look at that stone book, he just wanted the photographs."

Scott's brows lifted, but he didn't seem put off. Instead, his smile widened. "You came back to see my book? Just to see my book?"

Sam laughed and shook her head. "Not entirely, no. Don't get me wrong, I'd love to see it again, and anything else you might have that's like it, but I also wanted to talk to you. A man who could not only find all this, but see the value in it, is someone I'd like to talk to."

"I think I can help you with both of your...desires," he murmured, releasing her hands and placing his on the small of her back. "Come, you can have as much time as you like with the book. And I might just have something else you'd enjoy seeing," he told her as he guided her back to the clean room.

"Oh? And what's that?" Sam asked, forcing herself not to cringe away from his touch. Where she'd thoroughly enjoyed having Wade touch her wings, the simple hand against her back now made her skin crawl.

"I have quite a few artifacts that I don't put on display, either because they're in a fragile state, or because they're too valuable to have out all the time," he told her as they entered the clean room. "Such as the book. There are so few intact stone books, especially of that age, that I simply must protect them."

She looked up at him, her eyes widening. "Do you have more stone books?" she asked, losing the brisk tone. While she was a master at hiding her emotions and thoughts, she could only hope she was equally as skilled at hiding her utter disgust in a man.

"I might," he told her with a smile that made her happy she was a trained assassin. His hand slid down, stroking her butt, then squeezing it, before he went to one of the lock box filled walls. "I have to say, it's rare that a woman as beautiful as yourself is interested in artifacts like this," he said as he selected a box and used his thumb and key to unlock it. He paused in the act of drawing it out to glance over his shoulder and give her what he probably thought was a seductive smile. "If you thought the other book was impressive, you're going to love this one."

"I'm sure I will," she told him as she moved around the table to stand next to him as he set the box on the table.

It was clear that, at this point, he considered her a sure thing, because he wound one arm around her waist and pulled her into him while he used the other to open the box. Since Sam didn't know which book—if any—this box contained, she didn't remove his hand from his arm. Yet. Instead, she ignored that arm while he opened the box and revealed a stone tablet, extremely similar to the one she'd seen in the museum.

"Look all you like," he murmured as he drew her hair back from her neck and kissed it.

While she wanted nothing more than to ram her elbow into his gut, she drew on a technique that had saved her in the past and blocked him out and focused on the book. Besides, she'd take care of him before she left. If he was acting like this with her, how many other women had he gotten pushy with? How many hadn't been able to protect themselves? No, she'd definitely make sure he understood that just because a woman was interested in his artifacts, it didn't mean she was interested in him.

As her gaze slid over the carefully chiseled symbols, she smiled. Scott may be a creep and a thief, but this book was the right one. She didn't bother asking permission before she slid her phone out of her pocket. Wade had made sure she knew how to take pictures with it, and she took several now.

Scott lifted his head and frowned at her, but the hand that had wandered down to her backside didn't move. "What are you doing?"

She flashed him a quick, genuine smile. "I told you I was interested in stone books," she told him as she turned the page and took several more shots.

That wasn't what he wanted to hear. He drew her away from the table, his touch irritated rather than amorous now. "The book. You're here for the fucking book?"

Arching a brow, she shook off his arm. "Did I say anything that might have indicated I was interested in anything but artifacts?"

"Damn right, you did!"

Sam shook her head. "No, I didn't. I said I wanted to see the book and any like it, and that I'd like to talk to you about them. You just assumed that meant that you could grab my ass and whatever else you wanted."

"No," he protested in a snarl, though it lacked punch after Wade's. "You came in here, dressed like that, flirting with me. You lied."

He was only two inches taller than she was, so it was easy for her to get in his face. "I never lied," she snapped, fighting to keep her wings from bursting free. "But if you want to talk about people who have done wrong, let's talk about you, Scott Delaney. You, who clearly likes taking advantage of women. You, who steals artifacts from their rightful owners." Her head cocked and she smiled dangerously. "What else do you do to add to your collection, I wonder?" She closed her eyes and drew in a deep breath through her nose. "Murder," she said, and it wasn't a question. "I can't say I'm surprised."

"How dare you talk like to me in my home?" he demanded, but his voice had a quaver to it that it hadn't before. "And accuse me of theft and murder? I want you to leave. Now. Before I call the police."

Slowly, she shook her head. "Not yet." She moved back to the table and turned to the last page of the book.

"Now!" he roared, grabbing her arm to jerk her back.

She turned and rammed her knee between his legs. Not normally a defense she went with, but it seemed fitting, in the circumstances. "No," she told him as he dropped to his knees, cupping himself and gasping for air. "You've done so much evil in this world, you're going to let me take these last photographs so I can do some good." Which she turned to do now, making sure she had the entire thing on her phone. "And you won't call the police either, we both know that. Because they would end up coming in here and you'd have to explain how you have several artifacts that belong to other people, including one that's supposed to be in the Smithsonian museum. And I would be *happy* to point that out to them if you did, by some chance, call them."

Scott glared up at her, not yet recovered from the blow to his balls. "You're through," he wheezed. "I'll make sure of it. No one will hire you. And I'll make you pay."

She crouched down so they were at eye level. "Listen to me. Women aren't here for your amusement anymore than you're here for ours. Neither are artifacts like the ones you keep locked away in the dark."

She leaned closer, dropped her voice. "You aren't alone in the world, and you're not the king of it. It's time you learned that."

Standing, she looked down at him. "You should return that book to the museum," she told him as she strode out of the clean room, ignoring his screams of rage.

The butler appeared when she reached the entrance hall. Like her, he had to hear Scott's screams, but ignored them. In fact, Sam thought he looked a little amused. "Leaving so soon, madam?"

"It seems to that your employer is a little upset with me," she told him with a smile. "He might even need some assistance."

The tiniest of sighs slipped from his mouth. "I'm sure he does. Have a good evening, madam."

"You, too," she told him as he opened the door and she strolled outside. To her relief, he even opened the gate when she reached the end of the long driveway. Not that it would have stopped her, but it made things easier.

Now she just needed to find where Wade had hidden himself. He couldn't be far, and though he'd told her the phone could call him, she had dealt with technology too much for the moment.

"Wade?" she called out as she turned right and started walking. It didn't take long before she spotted his SUV.

When she climbed into the passenger seat, his hands were clenched into fists. "Did he hurt you?" he demanded, even as Keen threw himself into her arms.

She laughed and shook her head as she hugged the imp. "No, though I do definitely want a shower, and he's probably putting ice on his balls right now."

"He…" Wade trailed off, seeming torn between amusement and rage. He forced the latter down with several deep breaths and shook his head. "Are you okay?"

"I'm fine," she promised him as she handed him the phone and got Keen settled. "Can you show me the photographs on this thing? I remember some of what I read, but I'd like to make sure I'm translating correctly."

"It's the book?" he asked, momentarily distracted, but he took the phone and opened the gallery.

"First page mentioned a spear." She gave him a slow smile. "Specifically, a holy spear, one meant to kill evil."

"That's fucking amazing. Does it say where it is?" he asked as he handed the phone back to her.

She looked through the pictures. "Does land of the swamp mean anything to you? Not swampland, but land of the swamp?"

"A place comes to mind, but it's a state, and not really a narrow area to search."

"Does it help if I tell you this particular place has five burial mounds, spread apart? And there's a sixth one they kept secret in the center. That's where the spear is." She frowned. "It says something about a test, but it doesn't say what sort of test."

He waved that off. "I think the test will be the easy part. Though I actually think I know what the directions might be referring to. Suck it, Julian," he said with a grin. "Does it say anything else?"

"Not really. Whoever wrote this liked their words and didn't keep them to a minimum, so what I just told you is everything I see on these pages. He used ten words when one would have done fine."

"That's okay. We're strong, we're smart. We'll figure it out and get the spear. Now come on. My leg is killing me and I'm sure you're hungry. Keen, too."

"Hungry," Keen moaned dramatically, rolling onto his back and clutching his stomach.

She grinned at the imp. "You're not wrong about that. I wish we had more time for me to see these places, though. I really like seeing Earth. I like a lot about this world, in fact," she told him as they left the museum.

"You haven't even scratched the surface of what's out there. The good stuff. There's a lot of bad, too, but I don't think it's mostly bad."

"Like what? The good stuff, not the bad."

"You've never seen a movie or eaten cake. You haven't stood at the top of a mountain and looked at the world spread out in front of you, or seen a river so large that no bridges cross it. You haven't seen pyramids of stone, millennia old, standing tall in a desert, or a wall so long that it can almost be seen from space." He chuckled and shook his head. "No, you haven't even begun to see what this world has to offer."

She sighed wistfully. "That all sounds amazing. Though what are movies?"

He laughed. "They're sort of like the photos, but they're moving and have sound. They tell stories. All kinds of stories. I think you'd like them, just stay away from anything portraying demons."

"What? Why?"

He scratched the back of his neck. "Well, a lot of times, any kind of supernatural person isn't portrayed in the best light. Not just demons, either. The Arcane, too. Wolves, witches, we're all the bad guys in a lot of movies. Sometimes they twist us physically, make us monstrous. Though they're not too far off with some of the demons," he admitted.

She wrinkled her nose. "I don't think I want that to be the first movie I see."

"I don't blame you."

"So where do you think the spear is, anyway?"

"A place called Louisiana. I need to double check, but I'm pretty sure I remember the five mounds. I think they're pretty untouched, too. A lot of the mounds are. They can't explore them for some reason or another. Can't get the permits to dig, don't have the money, stuff like that."

She nodded, though she wasn't sure what money had to do with digging and exploring. "How far away is it? Will we be driving or flying?"

"It's just far enough away, and our deadline close enough, that I want to fly," he told her as he started back to the small airstrip where the plane waited. "And if we're lucky, by this time tomorrow, we'll have the spear."

Then they just needed to figure out where they would need to use it, and hope it worked as intended.

CHAPTER 12

By the time they reached the airport, Wade was honestly exhausted. Yes, he'd slept on the way to D.C., but he'd also woken up with a hangover and a half-healed hole in his leg. Then to jump back on a plane, drive to Scott's, then back to the plane? He needed more rest than he was going to get between here and Louisiana. Still, it was something, so he'd take it.

He parked and pulled himself out of the car, stretching some of the kinks out of his back. "I can't wait until we've killed Bellar. I'm going to sleep for a couple days straight," he told her with a wry smile.

"Same here," Sam agreed as she climbed out, Keen cradled lightly in the crook of one arm. The imp was out, but he'd already gotten more sleep than Sam and Wade put together.

They started for the plane, only to find out they'd been tracked down yet again. Fortunately, they weren't caught completely unaware this time. It was Wade who caught a glimpse out of the corner of his eye. The demon was armed, he could tell that much, but not what it was wielding. Halfway to the plane, he grabbed Sam's shoulder and dragged her down to the tarmac. The knife that would have embedded itself in his chest instead flew over their heads, missing by several inches.

Sam twisted to prevent Keen from getting crushed and hissed when her knee smacked sharply against the hard, rough surface, sending a bolt of pain up her leg. She didn't protest, just looked in the direction the knife had come from until she could see the same five demons Wade had spotted. Unlike the last batch, these she recognized, and icy fury poured through her and her wings shot out.

Her father had sent demons she had once trusted. Demons she had once, long ago, believed were her friends, before she realized that Bellar had control over what basically amounted to every demon on Olarid.

An angry sound, not unlike Wade's growl, vibrated in her throat as she pushed herself to her feet. She only had one knife on her, but she wouldn't need more than that, not to deal with these five. No, she wouldn't even need that for this group. While not the worst demons that inhabited Olarid, they were damn close, and they'd betrayed her, all for the chance to get closer to her father's inner circle.

Without hesitation, she let Keen take to the air before she stepped in front of him and Wade, though the wolf rose quickly and tried to move around her. "I've got this," she told him in a low voice, more dangerous and somehow more demonic than he'd heard from her.

"You sure?" he asked, though his attention was almost entirely on her. With her wings out and partially spread, her black eyes shining with power, she looked more magnificent than ever before and he realized he didn't care that she was a demon. He wanted her.

"I'm positive." Her voice rose as her lips curved. "You made an enormous mistake, Solnal. I thought I taught you to better weigh the risks before starting a job."

The demon who spoke had brown scales covering his body and two small horns located just above his temples. His smile wasn't any happier than Samara's, but it wasn't as fierce, either. "When our master promises a place beside him, all for returning his worthless daughter to him, how can I refuse?"

"If you had a brain in that thick skull of yours, you would have realized that Bellar knows I can take all five of you without breaking a sweat." She shook her head and began to slowly cross the tarmac toward the group. To her relief, Wade let her without protest. "At best? You're here to try to slow me down for a few minutes. But my guess—and my guesses are normally accurate—is that you're the distraction while he sends the real team meant to take me back." She laughed softly. "But you want to know what the really funny thing is?"

Another demon, this one with rough, dark gray skin, scoffed. "You're the stupid one if you think you're getting away."

"Shut up, Izlar," she said dismissively. "The funny thing is that all of you seem to have forgotten exactly what I am."

Solnal was the first one to realize exactly what she meant, but it was too late. Her gaze went from one demon to the other and power poured out of her, striking them despite the distance between them. She might not enjoy causing insanity normally, but in this case, she relished it and gave no mercy. She reveled in the sight of their eyes going wide in panic, and couldn't even mind when Solnal tried to rush her, his serpentine fangs bared. Nor was she worried when Izlar caused rocks to thrust up from beneath the pavement, forcing her to shift to maintain her balance, or when a third tried to fling lightning at her. With his grip on reality quickly disappearing, his aim was off in any case.

Solnal's steps slowed before he started to fight an enemy that didn't exist, grabbing and biting at the air. Izlar dropped to his knees and began to try to dig beneath the tarmac to find the stone beneath. The third curled up into a ball, his electricity crackling around him like a protective cocoon. The single female simply stopped, slipping into some kind of catatonic state while the last male actually displayed, in Sam's opinion, the most sanity when he turned and ran away.

Wade stepped up beside Sam and brushed his fingers lightly over her wing. "They're done," he told her. "I'll call Marco to clean up."

Samara's wings drew in against her back, but they didn't yet disappear. "No. Call Marco, yes, but I need—"

The bullet went through her bicep before she registered the sound of the shot. Then a second rang out, this one not just hitting Wade in the side, but grazing Keen's leg.

"Shit!" Wade snatched Keen out of the air and grabbed Sam with his other hand, pulling them back toward the cover of the car. They wouldn't make it to the plane, especially not since that was where this new group of demons was. He wasn't even sure they could make it back to his SUV.

The demons continued to fire—at least one of them with literal fire—as they ran. He felt the punch and heat as some of the magic connected with the back of his shoulder, but he didn't stop, not if he wanted to live past the next hour.

He released Sam, drawing his pistol. He hated the weapon, but since he knew he'd be fighting demons, he'd made sure to carry it. Unwilling to stop long enough to turn, he took the risk of firing behind him. It was unlikely he hit anything, but the shots from the demons did pause long enough for Sam to jump in the SUV. Wade was only a moment behind. As soon as the engine was on, he slammed it into gear and stomped on the gas. Right now he wasn't concerned with where he was going, just putting distance between them and the dozen demons rushing the car.

Keen crawled from Wade's hold into Sam's lap, whimpering at the pain from the graze. She was in worse shape but cuddled him close as she twisted to watch the demons.

"We need the Hunters here now. Even if we outrun them, they need to be dealt with before they attack anyone else," she told him.

"Agreed."

He used his car's system to call the Hunter and a moment later Marco's annoyed voice came out of the phone.

"What's going on, Wade?"

"Got demons at the airport."

"Dammit! How many?"

"Four insane, one insane and running, and…" He glanced in the rearview mirror but could only see a couple of the demons. "Twelve up and ready to fight. They were at the plane, but some are chasing us." After only a moment's pause, he added, "I'm not sure if the pilot made it out."

There was a quick curse then Marco said, "Call me when you're safe," before he hung up.

Wade glanced at Sam. "Watch for the Hunters."

"I am," she promised as she stared out the back. It only took a minute before she saw one of the demons who'd been trying to keep up by air fall. "I think they're here," she said, and the moment the last word was out of her mouth she saw two new people, clearly not demons, attack the red-skinned demon in the lead. "Should we stop and help them?"

"No," Wade said instantly. "Marco said to call when we're safe, and he's got hundreds of Hunters to call on. This is what they're trained to do. And we've got to get to that spear."

She turned back to him. "I'm guessing we're going to be driving now?"

"Yeah, but before we do a road trip, we need to get patched up. How badly are you and Keen hurt?"

Sam shifted Keen so she could look him over and he gaze her a sad, pain-filled look. "He's just got a shallow cut on his side. As long as we clean it, he'll be okay."

"And you?" he asked, daring to look away from the road just long enough to glance at her.

She smiled faintly at him and shrugged. "I've had worse. I'm just more concerned about bleeding everywhere."

"I want to put some more distance between them and us, then we'll stop," he promised, and hoped he could keep it before the blood loss forced him to pull over.

Marco had told him to call when he was safe, but it wasn't until the Hunter called him back about thirty minutes later that he started looking for some place to stop.

"Are you okay?" the Hunter demanded the moment the call connected.

"Yeah. Are you?"

"Lost one," Marco admitted, and Wade could almost hear the commander grinding his teeth. He hated losing men and women, especially in the line of duty.

"Damn, Marco. I'm sorry," he said, guilt curling in his belly.

"So am I," Samara added quietly.

Then Wade remembered Marco had one more person at that airfield. "What about the pilot?"

"He's okay. Was banged up, but we were able to heal him. And the demons have all been dispatched, aside from the one you said ran. I've got two trackers on that one."

"Thanks, Marco. Hopefully, our next stop will be the spear, but I'll keep you updated," Wade promised.

"You got the location?"

"Unless I'm way off base, yeah. Without the plane, it'll take us a day or so to get there."

"Got it." Once again, he hung up without saying goodbye, but Wade understood. Marco's priority now was his men, right where it should be.

No one said anything else until Wade pulled into a grocery store parking lot. He looked down at his side and grimaced. He was wearing a black shirt, so it wasn't too noticeable, but it was also bleeding, so he'd have to be quick.

"Can you keep Keen out of sight? Hopefully, I'll just be a few minutes."

"Sure," she agreed with a nod.

Fortunately, there were only a couple of people in the store and he was able to use one of the self check-outs, so there was no one to really pay attention to his condition.

When he returned to the SUV, he felt even worse than when he went into the store, and the wetness of his shirt and pants gave him an idea of how much blood he'd lost. Both new injuries were throbbing with pain, too, and he wasn't sure how they were going to make it to Louisiana at this rate.

Samara noticed.

"I don't know that you should be driving," she told him, her brow furrowed, lips thinned in concern.

"Yeah, well, unless you can learn to drive in ten minutes, we don't have another option," he told her, voice tight.

"It doesn't seem like it would be that difficult," she murmured absently as she reached over and drew his shirt up. The sight of the wound brought a small sound of dismay to her lips. "We need to take care of this first."

"Yeah." Fortunately, they were near the interstate, which meant truck stops, and truck stops meant bathrooms and showers. A quick check of his phone had his eyes closing in relief. There was one only a mile and a half away. He could make that.

He hoped.

Samara dealt with Keen's injury on the short drive, but the graze was superficial. Painful, certainly, but it wouldn't do him any lasting damage. Wade had gotten some pills called aspirin, and she gave one to the imp before he curled up in the back seat to sleep.

She finished just as Wade was pulling into the truck stop. He looked paler than she'd like and wondered just how severe the wounds from these bullets could be. After all, he wasn't a weak man, and for him to be looking like this meant he was in serious pain or more badly injured than he was admitting to.

Grabbing the bag, she got out of the car and went around to the driver's side, helping Wade out. She slid an arm around him—careful to avoid grabbing the gunshot—and half-supported him as they made their way inside.

"Gotta pay for the shower," Wade murmured to her, pausing to pull his wallet out.

"I'll take care of it."

He looked skeptical, but drew a slim rectangle from the wallet and handed it to her, explaining briefly how to use the credit card. Fortunately, the cashier seemed used to people acting a little oddly, so in just a few minutes she was back at Wade's side with a key.

After making their way into the shower, she set the bag of first aid supplies down and turned to him. She pulled her knife and carefully cut the shirt off so he wouldn't have to lift his arms. Now that she'd gotten a good look at both wounds, she winced sympathetically.

"Is it that bad?" he asked as he leaned against the wall with his good shoulder.

"Your back isn't," she began slowly. "It's going to be painful for a few days, though, unless you can find a healer." She lowered herself into a crouch so she could see the mess the bullet had made of his side. "This, however, isn't good. I can clean it and close it as much as I can, but I would definitely see if you can get a healer." Glancing up at him, she added, "If we're attacked again..."

He sighed and nodded. "I know." He grabbed his phone and hoped the demons wouldn't find them for at least the next fifteen minutes. This time he was well aware of how early it was in England, but while Suni was closer, she couldn't teleport.

"Wade, I'm really starting to hate you," came the sleepy reply from Julian.

"Give me the number of another healer who can teleport directly to me and I'll let you go back to sleep."

"Why do you need a healer?"

"Got ambushed on the way to the plane."

Soft rustling came through the phone, even as Julian whispered to Paige to go back to sleep, that he'd be back in a few. It was only another minute before the witch appeared in the bathroom, wearing only a pair of black pajama pants.

Samara and Julian stared at each other for a minute before he shook his head. "Later," he muttered before he turned to Wade. The gunshot wound was the first noticed and he, too, gave a sympathetic wince. "I never thought I'd see the day when demons started using our technology against us."

"Most don't, but please, can you just heal him?" Sam asked. Julian flicked a glance to her, then laid a hand on Wade's side, just next to the wound. To her relief, the skin began to knit closed. Wade's color would take a little longer to return to normal, but at least he wouldn't lose any more blood.

"He took a fireball to the back of his shoulder, too, and an arrow yesterday to the leg," she pointed out, and Wade helpfully turned to show the wound.

"You don't do anything halfway, do you?" Julian asked as he set about healing those, too.

"If I didn't, I'd be dead," Wade said dryly.

"True." Julian stepped back and studied Samara with a detached curiosity. "So what exactly happened?"

"Not yet." Wade inclined his head to Sam. "She's hurt, too."

"Oh, it's not that bad," Sam protested. Julian may have conceded to working with her to stop Bellar, but she doubted he wanted anything to do with her directly.

"You got shot," he snapped back. "Bad or not, it's still a wound. If you don't give a damn about your pain, fine, but we keep getting attacked by demons. We both need to be at the top of our game if we're going to get the spear and kill Bellar."

For a full minute, they stared at each other, neither willing to give first. Julian broke the standoff when he stepped between them. "Where?" he asked her.

She sighed and turned to show the hole in her arm. Did it hurt? Absolutely. But she'd also grown up in Olarid. This was far from the worst she'd suffered. She couldn't say it was nothing, but she had grown depressingly accustomed to existing with pain. Honestly, the awkwardness thanks to Julian was almost worse.

It took another minute before he reached out laid his hand on her arm. Only a moment later, he lifted his hand, but the pain remained.

"Why aren't you healing it?" Wade demanded.

Rather than responding, Julian stepped partially behind Sam and shifted her arm. "The bullet's still in her arm."

"What?" she asked, lifting her arm up to try to look at it.

Wade cursed. "How deep?"

Julian probed at her arm with more gentleness than she'd expected from him. "Not far." He glanced to Wade. "I can remove it with magic."

"Do it, please," Sam told him.

He nodded and held his hand over the entry wound. She felt something shifting beneath her skin, more uncomfortable than painful, then a tiny blob of metal flew out of her arm and into his palm. His other hand touched her arm and, this time, she felt the pain receding. "Better?"

"Much. Thank you."

"Good. Now will you tell me what the hell happened?" he asked as he turned back to Wade.

"We were walking from my SUV to the plane when we were attacked. First group of demons was…easily dealt with," Wade explained, looking to Sam, "but there was another, larger group. They were at the plane, so we made a run for it. Sent Marco to deal with the demons."

"Losses?"

"One."

"Damn. Was the trip worth it?"

"Seems to be. Book mentioned a spear in what I think is Louisiana. That's where we're headed as soon as we leave here."

Julian nodded. "You need anything from me?"

Wade considered, but ultimately shook his head. "The healing is good enough for now. Go back to Red."

"Are you sure?"

Before confirming that, Wade looked at Sam, who only shrugged. "Yeah, I'm sure."

"All right." Julian gave Sam another long look before he disappeared.

Without the witch causing tension, Sam moved closer to Wade, checking to ensure his wounds were healed. Satisfied, she inclined her head to the shower. "You should wash up before we go."

"Yeah. I'm going to need another shirt, too."

"Can I use that card to get one?"

"Yeah. Find something for yourself, too, since all our clothes were on the plane."

While he cleaned up, she found a tee-shirt and hoodie for him, and the same for herself. As an afterthought, she grabbed a blanket as well, just in case they needed to better hide Keen. By the time she returned to the bathroom, Wade was free of blood, his hair damp.

They changed into the new clothes, grabbed some drinks and snacks, then went back to the SUV. "I know we both want to rest, but I want to put some more miles between the plane and us, just in case," he told her.

"I know your leg is healed, but I wouldn't mind doing some of the driving if you tell me how."

He considered her over the hood for a moment. She was smart and had exceptional reflexes. Everything else had been picked up with relative ease, so he didn't see why this wouldn't be the same. It also meant they could take turns getting some rest on the road. "Let's get someplace with fewer cars and I'll show you."

He did just that, and she did indeed learn with minimal issues. When he got around to explaining speed limits to her, though, she was thoroughly confused.

"Why would you drive slow when there's nothing blocking you, though?" she'd demanded. Since he didn't really disagree with her, he could only shrug.

Once she was comfortable behind the wheel, he reached over to start tapping on the touch screen. "I'll set up the GPS, so it'll tell you when you need to turn, and it'll show a map if you need it. I think you'll be okay, but if you want to practice while I do some checking, go for it."

"Love to," she told him with a quick grin before she put the car in reverse and sped back in a half circle.

He rolled his eyes at her enthusiasm, but couldn't help but grin as he pulled his phone out. A few internet searches later netted him the information he was looking for. "Got it. This time tomorrow, give or take, we'll be at the mound and be able to start hunting for the spear."

"That soon?" Sam asked, surprised. "I thought that since we were driving instead of flying that it would take a lot longer."

"Depends on how fast you like driving, but yeah. That's accounting for us stopping for some sleep, too."

She stopped and was quiet for a long moment, staring at the steering wheel.

"Hey, what's wrong?"

"I just...Aside from the demon attacks, I've been enjoying myself, wolf. I don't want it to end," she whispered.

He stroked a hand over her hair and gave one of the locks a gentle tug. "Maybe it doesn't have to end. Let's not worry about what might be and just focus on the now, okay?"

She gave him a faint smile. "Yeah, okay. We should get going."

"I think I know something that'll make Keen happier about having been left in the plane and car while we were gone."

"Oh yeah?"

"My computer. I was too tired when I got home the night we met, so it's still in the back. It's a machine, sort of like the phone, and it can play movies. I've got a few on there that I could play for him while we're on the road."

Her smile firmed. "That's sweet. I know you don't really like Keen."

He shrugged. "It's not that I don't like him. I was surprised as hell to find him in my cabin, yeah, and I'd had a few too many surprises, but he's not a bad guy. When he's not trying to bite a chunk out of me, anyway."

She laughed and the sound made him smile. She hadn't laughed nearly enough. Hadn't had a reason to, he knew. "He's just protective of me and thought you'd hurt me. He doesn't just like biting you, I promise."

"That's a relief. I don't mind being a chew toy, but I generally prefer to be bitten by a gorgeous woman and not a tiny imp," he told her with a wink.

She blushed and he chuckled as he got out and walked to the back of the SUV, retrieving his laptop. Fifteen minutes later, the SUV was heading south and Keen had his eyes glued to the laptop, which was playing an animated movie.

It wasn't a bad start to a road trip.

CHAPTER 13

After they'd gotten out of the city and Wade was sure that Sam was confident behind the wheel, he called Julian again.

"Don't tell me you got the spear already."

"No, but I did want to talk about it a little more now that I'm back on the road and you're back with your books."

"Oh?"

"I told you I managed to pin down the location. I think. It's in a burial mound in Louisiana. There's a cluster of them that form a circle, and there's supposed to be one in the middle where the weapon is."

"And all it said was it was a spear?"

"No, it said it was a holy spear, but other than that, yeah."

"That could be...good and problematic."

Wade frowned. "Problematic?"

"Holy, Wade. Good for killing a demon, especially an evil demon, but not so great if a demon's trying to use it."

He hadn't thought of that, but it was also a moot point. "Not a problem. I'm going to be using it."

"What?" Julian yelled.

"You heard me. It's the best option since Samara physically can't do anything to harm Bellar thanks to an enchanted tattoo on her neck. And you know I've been in tough situations before."

"Not like this."

"Maybe not, but it's my choice, not yours. And I've made it. I'm just keeping you in the loop like you wanted."

Julian sighed. "Dammit, Wade. You know if anything happens to you that Paige is going to be furious."

"I know. It won't. Look, Julian, I gotta go. But I'll call you when we reach the mounds."

"You'd better," Julian muttered. "Stay safe."

"I will." He hung up the phone and sighed, rubbing a hand over his face.

"Everything okay?"

"Yeah, Julian just worries. He's worse than a mother hen."

"It's not a bad thing to have friends who worry about you. It's a precious thing, and you shouldn't take it for granted," Sam said, her hands tightening on the steering wheel.

"I don't, Sam. I promise. Julian's like a brother to me. Trust me, I know what I have with him," he assured her. Several minutes passed before he spoke again. "It sounds like a sensitive subject for you."

"Because it is," she said, voice clipped. When he said nothing, she sighed. "The five we first saw at the plane..."

"The ones you knew?"

She nodded. "Almost my entire life," she said quietly. "Once, centuries ago, I thought they were my friends."

"I take it they weren't?"

"No. They just wanted to get closer to my father. They wanted the power that would come with being at his side." She laughed humorlessly. "They used me. I confided in them. I taught them how to fight. Right up until it was more advantageous for them to screw me over as proof that they would do whatever Bellar wanted."

His gut twisted in sympathy and rage for her. "I'm sorry, Sam."

"Me, too."

Minutes passed and she decided to shift her focus elsewhere. "You said you helped Julian with his wife?"

"I did."

"Why aren't you married?"

Wade blinked at her. "That's a hell of a question to spring on a guy. And out of the blue, too."

Sam shrugged. "Maybe, but I'm curious. You're not a shy man, and obviously you're interested in women, so why aren't you married?"

"Loaded question," he muttered. "Best answer, though, is the simplest one. I won't marry the wrong woman. Sex, companionship, partnership…those are great things, sure, but they aren't good enough reasons to get married."

She nodded. "That makes sense. I'm sorry you haven't found the right woman yet."

He glanced at her, then out the window. "I'll find her. Don't worry."

Miles passed with only the sound of Keen's cartoons breaking the silence. Hours later, just before everything closed for the night, Wade said, "Why don't you pull off here? We'll find a place to get some supplies, then a motel so we can order some food and get some sleep."

Sam followed his directions off the interstate and to a large, well-lit building. He told her to stay there and he'd be back in a few. When he returned, he opened the back and put several bags in it before they headed to the motel. He checked in then led her and Keen to the room. Once inside, Keen flew to one of the beds and curled up around a pillow, dropping almost instantly into sleep.

"I guess he's not too hungry," Wade said dryly as he set his bag down on the dresser.

"He may not be, but I am. And I'd like to see one of these movies, too."

"That can be arranged. I'll order us a pizza then see what movie we can find on TV. Go ahead and get comfy."

By the time he'd finished ordering the pizza, she'd ditched her shoes, washed the blood from her arm, and stretched out on the empty bed.

"Food'll be here in twenty," he told her as he grabbed the remote and laid down beside her, with only a few inches between them.

"I can't wait to see what a pizza is. Is it as good as the chocolate?"

He chuckled. "I think so, and some think it's the perfect food, but we'll see what you think," he told her, flipping through channels. He struck pay dirt when he found a movie just starting. "Ah, you'll like this one. It's got most everything. Violence, explosions, magic, humor..."

She barely heard him. Her eyes were wide as she stared at the screen, enamored by the sight of her first movie. "That's amazing," she whispered, awestruck.

He only grinned and settled in to watch, though rather than watching the TV like she was, he watched her. Her reactions were so open, and he could see the sheer enjoyment and wonder on her face as the bad guy created chaos on the screen.

When the pizza arrived, they ate cross-legged on the bed, Sam still glued to the movie. She did, however, take a minute to express her great appreciation for the miracle that was pepperoni pizza coupled with a cold soda.

After the pizza was finished and the box cleared away, they stretched out once more. Wade couldn't have said if it was an accident or sub-conscious design that had them closer than they were before, with the line of their bodies touching, but he was happy either way. After that, it felt more natural than not to slide his arm around her shoulders and draw her in close, her head pillowed on his shoulder. She stiffened for a few seconds at first, but quickly relaxed. It wasn't quite so easy for him.

With her so close, his body had a mind of its own. He was happy that he'd turned the lights off so it was dark aside from the TV. Maybe she couldn't see that he was aroused by her closeness. The press of her against him, the unique scent that was hers alone, even her facial expressions as the superheroes fought to save the world. All of it had his need for her building. Yet he couldn't bring himself to distance himself from her, even if it would be more comfortable.

By the time the credits rolled and the final scene had played, Wade was in agony. He wanted nothing more than to roll atop her, claim her mouth with his, and sink deep into her. When she drew away from him and slid off the bed, he nearly wept.

"I liked that. A lot. I want to see more movies," she said with a big smile.

"I'm glad you enjoyed it," he replied, voice strained.

She lifted her arms above her head, fingers linked, and stretched slowly. "I'm think I'm going to take a shower then get some sleep. You're wanting to get going in just a couple of hours, right?"

"Hmm?" He'd gotten distracted by the sight of her breasts pressing against her shirt, and the smooth expanse of belly revealed by her stretching. "Oh, yeah. As early as we can."

Her arms dropped and she smiled. "If you're asleep when I get out, I'll see you in the morning." Unthinking, she started to untie her halter, only to stop when she noticed Wade watching her intently. "Sorry," she murmured. "On Olarid, nudity isn't uncommon, but it seems to be taboo here." It didn't make sense to her, but she didn't want to make him uncomfortable.

"Not quite taboo, but you shouldn't apologize. And you, of all people, have nothing to be ashamed of," he told her in a soft growl. Just the thought of her taking her shirt off turned him on even more. He was disappointed that she'd stopped. It was probably for the best though, since he was harder than steel at the moment.

She didn't know what to say to that and hurried into the bathroom. The moment the door was shut, she leaned against it and closed her eyes. This was getting out of hand. He only had to look at her, or speak in a certain tone, and everything in her ached for him. There was a needy throbbing between her legs and her breasts felt heavy, begging to be touched. All of her was begging to be touched. By Wade. The same man who said he couldn't touch her even as he looked at her. Even as his eyes flashed yellow as his wolf peeked through.

Shoving those thoughts aside, she got in the shower. Her motions were brisk, though it was tempting to linger and try to ease some of the need. She doubted it would actually help, so simply cleaned herself then dried off.

When she stepped out of the bathroom, a towel wrapped around her, she came face to face with Wade. She gasped and a hand lifted, clutching the towel against her chest as she stared up at him. "Wade—"

His hands sank into her wet hair and he lowered his mouth to hers. This kiss was unlike the last one. He didn't crush his mouth to hers, nor was the contact brief. There was urgency for both of them, but this was a marathon, not a sprint. His lips moved over hers until they parted so his tongue could slip between them. When she moaned, he swallowed it as his tongue teased and stroked against hers, beguiling her with each touch.

Her hands found his arms and she clung to him greedily. At her surrender, his hands loosened and he wrapped an arm around her, drawing her flush against his body. He groaned at the feel of her soft flesh against him, and it took everything he had not to yank the towel off her, especially when she trembled against him.

"Sam," he murmured into the kiss and she blinked up at him, her eyes dazed with passion. He stroked a thumb over her cheek and tilted his head to nuzzle at her throat, drawing a whimper from her. "Tell me not to stop, baby. Tell me you want this as bad as I do," he whispered against her skin before he lightly pressed his teeth against her neck, biting just hard enough for it to send a jolt of pleasure through her.

Her hands still held onto him. She couldn't seem to make herself let him go. She didn't want to let him go. "Please," she moaned, not knowing exactly what she was asking for, just wanting this burning need to be eased. She wasn't unfamiliar with the concept of sex, but she'd also never felt quite like she did with his mouth working magic on her skin.

He growled and undid her towel in record time, letting it fall to the ground. The sight of her nude, her skin still damp from the shower, was a feast for his eyes. This time, he let himself look his fill, unable to look away from her beauty.

Thumbs brushed over her nipples and her eyes fluttered closed. One of his hands cupped her breast and she arched, pressing against his palm. "Wade," she whispered, unconsciously rocking her hips. He smiled as his other hand slid down her skin and between her legs until his fingers could stroke across hot flesh. She cried out at the contact and bucked against his hand. "Wade!" she said again, more urgently.

"I know, baby. I know. I want it, too," he said in a low voice. He slid a finger into her tight sheath and almost lost it when he found her slick and ready for him. "You're killing me, Sam."

She shivered and dug her nails into his arms, hovering on the verge of something new, something amazing. When his finger pressed deeper, she forced her eyes open, to watch his face, only to see it transform from lust to shock.

He drew back so quickly that she felt more empty than she'd ever been before, and her body swayed toward his before she caught herself. "Wade?" The plea, the need, were naked on her face, quickly followed by confusion when he took a quick step back.

"Are you a virgin?"

It took a moment for her brain to process the words. "What? Yes. Why?" He cursed and it was her turn to take a step back, baffled by this reaction. A moment before, she'd been certain she was going to have what she'd been craving since she met him, and now he was looking at her like he would rather do anything but touch her. "What is it?"

"Why didn't you tell me? This isn't right, Sam," he snapped, stalking across the small room and back again.

Now uncomfortable with her nudity, she knelt and picked up her towel, holding it like a shield in front of her. "I don't know. I didn't realize it mattered. What's wrong with being a virgin?"

"Sam, you're a two thousand year old demon. I never, *never* expected you to be a virgin. Most people don't even make it to twenty with their virginity! How the hell did you make it two thousand years?"

She frowned and shook her head. "I still don't understand why it matters, but I wasn't interested in anyone on Olarid. They're all evil bastards I'd sooner kill than take to bed." Anger began to grow and she let her hands fist on her hips, not caring that it meant the towel dropped. "Why in the hell do you seem to think it's a bad thing that I've never been with a man? I thought that's what men on Earth wanted, not that I understand what's wrong with someone having as many—or as few—lovers as they want."

Pissed at himself for wanting to pick back up right where he left off, even with her confession, he shook his hand and slashed a hand through the air. "I'm not doing this. You should have told me. Period. I'm going to go for a walk," he growled at her as he stomped for the door, slamming it on the way out.

Suddenly exhausted, Sam collapsed onto the bed, trying desperately to figure out what had just happened. His words hadn't made anything clear. If anything, they'd only confused her more.

Maybe she'd been right to abstain all those centuries. If sex was this complicated, then she didn't know if she wanted any part of it, no matter how much her body argued.

She sighed and shook her head. Men, no matter the species, were entirely too confusing.

Heart heavy, she stood up and went to put some clothes on and braid her hair, happy that Keen had slept through the whole thing.

CHAPTER 14

The moment the door closed behind Wade, he stopped. He wasn't exactly sure where, exactly, they were at, and there wasn't really any place for him to go unless he wanted to find some bar, but the memory of his hangover prevented him from seriously considering that. While right now his body just wanted to go back inside and pin Sam to the wall, his mind wanted a cold shower—or for it to start raining. Since he couldn't have either shower or rain, he decided he was going to harass his best friend once more.

He growled under his breath and yanked out his phone. As the phone rang in his ear, he stalked away from the room. Then it occurred to him that it was, once again, around five in the morning in England. Unfortunately, that thought came when the call was connected and it was too late.

"This isn't going to become a habit, is it?" Julian mumbled, his voice slurred with sleep and annoyance.

"Sorry," Wade said, though he was too worked up to truly be apologetic. "Forgot the time. Again. Called to see if you'd learned anything new."

Julian wasn't a fool, and he'd known Wade for centuries. He knew when something was off. "Bullshit," he said on a yawn.

"Huh?"

"Bullshit," Julian repeated calmly. "Not only did you just talk to me a few hours ago, I know you. You wouldn't call this early just for an update. What's wrong?"

Wade clenched his teeth and glanced over his shoulder toward the hotel room. He pictured Sam in the room—confused, aroused, and angry—and sighed. How had the last ten minutes gone so wrong? "Personal problem. Nothing for you to worry about. Besides, we've got more important things to worry about. Like, you know, a demon who's wanting to take over the world."

"Yes, and? You've never kept personal problems from me before. You generally bitch, get it out of your system, sometimes get my input, and take care of the problem. And if you're distracted by whatever this personal problem is, you won't be at the top of your game. Since demons keep finding you, you need to be at the top of your game."

"This isn't a general problem, Julian. I'm not having trouble with a bounty or dealing with slow as shit contractors."

"Ahh," was said in such a knowing tone that Wade scowled.

"What's that supposed to mean?"

"It means I know the source of your problem. It's Samara, isn't it? I suppose it could be another woman, but I doubt you're traveling with more than just her, which means it must be Samara."

Wade frowned harder and kicked a rock. "And what if it is?"

Julian chuckled. "Then it means that turnabout is fair play, Wade. You do remember putting your nose into my business last year with Paige, right? You were extremely persistent about it, if I remember correctly, and I always remember correctly."

"Dammit, Julian, that was different."

"Yes, because it was you giving advice and me hating it. It's also different because she's a demon, and until recently, you hated any and all demons. My guess is you're still convinced you do hate them all. Not that I can blame you. None of us are fond of them. Are you alone at the moment?"

Wade glanced around, but saw no one nearby. He'd even wandered far enough away from the motel that no one in any of the rooms could overhear him. "Looks like it. Why?"

A moment later, Julian appeared in front of him, grinning like it was Christmas as he slid his phone into the pocket of his sleep pants. "Because if I didn't show up, you were going to hang up on me in a minute."

"Motherfucker," Wade said, resigned. He hung up the phone and put it away. "Is this really necessary?" he asked, folding his arms across his chest, grumpy now because Julian wouldn't leave until he was satisfied.

Julian shrugged. "Could be. So what's the problem with Samara? My guess is either that she's been hitting on you and you're disgusted because she's a demon..." He trailed off, smiled. "Or is she resistant to your wolfish charms? Don't tell me the infamous wolf has finally found a woman who is immune to him. Actually, no, do tell me that, because it would serve you right."

"No! Which is part of the problem. Sort of."

Julian's brow furrowed. "Okay, back up, because I'm confused. How is her being attracted to you a problem? Mutual attraction is usually a good thing."

Wade sighed and dragged his hand through his hair. He didn't think Sam would enjoy him telling Julian something so personal about her, but he had no idea what in the hell to do. Julian was as discreet as they came, and Wade's best friend, so really, she'd never know. With no better option, he shrugged and said, "Tell me, Julian, would you expect anyone who's two thousand years old to be a virgin? Add to it that said person is a demon and hot as hell, and doesn't it make it less likely?"

Clearly surprised, Julian just blinked at Wade. "No, I can't say I'd expect that, not from anyone other than a virgin goddess or two—and I have my doubts that some of those virgin goddesses are actually virgins, but I digress. How did you find out?" When Wade gave him an unamused look, Julian had to turn a laugh into a cough. "The hard way, hmm? I can see how it'd be a surprise, but I'm still not seeing what the problem is. Everyone's a virgin at one point. Even you were for a couple of years. I'm sure you were precocious, but you were also a child for a while. Besides, virginity doesn't mean anything more than a lack of experience. This isn't the seventeen hundreds anymore."

"I don't like the fact that you have a point, though it isn't the right point," Wade grumbled.

"So what is the point, Wade? Because I really don't see what the problem is. If you want her, and she wants you, then I see no reason not to give into what would make you both happy. Be gentle, of course, unless she won't let you, but I don't see virginity as a reason to back off when both parties are willing. The concept of virginity is honestly outdated, in any case. I'm surprised you care either way." Wade didn't speak, only glared at the ground like he was trying to crack the asphalt open with his mind. Slowly, Julian gave him a shit-eating grin. "You're intimidated."

Wade's head jerked up. "The hell I am," he snarled.

Julian wasn't bothered by the snarl. He knew this wasn't something Wade would actually attack him over. Besides, he was enjoying this. It really was amusing that Wade couldn't take what he dished out. "You are. You're intimidated that she's never had sex before and you could be her first. You're scared to death and covering it with grumpiness." He chuckled. "I thought grumpiness was my job, and yours was a zest for life."

Wade bared his teeth and growled at Julian, but it didn't bother the witch at all.

It took a minute, but Julian sobered. "Wade, I get it. There's a lot of pressure when you're someone's first. Or in your head there is, at least. You don't want to hurt her, you want it to be good, and you want it to be memorable. But I know you. You're not going to hurt her, or let her leave your bed unsatisfied. You just need to stop second guessing yourself. It was okay to be shocked when you first find out, but it's not okay to act like you blame her for not being experienced, or worse, treat her like a leper for it."

Wade let out a breath. "You're right. I hate it, and I'm tempted to kick your ass for it, but you're right."

"Of course I am," Julian said, smirking. "Like I said, turnabout is fair play." Wade just rolled his eyes and made Julian laugh. "Now, I don't have an update for you, so I'm going to head home before Paige realizes I'm gone. And you?" He shook his head. "I can't believe I'm saying this, but go in there, apologize to that demon, and make things right. I may not like that she's a demon, but she has been helping, and it's obviously you care for her. Besides, if you don't, I'll sic Paige on you."

The thought of small, sweet Red going after him made Wade smile. "Not that. You know I can't stand it when Red's pissed at me. Thanks Julian."

Julian clapped him on the back and told him, "Not a problem. Just remember what I said," before he disappeared.

The rain Wade had wished for began to fall as he walked back to his room. He stood outside the door for a minute, listening, wondering if Sam had fallen asleep or if she was still awake. If she was still pissed. No sounds came from the other side of the door, so he quietly unlocked and opened it, slipping into the room.

The TV had been turned off, but Sam had turned on the bathroom light and partially closed the door, giving him enough light to move around without bumping into anything. He could see that Keen was still snoozing away on the pillow, but was surprised that Sam hadn't moved over to that bed to sleep. Instead, he saw the outline of her body under the covers of the other bed. The bed where he'd held her while she saw her first movie. The bed where he'd almost learned what it would feel like to be inside her, to have her come while he held her.

He sighed. He'd really fucked this one up and wasn't sure how to fix it.

"Sam, you awake?" he asked quietly. If she was asleep, he didn't want to disturb her, but he didn't want to delay this, either. There was no reaction, and he was disappointed. He could be patient when he had to, he was a hunter, after all, but he hated putting things off when they really mattered. There was no way he was going to wake her up to apologize, though. That would be supremely selfish and only benefit him.

Instead, he went into the bathroom, stripped, and took his own shower. While he was tempted to do something about his lingering arousal, he refrained. It didn't seem fair to him that he should find some release when he'd denied Sam hers. So he finished washing up before he shut off the water and got out. After drying off, he put on a pair of sweats, but didn't bother with a shirt since he was just going to bed.

When there was nothing to do but go to sleep, he found himself with another problem. Both beds were occupied. While Keen took up less room, Wade didn't want to wake up because the imp had decided his arm looked tasty again. Nor did he want to piss Sam off by invading her space. Reluctantly, he glanced toward the two chairs in the room, but there was no way he could sleep in them. If he tried, he'd wake up stiff and probably with a crick in his neck. Going from that to hours in the car? Not happening.

Finally he said fuck it and grabbed one of the pillows from Keen's bed. He then slid into bed beside Sam and placed the pillow in the center of the bed, forming a barrier. There was also a good foot between them, and he was an early riser in any case. Chances were he'd be up before she was, so she'd never need to know they'd shared a bed, no matter how innocent it had been.

He rolled onto his side with his back to her and tried to relax, but it took almost an hour before he finally drifted off.

On the other side of the bed, Sam stared at the wall, still awake, still unhappy. But eventually she followed him into sleep.

CHAPTER 15

Well after the clock had struck midnight, but before the sky turned golden with dawn, Sam dreamed.

She stood in Olarid, in the middle of the most beautiful, most dangerous clearing she'd ever seen. Though it was night, she could smell the sweet fragrances of the flowers that still bloomed around her. The moons, for Olarid had two, were bright in the sky and cast everything in a dim blue glow and softened what few harsh edges existed.

She stretched her wings out and tipped her face toward the heavens. For a moment, she was tempted to smile. She enjoyed this place. Yes, it was deadly, but the beauty had been worth it at times when she needed to get away from her father. And that risk had helped hone her skill, just as much as her formal training had. The few fond memories she had of Olarid that didn't include her mother—or the brother she hadn't told Wade about—were here.

It was where she had hidden when she needed to escape the beatings meant to turn her into a weapon. When she needed to cry over the injustice of being born to a demon who had no regard for any but himself. When she had wanted to be anywhere else.

A figure walked out of the tree line, unrecognizable until he stepped into the moonlight. Her blood ran cold. There was no way she could mistake him for anyone but her father.

He was taller than her by a solid foot and a half, which put him two inches above seven feet. He was muscular, with black hair and wings that matched her own, right down to the gleam of purple when the light hit the feathers just right. Unlike her, his irises were red instead of black, but he was still the most handsome man she'd ever seen. But she knew that handsomeness hid a sinister mind and soulless heart.

"Bellar," she said coldly.

He tsked. "Samara, I've told you repeatedly to call me Father."

"And I've repeatedly told you that you're nothing more than the man who donated his seed to create me. I have no father." She gave him a dark smile. "Hopefully, one day, that will be literal and not just wishful thinking."

He sighed and shook his head as he approached.

Automatically, she reached for her knives, but her hands only brushed the leather of her pants.

Laughing, he shook his head. "Samara, you will never kill me. Didn't I make sure of that centuries ago?" He came closer and she tried to move, but her feet were fixed to the earth. Her heart pounded in her chest as he reached out and wrapped his hand around the back of her neck, covering the tattoo he'd forced upon her. His voice lowered so it was a threatening murmur. "No matter how much you may wish it, you'll never see the death of me. No one has the skill, the power to kill me." He smiled cruelly and shook his head again. "At least, no one other than you, and I've made sure you don't have the ability to do so."

He released her abruptly and began to pace in front of her. "I know what you've been doing," he told her with a sidelong glance. "Recruiting someone to kill me. But he's rejected you, too, hasn't he?"

Sam paled. How could he possibly know that? The idea that he could be somehow spying on her chilled her blood, but she forced herself to sneer. "You don't know what the hell you're talking about. As usual."

He laughed and the sound grated down to the bone. "I know exactly what I'm talking about. The wolf you've been falling for could have had you, but instead, he left. Just like everyone else has."

She shook her head emphatically. "You're wrong."

"Am I?" he mused. "Your brother needed no tattoo to serve me, and your mother? Well, you haven't heard from her in days, have you? I suppose you have that runt of an imp, but it's hardly worth mentioning, is it?"

"*He* is a good friend, no matter his size. And you're wrong about Evane. You're wrong about Mom. You're even more wrong about Wade."

"Wade? Is that the mutt's name?" He waved a hand in the air dismissively. "No matter. He'll be dead soon enough, and you'll be home where you belong."

"No. I'll die before I serve you again," she spit at him.

In a fraction of a second he was in front of her again, his face close to hers. In that moment, he looked truly demonic. The red of his eyes had spread to cover even the whites, and his incisors had lengthened into deadly fangs. "You will only wish you were dead," he hissed. "You are *mine*. My weapon, my assassin, and I will not relinquish you. But that doesn't mean that you can't be put in your place."

She saw the gleam of the blade only an instant before it plunged deep into her belly. She cried out and grabbed for the hilt of the knife, but Bellar only twisted it and dug it deeper into her body.

"Remember this, Samara," he said, clearly enunciating each syllable of her name. "I punish those who disappoint me. And your punishment will be greater than anyone's for your treachery."

"Samara…"

Bellar threw back his head and laughed as he stabbed her again.

"Samara…"

The knife pulled at her flesh as it was drawn out of her body, then thrust back in once more.

"Wake up, dammit!"

Her face was slapped and Sam's eyes shot open. She cried out and covered her belly with both hands, still feeling the phantom pain from her nightmare. The first thing she saw was Wade's face, pale and filled with worry. The next was Keen's just behind Wade's shoulder.

The imp crooned reassuringly at her as she slowly sat up. Her mind didn't quite believe that it had just been a dream, that she hadn't actually been stabbed. She drew one of her hands away, dimly surprised when it came away free of blood.

"You okay?" Wade asked as he reached a hand out to help her steady herself.

Keen wasn't so casual. He flew over Wade's shoulder and flung himself into Sam's arms. She wrapped her arms around him and shook her head. "No, but I will be."

"Want to talk about it?"

She started to refuse out of habit but reconsidered. If it had actually been her father in that dream, rather than a product of a stressed mind, then Wade needed to know. "Yes, but give me a minute."

He nodded and eased back. "Take your time."

She gently untangled herself from Keen and went into the bathroom. After splashing some water on her face and drinking a few handfuls, she felt a little better. Still not steady, but that would take time. Any interaction with her father took time to recover from, even if it had been nothing but her imagination.

She could still feel the knife stabbing her again and again, while the echoes of Bellar's laughter rang in her ears.

"Please let it just be a nightmare," she whispered as she stared at her reflection in the mirror.

She stepped out of the bathroom and saw that, while Wade had put on a shirt, neither he nor Keen had gone far. They both sat on the edge of the bed, and Sam was surprised to see Keen leaning against Wade. A corner of her mouth shifted upward a tiny bit. The two of them weren't exactly the best of friends, but they'd definitely begun developing a bond. The movies had certainly helped with that.

"I had a nightmare," she began lamely. When Wade didn't deliver a sarcastic comment about that obvious statement, she continued. "It was about my father." Wade's eyes narrowed as they flashed yellow and she caught a glimpse of the dangerous wolf that lay within him. "I'm hoping it was just a dream. Just something my mind made up to torment me," she tried to reassure him.

"What do you mean?"

She drew in a deep breath. "Because if he was actually in my dreams somehow, then he knows what we're doing. He knows about you."

A growl trickled out of Wade's mouth. "How in the hell could that fuckwad possibly know what we're doing?"

"That's the part that scares me. I can only think of one way he could have found out. My mother."

He frowned. "I thought she was on your side? You made it very, very clear that she was, in fact."

"She is, which is why it scares me. She's the only seer with any sort of real consistency or accuracy that we know of on Olarid. But if he found out from my mom, I can guarantee she didn't tell him willingly. I'm just afraid of what he might have done to make her talk." She shook her head, her brow furrowed with fear. "She's not a weak woman, wolf. She's much older than even I am, and has dealt with more shit than I care to mention. She wouldn't bend easily."

"You said imp-boy here can cross dimensions, right?" he asked, resting his hand lightly on the top of Keen's head. "Send him to check on your mom. If she's okay and hasn't told Bellar anything, then it was just a dream, right?'

She mentally kicked herself. That was an obvious solution. Most likely she would have thought of it eventually, once the haze of the nightmare had passed. "That's a good idea. Keen, will you go check on her?"

Keen got to his feet, a little unsteady on the bed, and smiled at her, flashing his fangs. "Course." His wings flapped furiously as he lifted off the bed so he could kiss her cheek. Then, with a soft *pop*, he disappeared.

"Thank you," Sam said as she hesitantly sat on the bed beside him. "I'm determined to end him, but I don't want to see my mom killed. Or you."

"Eh, I'm harder to kill than I look. But it probably was just a dream. There's no way the demons who came after us would know I'm a wolf, and even if they'd figured it out, most of them are dead."

"No, the ones at the airport couldn't have found out and told him, but there are always ways. Just because we can't think of them doesn't mean they don't exist."

"Maybe. But let's not go into panic mode before we heard back from Keen, okay? Was there anything else in the dream you wanted to tell me about?"

She thought of the cruel words Bellar had spoken. Not the ones about him owning her or using her, she was used to that. She was even used to him trying to convince her that her mother and twin brother, Evane, had turned against her. But it hurt to have him—even if it was her subconscious—rub it in her face that Wade had turned her down.

Deciding to keep that part to herself, she shook her head. "No. That was basically it. Some rambling, but nothing really important."

It didn't look as though he believed her, and she held her breath as she waited to see if he'd press. Rather than pushing her, he nodded and got to his feet. "Why don't we go get some breakfast, and when Keen gets back, we can get going?"

"That's fine. If he gets back before us, he'll just stay in here, but it might take him a little bit. Navigating to my mom, whether she's free or not, will take some time if he wants to get there undetected."

"He can't move freely?"

A hand lifted and wiggled back and forth. "Sort of? He's not a prisoner or anything, but he's small and weak for an imp and gets a lot of harassment because of it."

"Ahh. So that's why you're so protective of him."

"That and the fact that he's my friend," she said dryly. "But you have to remember that he can't go directly to my mom, on the off chance she's with Bellar or someone loyal to him."

"Fair enough. Let's go. I saw a diner nearby. We can walk there."

"Do you think they'll have more chocolate milkshakes?"

"I'm sure they do."

She smiled faintly and got her shoes on so they could go.

CHAPTER 16

The air was cool, and Sam could taste a hint of rain on the breeze. It added to her enjoyment as they walked the short distance to the diner. The events of the night before still stung, but she did her best to push them aside. Whether Wade wanted her or not wasn't important. Most likely, once Bellar was dead, she'd never see him again even if they both survived the attempt, and there was no guarantee of that. Killing the ruler of Olarid wouldn't be an easy feat, even if they found the spear and everything went according to plan. Especially since the plan included dealing with a potential army of demons.

They took a booth as far away from other customers as they could manage so they could have a little privacy. And, Sam had noticed, people tended to stare at her eyes. She knew dark eyes weren't uncommon on Earth, but perhaps they were far less dark than hers? Either way, she was content to avoid people for the time being.

"Want me to order for you? Meatloaf isn't really a breakfast food."

Sam frowned as she looked over the menu. "No, don't order for me, but maybe you could suggest something?"

"Easy enough. To drink, if you want something hot, go for the coffee or hot chocolate. Cold? Orange juice or soda. For food, you can't go wrong with pancakes, bacon, and scrambled eggs. Omelets are good, too. If you're really hungry, you could add some hash browns or grits."

Sam nodded and continued to browse the menu until the waitress came. She listened with half an ear as Wade ordered enough food for two, then she ordered the hot chocolate, chocolate chip pancakes and bacon. She wasn't very hungry, but the pictures of those foods intrigued her. Learning about new Earth foods was surprisingly enjoyable. And anything that said 'chocolate' was immediately something she wanted to try.

The drinks came first and her eyes widened at the scent of her hot chocolate. Even Wade's drink smelled good, though unusual, but not nearly as good as her chocolate. She lifted the mug and inhaled deeply before she took a sip. "Oh my. Nothing should taste this good," she breathed.

Chuckling, Wade added some cream and sugar to his coffee. "Remind me to get you some real chocolate sometime. You'll be instantly addicted." He sipped, then set the mug down and nudged it toward her. "You're welcome to try some of my coffee, too. Not everyone likes it, and everyone puts different things in it, but it's good."

Though reluctant to set aside the chocolate, she did and took a sip of his coffee. Her nose wrinkled, but she took a second sip before she offered it back to him. "I think I'll stick with the hot chocolate, thanks."

He smiled. "You might like it with different stuff in it, but like I said, it's not for everyone."

They focused on their drinks for a minute before Wade sighed and ran a hand through his hair. "Look, I wanted to apologize. For last night."

Sam went still and the chocolate no longer settled quite so well in her belly. Slowly, she set the mug down but kept her suddenly cold hands around it for the warmth. "There's no need," she said stiffly, looking out the window. "I'm a firm believer that people should be able to make their own choices. You're allowed to want what you want. Even if that's not wanting something."

He wanted to kick himself at the hurt in her voice. He certainly deserved to be kicked. "That's not it at all, Sam. Wanting isn't the problem. Believe me, I want you. I've wanted you since I first saw you, asleep in my bed. Hell, before I saw you. It only took one smell of you and I went hard as fucking stone."

It took a lot of willpower, but she turned to look at him again. "Then what's the problem?" she asked quietly.

"Look, you're a—" He cut his words off and leaned back when the waitress returned with their food.

She set it down and, with a decade of waitressing under her belt, accurately read the atmosphere at their booth. With just a quick smile, she left them alone.

Wade waited until she was out of earshot before continuing. "You're a virgin," he murmured. "I didn't expect it and it threw me off. Way off. And despite a lot of women thinking that all men want virgins, a lot of us don't. Virgins…" He swallowed and again shoved his hand through his hair. "They're fucking terrifying, okay?" he admitted.

Astonished, Sam could only stare at him. "Terrifying? What could possibly be terrifying about it? It's a lack of experience, not some sort of…of…man-killer badge or something."

A wry smile curved his lips. "As it was recently pointed out to me, it's the pressure that it puts on a man. The pressure to not hurt the woman, and to make her first experience as good as possible. And not everyone performs well under pressure. Not everyone *wants* to perform under pressure."

"That's..." So many words came to mind, but she decided to go simple and straight to the point. "Stupid. Utterly stupid. You told me no and walked away because you were scared that...what? I wouldn't like it?" she asked, astonished.

He frowned. "That...isn't exactly how I'd put it," he grumbled.

"It doesn't matter how you'd put it, that's what it all boils down to, isn't it?" she insisted.

"If that's how you want to put it, yes."

She sighed. "Stupid," she murmured. "Wade, I've never had sex personally, but I've heard about it. I've heard people tell me about having it. I know that not every time is fantastic, especially not the first time." He started to speak and she held up a hand. "That being said, I was thoroughly enjoying everything up until you freaked out on me and stomped off while I felt...I was enjoying it."

His ego was bruised by her blunt insult—he was man enough to admit that—but as he turned her words over in his mind, he began to slowly smile. "Maybe I'll have a chance to make it up to you."

One dark brow arched. "You're assuming I'll give you another chance?"

His smile shifted to a wicked grin. "I'm pretty damn persuasive. Now eat your breakfast. We've gotta get back to the motel room and meet Keen, remember? Pour some of the syrup over the pancakes before you eat 'em. You'll love it," he added, pointing to the bottle with his fork.

Wade had been right. Sam loved the pancakes and bacon, just as she'd loved the hot chocolate. By the time she was finished, she was pleasantly full and feeling mellow. Earth food definitely had a lot going for it. Food on Olarid wasn't bad if you ate at Bellar's table—and she was often forced to—but it lacked the flavors and variety found on Earth.

The moment they left the diner, Wade surprised her by nonchalantly taking her hand. His grip was light, and it was clear he wanted to make sure she knew she could break the contact at any time without a struggle. After stopping and looking at their linked hands for a moment, she decided that she liked holding hands with him. When she kept her hand in his and resumed walking, he flashed her a smile that had her heart beating faster. She even smiled shyly at him.

His seduction had begun and they both knew it.

They'd just made it to the motel parking lot when it all went to hell.

Wade jerked to a stop, his face tilted upward, nostrils flared, but he'd scented them too late.

A cloaked demon with dark green skin used the hood of a car as a springboard and launched himself at Sam, tackling her before she could so much as say a word. She landed hard with his bulk on top of her, but his momentum made them roll across the unforgiving asphalt. She used that movement and twisted until she could regain her feet. In the same movement, her fist lashed out, punching him in the throat. He made a choking sound, but responded by swiping a huge arm in a backhand that would have broken bones if it had connected. Sam was faster though, and jerked back, avoiding the blow by no more than an inch.

Upon getting her balance, Sam kicked, her foot landing squarely on the demon's chin, snapping his head back hard. She twisted and followed it up with a sharp kick that had her heel landing on his breastbone. Something cracked in the demon's chest and he fell onto his back, still. For all Sam knew, he was just knocked out, but she couldn't take the time to find out for sure. Not when Wade was fighting two more on his own.

Why just send three? she wondered as she watched Wade's nails lengthen and form sharp claws. Wolf claws. A passerby might not notice the change, but the demon who had those claws raked down his face and throat certainly did. It just wasn't enough to take him out of the fight.

The other demon came up behind Wade and caught him in a choke hold. It distracted him just enough that the first demon was able to deliver several punishing blows to Wade's stomach and ribs. Between the two, it was unlikely that Wade would come out the winner unless he shifted, and she knew he'd never risk that in such a public place. Not unless he had no other choice.

Sam cursed the fact that she'd left her knives in the motel room, but her sheaths weren't made for concealment, and she'd foolishly thought they'd be safe enough going the short distance to the diner.

Long legs ate up the short distance between her and the others, and her hands came down hard on the ears of the demon holding Wade. He let out a howl of pain and his arms loosened enough for Wade to slip free. He whirled on Sam and his fist lashed out, catching her in the jaw.

She tasted blood from her teeth cutting into the inside of her cheek and her lip splitting, but it didn't even slow her down. She darted around him, punching and kicking, enraging the demon. He kicked out at her and she had to jump back to avoid being hit. It was then that she spotted the knife hanging from his belt. No doubt he was avoiding pulling it because they were supposed to bring her back alive.

No one wanted to disappoint Bellar. It wasn't good for anyone's life expectancy.

She had to get that knife and took a chance, dashing closer to the demon. He wasn't surprised and punched downward with his fist, hitting an already aching cheek. She sprawled on the ground, blood filling her mouth. She spit it out before giving him a red-tinged smile. He may have landed a hard blow, one that had her head aching, but she had his knife in her hand.

"Not too bright, are you? But then, dear old Dad doesn't send his best and brightest, does he?" she taunted as she risked a glance behind the demon.

Wade and the other demon were trading blows. They were about equal in size and apparent strength, and both were bleeding. Wade was going to be heavily bruised when this was over, but she trusted him to survive this. He had to.

The demon Sam was fighting took a step closer to her and lifted a foot, bringing it down hard, but she rolled out of the way before it landed. The sudden movement caused the knife to nick her arm, but it was minor compared to what would happen if she lost this fight.

She flipped up to her feet and feinted to the left before stabbing out with the knife. After that, she poured on the speed, circling the demon, lashing out with the blade to leave cut after cut on the demon's skin. He was strong, but didn't have her stamina, and the blood loss would weaken him.

The demon wasn't so patient, and the fact that Samara was getting the best of him was pissing him off. He rushed her again, but left his right side unprotected in his haste to get his hands on her. She ducked under his arm and thrust the blade under his ribs, angled upward. A look of surprised slid over his face just before the tip of the blade reached his heart.

She yanked the knife free and turned to help Wade, only to see him break the demon's neck and let it drop.

He was breathing hard, but he wasn't done yet. "We have to get the bodies inside. We can't let the humans find them."

She nodded and grabbed the smaller demon under the arms and dragged him toward the motel room. He was heavy, but she was a great deal stronger than she looked. Some of that was her demon blood, but some was simply how hard she'd trained.

Five minutes later, the three bodies lay on the floor of their room and Sam stared down at them. "What are we going to do with them?"

"I'll call Marco. The Hunters are used to cleaning up demon bodies. They took care of the ones at the airport, too, remember?"

"Handy. How bad are you hurt?" she asked, looking him over.

His hand gently probed at his side. "Might have a cracked rib, but I'm hoping it's just bruised. Gods know there's not much of me that isn't bruised. Fucker had fists like bricks. You?"

"A little banged up, some cuts. Jaw's the worst of it, but since I'm talking, I don't think it's broken. I'm going to wash up a bit while we wait for Marco and Keen, though."

"Take your time," he told her as he pulled out his phone. "Marco? Got some more bodies for you." He shook his head. "It's not like I'm hanging out a sign that says All Demons Welcome, asshole." Except, he sort of was with the tattoo on Samara's neck. And he really wished there was some way of removing it from her skin. "Besides, it's three fewer bad guys you have to hunt. Oh, and I wouldn't feel bad if you brought a healer, either. No, jackass. I can function, but with as often as we're getting attacked, I'd rather not start a fight at a disadvantage, and if I call Julian again, he's going to teleport me back to Antarctica." He glanced toward Sam and saw that she'd retreated into the bathroom, but he still lowered his voice. "Yes, you have to heal the demon girl, too. She's helping us, remember? And I sincerely believe she's on our side in this." He closed his eyes in relief. "Thanks Marco. I owe you one." He let out a short laugh. "Fine, I owe you two."

He hung up and stripped off his torn and bloody shirt. There was no way it could be salvaged.

Sam came out of the bathroom, dabbing at her cheek with a damp washcloth. When she spotted Wade, she stopped in her tracks, staring at his chest. He wanted to believe she was ogling him, but he knew that his skin was already turning colors thanks to the blows he'd taken in the fight.

He started for the bathroom. "I'm going to clean up. If Marco shows up before I'm done, try not to hurt him?"

"You don't think you should be warning him not to hurt me?" she asked blandly.

He paused beside her and gave her a wolfish grin. "Baby, I don't think there's anyway in hell he could lay a finger on you unless you let him." As she flushed with pleasure at the compliment, he continued on.

CHAPTER 17

Sam stretched out on the bed, feeling each and every blow she'd taken only minutes before. They weren't bad, and she'd certainly had worse, a lot worse. They didn't even hurt as much as the bullet had, though they covered more of her body. Sometimes she was surprised she'd survived all the injuries she'd received through the years, but she didn't regret them. Each fight had made her a little stronger until she'd reached the level where she was now; strong enough to stand up to Bellar.

Strong enough to kill him. Something even he believed she was capable of. *No one has the skill, the power to kill me. At least, no one other than you.* He'd said that. He'd meant it. And she intended to make his words fact, even if she couldn't deal the final blow herself.

Now that her goal was so close, she was anxious to get there, to get it done, but was surprised that part of her wanted to draw it out. She was hesitant to even think it, but she knew it was because of Wade. Especially the Wade he'd shown her today, who was flirty, charming. Sexy as hell.

She sighed and closed her eyes, daydreaming about the wolf, though she knew she shouldn't.

Wade was still in the bathroom when Marco teleported in, accompanied by an older woman and a man about his age. Tense seconds ticked by as Marco and Sam stared at each other.

"Where's Wade?" he asked sharply.

Sam pointed to the bathroom door. "Cleaning up. We both got pretty bloody."

He nodded curtly before he drew in a deep breath. "Beth, would you heal her?" he asked, though it clearly pained him to do so.

Beth frowned and stared hard at Sam. "But she's a demon. Why are we helping a demon?" she asked, sneering.

Marco turned and pinned her with a glare. "Because you're a member of Venatoribus Noctu and your commander told you to."

For a moment, Sam thought Beth would continue to protest, but she stomped forward and laid a finger—just the tip of a single finger—against Sam's arm. There was the gentle tingle of the healing magic, but Beth pulled her hand back before all Sam's bruises were gone.

Sam chose not to complain about the way they were treating her. "Thank you," she said instead. Words wouldn't sway these Hunters into believing she wasn't the evil monster they thought she was, anyway.

Beth gave her a disgusted look and retreated several feet.

"Take the bodies back and—"

Marco was interrupted by a soft *pop*, one that signified Keen's return. When the imp saw the Hunters, he let out a squeak and dove for Sam, clinging to the back of her shirt and her braid, half choking her.

"Demon!" cried the man with Marco as he drew his sword and started for Sam and Keen.

"Don't!" Sam yelled as she lifted the bloody knife still in her hands. It didn't halt the Hunter in his progress, and her knife clashed against his sword before she lifted a foot, planted it in his belly, and shoved him.

Not expecting the attack, the Hunter fell back and landed hard on his ass. He snarled at her and lifted his free hand. Sam saw the first sparks of what would become an energy ball and shifted her grip on the knife to a throwing hold. She wouldn't—couldn't—let him harm Keen.

"Enough!" Wade roared from the bathroom door, just as Marco stepped between the Hunter and Sam. Everyone else stopped, the sparks from the fallen Hunter fizzling out. "What the hell, Marco? You're here what, two minutes, and already shit's hitting the fan?" he growled.

"Fuck you, Wade," Marco snapped. "You didn't tell me there was going to be another living demon here. My people were prepared to see one demon. Just one. And not one who actually looked demonic."

"He's not a demon," Sam said quietly, reaching back with her free hand to rest it on Keen's head. "He's an imp."

"Same thing," Beth hissed.

"Actually, she's right. Imps aren't exactly demons," Marco said. "I just didn't realize that was an imp. I've only read about them. I've never seen one." He still couldn't see much of the imp, who was still hiding behind Sam, but he was intrigued now, and wanted to know more about the creature, but now wasn't the time. "Beth, Pete, take the bodies, see that they're disposed of."

"Happily," Pete said as he got to his feet. He waited for Beth to lay a hand on the bodies, then both disappeared, along with the trio of dead demons.

With the unfamiliar witches gone, Keen peeked over Sam's shoulder at Marco. "He gonna hurt me?" he asked quietly, but the words carried to Marco.

"No, I'm not going to hurt you," Marco said, shaking his head. "You surprised me, but since you're known to Wade and...Samara...I won't hurt you. I would, however, like to know what's going on."

"First, can you tell me if you just sent the healer away?" Wade asked.

"Oh. I did, but I should be able to take care of bruises," Marco replied as he walked over to Wade. A moment later, the blossoming colors on Wade's ribs were gone and breathing became easier.

"Thanks man."

"No problem. Now...explanation?"

Wade looked at Sam, who shrugged and gently pulled Keen away from her hair so she could deposit him on the bed. "Keen's my friend. A very useful friend. He, like all imps, can travel through dimensions as easily as you teleport."

Keen eagerly nodded and puffed his chest out proudly. "I can, I can, I can!" he said happily and made Sam smile.

Wade wondered what Keen had found out, but wasn't sure if it was a good idea for the imp to report now, since it concerned Lilith. On the other hand, if their plans were known to Bellar, it was best that Marco was aware of it. He sighed and said, "Speaking of, what did you learn? Do they know what we're doing?"

Keen looked at Sam, and when she nodded, he told the wolf, "Nope. Looked like everything was same." He cackled. "But Bellar not happy. Keeps losing demons. Makes him mad, mad, mad."

"Not going to complain about an unhappy demon," Marco muttered, arms folded across his chest. "Are you telling me the—Keen—went to the dimension Bellar's from and scouted for you?"

Sam wondered if Wade had shared the truth of her parentage with Marco. It didn't sound like it, and she thought Marco would be even less trusting than he already was if he knew. "He did. We wanted to know if Bellar had somehow gotten wind of our hunt for the weapon."

The Hunter gave Sam a considering look. "Seems like you were telling the truth, Fury."

"Believe me, I want Bellar dead more than you can possibly imagine. And unlike him, I have no desire to conquer Earth or any other dimension. I just want to be left alone to live my life."

"As long as that continues to be true, I think we can work together." He offered his hand. "Truce?"

Sam knew it had taken a lot for Marco to make the gesture and took his hand. "Truce," she agreed.

"Even with this spear, Bellar isn't likely to go down easy. You said that his plan is to come here soon, right?"

"By the next full moon, yes," Sam confirmed.

"I'm going to gather a team, my best Hunters. When he shows up, we'll help stop him, even if it's just to overwhelm him with numbers and pin him down so the spear can be used."

Sam hesitated, but it had to be said. "I'm not trying to question you, or your people, but...I'd be careful who you selected for this team."

"What do you mean?" Wade asked.

"I told you that Bellar's the Lord of Evil Things. He can take even the tiniest bit of evil in a person's soul, grow it, and use it to control them. I'm not saying that your people have to be pure of heart, because meanness or vices don't necessarily lead to evilness, but if you have someone who seems to like hurting people a little too much or something like that, I'd leave them far away from Bellar."

Marco frowned. "I won't say that all the people I have are saints, but I see what you're saying. There are a few people I was planning to bring who might not be a good fit. How good is Bellar's control?"

Sam smiled sadly. "He's had thousands of years to hone his skill. He's very, very good, and very, very powerful."

He sighed. "That's good information to know." He gave her a considering look. "When Wade first stopped me from killing you, I thought he was making a huge mistake. I thought I'd either get a phone call telling me he'd had to kill you, or I'd find his body after you'd killed him."

The faint smile disappeared. "Even after you found out I was a Fury?"

"Even after, because you're still a demon," he said with a nod. "But I think I was wrong." The corners of his mouth tipped upward a fraction. "This time." He turned to Wade. "I'll pick my people and get them ready. Keep me updated and let me know if you need anything between now and then."

"Will do. Thanks, man."

Marco nodded, looked at Sam, then disappeared.

"That went a lot better than I was expecting it, too. Even with the man trying to attack Keen," Sam said as she sat on the edge of the bed.

"Honestly? Same here. Though I didn't expect Keen to show up after they had like he did." Wade turned to the imp. "You didn't mention Lilith. Is Sam's mom okay?"

The fact that he'd ask made something flutter in Samara's chest and she nearly smiled. He hated demons, even if he had come to accept her, so for him to sound like he cared about her mother meant a lot.

Keen nodded with big movements of his head. "She free. She okay. Not happy, but she never happy there 'less she with Sam."

"No, she really isn't," Sam murmured.

"You're doing this as much for your mom as you are just because you hate the evil son of a bitch, aren't you?" Wade asked gently.

"I am. It's been hard enough for me, being his daughter and assassin for two thousand years. I can't imagine how much harder it's been for her. She's been with him for more than twice as long, and she's his wife. Not that the title means that much. It's common knowledge that he's not faithful to her. Which isn't a bad thing."

"No, I don't suppose it is." He walked over to her and waited until she lifted her head to look at him. He brushed his fingers over her cheek. "We'll get him, Samara. I promise."

"I hope so."

"You ready to go? We still have a long way to Louisiana, and that's not including the time it'll take to actually find the damn spear."

"Yeah, I'm ready. Keen? Would you do me a favor?"

"Yes. What?"

"Would you go back to Olarid?" He started to pout and she smiled. "My mom needs your company more than I do right now, because she's stuck there. Make sure she knows I'm all right, have help, and will take care of Bellar if it's the last thing I do." She paused a beat. "Maybe don't say it quite like that, though. One way or another sounds better. That way she won't think about me dying."

He gave a long-suffering sigh but nodded. "Okay." He flew over to her and hovered in the air while he kissed her forehead. "Bye bye. Stay safe." Then, with the soft *pop*, he was gone.

"Why isn't his teleporting as quiet as when witches do it?" Wade asked curiously.

"Maybe because he's moving from one dimension to another rather than traveling on the same plane? I honestly hadn't thought about it much, though. It's just how he travels, so I'm used to it."

She got to her feet, but Wade hadn't moved and she found herself bumping against him. Before she could move back, he slid an arm around her waist. "I want you to get used to being close to me, touching me. I just want you." He kissed her with such tenderness that her knees went weak and she trembled, but he didn't deepen the kiss. "But I know now isn't the time to start anything I can't finish." He slowly smiled and made her breath catch. "Yet."

He drew back slowly, so his body slid against hers, then gathered up the few things that were spread across the hotel room.

It took Sam a minute to compose herself before she followed suit. "Why don't you drive this time?" She was entirely too stirred up to be confident behind the wheel of a car, especially as a novice.

The grin he gave her told her he understood exactly why she was asking. "I can do that."

She made it out of the motel room and into the car in record time.

Oh yes, the wolf was definitely a hell of a lot more dangerous than Bellar ever thought about being, just in an entirely different way. Bellar could only enslave her body. Wade could enslave her heart.

CHAPTER 18

Wade was amused when he joined Sam in the car a few minutes later. That amusement didn't fade as miles passed by, then states. He stopped when they needed gas or food, but was intent on reaching Louisiana before they stopped for the day. It would be tight, especially since the demon attack had delayed them a bit, but they could still make it on schedule.

At one point, he set Sam up with his laptop and showed her how to access the movies and use the headphones, and she'd spent the next five hours engrossed in the amazing new stories. It didn't leave much of a chance for them to talk—or for him to charm her, but she'd be more receptive if she was relaxed in any case.

After they'd gone through a drive through for dinner, such as it was, she set the laptop in the backseat. As amazing as movies were, they couldn't compare to a real-life person.

"If you're going to wield the spear, then I'm going to help you," she told him.

"How? You probably won't even be able to touch it," Wade pointed out.

"I don't need to. I can enhance the abilities of others, or had you forgotten?"

He had, actually. It had been shoved into a compartment of reasons why Bellar shouldn't get his hands on Sam, but it hadn't occurred to him that it would be an ability that could help him. "Sort of, yeah."

She rolled her eyes but smiled. "It'll help. You're good in a fight, I'm not saying otherwise, but he's seriously strong. So we'll make you as strong and fast as we can. It probably won't work as well as it would if you were shifted, but you can hardly use a spear against him when you're a wolf."

"Unfortunately, no. Which is a shame. I've felt cooped up, not being able to shift the last few days."

"Believe me, I know. It's probably the same general feeling I have with my wings. Why don't you shift tonight when we get to the motel?"

Because he could hardly seduce her if he was furry and running around on four legs, but he didn't dare tell her that. "Maybe," he said noncommittally. "Can you boost multiple people at once, or is a one person at a time thing?"

"I can do a few people, but the more people I enhance at the same time, the more...stretched...my power gets. Two or three probably would be okay, but if I tried for a dozen, they might as well get nothing at all from me."

"Damn. Makes sense, but I wish it were a little easier to share the love."

"Believe me, I know. I'd love to boost every single person Marco brings with him, but it just isn't possible."

The next several hours were spent in idle chitchat until Wade pointed to a sign. "We're in Louisiana now." He glanced at the GPS app on his dash. "Another forty-five minutes to the mounds. It's late, but that's probably better for us. Fewer people around, if any. Which means fewer people to ask us stupid questions we don't want to answer. Especially if we end up doing something that's questionable or flat out illegal."

"I'm fine with going when we get there. I'll feel better when we have the spear in hand." And it might not even be at this location, so better to find that out now. If it wasn't, then hurrying now meant they had more time to try and find the correct location. Now that they were so close, she felt an eagerness she hadn't felt in centuries. If this worked, it would be over. There would still be demons in Olarid who would cause trouble, certainly, but none came even close to the level of evil of Bellar.

"So, you said this place you found is a ring of mounds, right?"

"Yeah."

"But there isn't anything in your research saying where the sixth mound is?"

He glanced at her. "No," he admitted. "The five are common enough knowledge for people who are familiar with the history of the area, but I've never heard of a sixth mound, much less in the center."

Curious, she asked, "What makes you think it's here, then?"

He was quiet for a minute. "I'm no archaeologist. There are plenty of people who'll agree with me on that. I have helped some people who were archaeologists—or just really damn good at pretending—but that's as close as I get to any sort of training. But I've seen how centuries, or even just a few years, can cover something with so much green that it's impossible to detect unless you're right on top of it. I looked at a satellite map—a picture from space, very, very high up—and the center of the mounds is a hill that's absolutely covered in trees and shit. For someone who isn't looking for a mound, it would be very easy to miss one or mistake it for nothing more than a natural hill. It's our best bet, I'm sure of it."

Slowly, she nodded. "I haven't got any better ideas, so I'm certainly willing to try. Though I hope you're right. We've only got another ten days, at most, until Bellar gets here. It's not a lot of time if we have to start over."

"I know," he said grimly. "I'm just hoping we can figure out how to get into the mound, since we don't have any heavy equipment to move dirt with, or an earth witch I can trust to do it. Especially not without attracting attention to ourselves."

They arrived at the closest mound five minutes earlier than expected, but it was still dark when they pulled into the parking lot. "There aren't any roads that go to the center, it's all forest, so we'll have to walk from here," Wade said as he shut the car off.

"I guess there's no point in me trying to see anything from the air?" she asked.

"Sorry, I know you'd like to stretch your wings, but I think if it were that easy, the satellites would have spotted something."

Sam sighed. "I know."

"It's dark out though, and shouldn't be anyone around, so I don't think there would be a problem if you wanted to let them out."

She smiled. "I think I will. You can do the same with your wolf, you know."

He returned her smile. "I might just do that."

They got out and he moved to the trunk, grabbing out a backpack with hiking supplies in it. He'd also gotten a shovel, just in case digging was needed. The map was pulled up on his phone and he showed her how to use that app. Once she was comfortable with it she chose to carry the backpack in one hand so she could loose her wings.

After staring at them for a moment, Wade grinned and yanked his shirt off. "Yeah, I think I will be myself as well. If you don't mind carrying my clothes in the pack, anyway."

"Not at all." She took the shirt from him but didn't look away when he reached for the button on his pants. When he pushed them down, her mouth went dry and she temporarily forgot how to breathe. She'd seen his chest, sure, and it was magnificent. She'd seen other nude men, and some were well built. But Wade, even in the dark, was a revelation. He was covered in taut muscle from his broad shoulders down. The tattoos she'd seen on his arms and chest continued to his legs, which were just as well-muscled as his arms. He was like a work of art, even when she noticed that he wasn't exactly unhappy to be the subject of her intense scrutiny. And when her eyes landed on his half-erect shaft, they didn't wander anywhere else.

He really was glorious, and, though it was far from the right time or place, she felt herself go damp.

Then he groaned and shook his head. "Don't look at me like that, not right now. If you want to stare at me later, though, I'm absolutely down for that. Hell, do more than stare. But I can't focus on de-mon-killing spears with your eyes on me."

"Sorry," she murmured, but it took another minute before she could look away.

"No, don't apologize," he insisted. "Believe me, I enjoyed it. We're just postponing it." He shifted to his wolf form and padded over to bump her hip with his head.

A hand dropped to stroke over his fur and she smiled. "Later," she agreed before they left the heavily trodden paths to go directly into the woods. They used a flashlight, but neither actually needed one. As a wolf, his night sight was superb, and Sam's was just as good.

Unsurprisingly, Sam had no problem moving through the thick brush or over fallen logs, just as graceful here as she was in a fight. He didn't protest when she moved a few steps in front of him, but he could admit it was largely because her ass looked amazing in her jeans.

Twenty minutes later, she stopped and frowned. "Is that a hill, or the mound?" she asked, staring slightly off the right.

He moved up beside her and shifted back to his human form as he considered. "I don't think it's a hill. It's too sharp, and the curve around the bottom looks pretty uniform from here." He took the phone from her and checked the GPS. "It says we're here."

She glanced up at him and grinned. "We found it?"

Reluctant to dim her excitement, he smiled back at her. "Might have. Let me get dressed and let's see if we can find a way in."

He dressed quickly before taking the bag and slinging it over his shoulders so their hands were free.

"Let's split up," Sam suggested. "I'll go to the right, you go to the left, and we'll meet on the other side?"

The chances the demons could have found them so soon was slim, but their odds so far hadn't been so good. "Demons have found us pretty quickly before. This thing can't be too big, so let's stick together."

She frowned. "You're right. Okay. Let's go. Any idea what we should be looking for?

"Not sure. The others in the area have an opening of some sort, but this one? Since no one's figured out it's a mound and not a hill? There's no telling. Hell, since it holds a magical weapon, it could be sealed magically."

"I wish that book had been a little more informative and a little less of the author trying to feel important," she said with a sigh.

They moved slowly, searching for any sign of a break in the earth and trees.

"Wait a sec," Wade said after ten minutes of searching, and he moved closer to the sloping earth.

"What is it? What'd you find?" she asked, hurrying forward.

"Sorry, it's nothing. Just some rocks that must have fallen and stacked up here. It's not a way in," he answered, disappointed.

They continued on, but found themselves back where they'd started. They'd found a tree that had been split at some point, though the opening didn't go all the way through, but nothing else caught their attention.

"I don't understand. If something was put into the mound, they had to have some way of getting in and out. There's got to be a chamber or something in there, right?" Sam asked as she looked at the tree-covered rise of earth.

"There is, but again, magically sealed. For all we know, it was an earth elementalist who put it in there. They could have just swum through the dirt to the center, or carved out a hole then refilled it," Wade said, though he hoped he was wrong about that. Elementalists of any flavor weren't exactly common. In fact, he knew of precisely one, and he was a fire elementalist, which wasn't any help here. Elementals were more common, but as far as he knew, they couldn't have made a spear to kill demons.

"Let's pretend like that isn't a thing. Maybe we're just looking at it wrong," Sam mused aloud as she walked more slowly around the base of the mound. "Let's climb to the top. Maybe they put the entrance there?"

Getting to the top wouldn't be easy. Trees grew everywhere, and tightly together, so there was no way that Sam could fly through them to the top, and there wasn't a good path up. In fact, the closest thing he saw to a way up was by the pile of rocks they'd found earlier. "It can't hurt to try. Come on."

A minute later, they were studying the rocks. They were jagged and dangerous looking, but they'd provide a better handhold than if the surfaces were smooth. "Ladies first," he offered with a half grin.

She returned it and stepped up to the rocks. She reached out for a piece that jutted outward in a perfect handhold and pulled to lift her body up. A sharp edge sliced along her palm and she hissed in a breath at the immediate sting.

"You okay?" Wade asked, coming up behind her.

Before she could answer, there was a pulse of light from the stones. They lit from within, but it was faint and over before they could really process what they'd seen.

Sam released her hold and stepped back, ignoring her injured hand in favor of staring at the blood that coated the rock. "What in the hell was that?"

"I don't know. But I think we may have just found our magical lock. Now we just have to figure out the key."

"Maybe not," Sam murmured. "It's a holy spear, meant to kill demons. What if this is some sort of defense mechanism?"

"Then why didn't it hurt you? More, I mean." He shook his head. "A cut on your hand isn't anything, really, and wouldn't deter any demon I've ever met." An idea was forming in his head. What better way for the ones who had made this mound to ensure that a demon hunter gained access than by requiring the blood of a demon? Proof, perhaps, that they'd already killed one? Curiously, he reached out and grabbed the same handhold Sam had. He was expecting the pain, so his only reaction to being cut was a tightening around his eyes.

The pulsing this time was stronger, the glow brighter, but while it dimmed, it didn't fully fade away.

"Either it needed more blood, or a different type of blood," he told her while he examined the rocks. Nothing had moved as far as he could tell, but there was a faint tug of magic from somewhere inside the mound.

"Nothing happened, though. I still don't see any way in," Sam said, disappointed. "Unless..." She glanced up at him. "Do you think it needs even more blood? I'm willing to shed a little more if it gets us in, but neither of us can afford too much blood loss right now."

He shook his head. "If it needs more blood—and I'm not sure it does—I think it would want enough to kill. And I'm not about to sacrifice either of us for it."

"No, neither am I." Not unless it was the only way to kill Bellar.

They stood in silence for several minutes as they tried to figure out what their next move was. The tugging Wade felt grew stronger until it was like an itch beneath his skin.

"Something definitely happened. I can feel it, I just can't see it," he growled in frustration.

"Let's walk around the mound again. Maybe something changed somewhere else," Sam suggested.

Not having any better ideas, he agreed, though he didn't expect to find anything. To his surprise, something had changed. The split tree they'd found before was open now, and large enough for a man to pass through.

"Well, I'll be damned," Wade muttered as he stared into the dark hole.

"Probably," Sam agreed with a smile. "But let's wait until *after* we get in and get the spear, okay?"

He gave her a cocky grin and, after sending Julian a text to let him know they'd found the mound, climbed up into the tree, passing through it and onto packed earth. The moment his foot touched the ground, torches sprang to life, lighting a hallway that led toward the center. "Huh. Very cool. Let's go get this thing," he said as he turned back to her and offered a hand to help her.

Sam climbed up, her hands braced on the edges of the hollow tree, but the moment she tried to pass through the opening, there was a flash of blinding white light and she was launched backward. She was thrown with enough force that when she hit a tree behind her, she didn't stop, but tumbled in the air until she hit a second, finally landing in a heap on the ground.

"Samara!" Wade yelled as he climbed back out of the mound as fast as he could. In a flash, he was beside her and gently turned her onto her back, easing her hair away from her face. "Shit, Sam. Are you okay? Tell me you're fucking okay."

She groaned at the movement, but opened her eyes. They were full of pain, and he noticed her body was tense with it as well. "I don't think it likes me," she said, voice tight.

"Dammit. We should have thought of that. Of course it wouldn't allow demons inside." And he was furious with himself for not realizing that sooner. "Are you okay?"

"Will be. Feel like I just lost a couple of fights is all." Slowly, she moved until she was sitting up and leaning back against a tree. He helped her as much as he could without hurting her worse. "You should go. Get the spear."

He didn't want to leave her here, not in this condition, but he also didn't dare delay. He dug his phone out and offered it to her. "Fine, but I'm leaving you my phone. Call Marco. Tell him what happened and see if he can come heal you." She looked skeptical, but he continued. "I mean it. You need to be a hundred percent, and he knows it. And it's the only way I'm leaving you."

She sighed and took the phone. "Fine. Now go. Get the damn spear."

Still, he hesitated for a moment, before he nodded and returned to the mound.

Sam watched him disappear into the mound before she looked at the phone. It took her a moment, but she managed to dial Marco's number. "Hey, it's me, not Wade. Yeah, it's complicated. I need a favor..."

CHAPTER 19

Wade felt uneasy once he was back inside the mound. Somehow it felt more sinister now than it had a minute ago, probably because he'd just seen a very tough demon get seriously injured by its magic.

"Where the fuck is Julian when I need him? This isn't my shtick," he muttered as he crept down the tunnel. With the torches lit, he could see perfectly fine, but that didn't help with the fact that this place creeped him out.

The tunnel was narrow enough that he couldn't extend his elbows to the side without hitting it. Trying to fight in such confined quarters would be a nightmare, so he hoped it wouldn't come to that. The walls were packed dirt and he could see roots worming their way through it, somehow without actually dislodging any soil. Despite that, someone had managed to write on the walls. It almost looked carved, but he didn't think the walls were quite solid enough for that term to apply. Oddly, none of the roots had disturbed any of the pictographs that covered the walls. He didn't know what language they were, and they didn't exactly look like they originated in this area, but some of the images were pretty self-explanatory, such as the figure bowed back with a spear going through his body. Others were complete gibberish to him.

He really hoped they weren't warning him about traps or something he was about to run into, because if they were, he was screwed. He may not be a stranger to trapped places, not after his experience helping Julian the year before, but he didn't have as many tricks up his sleeve as witches did. He couldn't use magic to avoid a spike pit, nor did he have any backup.

Ahead, the tunnel curved, and he tried to picture the mound and where the opening had been. If he was right, that curve led toward the center of the mound. He approached cautiously, because this was likely where any trap would be placed. When he reached it he peeked around the corner and sucked in a sharp breath.

The earthen walls spread out and formed an almost perfectly spherical chamber. In the center of the chamber was a circle of light, though he couldn't tell where it came from. It resembled sunlight, but there was no opening in the ceiling that he could see. He didn't spend too much time on that, though, because, hovering in the light and resting diagonally to the floor, was the spear. The shaft was six feet long, pale, almost white, and perfectly straight and smooth. Dark, nearly black leather cords criss-crossed along the length of it before they wrapped around the base of the spearhead, helping to secure it to the shaft. The point was an oily-looking piece of dark metal, and even from where he stood Wade could see that it shimmered with green and purple.

Just like Sam's wings...

Without moving a step, Wade could tell it was powerful. The thing flat out radiated magic. But he feared what it was intended to be used for. He didn't believe in coincidences, not when it came to stuff like this, and for the spearhead to remind him so clearly of Sam's wings was worrying. Did fate intend for it to be used against her rather than Bellar? Part of him wanted to turn around, tell her the spear wasn't here, and that they'd need to find another way, but he made himself walk the last few yards to the chamber.

There was a faint vibration in the earth beneath his feet, almost a trembling. The power here was so strong he started to feel like he could suffocate on it. He had to force himself to take a step, then another, until he was only a few feet from the spear.

"Stop."

He whirled around toward the voice and saw a man there. No, not a man, he realized, as the figure wasn't quite solid. A ghost, most likely, though he supposed it could be some sort of illusion.

The man was old, though not frail or hunched over. He still looked strong despite the pewter color of his hair, hair which was done in two braids that passed his shoulders. His skin was dark, his features strong, but his eyes…The irises were black, just like Sam's. The appearance of another similarity to the demon waiting for him had his heart beating faster.

The clothing the ghost wore reminded Wade of what America's first inhabitants had worn, but there was something about it that was different. He couldn't put his finger on what exactly it was, and fashion wasn't his main concern. He didn't care where this man was from or what he was so long as he could help them stop Bellar. Without killing Samara.

"I don't mean any disrespect, but I've come for the spear, and I'm going to leave with it," he told the man, not bothering to reach for his knives. They wouldn't do any good against a ghost. Only certain powerful magics would, or salt, and he had neither at his disposal. And if he was an illusion, nothing Wade had on him would dispel it.

"That remains to be seen," the ghost said, his voice deep and strong. It surprised Wade. Ghosts were generally stuck near whatever had tied them to this plane, whether it was a person, place or thing, and this ghost had to be tied either to the mound or the spear. Being alone for so long should have weakened the ghost or driven him mad, but the man looked strong and sane.

"What's that supposed to mean?" Wade asked warily, calculating the odds that he could grab the spear and make it out of the mound without being killed.

The ghost smiled and walked around him, into the shaft of light encompassing the spear. His hand moved over the spear, with only an inch between his hand and the pale wood. "It means precisely that. You have gained entry to the spear's resting place, yes, but that doesn't mean you have the right to take it."

Wade decided to tread carefully here. He may not be able to affect the ghost, but the ghost might be able to affect him. They were often blessed with what humans called psychic powers, and sometimes those powers were as strong as any witch's or elemental's. Trying to just take the spear and run might work, or he might end up in worse shape than Sam. "And just how do I prove that I have the right to take it?"

The ghost let his hand drop and watched Wade over the spear. "I know you arrived here with a demon. A living demon. I know you tried to bring her with you into this chamber. You know that this spear is meant to kill her kind, don't you?" When Wade slowly nodded, the ghost went on. "No demon can touch this spear without suffering great agony. If they dared to try to hold it, even for a few moments, the spear would burn them from the inside out. Nothing so evil can stand for long in the face of something so pure and powerful."

"I know it's a holy weapon, but that's why I want it. There's a demon, one who controls evil, who *is* evil. I need this spear so I can kill him before he takes over the Earth. It might be the only thing that *can* kill him."

The man arched a brow, cocked his head. "And yet you travel with a demon? One not bound, not broken, but free? One who is a companion, not a prisoner?"

"She's different." When the ghost arched a brow skeptically, Wade insisted, "She is. She's the one who told me about the spear, and helped me find out where it is. She wants the other demon dead even more than I do. More than anyone else on the planet does. Without her, I wouldn't have ever found this place."

"So she would be willing to do anything to kill him, yes?"

"Of course," Wade answered without hesitation.

The ghost reached up and his hand closed around the spear. Wade was shocked when the ghost was able to not just touch the weapon, but hold it. That generally took an extremely powerful ghost to manage. He pulled it from the light and stepped closer to Wade, holding it out, parallel to the floor so the point faced away from both of them. "Then I will give you the spear, but under one condition."

"What condition?" Wade asked suspiciously.

"You use it first to kill the demon who lays outside the mound."

"What?" Wade yelled.

"Kill the demon and you will have the weapon you need to kill the other. You said she would be willing to do anything to kill this evil. Let her prove it while you prove your worth and rid the world of one more evil creature."

Wade shook his head as he took a step back. "No. Not gonna happen. She's not like the other demons. And yes, she may die in the fight against Bellar, but I'm not going to betray her trust and kill her just for a fancy sharp stick. If that's the price, then I'll find another way."

"And if there is no other way? If this is the only way to kill this Bellar and save Earth?"

"There has to be a way. There's *always* a way," Wade insisted.

"Yes, and this is the way," the man said calmly.

"No, it's not," Wade stubbornly growled. "I'm not going to let your prejudice kill a good woman, and she *is* a good woman, despite being a demon. Name any other demon and I'll track it down and kill it, but I'm not going to kill Samara. It's just not gonna happen."

To his surprise, the ghost smiled and rested the butt of the spear against the ground. "Your convictions are strong. Good. Nor are you easily swayed by the easier path."

"Easier my ass," Wade growled.

The ghost shrugged. "Easier to some. Kill a weakened target in order to gain an advantage over the greater threat. Most would have accepted my bargain without a moment's hesitation."

Offended, Wade shook his head. "Yeah, well, I'm not most, so you can kiss my ass."

The ghost laughed. "You are exactly how I'd hoped you'd be." Wade frowned in confusion so the ghost explained, "We knew someone would come to claim the spear in a time of great need. What we didn't know was what manner of person the seeker would be. How he would use the spear." All humor faded. "While it's meant to fight evil, in the hands of the wrong person it could be twisted toward darkness. If you had accepted my bargain, I would have been honor-bound to give you the spear, but I would have feared for the world."

"Wait, does that mean that you're going to give me the spear after all?" Wade asked cautiously.

"I am. But there is still a condition."

Wade sighed. "Of course there is."

"It's not such a hard task," the ghost said with a smile. "When you have killed Bellar, return the spear here. As I said, it could be twisted to darkness, and the longer it's out in the world, unprotected, the more risk there is."

"That sounds reasonable." He cocked his head. "Will you still be here when I return?"

Now the ghost looked weary. "I will. I'm bound not only to this place, but to the spear. As long as one or the other exists, I remain here, waiting." That sounded very lonely to Wade. He liked his solitude as much as anyone, but he'd go crazy without the option to interact with people when he chose. "Take the spear, but take it with a warning. The demon outside, she truly must not touch it. Even if she isn't evil like the demon you wish to kill, the spear will not react well to being handled by a demon. I don't know how intense the reaction will be, but it will not be good."

"I understand, and we'd already agreed that I'd be the one to use it against Bellar." Still, he hesitated for a moment before he reached out and took the spear from the ghost.

"Use it well, and good luck," the ghost said before his image faded, as did the light the spear had rested in.

Wade blew out a soft breath as he looked at the weapon in his hand. It hummed with enough power that it tingled against his fingers. He expected to feel some sort of triumph or relief now that he had it, but all he felt was urgency and concern for Sam.

"I'll be back," he murmured to the empty chamber before he turned to leave the mound and rejoin Sam.

CHAPTER 20

As soon as Wade had passed through the opening, he felt a shifting behind him. When he glanced back, he saw the opening had sealed itself and once more looked like nothing more than a hollow tree.

"You got it," came Sam's excited voice from behind him.

He turned and saw her on her feet, her eyes no longer clouded with pain. In his relief, he hurried toward her, but stopped at the last second when he saw Marco watching him with an odd look on his face.

"What?"

Marco shook his head. "Nothing. So this is the demon killing spear?" he asked with a nod toward it.

"Yeah." He lifted it so they could both see it more clearly. "Can't you feel the power from there?"

Brows lifted as Marco shook his head again. "Not really. I can feel something, but I couldn't pinpoint it as the spear. Still can't, even knowing what it is. Are you sure it'll work?"

"Positive. There was a...caretaker, of sorts, inside. A ghost, I think. He said the spear will hurt any demon who touches it, and the longer they touch it, the more it'll hurt, until it finally kills them. But stabbing Bellar should be a hell of a lot quicker." He looked to Sam. "And you don't touch it at all. It *might* not kill you, but let's not take that chance, okay?"

Sam's mouth tightened, but she nodded. "Okay. Though I really hate that I can't be the one to use it against him."

"I know, but some things we just can't change. This is one of those things." He shrugged. "Besides, does it really matter so long as he ends up dead?"

"I suppose not," she muttered, her tone so sullen Wade couldn't help but smile. He could understand her reluctance to not be the one to make the kill. It was a feeling he'd had several times himself.

"Did the caretaker say anything else?"

Wade hesitated. He trusted Marco, had worked with him for two hundred years, and oddly enough, he trusted Sam even more, but he was reluctant to share everything he'd been told. More to the point, he didn't want to tell Sam about the test the ghost had put him through. "I need to bring the spear back after we kill Bellar."

"What? Why? Sounds like it would make it a hell of a lot easier to kill demons." Marco paused, then halfheartedly told Sam, "No offense."

She shrugged and shook her head. "None taken. I know most demons are pricks. And he has a point, Wade."

"I know, and I see it, too, but apparently the spear can be altered to work *for* evil instead of against it. So the caretaker wants it brought back so it can be kept safe. He's afraid if I don't, it could be as bad as Bellar coming to Earth." But most importantly, "And I promised I would."

Marco sighed. "Fair enough. Though when you do bring it back, maybe you can ask him if there are any other demon killing relics out there? Julian's been looking, but so far it sounds like they were all destroyed. If this spear does as it's supposed to, then maybe it isn't the last one."

"Maybe it isn't," Wade agreed. "For now, though, I need some sleep, and I'm sure Sam does, too. We'll see if we can figure out where Bellar's going to portal in. Can you check with the seers, see if any of them know anything?"

"I can, though last I heard they hadn't seen anything useful. Watch your back." Marco directed his gaze at Sam. "Both of you." Not giving either of them the chance to react to his apparent concern, he vanished.

"Well, that was unexpected," Sam murmured. "I think I'm starting to grow on him."

Wade only smiled as they started back to the SUV. She was growing on him, too.

They reached the car without incident and placed the spear in the back seat. Wade didn't like how it was exposed, but he also wanted it close, just in case. He did cover it with a blanket, but it still stood out.

After stopping at a drive through and getting some food, they found a motel and checked in. Only once the spear was safely inside did they relax. "I don't think I'm going to be comfortable around that thing until it's back in the mound," Wade told Sam as they settled down at the small table to eat.

"How do you think I feel?" Sam retorted as she stared at it with both suspicion and relief. "You can at least touch it safely."

"Good point." He started eating, and the moment the first bite touched his tongue, he ate faster. Apparently bleeding for a mystical lock and dealing with a ghost were great for stimulating the appetite. "When we find out where the portal is, I'm going to call Julian."

"You said he's a demon expert, right?"

"Yeah. I kind of hate to do it, seeing as how he's still pretty much a newlywed, but I can't think of anyone on the planet who knows more about demons than he does." Sam cleared her throat and he gave her a sheepish smile. "Anyone who isn't a demon themselves, anyway."

"That's better. And I'm sure he and his wife will both understand. Besides, if we don't stop Bellar, both of them will be in danger anyway, along with the rest of the world."

"There is that," he conceded. "And he would do anything to keep Red safe."

"He sounds like a good man. But I was thinking that maybe we shouldn't wait for Bellar."

He stopped eating and frowned at her. "What do you mean?"

"I mean, maybe we shouldn't wait for him to come to Earth. If we lose him here, he has a whole world of people to try to corrupt. If we take the fight to him, though...Go to Olarid, find him, kill him before he has a chance to get here, then isn't that a better option? Fewer innocents at risk."

The idea had its upsides, Wade couldn't deny that. There would be fewer innocent people and less hiding of what they were, but it was also Bellar's home turf. And if something went wrong, then the spear would be out of the hands of the people who could use it. Yes, Sam had said there were non-demons on Olarid, but if they were slaves, would they be conditioned to blindly obey, or would they fiercely want freedom? And revenge.

"I'm not sure. There's a lot that could go wrong with that plan, but there's a lot that could go wrong with our current plan, too. Especially since we don't know where Bellar will portal in," he said as he got up to throw his trash away.

"Then let's do it," Sam said eagerly as she stood as well. "Call up Marco and Julian, get them to help us. When Keen gets back, I'll ask him to see if Mom's seen any portals in the next day or so. We'll take the advantage while we can."

Wade studied her face, the intensity on it, the hope, before he sighed. "Okay, fine. But we wait for Keen first. If there aren't any portals before the one Bellar's going to use, there's no point in making plans or getting Marco and Julian riled up. Because they won't like this idea at all," he warned.

"That's fair."

"Of course it is. Now..." He took the two steps which separated them and cupped her face. Her lips parted to speak, but his mouth covered hers before she could make a sound. Seeing her hurting earlier had affected him more than he would have liked, and having the ghost try to entice him to kill her had only made it worse. If things had gone wrong, he could have lost her. He had to touch her, to calm himself with the taste of her.

And he couldn't forget the way she'd looked at him when he'd stripped earlier.

He didn't go slow and couldn't be gentle, no matter how hard he tried. Part of him expected her to protest the treatment, especially when her hands lifted to his chest. But rather than shove him away, which she absolutely could have done, her fingers gripped his shirt as she returned the kiss. More sweet than experienced, it heated his blood and made him growl against her mouth. His hands released her face and wrapped around her, pulling her tightly against him so he could feel every curve. It was almost a mistake, though, when it brought her flush against his aroused flesh and made him ache with need.

To his delight and astonishment, she rubbed her hips against him and nearly brought him to his knees. It was almost too much, but no way did he want her to stop. He groaned her name and slid his hands down, cupping her rear and boosting her up. Automatically, she wrapped her legs around him, which made it easy for him to carry her to the bed.

There was nothing to stop him now. No more surprises, and he wasn't going to deny himself this. He wasn't going to deny himself her, no matter who or what she was. He wanted her, needed her, and the wolf that lived inside him demanded he take what was his.

He laid her on the bed and immediately covered her body with his own, unwilling to give up the feel of her against him. He pressed his hips more firmly between her thighs and nearly howled with satisfaction just from being so close to her.

Under him, Sam struggled to keep a thought in her head. She'd never been kissed like this before, much less had a man laying against her so intimately. It made heat and need pool between her thighs. Her arms wound around him as he broke the kiss and trailed his lips down to her throat. When he gently sucked at the sensitive skin there, she whimpered and her hips arched. The need she had for him grew stronger with each moment until she felt like she couldn't contain it any longer. If something didn't happen to ease it, she was going to explode.

"Wade...please," she panted as her head fell back.

He growled against her skin and eased his hips back enough to slide his hand between them. He'd just gotten the top button of her jeans undone when he heard a familiar *pop*.

His head dropped onto Sam's shoulder and he wanted to cry. Was he never going to have the chance to get Sam naked and beneath him? Or on top of him, he wasn't picky. "Tell me we can kick him out," he breathed against Sam's ear and made her shiver.

"He hurting you?" came Keen's angry voice from above Wade.

Sam closed her eyes and bit her lip as she struggled to remember that she loved Keen. It wasn't his fault that his timing was atrocious. "No, he's not hurting me," she told him, her voice huskier than normal. When Wade didn't move right away she pushed at his shoulder and he reluctantly scooted off of her. Even then, it was still hard for her to focus, the desire still rushing through her veins.

"You mom had a vision," the imp said as he slowly flew down until he could perch on the foot of the bed.

That hit Sam like ice water and she sat up, buttoning her jeans. "What was it? What'd she say?"

"Two days'n there'll be a portal."

Her eyes widened. "Bellar's coming here in two days?" That was not good. They were supposed to have another week.

Keen shook his head. "No, not Bellar. You." He wrinkled his nose and looked to Wade, who still lay mostly on his stomach. "And him."

"She wants us to go through a portal to Olarid?" Wade asked, lifting his head and arching a brow at Sam.

"Yep. But be careful. Very careful. Bellar not happy."

"I guess you were right, Sam. Where did she say the portal would be?" he asked as he sat up and turned to Keen.

The little guy looked apologetic. "Said it was in a dry place with lots of cows. Lots and lots. Near a fake man that's tall as a building."

"Did she describe the man?"

"Said he had a big hat? And big boots?"

Sam looked frustrated. "That can't be helpful."

"Actually, it can," Wade said thoughtfully. "People as tall as buildings aren't really common here, and I actually had a bounty over in Texas not too long ago." Okay, it had been a decade, but still, that wasn't long in the grand scheme. He grinned and explained, "Texas is a state, like Louisiana, and it has a hell of a lot of cows. Lots of ranches and stuff. And near Dallas is a fake man who's fifty or sixty feet tall, wearing a cowboy hat and boots. It's pretty hard to miss. I think that might be what she's talking about. It's not too far from here, either. Five or six hours. We can sleep here tonight and leave tomorrow and make it there in plenty of time."

Sam smiled. "That's fantastic. You should call Julian and Marco, let them know what's going on. Keen, you should rest. You've been doing a lot of dimension hopping lately."

"And what are you going to do?" Wade asked as he drew out his phone.

The smile she gave him now was completely different. Sensual, full of teasing promises. "Take a shower."

He groaned. "Wicked woman," he growled. "Go before I change my mind about making my calls."

She laughed on her way to the bathroom.

Keen was watching him and Wade frowned. "What?"

"You like her."

Wade shrugged. "Yeah. So?"

Keen slowly shook his head. "You *like* her," he said, putting extra emphasis on the middle word.

"Again, so? I'll admit we didn't get off to the best start, but we've been working together for almost a week. We've each saved each other. Hard not to like a person under those circumstances."

Keen smiled and moved to an unoccupied pillow. "Okay."

Wade rolled his eyes and dialed Marco, ignoring the sound of water running in the bathroom. He would not picture Sam naked. He would not picture the water sliding over her skin. He would not—

"Everything okay?" was how Marco answered the phone. "I saw you less than two hours ago."

Wade yanked his mind back to the here and now. "It could possibly be better than okay. There's a portal opening in a couple of days in Texas. Several people, including a seer, think we should go through and use the spear on Bellar before he gets to Earth."

Marco considered for a moment before he spoke. "That...plan does have merit, yes. If we fail there, we could still weaken him. If we succeed, he never reaches Earth."

"Exactly. Sam and I are going to head that way in the morning, but I wanted to give you and Julian a head's up."

"Appreciated. We don't want an army for this. I doubt we have enough men to combat an entire dimension full of demons, anyway. A small group with specialized skills, though? It could work," Marco said thoughtfully. "I'll figure out who to bring and meet you. When and where?"

"Dallas, Texas, in two days. At or near the gigantic ass cowboy."

"The what?"

Wade chuckled. "You'll see what I mean. Plan fast." He hung up but didn't immediately call Julian. Though he knew the demonologist would be an asset, he really didn't want to be responsible for making Paige a widow. He'd never forgive himself. But he also knew if he didn't call Julian, and something went wrong, Julian would always assume he could have changed things. Finally, he selected Julian's name in his contacts and hit call. The moment he pressed the button, he cursed. He'd done it yet again. He hoped he only woke up Julian this time.

"Seriously, Wade?" came Paige's annoyed voice.

At his most charming, Wade said, "Ahh, there's the lovely Red. I haven't talked to you in ages. You're not really going to be mad at your favorite wolf, are you?"

She sighed. "Make it quick. I want to have a full night beside my husband." Her voice softened. "And take care of yourself, Wade. Or I'll make you think you look amazing in a pink tutu and green mohawk."

Wade winced, because he knew that she could do as she threatened. "I promise. Can I talk to Julian now?"

There was some soft fumbling before Julian answered. "I told you not to make a habit of this."

"I know, and I'm sorry. I forgot what time it was."

"What's so important it couldn't wait?"

"We got the spear, and a new plan."

"That might get you out of the dog house with Paige," Julian said dryly.

"Really? A dog joke? You can do better than that, English," Wade said, though he was amused. Julian had only recently begun joking again, and it was good to hear. "But yeah, there's a portal opening up in two days, and we're going to go through it. Me, Sam, Marco, and a handful of Hunters. And you, if you want in. We're going to kill Bellar before he can find his way here." He paused, knowing Julian wouldn't want to leave Paige, and added quietly, "Before he can get anywhere near Red."

Julian sighed. "I want to hate you for saying that, but it's a good point. I don't want him anywhere near her. I'll be there tomorrow night, so we have time to plan before we go."

Which Wade knew meant he'd be spending the next twenty-four hours with Paige, loving her in case he didn't come back. Jealousy tried to dig into his belly, but he shoved it down. Julian deserved the happiness. He deserved everything he had. And Wade? Well, there was Sam...

Quickly, he turned his thoughts elsewhere. "You know how to find me. Give Red a hug for me."

"I will."

He put the phone down and looked toward the closed bathroom door. There was no way he was going to let Sam fall into the hands of Bellar again, and no way he was letting that bastard take his planet. He just hoped the spear was did what it was promised to do.

CHAPTER 21

Neither Sam nor Wade slept well that night. Sam was plagued by dreams which alternated between ones in which Bellar had her enslaved again and ones where Wade touched her in ways she'd never been touched before.

Wade didn't even make it to the point of dreams, too distracted by the fact that Sam lay only feet away, wearing nothing but a tee-shirt and some yoga pants. The combination wasn't good for his sanity, not when he couldn't touch her. Why in the hell had he suggested them when they'd been getting her clothes? The jeans were bad enough, but the yoga pants? They were torture.

Because of that, they were up before dawn. Keen was sent back to Lilith to keep an eye on things and let them know if anything changed. After that, they didn't speak much, due to both the exhaustion and the tension that sparked between them. They picked up breakfast and ate in the car as they drove toward Texas. Luckily, the drive was uneventful and they reached Dallas before noon. When they found a motel, they booked three rooms near each other so they could make sure that Marco and others had places to sleep. It wasn't ideal, but the motel only had the three available.

They dropped their bags and the spear into the room they'd chosen for themselves, then stared at each other awkwardly. They had no clear task, nothing to do until the Hunters and Julian arrived. Nothing to distract them from each other.

"So..." Sam began finally.

Wade cleared his throat. "We've got a couple of options. We can play tourist, let you see a little bit of Earth while we actually have some free time..."

She gave him a minute, but he didn't continue, just watched her with an intensity that she could feel. "What's the other option?" she murmured, her heartbeat quickening.

Rather than speaking, he just looked to the bed, then back to her and arched a brow.

She felt herself go damp just from the insinuation, and after they'd been interrupted not even a day before, she found that she couldn't resist. More, she didn't *want* to resist. She wanted everything his touches and kisses had promised. Wanted what she'd almost had twice before.

That explosion.

Silently, she undid her braid and shook her hair out before she reached for the bottom of her shirt and drew it up and off. Bras didn't exist on Olarid, and Wade hadn't introduced her to the concept either, so she wore nothing beneath. She heard his sharp intake of breath and kicked her shoes off before she peeled the yoga pants down her legs.

She'd barely straightened when Wade growled and rushed toward her. He picked her up and gently tossed her onto the bed. His shirt was torn off more than taken off, and when he stretched out atop her, he wore only his jeans. "If Keen, or anyone, interrupts us this time,

I'm going to get violent," he warned her as he pressed his groin against hers.

There wasn't any argument from her, as she'd probably get just as violent. Instead, she grabbed his head and drew it down so she could kiss him. He groaned against the kiss and sank into it. One of his hands slid between them until he could cup her breast. He felt her breath shudder out when a calloused thumb drew over her nipple. He loved how she reacted so much to everything he did, but still he teased them both and did nothing more than kiss her and gently stroke her breast for several minutes. She might respond so easily and eagerly, but he still wanted her comfortable and desperate before he slid into her. He was going to make this first time as good as possible, for both of them.

With her lack of experience, Sam didn't think it could get any better than this. She'd happily do nothing but this for the rest of the day, if it weren't for the restless feeling inside her. The feeling that craved more, demanded more. "More, Wade. Give me more," she murmured into the kiss, shifting to press more firmly against his soft touch.

His head lifted and he gave her the wolfish smile she'd come to love. "Grab the headboard. You're gonna want something to hold on to in a minute."

Her eyes displayed her confusion, but she did as he asked. When his mouth found her breast, she gasped and her back arched. His lips closed around her nipple and her eyes fluttered closed. He started off gentle, but slowly drew harder on her, until she was squirming beneath him, her breath coming in soft pants. But he didn't move any lower, no matter how much he wanted to. Not yet. Another time they could rush to the finish line, but for her first time, he was going to make it last.

Wade kissed his way to the other breast and gave it the same treatment until she gripped the headboard hard enough he swore he heard the wood crack from the pressure. He smiled against her flushed skin.

Slowly, his mouth trailed down her belly and he felt the muscles quiver under his lips. His eyes, gone solid yellow with lust, stayed on her face as he moved closer to the center of her body. Then he was done teasing her. He needed her to fall apart for him. His tongue flicked over her clit and she cried out in surprised pleasure. The sound cut off when he began to suck on the sensitive flesh. She bucked under his mouth and his arms wrapped around her legs, holding her immobile beneath him. Now he was merciless, tongue and lips working over her as the blissful pressure coiled within her, tighter and tighter until she finally reached that point she'd been reaching for. Until she finally shattered.

Her body bowed, her head was thrown back, and she cried out his name as her first ever orgasm sent pleasure spiraling through her body until it seemed to invade every nerve. This time the wood did crack beneath her hands, though she didn't let go until, with one last lick, he lifted his mouth. His cheek rubbed against her inner thigh before he nipped it gently and released her. He reached down and undid his jeans, shoving them over his legs until he could kick them off.

Wade moved up until he hovered over her and his cock rested against the slick folds he'd just feasted on. He slid against her, coating himself in her wetness, though even that drove him to the brink. "You good?" he forced himself to say, wanting to make sure she was coherent enough not just to agree, but to enjoy every moment. She couldn't speak, but gave him a nod as she looked up at him with dazed eyes. Slowly, he began to press into her, taking great care to give her body time to adjust to him. He hoped that the orgasm would make this as close to painless for her as possible, but he didn't want to risk hurting her. He didn't ever want to hurt her.

He stopped when he butted up against the proof of her inexperience and gritted his teeth. The need to shove deep and bury himself inside her was great, but it couldn't overwhelm how much he cared for her. His hand found her breast again, lightly pinching and tugging at her nipple, building her desire once more. Slowly, carefully, he withdrew, then eased back in, gritting his teeth as he fought his natural instincts. When she began to squirm against him, he kissed her, hard, and thrust as far into her as he could go, breaking through that fragile barrier.

Beneath him, she tensed and cried out, but the sound wasn't one of pain.

The groan he made, however, almost was. He'd never felt anything so good as her tight, wet body gripping him like a fist. Nothing had ever been as difficult as keeping himself from coming right then. It took a minute before he was sure enough of his control to start moving, and when he did, he was glad he'd held off. The feel of her was too damn good and he wanted to savor every second.

Sam released the headboard and wrapped her arms around him, and by the second stroke, her nails were leaving half-moon marks on his back.

He growled and arched into her again as he lifted his head so he could watch her face as they moved together. "Wrap your legs around my waist," he half-snarled, too far gone for his wolf not to show itself in his voice. The moment she had, letting him press deeper into her, he lost it. He drew back then shoved into her, moving faster, harder than before. Over and over again he drove himself into her while she clung to him.

It wasn't enough for him, though. He wanted to feel her come around him. He wanted to watch her face as she broke into pieces in his arms. His hand moved between them and his thumb found that sensitive spot once more, still swollen with passion. The whimper she gave him shot straight to his cock.

"Don't fight it, baby. Let go," he breathed, holding onto his control by a hair.

There was no way she could fight it. The sensations he was causing her to feel were completely foreign to her, and she had no defense against them. Her nails dug into his back when she climaxed again, more intensely than she had the first time. It felt as though she'd swallowed liquid fire, and it burned painlessly through her veins. Nothing had ever felt like this before, not even flying, which had been her greatest joy before this point.

Wade's hand fisted in the sheets beneath them but there was no way he could prevent his body's reaction to feeling her clenching around him. He managed one more stroke before he buried himself deep inside her and threw his head back, roaring his pleasure. Never before had he come so intensely, and by the time he'd emptied himself inside her, his arms shook with exertion. He managed to collapse beside her rather than on top of her, but he couldn't stop touching her. A hand rested on her hip, and he couldn't care that his touch was possessive. She was his.

His mate.

Later, he'd probably freak out about that, but for now it just felt right.

"If…" The word was raspy and quiet, and Sam had to swallow before she could continue. "If I'd have known…it would be like that…I would've tackled you…that first night."

He let out a short, breathless laugh. "Should have let you. I was a jackass."

She turned her head and kissed his shoulder. "Yes," she agreed. Lazily, she rolled over until she was pressed against his side with her head resting on his shoulder. "Glad I waited for you, though," she murmured.

He waited for the spurt of panic her words should have caused, but as with the idea that she was his mate, it just made him content.

"Still have a choice to make," he said a minute later, when his breathing was a little steadier.

"Hmm?"

"You could still play tourist, see Texas."

Her fingers traced lazy patterns over his chest, following the lines of his tattoos. "Do these have any meaning?" she asked, ignoring his suggestion. She still felt a little drunk and found she didn't want to leave the bed, much less the room, not yet. Not when she had him pressed against her and her skin still tingled with the memory of what they'd done together.

He smiled at the change in subject. "They do, yes." It wasn't one he shared often. Only Julian knew why he'd gotten so many tattoos that they covered his entire chest, back, and both his arms and legs, and even he didn't know the full story. "You may have heard me mention bounties before, I can't remember. While I'm primarily a tracker, I do take bounties at times and help put down serious threats. Sometimes I help the Venatoribus Noctu with demons, but sometimes it's rough shifters, witches, elementals…Anyone supernatural who could pose a serious threat to people, magical or otherwise."

Her head tilted back so she could see his face and she smiled. "No wonder you were so willing to help me with Bellar. It's what you do normally."

"Basically. Though sometimes I help friends on treasure hunts. And each of my tattoos tell the story of a hunt, be it for a person or a treasure. This one," he pointed to a spot on his right forearm that showed some sort of temple surrounded by vines and trees, "I got after Julian, Red, and I went to Brazil and found a hidden temple. Damn near died in that temple, but it was an important step. This one?" He pointed to a beautifully rendered tattoo of a tiger head swirling into a woman's face. "Tiger shifter who got driven insane. She killed three people without meaning to. I'm the one who tracked her down."

Sam stroked her fingers over the vivid colors. "Did you kill her?"

He shook his head. "No. I only kill when I have to. I managed to restrain her and had a healer look at her. They were able to lock away the part of her mind that thought solely like a tiger. She's alive and living a relatively normal life now."

"The more I learn about you…the more I'm happy that it was your home I ran to when I first came out of the portal," she murmured, splaying her fingers out as she pressed her hand over the image of the tiger.

He covered her hand with his, thumb stroking over the back of her hand. "So am I. I'm even happier that I didn't kill you after I knocked you out."

She snorted. "If I'd have thought you would kill me, I wouldn't have gone as easy on you," she said, though something told him she was only half teasing. But then, he'd wondered about that fight, especially after seeing her truly battle against someone when the demons had attacked. Now he knew that she truly could have killed him if she'd wanted to.

"We've got a couple of hours before Marco and the others are going to show up. I know you've hated having your wings locked away. If we're not going out, why don't you let them out?" he suggested.

She pushed herself up onto an elbow and gave him an uncertain look. "Are you sure? I know that a lot of people who aren't demons are a little...uneasy...around winged beings."

His brows lifted in surprise. "Don't you remember the plane when you had them out?"

A frown marred her brow. "I do, but you were drunk."

He shrugged. "So? Being drunk doesn't change who a person is. Mostly, it makes them more of who they are, especially if they're an asshole. Besides, I wasn't drunk last night. I like your wings. I think they're beautiful, like the rest of you. And it's pretty cool that they've got that rainbow sheen like crow feathers." It was his turn to frown. "The spear point is the same way," he whispered with a glance to the wrapped weapon. No, he wouldn't dwell on that, not right now. Not when she was naked and warm in his bed. "But I mean it. Free your wings. The worst that'll happen is I'll try to talk you into riding me, so I can watch your wings spread out behind you," he told her with a wicked smile.

Sam laughed and rolled her shoulders, setting her wings free. She pushed herself up until she could straddle him. "I think that could be arranged."

CHAPTER 22

By the time the Hunters and Julian arrived, Sam had been introduced to shower sex, sex against the wall, and the joys of taking control when riding a man. But Wade had found his favorite had been when she'd rode him, her wings spread out behind her. They were so responsive, and he'd watched as they twitched and flexed as he touched her, then stretched out fully when she came.

No sight had ever been as beautiful as that moment. Seeing her like that had touched something in him that no woman had ever touched before. Something he hadn't realized could be touched.

They'd only been dressed about fifteen minutes when the first of the others arrived. Wade tried to be annoyed at no longer being alone with Sam, but he was entirely too relaxed to be bothered.

"Hey Marco," he told the commander of Venatoribus Noctu and the two men and two women who'd arrived with him. "Have a seat. Julian should be here soon. We figured everyone would be hungry, so I just ordered a bunch of pizzas. Probably be an hour before it gets here."

Marco grimaced at the mention of pizza, but he nodded and sat hesitantly on the foot of one of the beds.

The four with him weren't even that relaxed. All four stared at Sam like they wanted to kill her here and now.

Wade felt Sam stiffen next to him and glared at them as he drew her in closer. He knew the obvious affection he was showing Sam would confuse and annoy them, but he wasn't going to let her be ostracized by the very people she was trying to help. "She's not the bad guy, and if I hear any of you say one wrong word to her, you'll be answering to me," he told them, a growl trickling out of his mouth.

One of the women started to speak and Marco held up a hand, silencing her. "I told all of you that Samara wasn't the enemy. She's helping us deal with Bellar. If it weren't for her, we wouldn't know his plans."

"How do we know she's telling the truth?" one of the men asked coldly. "She could have said anything. Just because Bellar's name is known doesn't mean the rest is true."

"Do you really think I didn't check every resource I have? Do you think I didn't find a seer and see if what she said could be verified? While no one had as much detail as Samara had, they verified the general plan. So if you can't work with her, then tell me now and you can go home. We don't need this bullshit, and I won't accept it," Marco said in a tone that made Sam realize just why he was the leader of the Hunters. He had a commanding way that made a person sit up and listen.

"I don't want to go home, and I won't cause any problems," said the other man, "but how do you have so many details?" The fact that he directly addressed Sam, and in a fairly neutral voice, earned him points with Wade.

Sam drew in a deep breath and glanced at Wade. He shrugged a little and smiled, leaving it up to her how much she shared. He wouldn't judge her if she told them the whole truth. It would be a big step. They might take her words to heart more if she knew, but they might also turn on her, all of them. But Marco, at least, was Wade's friend, and she didn't want to lie to him. The biggest problem was, she still hadn't told Wade about her brother, and he wasn't going to be happy, but it was time to come clean.

After turning to the Hunters, she straightened. "I've been in his service, unwillingly, for two thousand years. I was the one he used as an assassin when he wanted someone killed discreetly. I was his threat...along with my twin brother." She didn't dare look at Wade, though she could feel the tension that suddenly thrummed through him. The fact that his arm remained around her meant everything to her. "He made it so I couldn't strike against him, so he shared his plans with me. Mostly because he intended me to help him carry them out." She bit her lip before continuing, quietly, more hesitantly, "And more...he's my father."

"What?" shouted Marco, his single word heard over the sudden cursing of the other Hunters.

"Keep in mind that a person can't choose their parents, Marco," Wade growled. "And think of how much she's suffered at her so-called father's hands in *twenty centuries*. That much abuse would turn any-one against a parent. She's told us nothing but the truth about what he's planning. And in coming here, she took away the biggest advan-tage he had for conquering Earth. So think about all of that before you condemn her, again, for something she can't help."

Marco struggled visibly to regain his composure. "And what about his consort, Lilith? None of the intel you've given us has included her. At least none Wade has passed on."

Wade braced himself for Sam to go off on Marco, but was surprised when her voice remained calm. "That's because my mom isn't working with Bellar. She's most definitely working against him. Who do you think told me about the portal that brought me here? Or the portal that's opening tomorrow to take us there? She's even the one who told me where I could find a clue to finding the spear. She's helped more than anyone else, on Earth or Olarid. Whatever you *think* you know about her, I can assure you, it's wrong. If, after all this is over, you want to know the entire truth about her, I'll consider telling you, but it's not relevant to the situation now."

Despite his anger at her for keeping her twin a secret, Wade was proud of the way she handled the Hunters and gave her a quick squeeze. They'd hash out the other later.

"I will definitely take you up on that, but you mentioned that your twin is also used as a weapon for Bellar. What about him?" Marco asked.

Sam hesitated. "I don't know," she admitted. "Evane loves me, but I don't know if he'll fight us or just abstain from it all. But I do ask that, if he does fight...please, don't kill him. Knock him out if you have to, but I don't want to lose my brother because of the asshole that's my father."

All five hunters were quiet for a minute, exchanging glances, before Marco sighed. "We can't make any promises. If it's him or us, we're going to choose him, but I'll give the order. We detain if we can, and only kill as a last resort, but it's the best I can offer."

"I understand. Thank you."

Just then, Julian appeared. He took a quick glance around the room and arched a brow. "Dare I ask what I just walked in on?" he asked dryly. No one spoke immediately, and Julian crossed his arms. "Well, someone tell me."

Sam was the one who answered. "I just told them that Bellar's my father, Lilith is my mom, and I have a twin brother who was used as an assassin for our father as well. But my mom and brother aren't the enemy."

"Your mom may not be, but even you weren't sure of your brother," Marco corrected, and Sam reluctantly nodded. "We've agreed to do our best not to kill her brother, however."

"It sounds like I missed quite a lot." Julian looked at Wade. His next words weren't aloud, but projected directly into Wade's mind. "*Did you know about this?*"

"*Not the brother, no. But I knew who her parents were. And she's very adamant that Lilith isn't what we think she is.*"

"*Do you trust her on that?*"

"*Actually, I do.*"

"*That's good enough for me. I trust your instincts.*"

"Then, since that's all out in the open, why don't we figure out what the plan is for tomorrow?" Julian asked, sitting on the foot of the bed Wade and Sam reclined on.

"Right. Wade, you're insistent on being the one to use the spear, correct?" Marco asked.

Wade nodded. "I don't know if anyone else should. I was tested to get it, and I have to return it when this is done, so I'd rather not loan it out. I trust all of you, but you know how magical objects can be. Especially weapons."

"He's right," Julian agreed with a nod. "Most of the time, weapons like that *can* only be wielded by the one who won them. Some of them will actually attack anyone else who picks it up. I don't know if the spear is one of those, but there's no reason to take chances unless we have to." Since he was the de facto expert on relics, no one questioned him.

"We'll wait for the portal, then go quickly. Wade, Samara, you'll go first. Wade because he has the spear, and Sam because she's the only one familiar with this dimension."

"Olarid," she supplied helpfully.

Marco just nodded. "Once there, can you lead us to where Bellar is?"

"I can. And if I had some paper, I could draw you a layout. Everyone, other than a few...unusual people, live in strongholds or towns that are surrounded by walls. The wilderness is very unforgiving, and both the plants and animals will attack if they can. Bellar's in a stronghold. Lots of guards and fortifications, since he rules the entire dimension." She smiled tightly. "But I know the secret ways in and out. I know the place as least as well as Bellar. Possibly better, by this point."

"I'll get some paper and pencils," one of the women said. "And will we be underground at some point? If so, I can grab some lights, too."

"We will, yes," Sam confirmed. "And what's your name?"

"Bethany. I'll be right back." The woman disappeared.

"And the rest of you? It would be easier if I knew who to address. And it might help to know strengths, too, if you're comfortable sharing."

Marco nodded to them.

"I'm William," said the one who'd spoken out against her. "Witch. I'm good at immobilization and combat magic.

The other man said, "Dan, elemental. Anything electrical I'm good with. Lightning, electricity, the whole deal."

The woman didn't look as happy, but she said, "Caitlyn. I'm a healer, but my primary skill is telekinesis."

"Thank you. I don't know if Marco told you, but I'm a Fury," Sam began, but stopped when Dan nodded.

"He did." There was a quick pause. "I was wondering...we have Furies here, or at least in mythology from one part of the world that's several thousand years old. Are those demons?"

"I honestly couldn't tell you. There aren't many of us, but it's entirely possible some could have visited enough to start the legends. I can't say that I've ever met someone who wasn't a demon who had quite the same abilities we do, though," she admitted. "Some that were similar, or parts of our abilities, but none that were identical without the demonic blood."

"Fair enough."

Bethany returned then and offered a large pad of paper and a couple of pencils to Sam, who took them with a faint smile.

After moving to the table, Samara set the paper down and started to sketch the layout of the stronghold. "We'll be using a secret passage to get in. It doesn't come out as close to Bellar's quarters as I'd like, but he keeps that area patrolled more than some of the others. He's not as paranoid as he should be, but he doesn't take too many chances with the place where he sleeps."

"Does he trust his people that much?" William asked.

Sam snorted as she continued to draw. "Hardly. But when you're surrounded by evil people and you can control evil, it's not hard to ensure that they're not likely to attack you. Not only that, but he's the most arrogant person I've ever met. But if there's a change in routine there, if for some reason he increases his security, we should know."

"How?" Marco asked.

She glanced up briefly. "Keen. We sent him back to keep an eye on things. None of us want any surprises."

"I can see why you keep him around," he said with a nod.

"No, I keep him around because he's my friend. The fact that he can jump across dimensions is just a little something extra."

Wade chuckled at Marco's discomfort. There was a knock on the door, then, and he got up to answer it. The pizza was there, and he gave the delivery guy more than enough for the seven pizzas he'd ordered and shut the door. "I booked two rooms. They're not next door, but they're close. Why don't you guys get settled and eat, and when the plans are done, I'll let you know?"

Marco looked surprised at the suggestion, but Julian just smiled and took two of the boxes. "Sounds good to me. Marco, why don't we take one of the rooms, and your Hunters can take the other?"

After a bit of grumbling, all the pizzas but one were taken, they had their keys and room numbers, and they went off to their respective rooms.

"This will only take me another minute," Sam said with some surprise.

"I figured, but I wanted to talk to you."

Her hand stilled and she looked up at him. "About Evane."

"Why didn't you tell me you had a brother, Sam?" It hurt that she'd held it back from him.

She set the pencil down and sighed. "Evane and I...Things have been strained for a while. I really do believe he still loves me, and I love him, but..." She shook her head. "We both serve our father, but where Bellar had to tattoo me to keep me from killing him, I've never noticed such a tattoo on my brother. It doesn't mean there isn't one, but I've never seen or heard of it. Part of me is afraid he's more like our father than our mom."

He saw the pain in her eyes and his own hurt faded, replaced by sympathy for her. He set the pizza down and crossed to her, drawing her out of her chair. Once she was on her feet, he wrapped his arms around her and kissed her brow. "Bellar will be dead soon. Maybe when he's dead things will get better between you and your brother. Or maybe he's just making his own plans to kill Bellar and he's trying to keep you safe."

"Maybe..."

Though he hated to bring it up, he made himself say, "You should let us know what his abilities are. In case we do have to fight him. Being surprised would mean it's harder to contain him. Is he a Fury like you?"

"No, all Furies are women. I don't know why, it's just how it is. But you're not going to like this."

"Honey, I haven't liked any of this, other than you," Wade said with a wry smile.

"You know Bellar used me as an assassin. He trained me, thoroughly, to be his primary assassin. But Evane? His power is all about pain. Sensing it, causing it. He can ease it, too, but he wasn't allowed to do that often. And Bellar also had him trained in poisons so Evane could be his torturer."

Wade winced. "That's not good, but it's better than it could have been. The Hunters aren't weak. A little pain isn't going to stop them."

She shook her head. "Pain can have an extraordinary effect on a person, wolf. I've seen people die from nothing more than pain. It shut their bodies down somehow. Shock, I think. But it did take a few minutes to build up to that level."

"Okay, that's even worse. Let's leave that part out. I'm afraid some of Marco's people might panic if he hurts them with the pain and kill him to save themselves."

"Thank you," she whispered, leaning up to kiss him lightly.

"You're welcome. Now, finish those plans so we can all get a good night's sleep."

She arched a brow. "You were planning on letting me sleep?" she asked, a smile playing along her lips.

He grinned. "Eventually. Maybe."

CHAPTER 23

True to his word, Wade kept Sam up half the night, but she couldn't mind, especially after they fell asleep with their limbs tangled and one of her wings sprawled across them like a blanket.

The next morning, they headed out to the tall statue where the portal was supposed to open. Sam voiced her concerns about how suspicious they looked—eight people standing around, armed and carrying a long, blanket-wrapped bundle—but as it turned out, Bethany's major power was illusion. In this case, she was making them invisible to anyone who looked in their direction. Impressed and relieved, Sam subsided and told them about Olarid while they waited, warning them how they couldn't trust the beauty of the place and describing some of the larger threats.

Unfortunately, it was two hours before they felt the burst of power signaling an open portal.

"Hurry, we don't know how long it'll stay open," Marco said urgently, and he was right to be concerned. Some portals lasted only seconds, while others could linger for half a day or more.

Wade dropped the blanket around the spear and grabbed Sam's hand. "Come on," he told her, and they rushed into the shimmer that hovered in the air.

The sensation of passing through a portal was one of the oddest things that Wade had ever experienced. It felt like he was pushing through gelatin while a low electrical current ran across his skin. But even that couldn't compare to what he saw when he was on the other side.

Sam hadn't been exaggerating when she said Olarid was beautiful. It looked like some sort of Eden. Everything was so green and healthy, with alien flowers darting up, adding splashes of colors everywhere he looked. And those flowers put a delicious scent in the air, one that was relaxing and beautiful.

She also hadn't exaggerated the danger, though this particular danger wasn't one that she'd mentioned. Nine demons stood there, armed and dressed in Earth clothing, and they looked as surprised as Sam and Wade felt.

"Ronin," Sam snarled as she glared at the demon who stood in the front. He was a few inches taller than Wade, and more thickly muscled. Most unusual was that he was an albino. His hair, skin, and eyes were all completely white, aside from a black ring around the outer edge of his irises. It made him look otherworldly, which Wade supposed he was.

She drew her knives, all too eager to sink one deep within Ronin's chest.

Then the unthinkable happened. The portal closed behind them without allowing even one of the Hunters through.

Wade and Sam exchanged a look. They were screwed.

Ronin smiled. "Well, well, well. I expected to have to hunt for you. I never expected that you'd just come to me, but I like it. This makes things so much easier. I hate going to that wretched dimension. It's so…dull." He glanced at the knives in Sam's hands and chuckled. "You really want to use those? You'll take out a few of us, sure, we both know that, but in the fighting, I think your toy will have an accident." He grinned evilly. "It might even be fatal. But if you don't mind having his death on your conscience—since you apparently grew a conscience—then go right ahead and fight us. And don't even think about inflicting insanity on any of us. The result will be the same. And no matter what you do, I'm taking you to your father."

Sam's eyes narrowed as she considered all nine demons. "You're working for Bellar? I thought you were Evane's friend."

He arched a brow. "And Evane works for him. I don't see any problem here, except you're still thinking about fighting us."

She glanced to Wade, who looked like he wanted to tear into the demons as well, but she knew Ronin, knew his weaknesses, knew his strengths. Though he was certainly guilty enough for her vengeance magic, he was also immune to any sort of mental influence. A fact she'd learned the hard way. His men weren't immune, but he would still follow through with his promise to kill Wade if she tried that.

If they'd been on Earth and been cornered like this, she would have reminded Wade of his promise to kill her if necessary, but with them trapped on Olarid, she would have to improvise. "If we come quietly, do you swear you won't harm him? And I mean not a single hair on his head, Ronin."

"Sam…" Wade growled, but she just shook her head and kept her gaze on Ronin.

Ronin grinned triumphantly. "Of course. Surrender your weapons and I promise I won't hurt him."

That might still be tricky. If they touched the spear, they'd know it was dangerous. But they didn't have much of a choice. Hoping that Wade would follow her lead, Sam dropped her knives on the ground.

Wade glanced at Sam, but slowly released the spear so it clattered down beside the knives.

"Good girl. Your father will be pleased," Ronin said with a smirk.

"Fuck you," Wade snarled.

"Tsk. Your father won't be pleased with your choice of friends, though." He jerked his head. "You know the way. And if you even think of running, we'll put a knife in your friend's back, then take his head. Eventually. Are we clear?"

"Crystal," she replied, teeth clenched, as she turned to head toward the stronghold. Unfortunately, they were close to it, so there wasn't much time for them to escape if she decided to try. Fortunately, she saw all the demons follow after her without picking up any of the weapons that lay on the ground. Including the spear. If they could just get free, Sam knew how to get back to this place, so the spear wasn't lost.

She half wished that some of the others had made it through with them, but at the same time she was glad that Bellar's demons didn't have more prisoners. Knowing Bellar, he'd take pleasure in torturing the Hunters if he had them at hand, all to make her suffer.

As they walked, she glanced at Wade, but didn't dare speak to him. If Bellar found out how important Wade was to her, he'd kill her wolf, and it wouldn't be quick. Or worse, he'd plant a seed of evil within Wade and tend it until Wade was as against her as Bellar was. It wasn't an easy task, but it was a possibility she couldn't discount.

By the time they'd reached the gates and they'd been opened to admit them, she'd rebuilt the haughty shell that she'd had in place for most of her life. A few minutes later, when they were escorted into the throne room, her eyes were cold, her back stiff.

"It's truly sad when a demon's daughter has to be forcibly escorted back to her father," said the man who sat on the black and silver throne at the far end of the room. A woman sat on the arm of the throne, a blonde shifter that Sam vaguely recognized as one of Bellar's concubines. But then, essentially all females in the stronghold, aside from herself and her mother, were his concubines. Demon, human, witch...he didn't discriminate, and he didn't ask for permission. Then again, with his powers, he rarely had to ask. And the women were all too terrified of him to try to deny him, in any case.

The throne beside his, a smaller one made of gold that seemed to be made up of hundreds of snakes, sat empty.

Wade was surprised at his first sight of Bellar. The epitome of evil wasn't twisted and inhuman in appearance. Instead, he was perfect. His features weren't unlike Sam's, only more masculine, and the only difference in their hair was the length. Where Sam's nearly hit her hips, Bellar's was only a few inches long. Similarly, their wings were identical in color, though he had red eyes where she had black.

"When a daughter has a father such as you, who can truly blame her for not wanting to be in his presence for any longer than she must?" Sam replied in a bored tone. "You know I won't be staying long this time, either. Nothing has changed in the last week."

"No? I would say it has," Bellar said as his gaze shifted over to Wade. "You don't normally work with anyone, Samara. Or maybe you're not actually working with him. Perhaps he's...special to you."

Sam snorted. "Hardly. You cured me of wanting to let anyone be special to me long ago. But to annoy you, I'd work with absolutely anyone," she said, smiling sweetly.

His eyes narrowed for a moment. "Perhaps." He looked to the demons who stood behind Sam. "Ronin, choose five men and take my daughter to her chamber. The rest of you, lock the man in a cell. I'll deal with him shortly."

Sam had to fight not to protest, to keep her facade of disinterest. She saw the pain and shock that had flashed briefly on Wade's face when she said he wasn't important, but hoped that no one else had. Their best chance was for Bellar to think Wade was just someone she'd talked into helping her. Because of that, she went quietly to her room, though the fact that she hadn't seen Keen or her mother worried her. It wasn't that her mother often occupied her throne, but the imp was usually visible, if you knew where to look.

Outside her room was a single familiar face, though she was torn between happiness and upset at seeing him.

Her twin brother leaned against the wall, his arms folded over his chest. Hair identical in color to Sam's reached a chin that hadn't seen a razor for at least a few days. Like her, his irises were solid black, though they showed an aloofness that Sam only displayed for Bellar and his minions. And though his wings were hidden, she knew they were indistinguishable from her own. Unlike her, he stood half a foot over six feet tall, but it was the largest difference in their appearance beyond their genders.

"Sister," he said coolly.

"Hello, Evane," she replied quietly. "I'd ask how you've been, but no one who lives here is well, unless their name happens to be Bellar."

He shook his head and sighed. "You continue to rebel against our father. It's going to get you killed one of these days, Sam."

"Perhaps, but he can't control me in death, now can he? Though it would leave Mom without a child who gives more of a damn about her than they do power."

His eyes flashed red. "Don't speak about things you know nothing about, Sam.

It was her turn to sigh. "I don't want to fight with you, Evane. I never have," she said tiredly.

"Yet we end up doing that so often, don't we?" he asked as he pushed away from the wall and strode away toward his room.

Ronin shoved her into her chamber the moment Evane was gone and the door slammed behind her. She heard the sound of the lock being turned and groaned.

Home sweet home...

The rooms she'd spent her whole life in showed little of her. The walls were cold stone, just like the rest of the stronghold, and there was nothing personal anywhere in the room. Personal was dangerous, as it gave Bellar a target, a way to torment or punish her.

A bed sat against one wall, with a table beside it and a trunk at the foot of it. Within the trunk were weapons, nothing more. The single dresser held her clothes, but they all ran along the same lines; black leather pants and red or black halters that wouldn't hinder her wings. But there weren't any paintings or knick-knacks in the room. There weren't even any books. She had them, sure, but she didn't keep them here where they could be found.

The less Bellar had been able to learn about her, the better.

She moved to the trunk immediately and opened it up. Though she cursed when she saw it was empty, she wasn't really surprised. After closing it she straightened and put her hands on her hips. For the first time, she regretted not having more in her room. There wasn't much she could use to improvise a weapon, and she couldn't depend on her Fury abilities solely if she wanted to break Wade out of his cell.

Just a couple of minutes later, she heard her door being unlocked. She turned and braced for a fight, only to be relieved when she saw her mother slip into the room, accompanied by Keen.

"Mom," she breathed, and the second the door was closed, she was rushing across the room and flinging her arms around the smaller woman.

Though born centuries before Sam, Lilith didn't look even a year older than her daughter. Oddly, Lilith resembled Bellar a great deal and had, she was told, since before her mother had become a demon. Her hair was inky black and ruler straight as it flowed down her back past her hips. Skin as pale as moonlight showed not a single wrinkle or scar, but despite her perfect appearance, Lilith didn't look artificial. Sam always thought it was the warmth in her red eyes. Eyes that were sinister on Bellar were absolutely beautiful on Lilith.

The one flaw her mother had, if it could be considered a flaw, were the mystical black symbols that lay on both her palms. Sam had spent hours when she was a child tracing those marks, never knowing that they were signs of Lilith's tormented past.

Keen wasn't inclined to wait for them to finish their reunion and landed on Sam's shoulder, hugging both women as well as he was able with his short arms.

It was a minute before they drew back and Sam wanted to cry. Her mom looked tired. Visions could do that to her, she knew. "Are you okay, Mom?"

Lilith stroked a hand over Sam's hair. "As okay as I always am. And better now that I've seen you, though I would have preferred not to see you imprisoned."

Sam forced a smile. "You know it's temporary. He's never been able to hold me."

"I know. But I also know this time is different."

"How do you mean?"

"One way or another, this is going to be decided within the next week," Lilith said with a delicate shrug of her shoulder.

Sam was afraid she knew, but she asked, "By once and for all you mean..."

"Either we'll be dead, or he will. Perhaps all of us," Lilith answered. "I haven't seen enough to know for sure, and you know visions are generally more guidelines than anything set in stone."

"I know." She blew out a soft breath. "We need to get Wade out of his cell and get back to where the portal opened."

"Why? Another one won't open again there for a while. Maybe centuries."

"They were trying to use the portal right as we got there, so I dropped my knives in hopes that Wade would follow suit. He did, and those idiots left the weapons there," Sam explained.

Lilith smiled slowly. "The spear is here? And that close? That's certainly good news."

"Except demons can't touch it without suffering and eventually dying. And I don't know if anyone here who isn't a demon has the skill to use it on Bellar successfully."

"No, probably not," Lilith agreed. "Bellar is very serious that none of the slaves are allowed to learn how to fight with so much as a butter knife." She moved to Sam's bed and sat on it. "Getting the keys to the cell won't be difficult."

Sam instantly knew how Lilith intended to get the keys and felt her stomach turn. "Mom, no. I know how you hate using those powers on anyone." Though Lilith wasn't a succubus, she could create desire like one. Most of her powers she kept hidden from everyone but Sam, but that was an ability Bellar had bragged about. It was part of what had earned her the moniker Lady of Darkness and Desire.

"I do, but if it means the end of Bellar, then it's worth it." She smiled and patted the bed next to her and waited for Sam to join her. "We'll go down and I'll get the keys so we can get Wade out. You know the secret passages, so you should be able to escape after that. But after your escape to get the spear, it's likely Bellar will increase his security. You won't be able to get back into here to kill him. Your best bet will be to return to Earth and wait for him to go there. He'll be on unfamiliar ground, and he won't be able to carry his full army with him. Unfortunately, I don't know where another portal to Earth will be opening," she said apologetically.

"I don't know either, but I know someone who might. Someone who needs to know what's going on." Sam turned to Keen, who had perched on chest. "Keen? You remember Marco?"

"Hunter who don't like me?"

"He just didn't understand you at first. Can you go to him and tell him what's happened? Not only that, but see if he can figure out where a portal will be?"

Keen's wings drooped but he nodded. "Okay."

She smiled gratefully. "Thanks Keen."

He nodded once more then disappeared back to Earth.

"Good. We'll wait a few hours, let things calm down, then we'll get started." Lilith smiled. "Besides, I have a feeling you have a lot to share with me."

Sam laughed. "Mom, you have no idea." But her amusement died quickly. "I just hope Bellar takes his time in going to visit Wade." Because if he didn't, then Wade would be suffering while she was catching up with her mother, and she didn't think she could stomach that.

CHAPTER 24

I mps couldn't just travel between dimensions, but to people or places they knew in those dimensions. It was similar to how Julian had been able to teleport directly to Wade, and was how Keen kept appearing by Samara's side no matter where she was. And since he had met Marco before, even if it was only briefly, he was able to travel directly to the commander. The short jump took him back to the motel room that Sam and Wade had stayed in the night before. Marco, Julian, and all the Hunters were there, and they weren't happy.

When Keen popped in, those who were sitting shot to their feet and everyone braced for battle. Upon registering that it was Keen, they relaxed, but only marginally. Aside from Marco and Julian, they all looked at him with distrust. Julian, however, looked extremely curious, while Marco had a concerned expression on his face.

Marco was the first to speak. "Do you know where they are? The portal closed before we could make it through."

The anger in the man's voice had Keen darting toward the one person who had never threatened him—Julian—and taking refuge behind the man.

Julian looked bemused and glanced toward the scared creature who was currently clinging to the back of his shoulder. "We're not mad at you," he promised the imp. "We just want to know what happened."

Keen peeked around Julian, took in the angry eyes, and focused on Marco. "Demons. They wanted the same portal and were waitin' on the other side. They caught Sam and the wolf. Took 'em prisoner."

There was an outcry from every one of the Hunters, and even Julian let out a low curse. The reaction had Keen hiding again, now pressed against the small of Julian's back, trembling lightly.

"Is that it?" Marco asked, fighting to keep his voice as calm as he could.

Keen shook his head before he realized the others couldn't see it and slowly poked his head out again. "They alive. Sam's with her mama. They gonna get the wolf and escape. Demons left the spear, so they gonna go grab it. They wanna know if you can find 'em a portal. Can't get to Bellar anymore, so they wanna come back here."

"Shit." Marco began to pace. "Bethany, go talk to the seers. Let them know just how important it is that we find a portal, and soon. I don't care where it comes out, so long as it's in the next twenty-four hours. Twelve is better."

Bethany nodded as she stood, disappearing a second later.

"Did they say anything else?"

Keen thought for a moment then shook his head. "Nope. Just what I said. If you find a portal, I'll go tell 'em."

"Then we'll make sure that we find one so we can bring them back," Julian said. "Don't worry, we don't give up, and we don't back down easily." He looked up at Marco. "We'll get them back."

"Yes, yes we will," Marco agreed. He'd make damn sure of it.

"And I can stay and you won't hurt me?" Keen asked, glancing to the unhappy Hunters.

"Yes, you can stay," the commander said with a sigh. Then, more reluctantly, "And no one will hurt you."

"Yeah, you're our only link to Wade," Caitlyn muttered.

Marco gave her a sharp look. "I've already told every single one of you, keep your opinions to yourself. The imp and Samara are helping us."

"You sure about that? Samara told us about this portal and she took the spear that's supposed to be able to kill a demon right to him," she argued. "For all we know, Wade's already dead and Bellar's got the spear safely locked away—if it was really something that could kill him in the first place."

"Enough!" Marco snapped.

"She's right," William said softly, "Look, I like Wade. We've all worked with him before, but isn't it just possible he got taken in by this demon?"

Marco was getting pissed, and Keen hid behind Julian once again. The imp wanted, desperately, to defend Samara, but while he was impulsive, he knew he couldn't win against this many Hunters. As it turned out, he didn't need to.

Before the commander could speak, Julian shook his head. "I don't think he has, not like you're meaning." He saw their skeptical expressions and continued. "All of you know I've spent my life studying demons. I can't say I'd ever heard of a good demon before, but this one seems to be different." He paused, glanced toward the back of his shoulder. "These, I should say." He looked back to the Hunters. "She's had numerous chances to kill Wade or sabotage us, and she hasn't. I've personally seen how she's been injured and how she's done her best to care for Wade when he was injured. I really don't think this is a double cross."

Julian's support didn't fully appease Marco, however. "I don't expect any of you to follow me blindly, but I do expect you to trust me. If you don't trust me, then what the hell are we doing?" he demanded. "I told you I thoroughly checked her story. Not only that, but when I first met her, I was on the verge of killing her, and do you know what she did?" No one said anything and he went on. "She told me my need for vengeance was just, and that if killing her eased some of my pain, then she was happy to die. She bared her fucking throat and just waited for me to kill her. Does that sound like someone who would lure Wade into a trap?"

He couldn't have said whether it was his words or Julian's, but the Hunters looked like they were finally thinking.

"I don't know how I feel about the two of you defending the very thing we hunt," William began slowly, "but I think we can reserve judgment...for now. If Wade is dead in that dimension, we'll deal with it. But if he shows up intact, then we can reevaluate."

"That's all I can ask. And don't think I'm saying all demons are good, because there's no way in hell I'd ever say that. Just...this one seems to be the exception," Marco said with a curt shrug. Keen made a small noise and he rolled his eyes heavenward. "These two," he corrected wearily. "Now, assuming they are able to get back with the spear, we need to figure out exactly how we're going to take down Bellar."

"I've got some ideas on that," Julian said, hoping the distraction would ease some of the tension.

And Keen? He stayed behind Julian for the next hour, unwilling to put himself in the line of sight of the Hunters and risk riling them up again.

Wade had never been imprisoned in a dungeon before. He'd been in some tough spots before, sure, but locked in a cell, in the basement of a demon's fortress? He hated it. His wolf did, too, so the first half hour was spent pacing the eight by eight cell.

Where the hell was Samara? He knew Bellar wanted her to help him take over the world so wouldn't kill her, but that didn't mean he couldn't hurt her. For that matter, he was surprised he hadn't gotten a visit.

And he knew she'd been trying to avoid just that when she'd denied their relationship to her father. Oh, it had taken him a few minutes to figure that out. He'd first had to work past the initial anger and—he could admit it—hurt that her denial had caused, but it was the only thing that made sense. She hadn't been faking when she was with him, he knew it. And if Bellar was as bad as she claimed—and he had no reason to doubt it—then he would certainly hurt others to cause Sam pain.

But gods, he really wished he had Julian's ability to speak telepathically right now.

It was forty minutes later that the demons showed up.

Wade stopped and let out a low growl as he studied them.

There were three of them, two male and one female, and he couldn't have said which looked the most intimidating. The first man was seven feet tall if he was an inch, with long horns that curved back along his head. His entire body—including his eyes—was a gray so dark it was almost black. The other man was only a few inches shorter, though there was little about him that looked human. Instead of hair, he had mottled green scales and short horns that ran in two parallel rows from his forehead and to the back of his skull. His eyes were slit like a reptile's and his hands only had three fingers and a thumb, each tipped with a claw.

Next to the men, the woman looked harmless at first glance. She was tall and blonde, with all the curves a man could want. Her skin was smooth, her lips full, pouty, and red, her eyes a brilliant blue. Her clothing was almost identical to what Sam wore, except she'd opted for a red as bloody as her lips. The fact that she also had fangs, slender horns, claws, and leathery wings wasn't even the part that made Wade wary of her. It was the look in those pretty blues that said she'd love to hurt him. That and the aura that she gave off. It was close to the same feeling he'd gotten from Bellar. Pure evil.

"He looks like he's going to be fun to play with," she purred as she ran her fingers down one of the bars of the cell.

"Just remember, we need to get information from him before you kill him," the tall man said, unlocking the cell door.

Wade eyed all three demons and considered his chances. They were all visibly armed, with the big one having a sword almost as long as Samara was tall. He might be able to make it, but the odds weren't good. On the other hand, it was obvious they were going to torture him, possibly even kill him. If he tried to escape, at least he had a chance.

Before he could make a move, however, the reptilian demon opened his mouth and made a sound Wade had never heard before or wanted to hear again. It was somewhere between a shriek and a growl and it sent Wade to his knees. It was as bad as banshee screams were said to be.

While he was incapacitated, the big one grabbed him by the throat, lifted, and shoved him against the wall. Some magic of the prison had stone coming out of the walls and circling his wrists, holding him firmly in place. Once he was secured, the shrieking stopped, leaving Wade's head pounding. But he could still hear the demon tell the woman, "Have fun."

Wade tugged at the stone cuffs, not really surprised when he wasn't able to even budge them. "Sorry, I don't want to play right now. You'll have to find another friend," he snarled as the woman stepped inside the cell.

"Oh, you don't have any choice in the matter," she said with a laugh. He thought it was meant to be seductive, but after hearing Sam laugh, this demon simply grated on every nerve. She ran her hand lightly down his chest, pausing with it on his belly. "You're going to be my plaything until you tell me everything I want to know. Or until you die." She shrugged. "I don't care which."

Her hand lifted, but this time when it moved over his chest, she led with those claws, which ripped easily through both his shirt and the flesh beneath. He managed not to scream, but only barely.

She tsked playfully and shook her head. "Now, now. That won't do. If you don't want to talk, then you *will* scream," she promised.

Unfortunately, before she was done with him, she was right.

234

CHAPTER 25

S am had never held anything back from Lilith, nor did Lilith keep secrets from her daughter. Part of that was Lilith's trust in Samara, but it went deeper than that. Her mom was also Sam's best friend. At one point Evane had held that particular title, but that had been centuries ago, so Samara tried not to think of the loss too often.

While they waited for things to calm down, Sam distracted herself by sharing most everything that had happened since she left Olarid. She didn't go into the dirty details, as that would have just been weird, regardless of the fact that her parents were essentially an incubus and succubus. It partially helped keep her mind occupied. Knowing Wade was in a cell somewhere hurt and made it impossible for her to not want to go free him now. But it wasn't time. If she went now, she'd fail and they would both be worse off than they were now.

He might even die.

Unsurprisingly, Lilith was happy for her upon hearing what had transpired over the last week. For almost two thousand years, Sam had kept herself apart and allowed herself to get close to no one but Lilith, Evane, and Keen. The betrayal of her so-called friends had wounded her ability to trust that badly. Still, Lilith wanted more for Sam. She wanted Sam to have love, though she didn't dare use that term with her daughter. If she wasn't ready for the word, mentioning it would be the quickest way to scare her off. Which meant that when it was time to rescue Wade, Lilith was happy to end the discussion for the moment.

Lilith went first, peeking out the door to ensure that no guards had been posted. There weren't. Bellar was too arrogant to believe Sam could escape from his stronghold. He also probably believed she wouldn't leave without Wade—which she wouldn't—and had more guards on the wolf.

"Give me ten minutes, then follow me," she told Sam, who nodded.

Those ten minutes were agony. Sam knew her mom could handle herself better than all but a few people in the dimension, but she still worried. There was so much that could go wrong, especially this close to Bellar. He was sly and he was smart. He also had no morals whatsoever. If it strengthened or pleased him, it was right, no matter how horrible everyone else might view it.

Finally, she slipped out of her room. She moved quietly through familiar passageways and made her way down the two levels to the cells. It wasn't easy as demons patrolled most of the stronghold. Twice she was almost caught, and only her knowledge of the various rooms and tunnels kept her from being captured again. It took a good fifteen minutes before she was able to reach the cells.

Lilith was there, keys in hand, but the guard was no where to be seen. Unfortunately, she looked grim.

"What is it? Is the guard still there?"

"No, he's in his room, waiting for me to join him. Which I won't be, of course." She hesitated, then offered the keys to Sam. "Kilara had some fun with him," she said quietly.

Her heart stuttered in her chest. Kilara was almost as much a sadist as Bellar and had the power to ensure she could cause as much pain as possible. "Is he still alive?"

"He is, but he's not in the best condition."

Sam snatched the keys and stalked down the row of cells until she found Wade at the end.

He was slumped against the wall, his eyes closed, blood covering his face and most of his now exposed chest. His shirt was ripped in several places, as was the skin beneath. A few of his fingers looked as if they'd been broken, and two of the nails had been removed entirely. Sam was sure there was more damage that she couldn't see, too.

"Wade," she breathed, unlocking the cell and rushing inside. She dropped to her knees beside him and rested her hand lightly against his cheek. It was one of the few places that looked unmarked. "Wade?"

His lids fluttered briefly before one eye opened a crack. "Sam?" The eye closed again. "Thank the gods you're okay."

Never before had his voice sounded quite so weak, not even when he'd been shot at the airfield. Unfortunately, demons weren't healers, and few of the Arcane kept as slaves on Olarid had that ability. "I'm so sorry she got a hold of you," she whispered. She glanced back, saw her mom standing at the bars, looking at Wade with an expression of sorrow on her face. "Do you think we could get a healer in here? He can't fight like this. We'd never make it to the portal."

Lilith considered for a moment before she sadly shook her head. "You know he keeps close watch on those who can heal. I could give him some energy, but it wouldn't truly help him heal."

Samara sighed and rested her head gently against Wade's as she tried to think of some way to get him out of here and back to Earth.

"If I shift, I can heal faster," he murmured, lifting one bent and twisted hand to rest on hers.

And she would kill everyone in this fortress if it meant getting him out of here safe. "Okay, but you're getting a boost first, from both of us."

"Who's us?" he asked, eyes opening again as he frowned at her.

She tilted her head toward Lilith. "My mom. She can give you energy, and I can boost your strength so we can get out of here. But I'm afraid you can't shift until we're out of here."

"I can manage," he promised as he started to push himself to his feet. It put weight on his bad hand and he winced and he fell back to the stone floor.

"Careful," she cautioned as she wrapped her arms around him and eased him to his feet.

Once upright, he leaned against the wall and studied Lilith. She looked more like Sam's sister than her mother. The largest differences he could see was that Sam had half a foot on her mom and Lilith had red eyes rather than black. What surprised him the most was how human she looked, aside from the eyes. The woman who supposedly birthed monsters should look monstrous herself, shouldn't she? Not that it really mattered. Sam loved her and she was helping them. That was what counted.

Still, he wasn't sure how much of the legends were true. "How are you going to give me energy?"

Lilith smiled. "Nothing as heinous or intimate as you're thinking, I'm sure. You do belong to my daughter, after all."

"Mom," Sam protested, making Wade smile despite the pain.

"Don't argue with the truth," Lilith chided. "It only takes a touch," she promised as she stepped closer and offered Wade her hand. Slowly he took it, and instantly he felt better. The pain didn't dissipate, but no longer did he feel as though he were going to keel over at any moment.

"Whoa...That's potent," he said as his head swam at the sudden rush. It felt a little like he'd just downed half a bottle of whiskey mixed with a full pot of coffee.

"I wish I could do more, but the only person I'm able to heal is myself," she told him apologetically before looking to her daughter. "You should go. The guards won't stay away for long, and you need to get far from here before they discover you're gone."

"I know. And thank you, Mom." She left Wade against the wall long enough to wrap Lilith in a tight hug. "Hopefully, I'll be coming back in a week to get you and get you the hell away from here."

"If anyone can, it's you. Now go, be safe."

Sam took Wade's hand, though it wasn't strictly necessary in order to augment his strength. She needed to touch him, though, at least for a minute.

"Why haven't you done that before?" Wade asked her with a little smile as he straightened.

"You didn't need it before, or I didn't have the time."

"Fair enough. And thank you, Lilith. It does seem like everyone's misjudged you."

Lilith only smiled and stepped out of the cell.

"Neither the energy nor the boost will last long," Sam warned him, "so we need to get going."

Sam didn't immediately head for the secret passage, but detoured to the armory. "I know you come with built in weapons, but not everyone I meet is susceptible to my brand of magic," she explained as she selected two knives. She was skilled with all the weapons here, but knives were her favorite choice. They felt more like extensions of her body than separate pieces of metal, and if she was going to kill, for any reason, she wasn't going to leave herself any room to pretend it wasn't her hand delivering death. And, in a pinch, any knife could be thrown, with varying degrees of accuracy depending on the weapon.

To her surprise Wade took a pair of blades as well, though ones longer and heavier than her choices. At her curious look, he shrugged. "You never know."

She smiled and nodded. "Fair enough. This way."

Though they both knew speed was a good thing, Sam moved slower than he would have liked, and not just because of his condition. He understood why the first time they came across a pair of demons wandering the lower levels of the stronghold. While they could take a handful of demons, they didn't want to risk one of them being able to sound an alarm. They couldn't take on every demon here. If they ran right into a patrol, things could go bad, and fast, especially with Wade still so injured.

Over the next ten minutes, they came across more than a dozen demons, but Sam's anxiety didn't seem to increase at the sight of any of them. Lower level demons, he supposed, though now that he'd actually spent time around a demon, he wondered if the classifications he knew were at all accurate.

"Just right up here. No one uses this part of the fortress," she whispered to him. "I'd be surprised if he even remembers this particular bolthole, which means no one else should either."

"Good. I don't think I'm going to relax until we get the spear and get back to Earth," he admitted. He loved travel, but he was going to cross dimension hopping off his bucket list.

When they turned the next corner, Wade thought for sure that it was all over. Someone had beaten them to the bolthole. Someone who looked pretty damn close to the Fury by his side. "Sam?" he murmured, fingers gripping his knives tighter.

She sighed, but made no move to attack, or even prepare for one. Instead, her hands rested easily at her sides. "Wade...meet my brother, Evane."

Evane looked even more unhappy than Wade felt. He leaned back against the wall, arms folded over his chest, his wings out and half-extended. Like his twin, he didn't grab his weapons, though Wade saw a dagger and sword hanging off the demon's belt.

"Sam...what the hell are you doing?" Evane asked, anger and weariness mingling in his voice. "You're just daring him to kill you."

She shook her head. "That's as likely as me serving him willingly. He covets my power and what it can do for him. For all his arrogance, he doesn't want to leave anything to chance, so no, he won't kill me."

Evane inclined his head slightly, acknowledging the truth.

Her wings were suddenly free, mirroring Evane's. "You can come with us, Evane," Sam said, taking a step toward him. It hurt Wade to hear the plea in her voice and he wanted to beat the man to a pulp for putting it there. "There's no reason you have to serve him any longer. He has no hold on you."

"Like I said," Evane said without heat, "don't speak of things you know nothing about, Sam." He pushed away from the wall so he could walk slowly to her, stopping close enough to touch. "But I'm not going to hurt you, and trying to keep you here would result in one of us being hurt." They both knew that they were pretty damn evenly matched in both physical and magical prowess. There was no way of telling who would come out the worse in a fight between them.

"I've missed you, Vane," Sam whispered, taking that last step and wrapping her arms around him in a fierce hug. Because of that, only Wade saw the torment in Evane's eyes when he returned his sister's embrace.

Evane pushed back after a minute. "You should go, before one of the patrols finds you."

"I know. Will you do me one favor first, though?"

He sighed. "Let me guess. You want me to ease the wolf's pain?"

"Please. You know there's no way we're finding a healer until we get back to Earth."

"Fine." It seemed like he did little more than glance at Wade, but he scented Evane's power even as his own pain faded to nothing. While he knew he still had cuts and broken bones, he felt like he could breathe easier, move easier.

"Thanks."

Evane ignored him and again told Samara, "Go."

"We will. Be safe, Evane. Promise me."

"You too. Now go. I'll do what I can to keep you from getting caught, but that's all I can do."

"That's enough. Thank you."

Though Wade vaguely felt like he was intruding, he said, "We appreciate this."

"I'm not doing it for you," Evane hissed.

Wade shrugged. "We still appreciate it."

"Go," Evane told Sam again, voice soft.

Without another word, she glanced to Wade, then hurried down the hallway to the slender crack in the wall that led to a once hidden passage.

Seconds ticked by as Wade and Evane stared at each other before Wade moved past him to follow. Just before he entered the passage, Evane spoke again, his voice quiet.

"Take care of her."

Wade glanced over his shoulder. "I will."

CHAPTER 26

Wade didn't tell Sam what he'd seen on Evane's face, or those last words from her brother. This was hard enough on her as it was, and he didn't want to make it worse.

They moved quietly through the twisting tunnel that led them out of the stronghold. There was almost no light, but he could still see Sam in front of him, and she moved expertly through the passages. Clearly she'd had to sneak out more than once, to be this familiar with the route. He just hoped they got clear of the fortress before whatever the three demons had done to him wore off.

The passageway ended in a stone wall. Wade frowned when he saw it and ran his hand over the rough surface, searching for some hidden mechanism. "Did we make a wrong turn?"

Sam laughed and shook her head. "No, it's keyed, I guess you could say, to Bellar's blood. I don't know if he never expected to have children or just expected us to be more obedient, because it works for those who carry his blood, too. Namely, his children. Luckily, none of his concubines have ever managed to bear him children. In fact, in all of his long life, Evane and I are the only children he's ever had."

"He's married to your mom and he has concubines?" Wade asked, surprised despite everything he knew of the demon. Being unfaithful was one thing, but concubines? That was a little too overt.

The look Sam shot him over her shoulder said he should have known better. "You think a demon of evil is going to be faithful? Or even discreet? Everyone knows about his concubines," she said, and he heard how she fought against her anger. "It's part of what made me start to hate him at first, once I realized not all husbands acted like he did. Even before I knew she'd been forced to marry him, so he could try to steal her powers, I didn't like how he shamed my mom, though she preferred him being in anyone's bed but her own."

He ran a hand along the top edge of one of her wings. "He won't be in anyone's bed soon enough," he murmured to her.

"You're right." She sliced the tip of her knife along her palm, then pressed her bleeding hand on the wall. There was a soft pulse of magic before the sound of stone grinding on stone quietly echoed in the tunnel. Finally, it opened, but just far enough to allow them to pass through, one at a time.

Sam slipped out and Wade followed, though he had to turn sideways to manage it. He was surprised to see it was full dark. More time had passed than he'd estimated.

Olarid was more beautiful at night than he'd expected. He stared up at the sky, awestruck by the sight of not just one full moon, but two, both shining with a pale blue glow. About a hundred feet away lay the forest, as lush as he'd remembered from the few minutes he'd gotten to see when he first arrived. Only now there were tiny blinking lights flying around in the dark. Demonic fireflies, maybe?

"Careful. If you stare at them too long, you'll be helpless to do anything but follow them into the wilderness," Sam warned.

"That doesn't sound too bad."

"Then they'll eat you," she added.

"Oh." The image of a bunch of tiny, flying piranhas came to mind and his lip curled with a soft growl. He forced his attention back to her. "You know how to get to the spear?"

She nodded. "I know most of Olarid. As soon as I realized what kind of man my father was, I learned everything I could, and I've had centuries to learn this dimension. I can get us there. The hard part is getting there unnoticed, then finding a gate before we're found."

"Then let's go. After we find the spear, we can figure something out."

She led him toward the forest, though he noticed she veered around the firefly-like creatures. Just before they hit the tree line, he heard a shout. They had been discovered.

Sam glanced toward the sound and cursed. There were four demons, and all of them were heading their way. Just what they hoped to avoid until he'd been healed. "Hurry," she told Wade before she broke into a run.

He fell into step behind her and dropped his weapons. Their only chance was if he didn't slow them down, and the only way to manage that was if he shifted. Without losing a step, he took his wolf form while they ran. He was faster in this form, and more lethal. More than that, he moved better in the woods when he was on all fours and had full access to all the senses that came with being a wolf. The one problem would be the spear, but he'd carry it in his mouth if he had to.

She moved exceptionally quickly through the dense forest, weaving around trees, darting under branches, even leaping over fallen logs. Briars and sticks scraped at her skin as she passed them, but she didn't so much as wince at the sting. The only thing that gave her pause was when she glanced back to see a gray and black wolf rather than Wade. That was fortunate, as the demons chasing them weren't injured and wouldn't hesitate to attack anyone who stood between them and their master's orders.

But Wade stayed on her heels, flowing behind her like they were tethered. When she darted right, he did the same seamlessly, so they moved as one.

One of the demons fired an arrow at them and Wade let out a yelp when it sliced along his back leg. It stung, but it wasn't deep enough to cripple him, especially with Evane's magic still working on him.

"Almost there," Sam murmured, her breathing not yet labored, despite running full out. This wasn't the first time she'd run for her life, and she doubted it would be the last.

Another arrow was loosed, and this one hit Sam's wing. Her sharp intake of breath was only audible to Wade, but he wanted to turn and kill the demon who had fired it. No one caused Sam pain. No one. But she kept running, and he wasn't leaving her alone, not when she was surrounded by enemies.

They broke out of the trees and into the same clearing they'd arrived in. Sam's knives were still there, though in the short hours they'd been gone, the grass and vines had partially covered them. The spear, on the other hand, lay in a patch of empty dirt, like even the flora was too demonic to stomach its touch. It honestly wouldn't surprise him, given how vicious everything here was.

The head of the arrow in Sam's wing was broken off, and she yanked the shaft free with barely a wince and tossed it on the ground. "Shift back, use the spear," she told him as she dropped her borrowed weapons and yanked her abandoned knives out of the grip of the plants.

A sound that was dangerously close to a scream was heard at the tearing of the plants, but Wade couldn't be sure. He wasn't too happy about shifting and giving up the advantage that tooth and claw could provide, but they hadn't yet tested the spear on a demon since he'd refused to allow Sam near it. This would be a good opportunity to do so and their best chance to make it out of this alive.

He just hated fighting naked.

Another flash of magic had him standing on two legs again, though he swayed. Two shifts in such a short time while injured took its toll on him, though some of his wounds had healed slightly. Ignoring the weakness he still felt, he grabbed the spear before he turned to face the approaching demons. "Is there anywhere near here that portals seem to like?" Though portals were random, he knew there were some places that had portals appear multiple times. Not on any set schedule, but a patient person could generally find one there. Sometimes it just took a few years.

"Maybe. But let's take care of these guys first." Sam shot him a fierce grin. "I think we can handle four lousy demons, don't you?"

Wade barked out a laugh. She was going to have to carry the bulk of this fight, and they both knew it. "Damn straight, baby. Let's do this."

The demons rushed out of the trees and slowed, but they didn't stop. Wade had hoped they were stupid enough to just dive right in, but it seemed like they had at least some intelligence. Not much, but some.

Though Sam nearly vibrated with the need to fight, she waited for the demons to reach her before she sprang into action. They didn't go down quickly like most of the ones on Earth had, but displayed skill with their weapons, blocking most of Sam's attacks. She was relentless, though, and didn't get frustrated when all she managed at first were small, shallow cuts.

Wade held the spear ready while the Fury's knives flashed in the moonlight, and he growled at the demons who approached him. A spear wasn't his favorite weapon. He could count on one hand the number of times he'd fought with one and still have a few fingers left over. But all he had to do was touch the demons to cause them pain. Theoretically.

He lunged forward, thrusting the spear toward one of the demons. His opponent jumped back, but not quite far enough since the tip of the spear sank an inch into his body. That was enough.

The demon howled with pain and fell backward, landing hard on the ground. Where his eyes had held anger and a thrill for the fight, for killing, Wade saw something else now. Fear. Still he got up, and glanced at the other demon, before they split up, trying to get on opposite sides of Wade so one could attack behind and avoid the spear. "You'll give that to us now, or the bitch will die," said the demon Wade had stabbed.

Wade snarled at the insult as he moved in response to them, making sure he didn't end up caught between them. "You clearly don't know who she is if you think any of you will be able to kill her." True, Sam had a few cuts, but she was more than holding her own.

"Maybe the four of us can't, but we've got friends coming," the other demon said with a wide, toothy smile.

Shit. So they'd sounded the alarm. Unless it was all a bluff. Please, gods, let it be a bluff.

"Fuck this." Wade threw the spear at the demon who'd called Sam a bitch, and though the demon tried to dodge, it sank deep into his chest, just barely missing the heart.

The demon screamed in utter agony as he tried to pull the spear out of his body, but every time he touched it his hands were instantly burned and started to bleed, so he couldn't get a good grip on it.

Ignoring the screaming, Wade leapt at the other demon, shifting mid-jump. He felt a knife sink into his side, but it didn't prevent his jaws from locking onto the demon's throat. The knife was pulled out only to stab into his body again, but Wade didn't let up until the demon collapsed to the ground, until his heart stopped beating and he lay still.

He released his opponent and turned toward Sam, dimly noting that the screaming was still present, but fading. He took a single step toward her before it registered that the two demons she'd been fighting were on the ground as well. Relieved, he retook his human form and swayed once again. He was pushing himself entirely too far with his injuries, but there wasn't any other option. He pushed or he died.

"We've gotta go," he told her, hating that he sounded weak again. "They have reinforcements coming." He moved to the dying demon and grabbed the shaft of the spear. Unlike these demons, he wasn't cruel, and he didn't torture his enemies. Rather than leaving the demon to die a slow death, he twisted the spear until he found the demon's heart, ending his suffering.

Before they could even take a step back toward the trees, more demons found them, and this time, they were vastly outnumbered.

Sam and Wade glanced at each other, then turned to face the demons. There would be no running this time, but they wouldn't stop fighting. They couldn't.

"Put down your weapons and surrender, or we'll kill you," one of the demons said. "Well, we'll kill the man, Samara. You? We'll just hurt you and take you back to your father." And the cruel gleam in his eyes said he'd enjoy every moment of it.

"Fuck you, and fuck him," Sam spit. If she could inflict them all with madness, they could escape, but it took precious moments of concentration they couldn't afford. With this many demons, there was no way she'd get them all before they reached her and Wade.

Wade was game though, and shifted into a battle stance, spear held at the ready, ignoring the fact that he was still in the middle of a life and death fight without any clothes on.

Before either side could attack, every single demon screamed in pain. Weapons dropped as bodies contorted, then fell, only to writhe on the ground.

Shocked, Wade straightened and stared at the demons. If this was some sort of trick, he couldn't figure out what the point of it was. Baffled, he looked at Sam, who was just starting to smile. "What's happening to them?"

Evane walked calmly out of the trees, a hand extended toward the demons. "I am," he answered Wade, voice strained. "I can't hold this many for long, though." He gave his sister an apologetic look. "Is your offer still good?"

"What offer?" Wade snapped, still not trusting Evane. This could easily be a trap.

"The offer to go with her," Evane responded without looking away from Sam.

She nodded. "Yes, of course." To Wade, "He won't hurt me, and he can help us. A lot."

Wade noticed she hadn't said Evane wouldn't hurt him, but they were out of options. "Fine," he bit off. "Let's go before whatever you're doing to them stops."

Evane nodded and started to walk toward the far end of the clearing. Wade and Sam followed. "The moment I release them, run. It'll take them a few minutes for them to be in any shape to follow us." He dropped his hand and the screaming stopped, replaced by whimpering.

The three ran into the woods, moving as fast as possible, just wanting to put distance between themselves and Bellar's demons. No one spoke for several minutes until Evane asked, "Where are we going?"

"Ultimately? Not sure. For now? I know a private place that's hard to find. We can rest there and figure out our next move," Sam answered. "Ultimately, we need to find a portal back to Earth."

"Private place? You mean..."

"Yeah. There."

Wade frowned, but said nothing. If Evane betrayed Sam, it was going to kill her. And if he did, he wasn't going to see another day, even if Wade had to tear him apart with his bare hands.

CHAPTER 27

The private place turned out to be beautiful. It was a clearing surrounded by dense foliage on one side, with a pond and tall stone wall on the other. Inside that little bubble, it looked completely different from the area surrounding it. The trunks and branches of the trees were almost black, and rather than green leaves, they were red. At first it looked like he'd stepped in the middle of autumn in New England, but these leaves looked alive and healthy.

But as Sam had promised, it was definitely secluded. They'd had to fight their way through the plant life, and a gorgeous lily-like flower had nearly taken Wade's hand. Despite that, this was instantly Wade's favorite place in Olarid, especially when the pale blue moonlight broke through the canopy overhead and shimmered on the small pool.

"This place is amazing," Wade said, shaking his head. It seemed so wrong for such a beautiful spot to exist in a realm populated by evil.

"And as you saw, it's pretty well hidden. I've used it to hide out in the past, so we should be safe here for a little while," Sam told him as she knelt by the water and began washing her wounds.

Wade set the spear down and joined her, but rather than kneeling, he stepped into the pool. Not only was he not sure he could get back up if he bent down, it also wasn't like he had any clothes to worry about getting wet. One of these days, he'd find a way to shift without shredding his clothes. Maybe Julian or Marco could help with that. "How badly are you hurt?" he asked, glancing at Sam.

She shrugged. "Not bad. The wing's the worst, and it's already healing," she answered, shifting and extending her injured wing so he could see.

"How? You didn't heal this quickly back on Earth."

"Because it was on Earth," she pointed out with a small smile. "This is my home, like it or not, so I heal more quickly here."

Evane sat down on a short stone and watched them. "And why did you come back here, Sam? You were away from him. You were safe."

Wade snorted as he carefully washed the blood from his many wounds. "Safe? Do you know how many demons found her on Earth? She wasn't safe. It was only a matter of time before they caught us unawares and dragged her back here."

"He's right, Vane. They followed me through the portal and came every day or two after that," Sam agreed. "But we came here to try to kill Bellar."

Evane looked resigned, even sad. "Sam, you know you can't kill him."

"I know I can't personally, but that doesn't mean he can't be killed."

He looked at Wade skeptically. "So you think a wolf can?"

"He can when he's armed with a weapon that's deadly to our kind."

Evane's eyes narrowed and flicked to the spear. "That?" He didn't sound convinced.

Wade smirked. "Touch it if you don't believe me. But don't try to hold it."

Sam started to protest, but she knew her brother well enough to know that anything she said would fall on deaf ears. Even if she'd seen first hand what even a small poke from the spear could do.

Evane stalked over to the spear and bent down beside it. He wasn't so arrogant as to fully ignore Wade's warning, at least, and just laid his hand atop the spear. His teeth clenched, and he hissed out a sharp breath of pain, but there was no scream.

Wade had to give him credit for showing such a small reaction. When Evane drew his hand back slower than Wade expected, he had to wonder if Evane liked feeling pain as well as causing it.

"You might be right. If just the touch of that can cause that amount of pain…" Evane shook his head. "If you actually managed to stab him with that, it might do the trick. That's *if* you can get close enough to do it."

"That spear was made to kill demons and was protected from us. We'll find a way to get Wade close enough to Bellar to kill him," Sam insisted as she watched Wade carefully climb out of the water. Without his clothes to cover the injuries, she could see just how badly he was hurt.

Cursing, she moved to help him and eased him down to the ground in front of a tree. "You can't keep going like this."

"I can," he argued. "I kind of don't have a choice." Just like he didn't have a choice about being naked around Sam's twin brother. While he generally didn't care about his nudity, it was kind of weird in this situation.

Evane must have noticed the discomfort—or was just as unhappy to see Wade naked—because he drew a pack off his back where it had been hidden between his wings. "There's some food in here, but I also have a spare change of pants. I'd intended them for me, but I'd rather not have to stare at your hairy ass," he said dryly and tossed the bag over toward Wade. "Especially given the way you keep looking at my sister."

Wade wanted to snarl at him, but he opened the pack and dug out the pants. It took him a minute to get them on without standing up, but he managed. They were a little long, but otherwise fit okay. He may still be barefoot and bare chested, but he'd take it. He found the food, which consisted of bread, cheese, and jerky, and offered some to Sam. "You should eat while you can."

Sam accepted it but told him, "I'm going to go see if I can find something that will help those wounds heal a little faster."

He frowned and shook his head. "I thought you said everything here was deadly and wanted to kill you?"

She made a waffling gesture with her hand. "It is, but aren't there things on Earth that can be poison or cure, depending on how you use them, or how much of them you use?"

"Well, yeah," he admitted.

"It's the same thing. There's are a couple of things that tend to live in this area which can help, if I can find them. It won't be as good as a healer, but it'll speed up the healing and make sure your wounds don't get infected."

"And what if one of those patrols finds you?" he asked, really not liking the idea of her going hunting by herself. Could she take care of herself? Sure. But these weren't normal circumstances.

She smiled and bent to kiss him lightly. "I'm surprisingly good at being unseen in the dark. Don't worry." She straightened and looked at her brother. "Be nice."

"I make no promises," Evane said with a shrug.

"You start anything, I'll kick your ass," she promised before she slipped through the trees and into the darkness.

For several minutes, neither of the men said anything. Wade chewed on some jerky while he studied Evane. Yes, the man had saved their asses and seemed to care about Sam, but there was something bothering Wade. "What made you change your mind? About coming with us?"

"I don't see how that's any of your business," Evane said stiffly.

"When we're on the run from a dimension full of demons with no easy exit plan? Yeah, it's my business. She trusts you. I don't. I don't know the first thing about you," Wade said evenly.

Evane sighed and looked in the direction his sister had gone. "She asked me why I stayed when Bellar had no hold over me, but he did. He still does."

"What sort of hold? Did he give you one of those fucking tattoos, too?"

He shook his head. "No, he's never marked me, but that doesn't mean he doesn't have a way to control me." He looked back at Wade and smiled thinly. "He has two, actually."

Understanding hit Wade. "Shit. He threatened to hurt or kill them if you didn't fall in line, didn't he?" Evane nodded. "That fucking bastard!" Wade snarled. "I'm going to enjoy killing him."

"Not as much as I am," Evane said coldly. "He's been trying to play us against each other almost since our birth. It's why I stayed away from her when possible. If he thought I no longer gave a damn about her or Mom, then maybe he'd stop making so many threats."

"Even if you two acted like you hated each other—and your mom—he never would have stopped," Wade told him. "I don't know much about him, but I have no doubt about that. Even if he thought it was true, he would've saved that for a last resort. Or a punishment if you had disobeyed."

"Probably," Evane agreed without emotion.

"Still, can't say I blame you," Wade mused after a minute. "I'd have done the same in your position."

"Thank you for that. I'm not sure she'll see it that way."

"She will, it just might take a century or two."

Evane chuckled. "Probably. I almost told her a hundred times. The only reason I followed you two tonight was that I talked to Mom after she left." His lips curved into a wry smile. "She talked some sense into me, convinced me to help. I swear, that woman doesn't miss a thing."

"I think to survive this long with Bellar, you have to be either perceptive as hell or lucky as hell. Probably both."

"Probably." Evane's voice went low and dangerous then. "We have to kill him before he can hurt her. If he hurts one hair on her head—either of their heads—I'm going to make what I did to those demons earlier look like a mercy."

"You just did a reverse of what you did to me, right? When you tricked my mind into believing I wasn't in pain?"

Evane made the same 'not quite' gesture his sister had only minutes ago. "Sort of? You know about Samara, right? How she's a demon of retribution? Of justice?"

"She's a Fury, yeah," Wade said with a nod.

"Well, I'm a demon of pain. It's not so much tricking the mind as I simply cause it to manifest or vanish, depending on what I'm doing. The pain is real, it just doesn't have a natural cause."

"Remind me not to piss you off."

Evane arched a brow. "Don't hurt my sister, in any fashion, and you won't." He actually smiled, though it was a shadow of what it could be. "Though I think she'd take care of you before I could lay a finger on you."

A tiny smile ticked one corner of Wade's mouth upward. "She absolutely would, but it's not an issue. I'd rather die than hurt her."

"Good."

They fell silent, both lost in their own thoughts, though Samara filled both their minds. Evane was concerned about his sister, both for the path she'd chosen to take, and the wolf she had—at least temporarily—claimed as her own. He had to wonder if she realized exactly how she looked at him. Or how Wade looked at her.

It was the return of the woman in question that disturbed the quiet. To both men's relief, she didn't appear to have any new injuries. In fact, she looked pleased.

The moment he saw her, Wade's wolf sat up and howled within him, long and loud. In that instant, he knew—really knew—she truly was his mate. He closed his eyes briefly as he struggled with the sudden realization that he'd gone and fallen in love with a winged demon, a beautiful Fury. Unfortunately, now wasn't the time for such thoughts, important as they were.

"Any trouble?" Wade asked as he shifted to a slightly more upright position.

"Not unless you count catching this little shit," she said, lifting her left hand, which held something that looked like a weird cross between a rose and a rat, of all things.

"Is that a plant or an animal?" he asked as he eyed it suspiciously.

"Yes," she and Evane answered in unison.

"This is a weird fucking dimension," Wade muttered as he watched her pluck the leaves and tail off the...thing, and crush them with two rocks.

When it had been ground into a paste, she scooped it onto a leaf then sat beside Wade. "Sorry, this is going to stink, but it'll help," she told him.

He caught a whiff of it, and it smelled a lot worse than it looked. Somewhere between skunk and rotting pile of shit, if he had to describe it. "Go on," he told her anyway, hoping it worked as well as she promised.

The paste was surprisingly warm as she spread it over the worst wounds first. Unfortunately, the moment it touched his skin, he could almost taste it.

"You think we'll be safe here for the night?" Wade asked to distract himself from the stench. "I figure we should rest while we can, especially since we don't know where a portal will be opening."

"It should be fine. We can take turns keeping watch just to make sure," she said with a nod.

"I'll take the first watch since I'm not injured. You two sleep while you can," Evane said.

Sam glanced over to her brother, considering him for a moment before she nodded. "Keep an eye out for Keen. He's supposed to let us know if the Hunters on Earth hear of a portal opening soon."

"I will."

"Thanks." She finished smearing the last of his wounds before Wade lightly tapped her wing.

"Don't forget to do your own injuries."

Her nose wrinkled, but she complied before tossing the leaf away. "I always forget how much this stinks."

"I don't see how," Wade said dryly.

Safely on the other side of the clearing, Evane chuckled. "Go to sleep and you won't be able to smell it."

Wade doubted it, but the patch of grass he was sitting in was soft and comfortable, so he stretched out on his back, an arm pillowed beneath his head. To his delight, Sam laid down beside him, using his good shoulder to support her head with an arm wrapped carefully around his waist. He slid his free arm around her and drew her close. It wasn't perfect, since they weren't naked and her brother was here, but it was pretty damn good. "Wake me up for the next watch," he told Evane, but before the demon could turn away, he mouthed, "Don't wake her. Let her sleep."

Evane nodded. "I will."

After a few minutes, Wade felt Sam relax in his arms as sleep took her. He sighed softly and hope she slept through the night. The last thing she needed right now was another nightmare. The last week had been insanely difficult on her and wouldn't ease up until Bellar was dead.

Despite having Sam against him, sleep didn't come easily to Wade. He should have been thinking about Bellar and how to get back to Earth, but he was stuck dwelling on the realization that somehow he'd fallen in love with her. His whole life, he'd assumed when he found his mate that she'd be another shifter like him. The Arcane wasn't against mixed race couples by any stretch of the imagination, he'd just always assumed he'd find someone like him, a tracker, a hunter. Not a demon. Although she was hardly a silly or weak woman. She was strong as steel, smart, stubborn, and hot as hell. So what if she wasn't a wolf? She had wings, which felt amazing wrapped around him, and she was a hell of a fighter. That was enough.

He suddenly wanted to see her flying, and joy on her face as she soared.

"How is she, really?" Evane asked, his voice quiet. He'd moved to sit with the stone against his back so he could watch for anyone who might approach.

Wade glanced at the sleeping Fury, then to the other demon. "She'll be okay when this is all over with," he answered just as softly.

"We all will, but that's not what I asked."

Wade sighed. "It's been hard on her, but she's holding up better than anyone has a right to. We just need to kill Bellar as soon as possible so she can relax."

"And you?"

"What about me?" He doubted Evane was asking how he was do-ing. They had a truce of sorts, but neither trusted the other and made no effort to hide it.

"When Bellar's dead, are you done with her? Will you go back to your normal life?"

Wade's arm tightened around Sam and he bared his teeth in a barely audible growl. "I'll never be done with her."

Evane nodded like he expected that answer. "Good."

All the aggression drained out of Wade, replaced by surprise. "Huh?"

"Good," Evane repeated. "Her whole life has been hard. For most of it she only had our mom and Keen. She needs someone strong who will stand with her, against whatever comes. And while I really don't like thinking about what you've been doing with my sister, it's obviously made her as happy as the situation would allow."

"I really don't like you thinking about what I've been doing with her either," Wade said dryly.

Evane gave a little laugh and nodded. "Fair enough."

"Something's been bugging me."

"What's that?"

"How do you guys talk like you're from Earth? Not just English, since that's only one language on Earth, but the way you talk. The slang."

Evane shrugged. "I've been to Earth before, and quite a few of the demons here have, too. Since it's the dimension Bellar wants, it was adopted, sort of, as the official language of Olarid."

"So it's not your native language?"

Evane shook his head. "No. I guess you'd probably call that Demonish, but those of us who travel between dimensions or deal with assassinations tend to learn multiple languages, anyway."

That sort of explained how Sam had known languages no one else on Earth had known. Wade wondered if those books she'd translated had even been written on Earth, or brought from some other dimension. "What's Demonish sound like?"

There was a grimace, but Evane complied and spoke in what had to be his native tongue.

It wasn't harsh or guttural like Wade had imagined, but flowed like a song. It was kind of pretty, actually. "Do I wanna know what you said?"

Evane flashed a grin. "Probably not. Now sleep, wolf, while you can. Your watch will come soon enough."

Knowing he was right, Wade nodded and closed his eyes. Somehow, minutes later, he was asleep.

CHAPTER 28

When Wade woke next, it was morning. For some reason, Evane had opted to take the watch entirely solo. Though he wasn't sure why, Wade wasn't going to complain. He'd needed the sleep.

Sam was still curled up against him, and he carefully shifted her wing so he could look at the wound the arrow had left. It looked better now, which relieved him, but he wouldn't be happy until someone healed it completely. He checked his own wounds, startled to see that they looked as though they'd been healing for several days rather than a few hours.

"You should wake her so we can get going. Eventually they will find this place, however hidden it is," Evane said from where he was crouched by the pool, washing his face with the cool water.

"I just wish we knew where we were going," Wade said with a yawn before he gently shook Sam's shoulder. "Sam? Baby, it's time to wake up. We've got a portal to find."

She made a soft, protesting noise and curled more fully against him, her face buried against his neck.

Normally he'd love her doing such a thing, but with her brother only feet away, he gently untangled himself from her and kissed her cheek. "Come on, baby. Portals to find, demons to kill."

Lacking the warmth his body had provided, Sam's eyes fluttered open as she rolled onto her back. When she stretched, her wings flared outward as well, one of them smacking Wade lightly, almost hitting him in the face. "No one woke me for watch," she said before she sat up.

"Yeah, well, he didn't wake me either, so we can be lazy together," Wade told her with a smile, getting to his feet. He offered his hands to her and helped pull her upright, shocked at how much better he felt. "We should eat some while we can, then get going. Though do either of you have any ideas on which direction we should go? Keen hasn't popped in yet, so I'm guessing he hasn't heard from either side where a portal's going to be."

Evane shook his head. "I know a few places that seem to be exceptionally suitable for portals, but I've never been able to see the future, so it could be anywhere for all I know."

"That's what I was planning on trying. Chances are better if we head to those places than if we just wander and wait," Sam said as she cupped a hand in the water so she could drink. "But we can't stay anywhere too long. I'm honestly surprised no one found us in the night, what with the mark on my neck and all."

Wade had almost forgotten that the tattoo was a tracking mark. They'd been in the same place for hours, and they weren't that far from the stronghold. Why hadn't anyone found them? Then again... "Evane?"

"Yes?" Wade only cocked a brow and looked at the demon, but after a moment, Evane grinned and shrugged. "No reason to wake either of you for a pair of scouts. They're taken care of though. And I dealt with the evidence."

Looking toward the water, Wade grimaced. But where else would two bodies be hidden?

"Don't worry, wolf, they're not in the water. It's safe to drink."

"Then what'd you do with them? Or would I rather not know?"

"Since you don't seem to be the squeamish sort...I fed them to a rather large, rather hungry plant."

Wade almost bust out laughing. "Was it named Audrey?" Both demons gave him confused looks and he shook his head. "Never mind. Earth movie. Just gave me an amusing visual. Why don't we get moving before more demons show up, though? The food we've got is easy enough to eat while walking."

"That's a good idea, actually," Sam agreed.

"How far is it to the first hot spot?" he asked.

"A couple of hours. If we don't run into trouble, anyway."

"Is that likely? Bellar's demons shouldn't catch up with us that quick, should they?"

"It's not his demons you really need to worry about out here," Evane chimed in. "Didn't Sam tell you about Olarid?"

"Oh. Yeah, she did. I'm just not used to the wildlife being more dangerous than demons," Wade said. "I promise not to just assume something that looks like a squirrel is harmless."

"Good thing, too. The squirrels, as you call them, spit an acid so strong that it can eat through stone."

Wade grimaced. "Fun. But duly noted. Avoid all cute and fluffy animals."

"I'd just avoid anything that isn't Sam, our mother, or myself," Evane said with a wry twist of his lips.

"Sounds like the smart move, yeah." He picked up the spear and grabbed a handful of jerky while he waited for the other two to get ready. A few minutes later and they ventured deeper into the wilderness of Olarid.

It only took half an hour for Sam to get restless. It had been too long since she'd flown, and her wings nearly itched with the desire to be used. The problem was, she could either fly alone, which would mean leaving Wade and her brother alone, or Evane could fly with her, in which case Wade would be by himself on the ground. Neither option sounded particularly wise, especially since Wade wasn't quite back to full strength, so she contented herself with flexing them, letting them stretch out so the breeze could slide over her feathers. It was a poor substitute, but it was better than the alternatives.

Wade watched her shifting her wings and the longing that kept crossing her face. He knew that longing well, as he had similar feelings when he was unable to shift for too long. He was distracted by a loud screech from above them and stopped, aiming the spear in the direction of the sound.

"Calm yourself, wolf. That's one of the few things here that probably can't harm you," Evane told him as he pointed to a small, brightly colored bird. "It's a carrion-feeder. Sometimes it tries to lure a victim over a cliff or into the den of a more dangerous animal so it can feast on the corpse, but it can't harm you directly. Besides, you're not alone, so you're safe."

"Okay, this place is officially fucked up," Wade muttered, but he resumed walking.

Over the next few hours, he saw more than a few types of animals—and even a few plants—that made him yearn for the familiarity of Earth. He saw the squirrel Sam had warned him about, from a distance, luckily, and managed to avoid its acid. There was a dull-feathered bird that had started to sing the prettiest birdsong he'd ever heard, and he'd started feeling more and more relaxed until Sam pinned it with one of her knives, cutting its song off. Then there was a creepy as hell lizard spider. He couldn't think of any better way to describe the thing. The skin and general shape of it had resembled a lizard, but it had definitely had eight spider-like legs and two fangs. It had fallen out of a tree and landed on Sam's shoulder. Before Wade had even been able to move, Evane had slapped the thing off Sam and onto the ground. Taking over, Wade had pierced it with the spear. But the scariest animal he saw was a massive beast with six legs and two dull gray, feathered wings. It looked like a weird cross between a winged lion and a bear, and way more dangerous than either animal would be on its own. Wade wouldn't have been happy trying to fight it, not with the six inch long claws it sported on each and every one of its six feet. But while it was aggressive, Evane was able to make it leave them be with an application of his power.

"Are all dimensions as dangerous as fuck?" Wade asked after the lion-bear had slunk off.

"Some are, but not all. There's a lot of variety in dimensions," Evane answered with a shake of his head.

"Keen told me about one that was as beautiful as Olarid, but without the dangers. A true paradise," Sam added.

"That one I'd like to see. But...other than the demons, tell me what I've seen already is the worst that's here," Wade said, prodding suspiciously at a large-leafed bush.

"No, that would be the dragons," Evane said absently.

Wade stopped and gaped at them. "Dragons? You guys have actual living, breathing dragons here?"

"Of course," Sam answered. "Not that you'd want to get close to any of them. They're extremely vicious and very territorial. Even Bellar doesn't mess with them."

"I'd heard that Earth had dragons once, too, but if we did, they died long before I was ever born. Probably before you two were born, for that matter," Wade said, awed and secretly hoping that he'd see one before they left. Nothing said he had to get close to one, after all.

They spoke little for several hours, other than to warn each other about more dangers, and there were plenty of them. Not all were easy to spot, either, hidden as they were in the lush forest. Other than a few clearings, they hadn't come across a truly open area, and Wade realized the only one he'd seen was where Bellar's fortress was. Even that had probably been created rather than a natural occurrence.

When they reached the first spot Sam thought might have a portal, there was no tingle of magic that would have been there if one was open. Nor did Wade smell any residual magic to say one had opened recently. After taking a fifteen minute break, they continued on.

Sam was still playing with her wings an hour later when Wade bumped her shoulder lightly. "Why don't you fly for a while?"

"I couldn't," she said with a shake of her head, though her eyes filled with hope.

"Sure you can," Wade said easily.

"You sure?" she asked, glancing at her brother, then back to Wade.

His lips twitched. "I think Evane and I can keep from killing each other long enough for you to really stretch your wings. And I've never seen you fly. You're not going to deny me the pleasure of seeing it, are you?" he asked, stroking a finger lightly over a long feather.

"He's right. I know how much you love flying, which is precisely why Bellar refused to let you whenever possible. Go fly, just stay in sight. And I promise not to harm a patch of fur on your wolf," Evane promised.

The joyous smile she gave both of them made the awkward conversation to come entirely worth it. She ran forward to a gap in the trees and her wings thrust downward, lifting her into the air as she laughed in delight. Once above the trees, she spun and soared and dove to skim along the leaves.

No matter how awed Wade had been at the thought of dragons, the sight of his Fury joyously flying was so much better. Nothing was more magnificent than watching her defy gravity and rejoicing in it. In fact, he realized the only time he'd seen a look like that on her face was when she'd found release in his arms.

The thought made him smile.

"That was a good idea," Evane said as they resumed walking.

"She'd been twitching her wings all damn day. I remembered her saying she didn't get to fly as much as she wanted to and…" He trailed off with a shrug.

"It was a good idea," Evane repeated. "She hasn't had nearly enough happy, certainly not as much as she deserves."

Wade nodded his agreement, but fell silent, his attention split between watching Sam and keeping an eye out for threats.

Despite the pleasure it gave her, she only flew for half an hour. Her wings needed more exercise to keep her weight aloft for longer than that, but even once back on the ground she looked happier than she had. Freer.

The first of the two moons was high in the sky when Wade stopped, every muscle in his body alert. He tilted his face toward the faint breeze and drew in slow, deep breaths.

"What is it?" Sam asked when she noticed he had stopped.

"Magic. Portal magic. I just can't pinpoint where, exactly," he explained as he turned in a slow circle, trying to figure out which direction it was coming from.

"Vane, give me your shirt."

"What?"

"Do it, quickly," she snapped.

He frowned, but tugged his shirt off and handed it to her without questioning her further.

"Wade, give me the spear and give your pants to Vane," she said as she wrapped the cloth around her hand several times before taking the spear. Even with the shirt keeping the weapon from touching her bare skin, it still burned, like she'd grabbed hold of red hot metal dipped in acid. Knowing how protective the two men were, though, she kept herself from wincing and didn't make a sound.

Unfortunately, she couldn't quite hide it from Evane. With pain as his power, he could sense it in her, and gave her a sharp look. Ultimately, he said nothing after she gave him wide, pleading eyes and a quick shake of her head.

Catching onto her plan, Wade grinned and had his pants off in seconds, only to toss them at Evane's head, though the demon caught them just before they hit him in the face. Free now, Wade transformed into a wolf, his senses instantly sharper. It only took a quick sniff before he darted off to his left, pushing through thick foliage. The twins were close on his heels.

The closer he got to the telltale 'scent' of the portal, the faster he ran. He burst out of the trees only to find a cave that was barely big enough for him in this form, but he could see the shimmering of a portal inside. A quick glance showed that Sam and Evane were still with him, and he moved right to the edge of the portal.

"It's going to be a tight squeeze for you, Vane," Sam said with a grimace before she wiggled into the cave and through the portal with the spear.

"She's right. I may not make it through, so you go first, Wade. If I can't make it across, keep her safe," Evane said, nodding toward the portal.

Wade whimpered, which was the best way he could convey his thoughts on leaving one of their group behind, even if he didn't trust Evane a hundred percent yet. But he understood the reasoning and darted through the portal after Sam.

CHAPTER 29

Sam had already moved out of the way to make room for Wade and Evane, but the moment Wade came through, she dropped the spear so she could wrap her arms around his neck, her face pressed against his fur. "Is Evane right behind you?"

Wade shifted back to human with her still holding him. "I hope so," he said grimly.

A heartbeat later, Evane crawled through the portal, frowning. "Really? You couldn't have waited before shifting back? The first thing I have to see is your hairy ass, wolf?"

"Sorry," Wade said cheerfully and with complete insincerity.

Evane stood and tossed the pants back at Wade. "Apology not accepted. Now, cover yourself."

Sam released Wade and threw her arms around Evane now. "No more worrying me!"

Evane hugged her tightly. "I'm trying not to. Now, does anyone know where we are?"

Fastening the pants and picking the spear back up, Wade looked around.

They were in a forest, but that didn't narrow things down much. It didn't even tell him if they were on Earth or not, though it certainly smelled like Earth. It was also a hell of a lot colder than it had been back home, which told him they were farther north than his cabin. "Canada, maybe? Could be Russia, though, I guess." He reached into his pocket only to growl. He'd lost his phone when he'd lost his pants, which meant no calling for transport out. "Okay, here's the plan. First, you two need to hide your wings. If we are on Earth, the only things that have wings here are birds and bats. We're going to head south, and quick. None of us are dressed for this kind of cold. As soon as I find people, I'll go in, borrow a phone, and call Marco." He focused on Evane. "He's going to be a dick to you at first."

"Let me guess, demon hunter?" Evane asked with a sneer.

"Better. Head of the Venatoribus Noctu."

"Shit, you're calling in the boss Hunter? Fantastic."

"Hey, he can get us out of here and he's invested in killing Bellar. Just don't use your mojo on him and we'll get through it."

Before he could say more, and just as Samara remembered the phone Wade had given her, Keen popped in and suddenly had three pairs of eyes focused on him.

"Keen!" Sam reached for him and cuddled him against her, happy to see the imp.

"Guess you no need my help?" Keen said mournfully. "Already on Earth."

"That's really good to know. And actually, Keen, you've got really, really good timing," Wade said with a grin. "We don't know where we are, and I don't have my phone to call Marco. Could you let him know we're back on Earth so he can send someone to teleport us the fuck out of here?"

Perking back up now that he had something helpful to do, Keen nodded eagerly. "Can do! Be back!" he said happily before he disappeared out of Sam's arms.

"That solves that problem, though you two still probably want to put your wings away," Wade told them.

Neither looked happy, but they complied. "There's less than a week left until the full moon, which is the deadline for when Bellar's going to come through," Sam said with some worry.

"I know, but don't worry. We'll figure this out. And we've got the spear. Better, we know that it does act just like expected toward demons. It should work even better on Bellar. I mean, holy spear, right? Wouldn't it be more deadly to more evil demons?"

"That does sound logical," Evane agreed.

Marco and Julian showed up a moment later, along with Keen.

"About time you guys showed up. I'm freezing my ass off," Wade told them. Wearing nothing but a pair of pants in temperatures just below zero wasn't fun.

"Happy to see you, too, Wade," Julian said dryly.

"First, I want to know who he is and why I shouldn't leave him here," Marco said as he eyed Evane.

"He's my twin. He helped us escape and he wants Bellar dead just as much as the rest of us do," Sam said quietly. "I know you don't trust us because we're demons, but you agreed to work with me. He's no different."

Marco wasn't happy, but he nodded.

In an attempt to make things easier, Julian laid his hands on the demons' shoulders. "I got them, you get Wade, and we'll meet at Wade's place?"

"Fine," Marco bit off, but he touched Wade's shoulder and tele-ported to the cabin.

Julian, the demons, and Keen popped in only an instant later, all of them appearing in the front yard.

It felt good to be out of that frigid place, but Wade wasn't quite comfortable yet. "Before we do anything else, can one of you guys give Samara and I a heal?"

"I was going to ask," Julian admitted, eyeing the partially healed cuts on Wade's torso. To try to avoid more drama, he placed his hand back on Sam's shoulder, letting Marco take care of Wade. Sam was healed quickly, though it took a little longer to take care of all the damage Wade had suffered.

"That's better. Thanks. You got the dead demons out of here, right?" Wade asked Marco as he went for the front door.

"Of course," Marco said as the rest of them fell into step behind Wade.

"Good. Then you guys can all sit and try to relax while I take a shower and put on some clothes that are actually mine," Wade called over his shoulder as he started for the bathroom. Halfway there, he paused, then veered off for the fridge. He got sandwich fixings out and laid them on the counter, then added a couple of bags of chips. "You can all chow down, too, but that's the best I've got unless someone's gonna cook."

"I think we can manage," Julian said. "Besides, Marco and I have eaten. Keen, too."

"Great, then you can teach Evane how to make a sandwich," he said cheerfully.

Lips twitching, Julian arched a brow. "Just Evane?"

"Sam needs a shower, too. Don't you, baby?"

Evane glared at him, hard enough that Wade thought it was a good thing that looks couldn't kill—and that Evane didn't decide to use his pain magic on Wade—but he ignored the demon, focusing on his Fury instead.

"I do, though it seems a shame to take a shower just to put dirty clothes back on," Sam agreed.

"Julian can teach sandwich making, but I can go to the hotel you two were at and grab your clothes. We kept the room just in case," Marco offered. Everyone knew he needed a minute after finding himself working with another demon, but no one dared to actually say it aloud and spoil the fragile peace.

"That'd be great. You can just leave them in my room." Which was the first place Wade went so he could set the spear in a corner where neither demon would accidentally touch it. After, he peeked back out into the main room, and saw that Marco had already left, and Julian, Keen, and Evane were in the kitchen. There was some tension there, but nothing major, so Wade took Sam's hand and drew her into the bathroom.

"I don't know about leaving Evane alone..." she said hesitantly.

He chuckled as he untied her top and drew it off of her. "Baby, he's a big boy, a fully grown demon, and Julian is an Englishman. He mostly does what's proper, and proper isn't killing an ally. Besides, Julian's a demonologist with the chance to actually talk to a demon who's not only *not* trying to kill him, but is also on his side. Evane will be fine while we shower. Especially since it won't be as long a shower as I would like."

"Oh?" Sam asked as she undid her pants and started wiggling out of them, which made him instantly hard.

Ever since he'd realized he loved her, he'd wanted to take her to bed. Any bed, but especially his. In lieu of that, he just needed to be inside her. "Yeah. Considering the last time we were right here was the first time I ever saw you naked? I want to do all the things I thought about doing then." Wade sighed as he stripped off his borrowed pants. "Unfortunately, with company waiting, we'll have to settle for a quickie."

Sam slowly smiled, hot enough that Wade's cock jerked. "You sure you can keep from howling, though? Don't want to scare off the company," she purred.

Gods help him. Sam had been sexy as hell to begin with, but now that she was learning to flirt and tease? She was going to be the death of him. And he loved every single torturous second of it.

He growled, slipped an arm around her waist, and pulled her up against him. "I don't think I care if I scare them off," he told her as she wrapped her legs around him and linked her fingers together behind his neck. With her pressed so intimately against him, it was hard to remember to turn the water on, or what he went into the bathroom for, but somehow he managed.

While he waited for the water to heat up, he grabbed hold of her braid, just hard enough to make her breath catch. "Besides, I may howl, but you're the one who's gonna be screaming."

She bit her lip and ground herself against him, angling her hips just right so he could feel that she was already wet. "Maybe we'll both scream," she panted softly

He quickly stepped into the shower. Under the spray, he pressed her against the wall, sank into her, and took her mouth in a scorching kiss.

Every time was better than the last. Sam felt full, complete, and couldn't stop herself from grinding against him. When it made him shiver, she felt powerful. Then he started to move and she felt blissfully weak. His hips drew back then thrust in hard, making her forget to breathe under the sharp rush of pleasure. Over and over he arched into her, until she couldn't do anything but cling helplessly to him while she kissed him like it was their first time. Or their last.

Then the kiss gentled. He was still pounding into her in a way that sent tendrils of fire through her blood, but there was something sweeter about the way his mouth moved over hers, the way his tongue stroked and teased hers. It consumed her senses and muddled her thoughts, so when her climax rushed over her, she was unprepared. She cried out, the sound caught by his kiss and muffled by the sound of the water.

Wade lifted his head, watching her face as the release rolled through her, but the sight was enough to push him over the edge. He pressed his face against her throat, growling as he buried himself to the hilt, pouring himself into her. It was tempting to sink his teeth into her throat, to mark her as his, but held off. Barely. When he marked her, he wanted her to know exactly what he was doing, and why.

Even once he was empty he didn't move, unable to make himself draw out of her. In any case, it was going to take him a minute to be able to move after he'd come so hard. Being with Sam was so much more intense than it had ever been before, and he didn't think it could ever become dull or routine.

With his body still not quite steady, he slowly let her slide down until her feet touched the shower floor. He kissed her softly before rubbing his cheek against hers. There were so many things he wanted to say, but now wasn't the time. Not in the shower, with her brother, their best friends, and Marco waiting outside. She deserved better than a quick declaration after she'd had a lifetime of suffering.

And he didn't want it spoiled by the threat of Bellar looming over all of them.

So he drew back and gave her a lazy grin. "Turn around. I'll wash your hair for you."

Sam looked up at him for a long moment before she slowly turned. As he started to undo her braid, she said, "I think I like quickies."

His lips twitched. "You only think you like them?" he asked, running fingers through her hair to separate the strands.

"Mmhmm. I'm not quite sure, though. I'll have to try it another seven or eight times to make sure. Could be more. I'm very thorough when it comes to making decisions."

He laughed and poured shampoo into his hand, then started to lather it into her hair. "I think that can be easily arranged. Any other type of sex you're on the fence about? Because I'll be more than happy to help you out with those, too."

She leaned back against him and smiled. "I'll let you know." Her head tipped back to rest against his shoulder, and her gaze lingered on his lips.

Unable to resist her, he brushed a light kiss over her mouth. "That's all you get for now. Unless you want to leave Evane alone even longer. Which, don't get me wrong, I'm on board with. I am feeling kind of tired, so if you wanted to go straight to bed..."

Knowing he was at least partially teasing, Sam only laughed and straightened. "After we talk to them and figure out what we're doing, absolutely."

"I'm holding you to that, just so you know."

"Here I was hoping you'd hold me to you. That's a lot more fun."

"Good gods. You're going to drain me dry."

"Isn't that the point?" she asked, feigning an innocent smile, one spoiled by the wickedness in her eyes.

He growled and leaned in, nipping her shoulder just hard enough to make her shiver. "Be good. For now."

"I'll try, but I make no promises."

The rest of the shower was tense with building need, especially since neither could keep their hands to themselves, but fifteen minutes later they were drying off and preparing to rejoin the others.

CHAPTER 30

When Sam and Wade finally emerged, clean and clothed, they found a very tense room. Evane was standing, his back against a wall. Marco was perched on the arm of the single couch, body stiff, staring at a knot in one of the floorboards. Julian looked resigned as he lounged in a chair, with Keen sitting on the arm of the chair.

"Well, this looks like fun," Wade said dryly, folding his arms over his chest and considering all three men.

"There's no blood yet, so give credit where credit is due," Julian said with a shrug.

"Marco...seriously? You've got to get rid of this prejudice you have against all demons," Wade said as he headed for the fridge. He grabbed out two beers, giving one to Sam before he opened the other and took a deep drink. He saw that the fixings for sandwiches had been left out and started making a couple for himself and Sam.

"I'm here and not killing either of them. Isn't that enough?" Marco grumbled.

Sam took a sip as she leaned against the counter, studying the head of the Hunters. "Marco...I know you don't like us, and for most demons, that dislike is entirely justified. But you know I'm not one of the bad guys, right?" He just grunted, but she took it for assent. "Vane is the same way. We've both suffered under our father's rule, and we're tired of seeing our mom suffering, too. We're going to kill Bellar, but we don't have to put up with this attitude. I offered you vengeance and you refused it."

"Because you're not the one who killed my family," Marco snapped.

"Exactly my point. And neither is Evane. So give us a break, okay? Just tone down the hostility and when Bellar's done, you never have to see either of us again."

His gaze slowly shifted to Sam, and it was clear he was contemplating her words.

Out of the corner of her eye, Sam saw Julian focusing on Marco as well, before Marco relaxed. It wasn't a complete change by any stretch, but some of the tension around his eyes and mouth disappeared.

"Fine. Now let's figure out what's going on with Bellar," Marco said, and he even sounded less hostile.

Julian had to have done something to his friend, but since it seemed to be just a lessening of the man's anger, Sam said nothing about it. "First...Keen? Can you go back to my mom? Check in once a day, but come back the moment you find out anything important, okay?"

"Okay!" the imp said as he stood up and almost smacked Julian in the face with his wings. "Bye!" he said cheerfully before they heard the familiar *pop* and he was gone.

"With our escape, Bellar's probably going to be more on guard," Wade said as he handed Sam a plate with two sandwiches. "Luckily, since they left the spear at the portal, he doesn't know anything about it. He should just think that we're going to fight him the way most demons are fought; with weapons and magic."

"Don't underestimate Bellar," Evane warned. "He's arrogant be-yond belief, but he is smart. If he wasn't, he wouldn't have been able to hold on to Olarid, even with his powers."

"I thought that was how he was holding Olarid," Julian said.

"No, though don't misunderstand me, it helps. But anytime some-one would gain enough power and ambition to become a threat, he had them dealt with."

"What my brother isn't saying is that Bellar would make me go kill them," Sam said quietly.

Wade stepped over to her and kissed her cheek. "In the past, baby," he murmured against her ear. "Don't dwell on it."

She gave him a faint smile before continuing. "Vane's right, though. He's good at figuring out weaknesses and striking at them. Our best bet will be to figure out which portal he's going to use, and get as many people there as we can, because I guarantee he won't be coming alone."

"Last I heard, he was planning on a dozen or so demons, but that was before Sam and the wolf escaped, so he might double that number now, if the portal will stay open long enough," Evane added.

"We can handle a couple dozen demons, so long as they're not all high level demons," Marco said. "There are enough Hunters for that."

"That depends on what you consider high level," Sam said slowly. "He has some powerful demons working for him, but none as pow-erful as him. Not unless you include Evane and I. Our mom is pretty powerful, too, but she has never willingly helped him."

Marco looked skeptical, but he nodded. "My Hunters are already on alert. The moment we figure out when and where he's coming through, we'll gather there and wait. I just hope that it's someplace secluded. I can't imagine the backlash if he shows up in the middle of

New York City or London or something. We'd have a hell of a time keeping it from the humans."

"That would be a bloody disaster," Julian muttered. "Fortunately, most portals don't open in large cities. I don't know why, but it's a good thing for us."

"Agreed," Wade said. "The seers are already trying to pinpoint the location, right?"

Marco nodded.

"Lilith is, too, so we're doing all we can for the moment," Wade said. "So for now, Julian, why don't you go home to Red so she can relax? Marco, go brief your team, including the fact that there are now two demons on our side. Evane...well, you can crash here. No reason to move you when Sam's here and it sounds like you two have some catching up to do."

Sam smiled brightly at him and gave him a quick kiss. "Thank you."

Evane glared at the kiss, but he nodded. "That's generous of you."

Wade grinned at Sam before he gave Evane an amused look. "You might rethink that after a night on the couch. I've just got the one bed, and I don't like you enough to give it up," he said, but the twitch of his lips said plainly that he was kidding. Mostly. He really wouldn't give up his bed, especially not when he could have Samara in it. Finally.

Evane shrugged. "I'll survive. It's not the worst thing I've slept on. And so long as I have food in my belly and can make use of this shower I've heard about to get clean, I'll manage."

"Good. Now that that's settled, I'm going to go have a nap with my wife," Julian said as he stood. "Evane, glad to have you on board. And everyone else? Stay safe," he said before he teleported back to his home in England.

"I know I've been a dick, but I promise not to stab either of you when you're not looking," Marco said as he stood as well. "I'll keep you informed," he promised before disappearing as well.

"I'm going to be so fucking happy when Bellar's dead and I don't have to keep shoving you two in the same room as Marco," Wade said, shaking his head. "Though he's acted a hell of a lot better than I expected."

"Let's not talk about that anymore," Sam said. "You eat your sandwiches. I'm going to show Vane how to use the shower."

"One sec. Let me grab some clothes for him to put on," Wade said, heading into the bedroom. He emerged with a pair of sweats and a tee-shirt, which he handed to Evane.

"Thanks."

"No problem," Wade said, grabbing his plate and moving to the couch. It didn't take long for him to start devouring the sandwiches.

Sam grinned as she showed Evane how to use the shower and left him to enjoy one of Earth's little luxuries. When she returned to the main room, she settled herself beside Wade. "Thank you for letting him stay," she told him again.

"It's not a big deal. It's just a couch. And I'm not going to be the ass who makes you choose between staying with me or staying with your brother. I'm a wolf, not a dog."

Sam touched his cheek and gently turned his head to face her. "It is a big deal. I know you don't entirely trust him, so it means a lot that you'd put that aside for me."

"Yeah, well, I plan on making you moan and scream all night, so maybe it's just my way of torturing him," Wade joked.

She grinned and shook her head. "That's just a bonus," she said astutely.

"True," he admitted. "But I'm finding there's not a lot I wouldn't do for you," he told her seriously.

Her heart skipped a beat. "There's not a lot I wouldn't do for you, either," she said quietly, stroking her fingers over his cheek.

He set his plate aside, then hauled her onto his lap, his arms wrapped around her waist. "Careful now, or we'll start leaving the sexy conversation for the sappy one," he murmured as he nuzzled her neck.

She tilted her head to give him better access and gave a contented hum. "I know I'm stepping into dangerous waters saying this, but...you started it," she murmured, only to give a surprised squeak when he nipped her throat. When he did it a second time, she moaned quietly.

"There, that's better," he whispered. "But that's all you get until we go to bed. I'm not gonna risk having your brother catch us in the act."

Sam started to scoot off his lap, but he held onto her until he could give her a short, hard kiss. "I don't particularly want my brother to catch us, either. That would just be..." She trailed off and wrinkled her nose.

Wade chuckled. "Then think about something else."

She sobered. "I'm worried about my mom. He has to know that she helped us escape. I know she's powerful and he can't kill her, but that doesn't mean he can't hurt her."

He looped an arm around her shoulders and gave her a warm squeeze. "Hey, stop that. If she's anything like you, she's smart, strong, and stubborn. I'm not saying he won't be able to lay a hand on her, but if it's a case of like mother like daughter? Then I'm putting my money on Lilith. And she's not alone. If things get bad, you know Keen would let you know," he pointed out.

"Yeah, that's true." But she still sounded worried.

"I've got an idea…When Evane gets out of the shower, why don't you guys go fly for a bit? We're far enough away from any neighbors that no one's going to see you, and you said you needed to work your wing muscles." And he'd seen the joy she felt while flying. Doing so with her brother might help her release some of the tension she was carrying. At the very least, it would give her a much needed distraction.

Just as he hoped, she brightened. "Really?"

"Yeah. I'll be here when you guys get back."

She cupped his face and kissed him hard. "You are the most amazing wolf I've ever known." She scrambled off the couch and hurried to the bathroom door, pounding on it. "Vane! Hurry your ass up! We're going to go flying!"

The door cracked open enough to reveal Evane's face. "Flying? On Earth?" he asked skeptically.

"Wade said there aren't any people nearby, so no one's going to see us. Besides, our wings are black. So put those pants on and let's go," she said urgently as she loosed her wings.

"Two minutes," he said and closed the door in her face. He only used half of that before he emerged wearing the sweat pants. His hair and chest were still damp and he was barefoot, but his wings were out.

Sam wasn't the only one who had missed flying, it seemed, and Wade was happy he'd suggested this outing.

"If you two head north," and he pointed out the direction, "you'll be less likely to run into anyone if you have a long flight, though the closest neighbor in any direction is a good ten miles."

"Thank you," Evane said as he followed Samara out of the cabin.

Wade got up and walked to the window. He got there in time to see the siblings leave the ground and head north along the tops of the trees.

Smiling, he grabbed his beer and sat back on the couch. It wasn't how he planned on spending his evening, but it was worth it.

CHAPTER 31

When they returned, Wade was stretched out on the couch, dozing. He woke instantly and studied both their faces. The flight had clearly done them both good, and they were smiling when they went to bed, even though Evane's frame was too long for the couch.

To Wade's delight, Sam not only stripped before getting into bed with him, but settled herself over his body and slid onto him, riding him until pleasure washed over them both. It wasn't fast and almost feral this time, but lazy and comfortable. After, exhausted from both the flight and lovemaking, she simply collapsed against him and fell asleep.

He smiled and wrapped his arms loosely around her waist as he closed his eyes. He was going to have to make sure she went flying more often. Every day, if he could manage it. Maybe twice a day.

Only moments after that thought, he fell asleep with her still sprawled over him.

When he woke, she'd partially slid off him, so one leg and an arm were draped over him, along with a wing. Since she'd fallen asleep with pleasure still coursing through her, he decided to wake her the same way.

Gently, he rolled her off him and onto her back, but she barely stirred. Even when he settled himself between her legs, her wings only twitched. Smiling, he kissed across the tops of her breasts then slowly made his way down her body. He wasn't in any rush and wanted her fully awake before he was inside her. By the time he made it between her thighs, she was beginning to stir, and when his mouth found her, she moaned and her eyes fluttered open. No words were spoken as he brought her to that first sweet peak, one that had her gasping and arching. Only then did he stretch out over her and slide smoothly into her.

She groaned and arched against him, pressing him deeper. Her eyes looked into his, already amber with passion, and she sighed, stroking her fingers over his cheek. "Wade," she breathed as he withdrew, then sank into her once more.

His lips claimed hers in a tender kiss that made her chest tighten with emotion, and she wrapped her arms around him, hands stroking down the hard muscles of his back. They moved together in the soft orange glow of dawn like nothing else existed in any dimension but for the two of them.

For Wade, nothing else did exist. There was only her. The feel of her body beneath his, the press of her hands against his skin. The warm, dazed look in her eyes as she watched him.

When she reached her climax, it wasn't the explosion it had been in the past, but more like sliding into pure bliss. Her arms tightened around him, anchoring her to her body as pleasure washed over her again and again before leaving her sighing beneath him.

She murmured his name as he lifted his head.

Still moving, slow and sweet, he lifted a hand to cup her face, thumb stroking her cheek. "I love you, Samara," he said quietly.

Her eyes widened with surprise before they darkened with emotion. Her reaction to hearing those four words went beyond the mental, or even the emotional. Combined with the steady rocking of him into her, it shot her to another climax. This time she drew him along for the ride and he groaned. Unable to resist any longer, his teeth found the curve where her shoulder met her throat, biting just hard enough to mark her. Any pain she might have felt was lost in the pleasure, and she only arched beneath him and moaned. He managed only two more thrusts before he stilled and simply held her while they trembled together.

Wade rolled onto his side and drew her with him, unwilling to give up the closeness just yet.

"Do you really love me?" Sam asked a moment later when she had enough breath to speak.

He brushed his lips over hers. "I do." The look on her face floored him. He saw awe, tenderness, shock, and even a little fear.

"And that's why..." Her voice trailed up and her fingers brushed lightly over the bite mark.

"It is. I couldn't not mark you as mine," he admitted, watching her eyes closely to see if she would mind the visual proof of how he felt.

Her hand lowered. "No one's ever loved me before," she whispered. "Just my mom, Evane, and Keen, but that's different. That's family."

"That's because they were all jackasses who couldn't see what was right in front of them," he said, rubbing a hand soothing up and down her back.

One corner of her mouth threatened to tip up into a smile, but didn't. Instead, she solemnly watched him for several minutes while he did nothing but hold her and try to soothe her tangled emotions. When she did speak, it was so quiet he barely heard it. "I love you, too."

Wade felt like his heart was about to explode from his chest. He couldn't resist kissing her again, putting everything he felt into it; the happiness, the protectiveness for his mate, and the pride that someone as strong and amazing as Sam loved him back.

He hadn't been looking for his mate and couldn't have said he'd been unhappy before he met her, but this? He understood, completely, why Julian got so pissed when he was pulled from Paige's side.

A knock at the door interrupted them and Wade growled angrily, "What?"

"Are you two going to laze around in bed all day?" Evane asked.

Sam laughed softly against Wade's shoulder, which soothed the worst of Wade's annoyance.

"We'll be out in a few," he called back. After giving Sam one more—brief—kiss, he reluctantly drew away from her and pulled on a pair of pants and a tee-shirt.

She grabbed a pair of yoga pants and, after a bit of hesitation, put her wings away so she could toss one of Wade's shirts on as well. It hid his mark, but since she was wearing his shirt, he couldn't mind too much.

"You know, I've seen a lot of women wearing a lot of sexy clothes, but I think the sight of you in yoga pants and *my* shirt beats them all," Wade told her with a familiar rasp in his voice that told her he was aroused.

Part of her wanted to be jealous of the other women he'd known, but she couldn't find it in her to give in to such an emotion. Not after he'd woken her in such a wonderful way, and especially not after he'd told her he loved her. She grinned. "I'll keep that in mind," she told him as she left the bedroom. "Do you have any of those pancakes? They were really good, and I'm starving."

Evane leaned against the wall just outside. "Flying always makes me hungry. I was just too tired last night to even think about finding food."

"Not a problem. I can whip up some pancakes. They're from a box, but they're pretty good," Wade offered as he headed for the kitchen. "Anything you two want to do today since we're pretty much on standby until someone figures out where we need to go?"

"I'd like to show Evane a movie," Sam said. "Do you have any of them here? I don't see the bag you had that computer thing in."

"It's probably still back in the motel room, but we can do movies here, no problem." Though he made a note to ask Marco or Julian about his computer. The clothes were easily replaced, but the computer would be a hassle if a human found it. He also needed to replace his phone, since his was in Olarid.

"What's a movie?" Evane asked, and Wade grinned as Sam not only explained what movies were, but relayed almost the entire plots to the movies she'd seen already. He'd have to make a note to talk to her about spoilers later.

When they sat down at the small table with pancakes, eggs, and bacon, Wade realized that it wasn't just Sam who was entertaining to watch when trying new Earth food. It was all demons. Hopefully, the introduction to movies would be just as amusing.

Except they never got to the movie.

Wade had just turned the TV on when Keen popped into the room looking frantic. He immediately dove at Sam and clung to her shoulder and hair.

"Keen? What's wrong?" Sam asked, rubbing his back.

"Twelve hours. He has his best demons getting ready," Keen said, his voice trembling, and Wade had to wonder exactly what had happened to terrify the imp so badly. Though part of him was just as scared. Twelve hours? They were supposed to have more time. Twelve hours gave them some time to plan and get into position, but they might be cutting it close. And that was if the seers had figured out where the portal would be opening.

Another burst of magic had Marco teleporting in, and where Keen looked scared, Marco looked grim. "We know the where, but not the when," he said before anyone had a chance to speak.

"We know the when," Evane told him.

"What? How?"

Evane inclined his head toward Keen. "He just showed up. Bellar's getting his demons ready to come through a portal in twelve hours."

"Fuck!" Marco snarled. "Okay, do whatever shit you need to do and be ready to go in an hour, just in case he comes early. I'm sending the bulk of my team there now. Wade, can you call Julian, so he can get ready?"

"Sure. Give us thirty and we'll be ready to go," Wade said with a nod. "But Marco, where's he going to be?"

"Utah, and no, it's not near a city, so we lucked out there."

"Good. Go, we'll be ready."

Marco nodded once, glanced to the two demons, then disappeared.

Wade ran his hand through his hair. "Shit. Okay, we'll do the movie to celebrate after this bastard's dead. What do you two need before we leave?"

"I've got my weapons, but a change of clothes would be appreciated," Evane answered.

Samara shook her head. "I just need to change." But Keen was still holding tight to her. "Is it okay if Keen stays here when we head to this Utah?"

"That's fine. Keen, I'll make sure there's some food out for you and get a movie set up for you," Wade said as he headed for the bedroom first. His pants were all going to be a few inches short on Evane, but it was better than nothing. He was clueless on what shirt would work if Evane wanted to have his wings out, so he just grabbed a tee-shirt and gave it to the demon, who disappeared into the bathroom to change.

By the time the twins had gotten ready, Wade had done as promised for Keen, then went to change himself and arm up. Though he was going to be primarily fighting with the spear, he grabbed some knives just in case he got disarmed and dressed in clothes that could be shredded if he needed to shift. He'd been in way too many fights to assume this one would go according to plan. They *never* went according to plan.

Ready to go, he glanced at Sam, who was busy trying to reassure Keen, then motioned Evane over.

"What is it, wolf?" he asked, all trace of the more relaxed demon gone, replaced by the man ready for battle.

"My job in this fight has to be trying to get to Bellar and kill him, I know that. But I'm going to worry about Sam," Wade said quietly.

"She's a formidable warrior, but yes, I understand," Evane said, watching his sister.

"Will you keep an eye on her? My guess is Bellar's going to be pissed she escaped and will try to punish her for that."

"Your guess is probably right. I'll definitely do my best to keep her safe," Evane said as he turned back to Wade.

Again Wade found himself startled. He knew that his eyes shifted to a wolfy gold with strong emotion, but he thought that was a trait reserved for shifters. Yet Evane's eyes had changed. The black of his irises had spread outward. It didn't envelop the whole eye, but darted outward in jagged paths that looked like lightning bolts. And, judging by the quiet anger in Evane's voice, Wade assumed it was a similar cause to his own, even though Sam had never displayed such a trait. It was a little eerie, but he couldn't say anything. His eyes changed, too, and their goals at the moment were the same.

"We'll kill Bellar and she'll be safe," Wade told him before Marco returned with another witch.

"You ready?" Marco asked as he glanced around.

"I am," Sam said, giving Keen one last smile before she moved to stand by the witches.

"As am I," Evane said with a nod.

Wade grabbed the spear from where he'd leaned it against the wall, then joined the loose circle. "Let's go."

The witches laid hands on shoulders and took them all to Utah.

CHAPTER 32

They appeared in a relatively flat stretch of land filled with dry dirt and short, scrubby bushes. There were also more than two dozen Hunters already there, along with Julian. They weren't all armed, but Wade knew that most of them would be fighting with magic rather than physical weapons. There were full packs scattered about, which made sense given that the portal wasn't slated to open for almost eleven hours. They'd still need to eat and drink to keep their strength up while they waited, but no one wanted to risk Bellar coming through early without a team in place.

There was a moment of tension when they first appeared, though the Hunters relaxed when they saw familiar faces instead of Bellar.

"Hunters," Marco called, voice carrying to reach everyone. "We should have some time, but I want to make sure we're all clear and have all the information we need now, just in case. Again, Bellar, a demon of evil, will be coming through that portal with plans to conquer Earth. He won't be alone. Wade has a spear which is supposed to be able to kill him. If you can get Wade to Bellar, then do whatever you can to make it happen. If he falls, grab the spear and do your best to use it. We cannot let Bellar escape us!" he said fiercely.

He glanced back to where Sam, Evane, and Wade still stood, clustered together. "Can you tell us anything else that will help?"

Sam and Evane exchanged a look before Evane nodded and stepped up beside Marco. "Bellar will greatly resemble me," he began, which had some of the Hunters eyeing him suspiciously, but he didn't pause. "But most of his demons will probably look more demonic. And while he can fight, he'll probably just try to corrupt anyone he can, turning them toward evil, and if he succeeds, he'll be able to control you. Completely. But his demons will all be extremely lethal and with a variety of powers. We don't know who exactly he's bringing, unfortunately, so we can't give you anymore information than that."

"And don't go attacking these two demons," Marco said, though Wade heard the tightness in those words. Marco trusted them, to an extent, but he still didn't like working with demons. "They've given us a lot of information, and they're on our side. If any of you attack either of them, you'll answer to me. Now, rest while you can, but stay alert. At the first sign of the portal, I want people in a circle around it and ready to fight, with these three in the front."

Some of the Hunters remained standing while others sat down, or even laid down, using their packs as pillows.

Julian joined Wade's group, but he was paying more attention to the spear than the three people standing near it. "Can I take a look at it? I know you said it needed to be returned to the mound after Bellar was dead, but I'd like to see it first."

Considering Wade had helped Julian reassemble a relic, he knew how interested Julian was in magical objects, and that he wouldn't do anything to harm it. "Sure, but you're not using it against Bellar," he said, only half-joking as he offered the spear to the witch.

"Yes, yes. I wouldn't even if you hadn't said that. One, you're much better with weapons than I am, and two, Paige made me promise the same thing," Julian said with a faint smile. He ran his fingers over the spear, examining every inch of it before holding it loosely in both hands and focusing his magical senses on it. After a minute, he sighed. "I kind of wish she was here, actually. I get very little from it. I know it's magical, and powerful, but it also feels cloaked."

"Why would you want your wife to see it?" Sam asked curiously.

"She's a powerful psychometrist. She can hold things and see all sorts of images and emotions about them, or just know something about them," Julian explained.

"I'd be curious to know what she'd get from it, too," Wade agreed. "Though I bet she wouldn't see its power as cloaked. I mean, the thing was hidden in a magically sealed burial mound, guarded by a ghost, and hovering in a shaft of light. That doesn't point toward a weak artifact."

"Oh, I agree," Julian said with a shrug as he handed the spear back to Wade.

"As long as it kills Bellar, I don't give a damn what it is," Evane said blandly.

"Right there with you," Wade said as he lowered himself to the ground and sat cross-legged, the spear across his lap.

"Now we just have to wait for him to get here," Sam said with a sigh.

The wait had everyone tense, and it only got worse with each passing hour. To Sam's surprise, however, the Hunters actually started to relax around her and Evane. A few of them even wandered over to talk to them. Some asked about Bellar, his demons, or Olarid, while some were curious about their wings. One even asked to see them fly, and the twins were happy enough to comply. It helped burn off some of the stress and warmed their muscles. And they couldn't see the suspicious looks others gave them when they were in the sky.

One of the Hunters who Sam had met before, Dan, seemed very interested in them, though after he'd explained that he was an electricity elemental, it made more sense. He could fly, after a fashion, but only if he transformed his body into lightning.

Other Hunters grouped up, chatting, and Sam saw one pair drag out a deck of cards and killed the time that way.

But the closer it got to the twelve hour mark, the less conversation happened, and the more the Hunters stayed close.

When it came down to only minutes, everyone stood and gathered what weapons they'd brought and waited.

"Portal," Wade growled as he caught the first whiff of power. He gripped the spear tightly and knew without being told that his eyes were solid gold. His wolf loved a good fight, and this was bound to be a massive battle. He was also fighting to protect his mate, which the wolf part of him saw as a higher priority than literally everything else. Including himself.

The first demon came through the portal a moment later, and Wade was surprised to see that it wasn't Bellar, but the same albino demon who'd captured him and Sam in Olarid, the one she'd called Ronin. Despite the Hunters who ringed the portal, Ronin looked smug, and when more demons started pouring out of the portal, Wade understood why. Bellar really had brought an army.

The last two who came through were Bellar, looking supremely arrogant...and Lilith. That surprised Wade until he saw the chains. Shackles rested on her wrists and ankles, with too bright links of metal connecting them and wrapped around her body, connected to a single length which Bellar held like a leash. The look on her face was absolutely miserable, and she gave her son and daughter an apologetic look.

Bellar's gaze immediately found Sam and Evane and his eyes flashed with rage. "Betrayed by my own children. I wish I could say I was surprised, but that's why I brought a little insurance," he said and jerked the leash, which made Lilith stumble and fall to her knees on the hard, packed earth. With her wrists bound as they were, she was unable to catch herself and her face ended up in the dirt.

Sam took a step forward, and in that moment Wade thought she'd never looked more like a Fury—beautiful, wrathful, dangerous. "You'll pay for that. You'll pay for every evil you've ever committed, for making our lives a living hell. But you'll mostly pay for what you've done to my mother."

At a silent signal from Marco, the Hunters surged forward, physically and magically. The air was suddenly filled with fire, lightning, and ripples as magic shot between the two armies. The ring of metal clashing against metal formed a harsh symphony that was almost deafening, and the dry, drab dirt was painted red from the blood that was rapidly being spilled.

That was when things started going wrong.

Marco had assured Wade that he'd chosen only people who had no evil within them for Bellar to tap, but apparently there were a few Hunters he didn't know as well as he thought he did. The witch he'd introduced as Caitlyn froze and the demon she'd been fighting smirked and moved onto someone else, assured that Caitlyn wasn't a threat any longer. It surprised Wade, since she was supposed to be a healer. In his experience, healers tended to be kind, compassionate people, but he supposed there were always exceptions.

"Immobilize Caitlyn!" Wade yelled as he made his way through the horde toward Bellar.

Even as he gave the warning, Caitlyn turned back on the Hunters and made a lifting motion, which had two of the group rising in the air, higher and higher.

William had been focused on grabbing demons before they could strike killing blows, but at Wade's shout, he abandoned the demons and gave his full attention to the controlled witch. He stopped her in place, and it seemed to affect her magic as well because the Hunters fell back to the ground. Fortunately, they'd only risen ten feet, so they were able to get back up and continue fighting.

Sam and Evane stuck close together, and it was obvious that they'd fought together on a number of occasions, even if it had been a while. They moved as a unit and used a mix of their powers and the weapons they held. None of the demons could stand when the twins focused on them, and Wade noticed that most of the demons were reluctant to approach the pair. Since screams of pain filled the air as demons were struck by pain or with one of the blades, he could understand why.

They mostly cleared the way for Wade, though there were enough demons on the other side that he had to fight his way through. The spear was an astonishing weapon, though, cutting through the demons like they were powerless.

And Bellar noticed. As demons fell around him, he stared at the spear. There was a flash of fear in his eyes before it was replaced by the usual arrogance. It didn't stop him from yanking Lilith in front of him and using her as a shield.

The demons all broke off from the Hunters they were fighting and swarmed to Bellar, forming a living barricade. Behind the mass of bodies, Wade saw Bellar's wings stretch out and he hurried toward the demon.

"He's trying to escape!" Wade yelled as he thrust the spear deep into the belly of one of the demons.

Every Hunter heard him and they fought harder against the ring of demons, trying to get to Bellar. Except there were too many enemies standing in the way for them to make much progress.

Bellar wrapped his arm around the immobile Lilith and his powerful wings swept downward, carrying him up, away from the fight below. He'd gotten a knife from somewhere and lifted it to Lilith's throat. As he hovered in the air, he looked down at his children, who were preparing to take to the air to chase him. He shook his head. "If you follow me, if you put one feather-width between you and the ground, I'll kill her," he called down, and just to prove his point he made a shallow cut on Lilith's neck, just deep enough to draw blood.

Sam looked devastated, and even Evane's stoic features broke into a mask of pain. They wanted to follow, they wanted to end this now, but neither could take a chance with their mother.

Dan shot Sam a pointed look, but she shook her head. She couldn't risk Bellar's hand twitching when he got hit by electricity. It wouldn't take much to slice Lilith's throat. She was tough, but sometimes, something as simple as a cut throat could kill a demon.

The agony of having to watch her evil father fly away with her mother only made Sam more dangerous. She took half a step back, but she wasn't retreating. There were fewer demons alive now, and she was surrounded by allies. Better, she had a moment where she could concentrate without opening herself for a killing blow. She lashed out with her power and touched the demons who remained on the ground. Each and every one of them had committed indefensible acts, each was deserving of the retribution she sought. She could feel the sins they'd committed, each one heinous. Minds cracked and broke under the weight of her power, leaving once powerful demons helpless against the hunters. But where she focused on the demons on the ground, one of the Hunters was still focused on Bellar. She didn't care about Lilith, only about stopping Bellar here and now.

Samara saw the ball of crackling energy begin to form in the woman's hands, saw her gaze firmly fixed on Bellar, and knew what she intended. While it might weaken Bellar, it could also kill her mother.

"No!" she snarled and, lacking any faster means of preventing the attack, shoved herself between the Hunter and her parents, just as the energy was loosed. It hit her just to the left of the center of her torso, with enough force and power to throw her back twenty feet. Though it hurt, intensely, it also knocked all the air from her body so she couldn't so much as gasp, much less scream.

Though she couldn't make a sound, Wade still knew the instant she was hurt. He pushed through the remaining demons and Hunters, not caring who he shoved out of the way. Enough of his mind was clear that he managed not to use the spear on anyone but the demons, but he wasn't gentle with the Hunters, either.

Above them, Bellar laughed as he rose higher, the sound trailing off as he put more distance between him and his children.

Wade dropped to his knees beside Sam and gathered her into his arms, snarling at the Hunter who looked pissed off rather than remorseful. To his horror, Samara didn't move when he picked her up. She didn't even open her eyes.

"Sam? C'mon baby, open those pretty eyes for me. Unless you want me to slaughter a Hunter, you better open your eyes," he warned her. Despite his words, he was gentle with her, carefully shifting what remained of her shirt to check the skin beneath. Seeing the blackened, raw hole in her chest, it took everything he had not to shift and destroy the Hunter who had caused it.

The fight continued around him, but he couldn't focus on it. Evane had noticed his sister's injury, though, and quickly moved to protect Wade and Samara.

In only minutes, the rest of the demons lay dead upon the ground, along with the Hunters who had fallen.

"I need a healer!" Wade yelled as he looked at the nearby Hunters. No one moved. As though she were fragile, he eased her off his lap and to the ground so he could stand. "Someone is either going to heal her, or I'm going to go biblical. In case that isn't clear, I mean an eye for an eye," he growled, looking pointedly at the Hunter who'd hurt Sam.

"You'd kill one of us because of a demon?" a man Wade didn't know asked, sounding disgusted and angry at the mere thought.

"Hell yes, I would," Wade replied without hesitation. "She's done nothing but try to help you fuckers, and now that she got hurt, none of you will lift a finger to heal her? If you won't help her, then why should I give a damn about any of you?"

"She protected him!" the Hunter who'd thrown the energy ball snapped.

"No," Wade growled as he took a step toward her, which made her retreat a step. "She protected her *mother*, another person who's been helping. So one of you get over your fucking prejudice and heal her!" The last two words were roared. Never had he been this angry. His eyes were a brilliant yellow and his hands had partially shifted, so his fingers were tipped by dangerous claws.

"Calm down," Julian said evenly as he cautiously approached the half-feral wolf. He'd never actually been afraid of his best friend before, but he knew what Wade was going through. "I'll heal her."

Wade could only nod sharply and watch as Julian knelt beside Sam. He hovered as the witch laid his hand on Sam's cheek. Though he scented the magic, the wound didn't seem to improve much. A growl trickled out before he could stop it.

Though Julian hadn't seemed worried when he spoke, he did now. He recognized the signs of a shifter who had chosen his mate, and knew that if he wasn't able to heal the demon, if—gods forbid—she died, then Wade would go crazy trying to avenge her.

"Marco," he said before trying again.

Reluctantly, Marco crossed to him and bent to add his healing to Julian's. He had other, more powerful healers, but he wasn't sure if Wade would let them close at this point. No, he didn't have any affection for the demon, but he could hardly tell his Hunters to deal with these two and not do the same himself. He was many things, but he sincerely tried to never be a hypocrite.

With both witches working on Sam, the wound began to close, though they knew they weren't sufficient to heal it completely. Still, she would live.

Her eyes slowly opened and she frowned at seeing the witches above her. "What…"

Wade shoved Marco unceremoniously away so he could take the Hunter's place. "Sam." He drew her into his lap again, holding her close. It took several minutes before he began to calm and he pulled her back just far enough for him to look at her. "Don't you ever fucking do that again!" he growled before yanking her close again.

Sam gave the barest of laughs as she closed her eyes and laid her head on his shoulder. "Can't promise that. I'd do the same to save Evane…or you."

"He can take care of himself," Wade protested.

Hearing that, Evane shrugged. "I can, but it's never a bad thing to have someone willing to protect you. Though I'm wondering why she's being lazy and just sitting there when we still need to deal with Bellar."

That reminded both Wade and Sam that Bellar had not only escaped, he'd taken Lilith, too. "We'll get her back," Wade promised Sam, seeing the look on her face.

"Yes, we will," Evane agreed as he looked toward the last place he'd seen Bellar, but the demon was no longer anything but a speck in the sky. "We'll get her back," he whispered.

CHAPTER 33

W ade eased Sam down to the ground. She wasn't moving, just trembling with shock, enough that he worried about her. He knew she was still injured, but the loss of her mother was more devastating than any physical injury would have been. He was reluctant to let her go, but she gave him a tiny smile and stepped a few feet away. He got it. She needed a minute, so he'd give it to her.

Around them, Hunters dealt with healing the injured and separating the fallen from the dead demons. Julian approached and laid a hand on his shoulder. Only when the pain in his side and arm had stopped did Wade realize he'd been hurt as well.

"How's Caitlyn?" Wade asked and glanced around for her. She was sitting down now, looking mortified, her head hung low. It was obvious she was trying very hard not to make eye contact with anyone.

"I don't think she's going to be a Hunter for much longer," Julian said quietly. "It's fairly common for some Hunters to take too much pleasure in killing dangerous demons, but that's not usually enough to darken their heart."

"I thought healers tended to be the type who wouldn't get corrupted like that."

"Usually, but some use those gifts to hurt as well." Julian looked to the four Hunters who lay side by side, well away from the demons. "But it could have been worse. You spotted her before she could seriously injure anyone. And with as many demons as we were facing, we could have lost a lot more people."

"True," Wade said, though he looked back at the woman he wanted back in his arms.

Marco stalked over looking absolutely pissed and Wade couldn't blame him. A dangerous demon was loose on Earth and four Hunters had died in the fight. "We have to find him, and soon. If he could do that to a Hunter who was trained to fight demons, then there's no way the people of this planet are going to be able to resist him."

"He doesn't know Earth, so that will help," Evane said. "This is his first time here. He's talked to demons who had been to Earth in the past, so he knows a lot about it, but it's different from being here, believe me. I'm honestly not sure why he decided to conquer a dimension he'd never visited."

"Where would he go?"

Evane glanced at Sam, but she was still trying to recover from the extreme use of her power as well as her injury. "A large city, especially one where there are wicked people," he told them.

Julian grimaced. "That doesn't narrow things down much. I can think of several just here in the United States that could fit that bill. New York, LA, Chicago, Vegas, Atlanta…They're all big and they're all full of criminals."

"What sort of criminals? He'd prefer those who commit murder or indulge in lust."

"He's not just a master of evil, he's also what you might term an incubus," Sam said quietly, and Wade drew her closer.

"Vegas," Marco decided. "It's actually nicknamed Sin City. There are lots of places to see women stripping, and if you go outside the city, you can find legal brothels. If he wants lust, and wants to stay close, then that makes the most sense."

"Yes, close is better. Traveling farther distances would be hard given that he's using his wings and carrying...carry my mom," Evane said with a nod. "How far away is this Sin City?"

"I don't know, three, four hundred miles. But enough of us have been there at some point that we can teleport there."

"It'll take him a while to get there, then, even flying."

Marco looked to his fallen Hunters. "Then we've got a little time. Enough to pay respect to those we lost...and torch the demons." He hesitated then turned back to the twins. "I wanted to apologize, and to thank you."

"Apologize?" Evane asked.

"I treated the two of you like shit just because you were demons, and you stood beside us and fought against your own father. The two of you took down more of Bellar's demons than the rest of us combined. And I didn't believe you about your mother, just based on who she is, but I clearly saw that she wasn't a willing participant in this. The myths about her might be...skewed."

Knowing just how prejudiced Marco was against demons, Sam understood just how much it cost him to say those words. "Thank you, Marco. For that and helping to heal me. And we will help you find him."

"I know." He offered his hand out to Sam, who took it. "We'll save your mom, too." His hand was offered to Evane next, who hesitated a moment before he took it. "I'm going to send a few scouts ahead to Vegas, to keep an eye out for him. I'll send people to other cities, too, just in case we're wrong about where he'll go."

"I don't think we are, based on what you told us about this Sin City, but that's a good idea," Sam agreed.

"I'll take care of that now, and when everyone's healed, we'll deal with the bodies." He walked away, motioning for several of the Hunters. A few minutes later, four of the Hunters disappeared.

"I've sent them to Las Vegas, LA, New York, and Chicago. They have orders to report any sign of Bellar or increased demon activity," Marco told them when he returned. "I know you need to rest, but will you stay while we bury our fallen?"

"We will," Sam said after a quick glance at Evane and Wade.

He nodded and strode away. Before dealing with the Hunters, they piled the dead demons into a pile and one of the elementals set them ablaze. No one said any words of mourning, they just stood or sat around, resting after the fight while the healers took care of the last of the injuries. There were enough that the healers were wiped by the time they finished.

"You should have time for a quick shower and at least a few hours before Bellar gets to Vegas, if that is his destination. Even flying, I can't see it taking him less than that, especially since he's carrying your mother," Julian told them.

"Good. We'll need it. I've never visited vengeance on so many at once. It's exhausting," Sam admitted.

"I don't doubt it. My wife can do something similar, and it leaves her the same way," he said with a nod.

She considered him for a moment. He was talking to her like she was any other person. It might be because of how close he was with Wade, but she found she liked him better for it. And given that he did seem to be Wade's best friend, she wanted to get to know him a little better. "I'd like to meet your wife sometime. Wade speaks highly of her."

Julian laughed. "He'd better. I think she'd like to meet you, too. And she's always happy to see Wade, though I can't imagine why," he joked.

"Because she has excellent taste, of course. Not fantastic, since she picked you over me, but excellent," Wade shot back with a grin. "When this is all done, we'll come out, spend a few days at Mooreton, visit with you both."

Wade noticed that Evane looked uncomfortable, and he realized that the demon was probably worried about what would happen to him after his reason for being on Earth was done. He decided to take pity on the guy. "Hey Evane?"

"Hmm?"

"You know you're not going to just get ditched and forgotten about, right? You've fought by our side and you're Sam's brother. We'll help you figure shit out."

Sam smiled at him, then Evane, who looked relieved. It was a minor change to his features, but Wade noticed. "Thank you, wolf."

He returned the smile and slid an arm around her to draw her against his side. "No problem."

Marco walked back over to them. "We're ready."

They stood and joined the group of Hunters, which included a still subdued Caitlyn. In front of them were four cloth wrapped bodies. Behind them were two men, solemn looks on their faces. Marco stepped between the mourners and the bodies and pitched his voice to carry to everyone.

"Today, we ended the lives of many dangerous demons and protected Earth. We fought well, we fought bravely. Despite this, we suffered losses. They didn't die in vain, though. They gave their all to do the job they'd pledged their lives for. They died in defense of our world. And we will not forget them," he said fiercely. "Their names will forever be etched into our memories, and we will honor their sacrifice. We will finish what they began today. So stand with me while we say goodbye to our friends." Though most were already standing, he waited for the rest to join them before reciting the names. "Elijah, Eddie, Roseanne, and Tim. Our allies. Our friends. Our family."

He turned and nodded to the men behind him. One of them lifted his hands, palms up, and had dirt lifting from beside each body, forming a rectangular hole roughly six feet deep. The earth hovered in the air while the second man used his power to gently lift the bodies one at a time and lay them carefully within the graves. The dirt was then lowered to cover each of the fallen, leaving four graves that were indistinguishable from the ground around them.

Wade knew that no markers would be placed here. It wasn't disrespect—Marco meant every word he'd said—but safety. Two of the dead were witches, one was an element, and one a shifter. While their biology was very similar to a human's, it was just different enough that if anything more than bones were found, it would send a shock wave through the scientific community. Any sort of supernatural would be hunted so they could be studied, and no one wanted to risk that. The bones were generally safe, though, so it was likely a spell would be placed on the area to keep people away for years to come.

A few minutes of silence were given before Marco turned back to the living. "It's likely Bellar is going to Vegas. You all have an hour to go home and take care of whatever you need to do, then I want you heading to Vegas. I'll have rooms for all of us while we wait for Bellar. You can sleep and shower there, so don't waste time with it now. I want everyone available the moment Bellar shows up. In one hour teleport to me, or call if you can't teleport. Dismissed."

Alone and in pairs, the Hunters disappeared until just Marco, Wade, Julian, and the two demons remained.

"I'm going to check in with Paige, but I'm thinking we might want to call Suni in," Julian said.

"True. Fighting Bellar isn't going to be easy and the Hunter's best healer is lying in the earth now, while our second best's faith in herself is shaken," Marco said with a sigh. "Mine is shaken as well. She can't be in this if she can be so easily swayed."

"Give Suni a call and I'll grab her on my way to Vegas," Julian offered. "Just don't fight Bellar without me. Tim was a good friend, and I want to give him justice."

Marco smiled faintly. "I won't. Give Paige our love."

"I will." And Julian was gone.

"I take it you three want to come with me?" Marco asked when his focus shifted back to the remaining three.

"Yeah. Seems easiest. And that way Sam can get a nap ASAP," Wade said, nodding as Sam and Evane put their wings away. "I also want Suni to finish healing her when she gets to Vegas."

He nodded and reached out so he could touch all three of them, and took them to Sin City.

CHAPTER 34

"I really don't think I like teleporting," was the first thing Sam said when they arrived in a deserted alley. "Flying is much less disorienting."

Wade grinned and slid an arm around her waist. "But you can't fall when you teleport."

She narrowed her eyes at him. "I've never fallen," she told him indignantly. "I have wings."

He chuckled. "Fair enough. Marco, where are we going?"

"Just around the corner," Marco answered. "There's a hotel there run by a siren. It's off the Strip, but she doesn't ask too many questions."

They followed him to the hotel and inside. The woman at the front desk blinked at the spear and state of their clothing, since they hadn't had time to wash off the blood or dirt, but she smiled when she saw Marco. "Welcome back. How many rooms do you need?"

To Sam, who had never dealt with sirens in the past, the woman's voice was a pleasant surprise. It was melodic and beautiful, soothing some of her frayed nerves.

"Hey Tess. How many do you have all on the same floor?"

Her eyes widened. "Crap. Should I be worried?" she asked, even as she tapped on her keyboard.

"I wouldn't wander around too much until we leave," he admitted. "It could get dangerous, but I can't say for sure."

"Noted. And I've got seven rooms on the third floor, all with two beds each. Will that work?"

"That'd be great. Just charge the card on file, will you?" In every major city, the Hunters found at least one hotel that could be used if needed, and kept a card on file in each one. Marco made sure to take care of his Hunters, even if it was just giving them a safe place to rest when they were hunting.

"Sure thing." She handed over a key card. "This is for room 304. I'll send the other cards up in a few. You guys go wash up and rest."

"Thanks, Tess," Marco said with a smile before he led Wade and the demons up to the room.

It was a typical hotel room with a dresser, TV, two beds, a night-stand, couch, and small table, along with an attached bathroom. Nothing but the basics.

"I'm going to wash up," Sam said the moment they were inside and hurried into the bathroom, shutting the door behind her.

Wade started to follow her, but Evane laid a hand on his arm and shook his head. "Give her a few minutes."

Reluctantly, Wade nodded and moved further into the room, setting the spear in a corner.

Marco turned on the TV and sat on the edge of the bed as he turned it to the news. He didn't expect there to be anything yet, not when Bellar had only escaped an hour and a half before, but this way they weren't likely to miss any reports. Just to be on the safe side, he pulled his phone out to search for any breaking news stories in the city. Nothing yet.

Wade pulled his stained and cut shirt off and tossed it into the tiny trash can in the corner. "Don't suppose you can tell any of your Hunters to bring some clothes with them?"

"That would be very appreciated, yes," Evane agreed, though his shirt was nowhere near as dirty as Wade's had been.

"Not a problem." Marco started texting one of the Hunters when someone teleported in. He tensed and glanced up long enough to see that it was Julian and a tiny woman he recognized instantly. "Hey Suni."

She barely topped five feet, and though she had the bone structure and coloring of a Native American, her eyes were a vivid blue. And when she smiled, like she did now, they sparkled. "Hi Marco, Wade." She glanced to Evane and stilled.

Wade glanced between them as they stared at each other, and he wondered at their reactions. Evane's wings were hidden, though he supposed Suni could be reacting to the black eyes. But surely Julian would have warned her that there would be two demons here. Then he slowly smiled. No, it wasn't discomfort from being in the same room as a demon. He could scent the attraction radiating off both of them. "Suni, this is Evane. His twin sister, Samara, is washing up. They're the ones who gave us the most info on Bellar. It's also their mom that Bellar's holding hostage," he said, doing little to hide his amusement at their reactions.

Julian and Marco glanced at him, the former arching a brow, before he caught on. Julian knew full well that Wade could smell more than any witch, and he tried to hide his smile.

"It's a pleasure to meet you, Suni," Evane said, inclining his head deeply enough it was almost a bow, though he didn't take his eyes off Suni for even a second.

Suni bit the corner of her mouth before she smiled. "Nice to meet you, too, Evane."

"Please, call me Vane."

"Vane, then." She realized then that Julian, Marco, and Wade were all staring at her and Evane, and she cleared her throat and purposefully broke eye contact. "Do any of you need healing?"

Marco glanced to each of the other men before he shook his head. "No, I think we're good. We had healers there. They may not be you, but most of the injuries weren't too bad." His face tightened and they all knew he was thinking about the Hunters he'd lost.

Suni rubbed a hand over his arm and gave him a cheeky smile. "No one's me. That's why you all love me." Normally she didn't joke much, but as a healer she worked to help the mind as much as the body, and knew Marco needed it.

He smiled a little, just as she'd intended. "It's probably part of it, yes."

"Sam will need healing when she's done showering," Wade said with a glance toward the bathroom.

"She needed more than your healers could provide?" Suni asked Marco with some surprise.

The commander didn't look completely comfortable, but he nodded. "Julian and I did what we could, but the injury was severe."

There was a discreet knock on the door and Marco broke off from the conversation to open it, getting the rest of the key cards from Tess. "Thanks."

She smiled and slipped away without a word.

Sam came out of the bathroom. She'd not only showered, but had done her best to clean her shirt, so both her hair and shirt were damp. Her wings were out again, though they were tucked in against her back so they didn't hit the door frame. When she spotted Suni, she stopped and glanced questioningly to Wade.

The fact that she looked to him rather than her brother for confirmation that Suni was okay made his chest swell with pride. He walked over to her and stroked a hand down one of her wings before he wrapped his arm around her waist. "Sam, this is Suni, the healer we were talking about earlier. She's okay and knows what you and Evane are."

She nodded. "Hi Suni. It's good to have another healer around. I expect there'll be quite a few more injuries before Bellar is killed."

"Unfortunately, that's generally the way it is when powerful demons are confronted," Suni agreed with a nod. "I was told you need some healing?"

Sam hesitated a moment before she nodded. "I'm in no danger of dying, but some healing would be appreciated."

Suni smiled and crossed to Sam, resting a hand on the demon's arm. After a moment, the pain Sam had been trying to block out disappeared. She sighed almost inaudibly at the sudden relief. "Thank you."

"You're welcome." She stepped back and glanced to the men before her gaze returned to Samara. "Do you have any idea where he's gone yet?"

Marco shook his head and pointed to the TV. "I'm monitoring the news and waiting to hear from my scouts, but so far, no one's seen him."

"I'm positive he's going to come here based on what you told us about this town, especially if it is the closest of the big cities to where we were," Evane said as he headed for the bathroom so he could take his turn washing up.

Wade frowned as a thought occurred to him. What if Bellar had shown up, but he'd taken care of the scouts before they could contact Marco? "I'd check in with your scouts now and again."

Marco grimaced as he caught on, and his fingers started moving over his phone. Times like this, he wished he had more skill with telepathy. He could contact them, but it was draining for him even though it was infinitely quicker. One by one, the Hunters he'd sent to the various cities started to respond with a mixture of telepathy and technology, until only the Vegas scouts hadn't checked in. When several minutes had passed with no answer, he looked up, his face grim. "No word from the Hunters here in Las Vegas, but everyone else is okay."

Julian cursed while Wade fought the urge to put his fist through the wall.

"He's here," Sam said quietly. "He's either killed them or turned them, depending on whether or not they were easily turned. He'll be wanting to build his army rapidly, so I doubt he'll take the time to work too hard on anyone unless they are someone who can benefit him in some way."

"She's right," Evane agreed from the doorway.

"Shit," Marco muttered as he stared at his phone. "News report just hit. Body was found just outside a strip club on the edge of the strip.

The club's abandoned. No one closed up or locked up, they just all left. Not a normal occurrence at eight on a Friday night."

"He's already started rebuilding his army," Julian said. "He doesn't have access to his demons, so he's just taking humans. Probably for cannon fodder."

"But where would he take them? He didn't hole up in this club and you didn't say there were reports of a crowd of people moving around the city, so they went somewhere," Sam said.

"Hell, they could be anywhere," Wade growled as he started pacing. His wolf wanted out. Wanted to hunt down Bellar and tear him to shreds. "They could've gone into the desert, found an empty building, or found some twisted fucker with a house they could use. Hell, he could've turned the owner of one of these huge hotels and they've taken over one of them."

"We'll keep watching the news, and the rest of the Hunters will be here soon. I'll send them out in teams scouring the city and make sure every team has a tracker."

Though Wade wanted to be searching for Bellar with Sam, he knew they needed to separate so they could cover more ground. He nudged her until she looked up at him.

After a moment, she sighed and turned to Marco. "Put us on different teams. He can use his wolf senses, and I know how to spot someone being controlled by Bellar."

"I can help, too," Evane said as he stepped up beside his sister. "It'll probably help any Hunters we're paired with stay alive, too. Bellar's tried for centuries to turn our hearts as evil as his, and he's failed."

Suni arched a brow. "Centuries? How old are the two of you?"

"Somewhere around two thousand," Evane answered.

She nodded and motioned for Marco to continue.

"That's a good idea, and I'll take you up on that." His phone chimed and he glanced down at it. "I need to go pick some Hunters up. When I get back, I'll start assigning teams. Keep an eye on the TV just in case there's more news."

"We will. Go get the rest of the team," Wade said, waving the man off. Once Marco had gone, he turned to Sam, pulling her into his arms. "You be careful out there, okay? I'm not worried about the humans. I know you can take any human stupid enough to come at you. But promise me, if you find Bellar before anyone else, you call in backup first. You call me." Except he remembered that his phone was still on Olarid. When he went out to scout, he'd have to pick up a prepaid one just so he could stay in contact.

She rested her head against his chest. "I don't know that I can promise that," she whispered.

"Yes, you can, because you know that there's a better chance we'll get your mom back safe if you have more than a Hunter or two helping you." It was a low blow, he knew, but it was also true. More, he knew she'd never forgive herself if she rushed in and Lilith got hurt because of it.

Arms tightened around him as she closed her eyes. "You're right. I hate it, but you're right. I promise to call you." She lifted her head so she could look at Evane. "You promise, too."

Evane nodded. "I do, and no, I don't like it anymore than you do. But I'll do whatever it takes to see Mom safe."

Sam drew away from Wade and went to Evane to hug him tight. "Me too. I hope Marco gets back soon with the other Hunters."

"It doesn't take long to teleport," Julian said. "Most likely, he's just taking them to the other rooms so they can put their things down first." When the door opened, he smiled. "And there he is."

Marco was accompanied by four Hunters, so the room was immediately cramped. "Wade, you're with Duncan. He's got telepathy, so he's going to help coordinate between the teams. Sam, you're with Cassidy. She's a witch and a hell of a tracker. Evane—"

Suni interrupted smoothly. "I can go with him. I know Vegas, and it leaves more of the Hunters free for other groups." Marco hesitated and she arched a brow. "I'm a healer, but I'm not incompetent. I'll be fine."

"Fine. Julian, you're with Ella," he said, nodding to a woman Julian knew to be a siren. "Jarred, as soon as someone else arrives, you'll be with them. I'm going to stay here to send people out as they get in. If you get hurt, get back here and we'll get Suni back to take care of you. And remember, the first sign of Bellar, you let me know. You follow, but make sure you're not seen. And *do not engage*," he stressed. "We hit him as one. You go in early, I'll kick your ass. Got me?" Around him he heard assents and saw nods. "Go on, and be safe," he added, motioning for the door.

"They'll be fine," Julian murmured as he passed Marco, following the others through the door and out into the city.

"I hope so," Marco whispered when he was alone. But he knew that, by the end of the day, he was probably going to lose more of his people.

CHAPTER 35

O nce out on the street, the four teams separated, going in four different directions, though not without a long look exchanged between Sam and Wade.

Waiting until they were out of earshot, the siren Julian was paired with finally spoke. "Is she really his daughter?"

Though Julian had met sirens before, including the owner of the hotel they were staying in, the sound of a siren's voice never failed to surprise him. It was almost tactile. Like something that could literally brush against the skin. "Both of them are his children, yes," he said, glancing to her. "I hope you're not going to hold that against her, though."

Ella was quiet for a few minutes. "Not exactly. I don't trust her because she's a demon, and I'm a Hunter, but I don't blame her for who her father is. It's not like she had a choice about it. And she is trying to kill him, so that gives her some points. But unless this guy actually dies without her trying to save him, I'm not going to believe that she's actually a good guy. More...an enemy of my enemy thing."

"That's fair," Julian agreed easily. "I understand how hard it is to trust a demon. I don't have the same bone-deep hatred for them that Marco or most of you Hunters do, but I've spent my whole life studying them, and I can't say I've heard of any good ones before the last week. Except Samara and her brother seem to be just that." He smiled faintly. "But it's not easy to reconcile centuries of experience with someone who appears to be the exception. But...she is one of the good ones," he insisted. "I know you're not just going to take my word on it, but you'll see by the time this is over. If she could handle the spear herself, I guarantee she'd be putting it through his heart personally."

"I hope you're right, considering the way Wade was looking at her," Ella said quietly.

Julian had noticed as well, but rather than feeling concerned like Ella did, he was just happy for Wade. It was time for the wolf to find his mate. He'd be happier if he knew that they were both going to survive this fight, but at least it had happened for his friend.

Although, he had no idea if Sam was going to stay on Earth when Bellar was dead. He hadn't spoken with her at length, and for all he knew, she would be returning home. He hoped not, for Wade's sake.

"Let's check down here," he said, pointing to an alley that ran down to another street. "I think this leads closer to the strip club Bellar cleared out."

"Works for me." Ella cocked her head and closed her eyes as she listened. "I don't hear anything out of the ordinary yet, but there might not be anything outside of where they're hiding out."

"Just keep an eye out."

Wade and Duncan headed south, though Wade couldn't help but glance back until he couldn't see Sam any longer. Though she'd promised to be careful and not go after Bellar by herself, he still worried. He didn't know if he'd have the strength to step back if someone had kidnapped his mom. But she was the strongest woman she knew, so he had to hope.

He swung into the first place he saw that had phones and quickly bought one. As they walked, he set it up, then texted Julian and Sam so they'd have his number. That done, he gave his full focus to hunting for signs of Bellar.

"So that spear I saw back in the hotel, that's supposed to be the key to ending this guy?" Duncan asked.

"Supposedly, yeah," Wade said with a nod. "It works pretty well on every other demon I've used it on, and burns them just to touch it, so I don't see why it won't. But there's not really any way of knowing until it's actually buried in his heart." And he was looking forward to that moment more than he cared to mention.

"Why leave it in the hotel room, then?"

Wade looked at Duncan, amusement shining in his eyes. "You must be a new Hunter."

Duncan frowned. "Not that new, but what makes you say that?"

"When Marco makes a threat, he follows through. He won't hesitate. But he only makes threats like he did back there when it's something really important, and this is. Bellar's gotten an army together.

Of humans, yes, but we're just two people, and there's no telling how many people he's got surrounding him. They could overwhelm us with sheer numbers, and then the spear would be in Bellar's control. And, oh yeah, we'd be dead. Or worse." He shook his head. "No, I'll take the spear when we find Bellar. Not to mention I'd look pretty fucking ridiculous wandering around Vegas with a spear almost as long as I am tall. And that's if I didn't get arrested."

"Okay, good point," Duncan said. "Sorry, I'm not big on tactics. My job's normally the same that I'm doing today—coordinating with people telepathically. Or tracking, though that's a lot easier when I've met the person I'm tracking."

Intrigued, Wade made a 'go on' motion. "How does that work?"

"Not too differently than your tracking, I imagine. Every person has a unique scent, right? So once you know how they smell, and if you find that scent in a crowd, you can pick them out, even if they're disguised? Or you can follow their scent to them?"

"That's close enough, yeah. Though I've met a few people who could disguise their scent, too."

"Happens to me, too. But every person has a unique mind, too. It's not a scent or anything, not even really a feel, though that's the closest I can describe it," Duncan explained. "Hell, different types of people have similar minds, like how humans all smell human, dogs smell like dogs, cats smell like cats, and so on."

"Wait, so you can tell what a person is just by how their mind feels?" He wasn't sure how he felt about that. Maybe it was a rare ability? He'd have to ask Red if she could do the same thing. Since she was the most powerful mental witch he'd ever met, she should be able to unless it was a specialized talent, like how he smelled magic.

"Most of the time," Duncan confirmed. "Some people have really weird minds that I can't figure out, but generally people are just people."

Impressed, Wade said, "That's handy for a tracker."

"Usually," Duncan agreed with a grin. "There are six more teams out, by the way. And Marco's sending for more. With an unknown number of humans, he wants at least twenty people on the ground here, and that's just scouting."

"That's smart. Half of us will probably just be trying to take the humans out without killing them."

"That's what he's concerned about, yeah."

Wade sighed. "Let's hurry up and find this bastard. Any demon minds around?"

"Not since we split up."

"Damn."

The first few minutes that Suni and Evane spent searching Las Vegas were quiet. After their greeting, neither had spoken directly to the other until Evane broke the silence.

"Marco called you a healer, so I take it you're a witch like the ones who healed us after the fight?" he asked, glancing down at her.

He couldn't keep his eyes off her. There had been many beautiful women on Olarid, and he'd visited Earth a few times and met more, but there was something unique about this petite woman that called to him. Under normal circumstances, he'd have tried to seduce her, but he couldn't do anything while his mother's life was on the line.

But the moment Bellar was dead…

"I am, yes. I'm not officially affiliated with the Venatoribus Noctu, and they have their own healers, but they call me in when there are too many injured for them to deal with or the injuries are too severe," Suni confirmed with a nod.

She wasn't sure why she was out here. She wasn't a tracker, and though she could hold her own against a human, she wasn't a good enough fighter to go against a demon. And yet she'd offered to team up with a demon, which was the height of stupidity. Yes, she trusted Julian's judgment, and he had said Evane and Samara weren't typical demons, but she should have stayed back at the hotel room. It was where Marco had intended her to be, she knew. She was too valuable a healer to risk. But when Marco had been about to pair Evane with Jarred, she'd been unable to resist offering herself instead.

Sure, Evane was undoubtedly attractive, but she had a feeling he was well aware of that fact. She was no blushing virgin, but as a rule, she avoided men who were the type to rack up as many women as possible. No doubt Evane was one of those, but she was more than a notch on a bedpost.

"You must be skilled indeed, then," Evane said, pulling her out of her thoughts.

"Why do you say that?"

"The healers I met earlier seemed very good at their jobs. There were some serious injuries, but they saved everyone except those who were already beyond healing. So for you to be the…big guns, I believe the phrase is, makes you quite a healer."

Suni felt herself blush and called herself a fool in three different languages. "I've had a lot of time to hone my talents," she said aloud.

Curious, he cocked his head and studied her. "You don't look any older than they did. A few looked older, in fact."

She only shrugged and peered through the window of a cafe as they passed it. "Do you see anything out of the ordinary?"

Evane's lips twitched. "Considering I've never been in this city, I don't really know what ordinary is. But I'm not seeing any signs that lead me to believe my father is here, no."

"Maybe one of the other groups is having more luck," she said.

"Perhaps. But if they're not now, then someone will. Bellar isn't the type to stay hidden for long. He enjoys his power too much, and is too arrogant to think that we'll beat him in the end. He'll make a move sooner or later."

Suni grimaced and nodded. "Yes, but if it's later, it probably won't be a move we'll enjoy."

Though Sam knew that Marco had spoken to his Hunters, the witch she was partnered with kept a good amount of distance between them. More, she kept watching Sam like she expected to be attacked at any moment. For the first half hour, Sam said nothing, just searched for any sign of Bellar or those being controlled by him. But after Sam had moved a little too suddenly for the witch and almost got singed feathers for her trouble, she stopped and turned to Cassidy, sighing.

"Look, this isn't going to work if you're more focused on me than on finding Bellar."

Cassidy narrowed her eyes at Sam. "What good does finding Bellar do if you kill me to cover it up?"

Sam glared. "Are you kidding me? I'm getting really fucking sick of this. Do you really think that Marco would intentionally pair you with me if he thought I was just going to kill you? For that matter, do you really think that he'd be working with me if he didn't trust that we were on the same side?"

Cassidy didn't have a good response for that and frowned.

"Exactly. Now trust me, I want this demon dead more than any of you Hunters do, so you've got two options. One, you stop watching me like I'm going to bite you and we keep going, or two, you go back to the hotel and tell Marco you can't do your job. I don't really give a damn which choice you make, because I'm going to keep looking for Bellar either way." She crossed her arms over her chest and gave Cassidy an annoyed look. "So what's it going to be?"

For a minute Cassidy studied her, but for once Sam thought she might actually be thinking. Slowly, the witch nodded. "Fine. I'll pay more attention to tracking Bellar."

"Thank you." Sam started walking again. "What sort of tracker are you, anyway?"

Cassidy fell into step beside her. "The traditional kind, for one, though that does no good in the city. But I also notice things other people miss. Sometimes it's a track, sometimes it's a pattern that's only barely there."

"So you might notice the signs of a bunch of people moving as one to wherever Bellar's decided to hole up?"

"I might," Cassidy said uncertainly. "A group of people doesn't look much different than a bunch of random people moving the same way, but trust me, I'm trying. Especially since we're reaching the city limits. Do you think he'd leave the city?"

Sam frowned as she thought. "He might, if there was a good reason to. Something he wanted, or a safe place for him to gather his army. What's outside the city?"

"Mostly it's desert. There's a lake and some state parks, but not a whole lot besides that, I don't think."

She shook her head. "He wouldn't be interested in either of those. He doesn't like denying himself comforts. No, if he's going to go somewhere that isn't palatial, it'll be someplace defensible."

Cassidy slowly smiled. "Palatial, huh? Girl, have I got good news for you. One of the sins of Sin City is the gambling, which means there are a lot of rich people around here. And where do rich people live?"

"You're kidding. Are you telling me that there are palaces here?" Sam asked, and she felt her adrenaline start to build. That was exactly the sort of place he'd go.

"Not quite, but some of them are as good as. Huge houses with every comfort known to man, and some of them aren't too far from here."

"Lead the way. I'm going to call Wade and tell him to pass on the word to look for these houses," Sam said as she dug her phone out.

"You can call him if you want, but there's no need."

"Why not?"

"Duncan's helping to coordinate, remember? I let him know," Cassidy explained. "Everyone's going to pay close attention to any of the mansions."

Remembering the wall around Scott Delaney's house, Sam said, "Focus on those that have walls and gates. It's an extra layer of security. He'd like that, especially since this is his first time to this dimension."

"Good point."

With the word out, they quickened their steps.

The first house that met the main requirement of large and extravagant was a bust. Whoever owned it wasn't there, and neither could detect the presence of a single person, much less dozens of people. They had hopes for the second, but it turned out that it was a normal party the owner was throwing.

Twenty minutes later, they struck gold.

The house had a stone wall around it, but through the iron gate, they could see several people patrolling the grounds, armed with guns.

"Is that normal?" Sam whispered to Cassidy.

"Definitely not," the witch said with a shake of her head. "Some criminals might have guards patrolling, and they'd be armed, but no one's going to be that obviously armed. It's just asking for the police to raid their house." They watched in silence for a minute before she added, "You see any signs of your d—of Bellar?" she corrected.

Sam smiled faintly, glad for the change of heart. "No, but then, he'd be inside, either toying with the women, getting pampered, or..." She trailed off, unwilling to think of what he could be doing to her mom right now. "Give me a second, though. If he's in there, I might be able to sense him from out here."

It wasn't a normal use of her power. Usually she just happened to notice if people around her were guilty of some crime that demanded justice, but Bellar had always made her Fury powers scream with the need for vengeance like no other could. Her eyes closed and she concentrated on that single aspect of her power, stretching it as far as it would go. When it brushed against Bellar, she gasped and her eyes flew open.

"Hey, what is it? You okay?" Cassidy asked, frowning in concern.

"He's in there. And he's done a hell of a lot more than he had last time I sensed him," Sam whispered, vibrating with outrage. Loose on Earth, with this many humans serving his every whim, he'd been indulging himself. "Tell Duncan to let the others know to meet us back at the hotel. We've found him."

CHAPTER 36

Even with the anger and adrenaline that pushed Sam, she and Cassidy were the last two back to the hotel. The room was cramped, given that there were now twenty Hunters in addition to the original group, but not a single person voiced a complaint.

"We found him," Sam said the moment the door shut behind her.

"Did you see him?" Evane asked as he pushed his way toward her, right behind Wade.

"The only people we could see were guards. They were patrolling inside the wall with guns. Knives, too, probably, but they were really obvious about the guns," Cassidy said.

"He's in there, though, trust me," Sam insisted. "I could *feel* him in there." She accepted Wade's comfort when he wrapped his arms around her, and leaned into him. "I don't know what he's planning, exactly, but he's definitely enjoying himself."

"What do you mean, enjoying himself?" one of the Hunters Sam hadn't met asked.

Her mouth tightened and she glanced at Evane. On his face, she saw that he understood what she meant. "Let's just say he's been a very bad boy and needs to be put down as soon as possible," she said finally. They didn't need to know the details, that he'd probably been torturing, raping, and killing—and not necessarily in that order. He truly was evil.

"You said it was a walled estate. Is it on the fringes of the city, then?" Marco asked. Hearing about Bellar's evil wouldn't kill him any quicker and he didn't need his Hunters distracted with rage. He just wanted the tactical details.

"It is. The back wall faced out into the desert, though there are neighbors on one side," Cassidy confirmed.

"How many guards?"

"How many do you think?" she asked Sam, who frowned in thought. "Somewhere around twenty, just on the outside, right?"

"Yeah, that sounds about right." Sam shook her head. "He's already gotten more people than we expected, though. And they're not good people."

"How many more did you sense?" Evane asked.

"It's hard to count, but probably another thirty or forty in addition to the ones we saw," Sam answered, resigned. "Mostly humans, but I'm pretty sure there are some others there, too."

Something in Sam's voice had Wade's arms tightening around her and he bent his head to whisper, "What is it?"

"A few of the people he's gathered are almost as horrible as he is, Wade. Even before he used his power on them, they'd still done some truly evil things," she murmured.

He wasn't really surprised, but nodded and stroked a hand over her head and down her braid. "We'll take care of it."

"Okay," Marco said, voice carrying over the low conversations that were happening all over the room. "We're going to split into two teams, front and back. Front team, you're to engage the guards and do your best to immobilize them without killing. We just need a distraction and to get the threats neutralized, we don't want to leave behind dozens of dead humans, especially if they're innocent." Sam snorted softly and he corrected himself. "Not willingly involved. And we'll get the worst offenders to the proper authorities, whether it's us or the human cops."

"Thank you," she said gratefully. She could, and had, carried out justice herself in the past, but it wore on a person. And she wasn't on Olarid now. Justice wasn't quite the same on Earth as it was on Olarid. Here there were jails and judges and trials. On Olarid, there was only death.

"You're welcome. Back team's Sam, Wade, Evane, Julian, Suni and myself. We're going to do our best to sneak in and catch Bellar before he realizes he's being attacked on two fronts. Suni, you stay back and just get ready to heal. The rest of us will do everything we can to get Wade and that spear to Bellar." He slowly looked around, noting the face of every person here, Hunter or otherwise. There were grim faces, yes, but there was determination on each one. "Any questions?" No one spoke up and he nodded. "Duncan will give the word to go on my signal, then. Let's go."

Those on the front team filed out first. Wade grabbed the spear and looked at Julian and Marco. "We should probably teleport there. The other team can split up and not be conspicuous, but a pissed off dude carrying a spear's going to attract attention."

"We will. Let's give them a few minutes to get closer first," Marco said with a nod. "Was there anything else you needed to tell us, Sam?"

"No, but I do want to thank all of you. I have the desire and drive to kill Bellar and save us all, but not the ability. So whatever happens tonight, thank you," Sam said, her tone sincere, her eyes earnest.

"Though you're welcome, there's no need for thanks," Julian said with a shake of his head. "He's a dangerous demon threatening Earth. It's Marco's job to eliminate that threat. The fact that he's helping someone is just an added bonus."

"Of course, there is the fact that you're *not* killing two particular demons," Evane drawled. "I'll tell you, I really appreciate that bit."

Sam smiled a little before she sobered. "We should get going. He could decide to move, and if someone isn't there, we'll have to track him all over again."

"Agreed." Marco laid his hands on Sam and Wade's shoulders, while Julian took Evane and Suni. "Think about the place, especially the back wall," he told Sam. She complied and he eased into her mind before he shared the image with Julian. One moment they stood in the hotel room, and the next they stood behind the high walls of the estate Bellar had taken over. "Is this it?" he murmured, just to confirm.

"It is. We saw a small gate over there we can use to get in if you don't want to go up and over the wall," Sam whispered back.

"Not all of us can fly, remember?" he asked with a quick half-grin.

She returned it and shrugged. "Pity. You'd like it."

They crept to the gate and Wade peeked inside. "Looks like you described it. Guards patrolling with guns," he confirmed.

"We're in position and waiting for your signal," Duncan thought to Marco.

"Everyone ready?" he asked.

Sam and Evane drew their weapons before Sam nodded. "We're good."

"Go!" he sent back, and a moment later, the sounds of a fight carried back to them. "Let's go," he said aloud as he blasted the gate open and rushed in.

About half of the guards had already started rushing toward the front of the house to join the fight. The rest turned toward the six people and started firing.

Julian held his hands up, palms facing the guards, and put up a shield, but not before a few bullets got through. One grazed Evane's leg, while another went through the fleshy part of Wade's arm. Fortunately, both men were used to injuries, and the relatively minor wounds didn't slow either of them down.

"I've got these guys. You go inside and find Bellar," Evane told the others as he stretched his arms out. One by one, the guards stopped shooting as they cringed and cried out in pain.

When the first man hit the ground and curled up into the fetal position, Sam turned to her brother. "Come find us as soon as you can. And don't die."

"I won't. I'll be along as soon as you're all inside. Now go," he told her, voice strained with the effort of sustaining his power on so many at once.

"Be careful," Wade growled before he hurried after Sam and Marco, with Julian and Suni behind him.

Sam didn't even attempt to see if the French doors were locked, but planted her foot against them with enough force that wood cracked and glass shattered. The lights were off inside, but it didn't even make her hesitate before she ran inside.

Before Suni disappeared into the house with them, she glanced back at Evane. As a healer, she should be enraged at what he was doing to the guards, but she understood that it was a non-lethal way of getting them out of the way. But she also found herself worried for the demon.

"Stop this, Suni," she muttered to herself before following the others inside.

A panther shifter in its animal form leapt at Sam, but a quick burst of magic from Julian had the feline lifted and slammed against a wall. When it didn't knock the panther unconscious, Wade strode forward and punched it in the muzzle. This time, its eyes rolled back in its head and it passed out.

"Where would he be?" Wade asked Sam.

"I don't know. He could be anywhere," she answered, shaking her head. She didn't understand the layouts of homes like this, which meant she didn't have any clue where Bellar would likely be.

He growled but nodded and hurried out of the kitchen. He could hear the sounds of fighting outside, and a glance out the window showed that a majority of Bellar's guards had gone out front to meet the Hunters. A majority, but not all. A human guard yelled and rushed at him with a butcher's knife, but he just reversed the spear and slammed the shaft against the side of the man's head, knocking him out. "Let's try upstairs," he told them as he made his way up the ornate staircase to the second floor.

The six guards who were waiting in the second-floor hallway made him growl, but if they were here and not outside, then they were probably protecting Bellar.

Sam ran in front of him and engaged the guards. She kicked, she punched, she slammed the hilt of her knife against temples, and had every human in the hallway on the floor in a minute flat. But that didn't clear their path.

Most of the supernaturals Bellar had called to him stepped out of one of the rooms, and they were prepared for war. One of them was a bear who almost reached the ceiling. Another was a stone elemental, who had already transformed into his sturdier form. A few others were likely witches but could have been anything, and somewhere Bellar had managed to find two demons to replace the ones he'd already lost. One of the demons rivaled the bear for muscle, had claws, and bone spikes protruded from his shoulders. The other was thin to the point of emaciation, but his movements were even more graceful than Sam's, and like her, he carried blades.

Marco hit the landing and threw his hand out, sending a blast of kinetic energy toward the elemental. It knocked the stone figure back, but didn't topple him. He lumbered forward and swung a heavy arm out. Marco barely managed to avoid having his head ripped off with a well-timed duck. They played a dangerous game as they circled each other, with Marco hitting him with magic while the elemental tried his best to pound Marco into dust. Only once did the elemental touch Marco, but the blow to his side was devastating and knocked Marco back, his ribs broken.

Suni darted forward and crouch over Marco protectively as she shoved her healing into him, repairing his ribs.

Julian noticed and broke off from fighting the bear in order to protect his friends. He blasted the elemental over and over again, pushing him just a little closer to the stairs with each blow, until the stone man lost his balance and tumbled down the stairs, landing with a loud crack on the marble floor beneath.

Sam had engaged the witches, leaving Wade with the demons. The spiked demon went down surprisingly easy. He'd seen the spear and scoffed at it until it had sank deep into his shoulder. Though it hadn't hit anything vital, it blackened the skin where it touched and the burn spread outward from the point of impact. He died screaming, but Wade was already moving on.

The other demon was much more cautious. He waited and watched, avoiding the spear as easily as he might swim downstream in a fast current. When the witches had fallen and the bear's fur had receded with unconsciousness, the demon simply smiled. It was toothy and sly, and something about it made the hair on Wade's neck stand up.

Wade thrust out with the spear, but the demon flowed back and didn't stop until he'd gone through a door at the end of the hallway. It wasn't the same door he'd emerged from, but perhaps it was the room Bellar was in.

He glanced back and saw that the others were on their feet. Julian and Marco looked exhausted, and Sam had a scorched wing and what looked like deep nail marks on her neck, but they were all alive, they were all conscious. Evane had even dealt with the guards in the back and came up the stairs to join him.

Though the demon had left them a trail a blind man could follow, Wade didn't trust him. Every single door was opened as they reached it, and the room inside checked. Each one had clearly been used in one form or another, since they all had rumpled sheets or blood stains, but they were all currently empty of life.

One door he closed abruptly the instant after he opened it. Sam had looked at him questioningly, but he only shook his head. She may know that her father was an evil bastard, but she didn't need to see any more bodies that proved it.

Finally, they reached the last door, the one the demon had escaped through.

"Ready?" Wade mouthed as he laid his hand on the knob. They all nodded, and he shoved the door open. He was the first to step inside, and noted, with relief, that Suni hung back.

Wade expected this to be a trap or some game, that they'd just find the demon, but they found Bellar as well, along with a still chained Lilith.

Bellar stood in the middle of the room, and though he retained his usual arrogance, it was obvious that their attack had royally pissed him off.

Good.

Just behind him, but standing to one side so they weren't hidden behind his large frame, were the other demon and Lilith. Blood had dried beneath her nose and at the corners of her mouth, and she looked bruised and beaten. She was being held by the demon, who had knives pressed against her throat and back. Worse, he was still smiling that creepy smile.

Sam and Evane stepped up beside Wade, and he didn't need to look to know that they were absolutely furious and fighting not to rush forward.

Bellar smiled. "Hello, children."

CHAPTER 37

T he sight before Sam enraged her more than any in the past had. She didn't know the demon who held her mother, but Bellar wouldn't have entrusted something like this to a weak demon, or one whose morals didn't fully align with his. Which meant her mother was in a great deal of trouble.

"Let her go, Bellar," she said, her voice shaking with anger.

Bellar folded his arms over his chest and seemed utterly confident in his position. "How many times do I have to tell you to call me Dad?" he taunted while the demon stroked the tip of the knife across Lilith's skin. Like Bellar, he didn't seem the least bit worried, but appeared to be fully enjoying himself. "And no, I won't let her go. She's my wife, after all, and the reason why I'm having all this trouble with my children and their..." He swept a disgusted look over Marco, Julian, and Wade, "pets."

"No," Evane disagreed, shaking his head, "the reason you're having trouble is that you were a shit father and have always been an evil bastard. Did you really think all the demons on Olarid follow you out of loyalty?" he sneered.

Bellar waved a hand dismissively. "I don't care why they follow me. It's enough that they do. Now leave, or you'll see your mother in pieces."

"Not happening, Bellar," Wade said as he took a step forward, gripping the spear. The odds weren't fantastic, he knew that. Yes, they had numbers, but if Bellar was as powerful as Sam and Evane believed, then they might be outclassed, especially with Lilith being used as a hostage. That wasn't going to stop him from shoving the spear into Bellar's chest and seeing him incinerated, it just might take longer than he would like. "You're not leaving this room alive."

Bellar sighed and shook his head. "I should have killed both of you at birth. I never could have predicted that children of my own would be so...weak." He gave another sigh and let his arms drop. "Fine." He glanced at his demon and smiled cruelly. "Don't kill her quickly," he ordered before he surged forward to meet the Hunters. As he moved, he pulled a sword from behind him and swung it at Wade.

Though Wade lifted the spear and deflected the worst of the blow, his forearms were slashed by the quick, vicious attack. Bellar was a great deal stronger than any foe he'd fought in the past and he couldn't avoid taking some damage. Before he could regroup or do anything else, the sword was moving again and cut across his belly despite the shaft of the spear being held partially in front of him. Bellar didn't stop there, either.

In an instant he realized that, while Sam and Evane were both exceptionally skilled in a fight and surpassed him by a mile, Bellar far outclassed both of them. But Wade wasn't alone, and Evane caught the next strike with his knife and shoved the sword away from them.

Marco took the opportunity to blast Bellar, but it only shoved him back a single step.

Knowing she couldn't actually harm Bellar, and unwilling to sit back and do nothing, Sam focused on the demon holding her mother. He'd taken Bellar at face value and was cutting Lilith up, the wounds deep enough to make the millennia-old demon cry out in pain.

"Mom!" Sam yelled as she rushed over. It might have gone badly, but Lilith met her gaze then feigned unconsciousness and slumped in the demon's arms. He didn't release Lilith, but it did throw his balance off just enough that Sam was able to stab him in the side. His hold tightened on her mom, so Sam bared her teeth and twisted the knife, grinding the hilt against him until he released Lilith.

The ancient demon fell to the floor unceremoniously, whimpering weakly as she landed on one of her many wounds, but she crawled away from Sam and the ill-looking demon, removing herself as an easy target.

With Lilith out of the way, Sam went wild as she attacked the demon. Since she couldn't go after the true source of her rage, she unleashed it upon the man who had dared to hurt her mother. Who had sided with Bellar against everything and everyone she loved. Ignoring the wounds she sustained, she rained blows down on him, slashing and stabbing with the knife, before she was able to lift her foot and kick him square in the chest. It knocked him back onto the bed and she dove after him. He angled his knife upward so it sank deep into her belly, even as she brought one of her knives down hard, square over his heart.

Sam tasted blood as she bit her lip to prevent herself from screaming and distracting Wade and the others. She pressed down and stared at the demon beneath her. The light faded out of his eyes even as her blood poured out and over the dead demon. Whimpering, she leaned back and drew the knife out of her body, dropping it on the bed. She was long-lived, yes, and could potentially live forever, but only if something didn't kill her. This wound was deep enough that, if not treated, it might be the thing to end her. But she couldn't stop, not as long as Bellar was alive and the people she cared about were in danger. Nor could she call for Suni. The healer had to be available to those who could wield the spear.

She crawled off the bed and glanced at Lilith. It tore her up to see her strong, powerful mother laying so still on the floor, bleeding, battered. But right now, she couldn't focus on that. If she did, she'd be dead. They all would. Her head slowly turned toward the fight and her heart skipped a beat.

While she'd been busy saving her mom, Bellar had done quite a lot of damage to the four men. One of Julian's arms hung uselessly at his side, blood dripping from his fingers, and his nose had been broken. Marco lay slumped against the wall, only half-conscious. He still tried to fight, but his movements were sluggish and weak. Evane's wings looked half-plucked and his shirt was cut open, the flesh beneath ripped and covered in blood. Wade wasn't in much better shape. He'd received multiple cuts and his hands were so bloody that he could barely hold on to the spear, even with the leather lacing on it. Yet he looked the least injured of them all. A testament to his skill, she knew—or the power of the spear—since she was aware of just how good her twin was.

But worse than the men's injuries, however, was the fact that Bellar had only a single, small cut on his cheek.

Sam wanted to slice the tattoo off her neck once again, but knew that it would be just as futile now as it had been every other time she'd tried. But she had to do something or they were going to be slaughtered. And she didn't have a lot of time to act.

Bellar lifted his knife and brought it down toward Wade. Sam acted before her brain had even processed it. She couldn't let Bellar kill Wade. Not because Wade had the spear, but because she couldn't see the first man she'd ever loved killed by her father. She leapt between them, so the blade sliced down her side to her hip but missed Wade entirely. This time she was unable to silence her scream as she felt the metal rip through her, felt the blood pouring from the cuts.

"You stupid bitch!" Bellar yelled, and when she landed on one knee on the floor in front of him, he kicked her hard in the ribs and sent her sprawling on her back. "You had one job, and if you would have done it, I never would have touched your mother!" he screamed as he kicked her again. When he pulled his leg back to kick her once more, Evane slammed into him and threw his aim off. Unfortunately, it didn't take the other demon down entirely, but it did draw his attention away from the barely conscious Samara.

Evane and Wade worked side by side, trying to get past Bellar's defenses or at least tire him out, not that the latter seemed likely.

Sam lay on the floor, unable to get up. She'd lost too much blood, and there was no telling how many bones Bellar had broken with his furious kicks. Suni had entered the room, but she was busy healing Julian. Since Julian could harm her father, he was the priority. Her gaze shifted over to Lilith, and she watched as her mom crawled to Marco. One pale hand stretched out and laid over Marco's. He gasped and his back bowed while Lilith's eyes fluttered closed. She was drawing energy from Marco, Sam knew, and saw a way she could help.

Slowly, she pushed herself up enough to see and focused on Wade and Lilith, amplifying their powers, their strength. That, combined with the energy Lilith had taken from Marco, worked wonders on the queen-in-name-only of Olarid. Doing so drained Sam, but she'd do anything to stop Bellar here and now. If she needed to die to achieve that goal, to save Wade and her family, she would. Her gaze flicked to Wade. She would regret not getting more time with him, but as long as he survived, she was content with her choice.

Lilith got to her feet and turned toward where Bellar still fought the Hunters. Darkness began to form around Bellar, covering him like an inky shroud. He roared and slashed out blindly, but he got lucky, hitting Wade's arm, cutting deep enough that the shifter lost his grip on the spear. It fell to the floor and got kicked aside before Wade could reclaim it.

It rolled until it bumped against Lilith's toes and she looked down at it.

Sam saw the intention in her mother's eyes and it roused her enough for her to shake her head. "No, Mom, don't. It'll kill you," she pleaded and tried to crawl close enough to grab the spear, but she didn't make it.

Lilith bent and picked up the spear. Every muscle in her body went rigid as the spear burned her skin. "Wade," she said, her voice quiet amid the sounds of fighting, but he heard and glanced back.

"You can't," he argued, but she just shook her head. Knowing how stubborn Sam was, and that she had to have gotten it from somewhere, he focused on distracting Bellar, keeping him turned away from Lilith to give her the best possible shot at not just hitting Bellar, but killing him.

Lilith let out a yell that contained all the rage, all the pain, all the suffering Bellar had caused her over the centuries. Every single time he'd abused her, humiliated her. Each time that he'd hurt her children. All those emotions and memories gave her strength and she ran forward. The tip of the spear hit Bellar, but she didn't stop, not until it sank deep into his body, penetrating his heart and protruding out the other side.

The sound Bellar made was loud, inhuman, and painful. It was beyond the scream of a wounded animal and somehow as bad as a banshee's shriek. Everyone but Lilith and Samara cringed with their entire bodies and covered their ears. While Lilith may have simply been too strong to be bothered, the only reason Sam didn't react was that she couldn't. She was dying, as surely as he was, and didn't have the strength needed to lift her hands even as far as her head. All she could do was stare into the inky cloud as every part of her throbbed with pain.

The darkness slowly dissipated to reveal a shocked looking demon, his once perfect flesh turning black, radiating outward from the impact point of the spear.

Lilith released the spear then, though it was difficult as her burned skin tried to cling to the wood. Wade gently drew her back as they watched the spear's power destroy Bellar from the inside out. It spread until his body fractured into large pieces, which then disintegrated into gray dust, allowing the spear to fall to the floor with a muted thunk.

"It's over," Lilith breathed, her eyes closing. Though her lips curved, the smile was tight and tears slid down her cheeks. "It's finally over."

CHAPTER 38

For a moment, no one did anything, then Evane limped to Lilith and took her from Wade. "Help Sam," he murmured as Lilith collapsed against him, her body wracked with silent sobs.

Wade knelt in front of Sam and carefully wrapped his arms around her, pulling her into his lap. She was so still, so pale, that his heart nearly stopped. "Suni? She needs help, now," he called, trying not to sound as frantic as he felt. He could feel how slow her heart was beating, and some of her injuries looked deep. Back in the desert had been bad enough, but this? She was so close to death.

Suni left Julian's side and hurried over to Wade and Sam. She didn't have the same prejudice against demons Marco did, and as a healer, it wasn't in her to watch anyone suffer, no matter who or what they were. "Oh gods," she whispered when she saw the condition Sam was in. Before she could lay a hand on Sam, the Fury's body started to shake and she screamed in pain.

"What is it? What's happening to her?" Wade asked, holding her closer.

Sam weakly lifted a hand and reached for the back of her neck before she passed out.

"Lift her up, quickly," Suni ordered, and when Wade complied, she shifted Sam's braid away to see curls of dark smoke rising from now blackened skin. "It looks like her neck's burning."

"All of her neck, or the tattoo?" Evane asked as he half-carried Lilith over to the trio.

Suni leaned a little closer. "You're right, it does look like it's just a tattoo that's affected. Is this significant?"

"It is. Bellar put it on her," Wade said quietly as he kissed Sam's forehead. "Heal her now, Suni, please." He didn't want to go through what Julian had, watching the woman he loved die while he was helpless to do anything to help her. He'd seen what it had done to his friend and he wouldn't have wished that on anyone.

She nodded and laid a hand on a small, unmarked patch of skin. "So much damage…If she wasn't as strong as she is, she wouldn't have held on this long," she told them grimly. Even with her skills as a healer, it took some time to heal Sam completely.

Sam's body relaxed against Wade and a minute later, her eyes fluttered open. "What happened?" she asked, voice low and hoarse.

"The tattoo burned off," Wade told her.

"Good." She curled herself more fully against him and closed her eyes. The peaceful pose only lasted a moment. "Mom!" she cried as her eyes opened and she jerked upright.

Lilith was barely managing to stay on her feet, but she gave a faint smile to her daughter. "I'm here. I'm all right."

"No, you're not. Suni, please, help her. She held the spear," she said urgently.

"Of course." Suni rose to her feet and moved to stand in front of Lilith. She could see that the demon's palms were completely burned, but there were dozens of cuts all over her body as well. She winced in sympathy. "I can see why she's concerned," she told Lilith as she gently laid her fingers on the tops of Lilith's hands. "Your hands aren't going to heal completely," she murmured apologetically after a quick magical check, "but I can take care of the worst of the pain and make sure it doesn't get any worse."

"Why won't it heal?" Evane asked as he moved closer to his mother's side.

"Powerful magic won't always heal completely by other magical means. It should heal on its own, though, especially after I get it started."

"That's fine. It's already feeling better." And Lilith did look improved. Her face wasn't completely devoid of color any longer, and she wasn't swaying with exhaustion and pain.

"If you don't mind me saying," Julian began, "I'm surprised you're still alive after holding it for so long. I thought it would kill any demon who touched it."

Lilith glanced at her children questioningly. When they only shrugged, and Sam said, "It's your choice," she smiled. "I don't know how much of my past has survived to modern times without being...warped, but I didn't begin life as a demon. Even now I'm not wholly demonic."

Marco snorted softly. "You seem demonic to me," he muttered.

Julian shot him a dark look then turned back to Lilith. "Then, if you don't mind telling us, what else are you?"

Lilith studied Marco for a moment before she answered Julian. "Before I was forced to Olarid, I had a name other than Lilith. Before I became Bellar's consort...I was called Echidna."

Neither Evane nor Samara looked surprised at the news, but Wade was the only other one not to react, simply because he didn't recognize the name as anything but some sort of animal.

"The mother of monsters?" Marco asked at the same time Julian's eyes widened and he blurted, "The goddess?"

She inclined her head regally to both men. "Which meant that, while the spear was painful to me, it couldn't kill me unless it was used to strike a lethal blow."

"Wait, if you're a goddess, what does that make Sam?" Wade asked, looking down at the woman in his arms.

"I'm still mostly demon," Samara admitted, "as is Evane. Whatever divine blood was passed to us from Mom is diluted. It might make us a little stronger than other demons, but that's it."

"That...I would love to speak with you at some point," Julian told Lilith, excitement flashing in his eyes.

"Later," Suni said as she released Lilith's hand and took Evane's instead. "You all took quite a beating," she told him as she worked on healing his many injuries as well.

"We did," Marco said from where he still sat against the wall, staring at Lilith, "but Bellar's dead now." He closed his eyes and focused. "Duncan reports that the humans—most of them—just stopped fighting when Bellar was killed. They're confused, and some are hurt, a few of them badly, but shockingly, none of them were killed. They're going to take care of them and do what they can to spin this to something they'll easily believe before taking them home."

"That's good. Though it's surprising no one was killed," Julian said.

"It is." His gaze moved to the three demons—nevermind that one of them was part goddess—and his mouth flattened into an unhappy line. "Are you planning on going back to Olarid?" he asked, his attention lingering on Lilith. He didn't know what she'd done to him, but he didn't like it. It had felt amazing for the first few seconds, then it had felt like hell. He wanted her gone, away from the world he'd vowed to protect. Away from him.

"Would you want to go back?" Lilith asked, one brow arched in challenge. "To a world that you were forced to go to, then essentially imprisoned in all of your life? A world where you were tormented for thousands of years by someone who forced you into a sham of a marriage? A world that means blood and pain and death to you? A world that tried to drive everything good and loving out of your children?" She shook her head slowly. "No, I have no intention of returning there. Besides, Earth is my home, even if most of my life was spent elsewhere."

"I don't want to return either," Evane agreed. "Olarid may have its beauty, and I may have been born there, but it's not home. It never was."

Sam stayed quiet, but her arms wrapping tightly around Wade gave her answer clearly enough.

Marco growled softly. "So you want me to just agree to allow three demons full access to Earth? To let you run around doing whatever it is you do?"

Evane's eyes narrowed. "Some gratitude you show after these three demons helped save your ass. My mom and sister nearly died destroying a threat to *your* world."

"They're right," Julian broke in, his voice calm. "I think they've proven themselves, don't you?" Marco gave him an incredulous look, but he only shrugged. "Sam's been helping us since the moment she got here. You said she warned the Hunters guarding the gate to run, right? And she helped hunt down the spear that ultimately killed her *father*, which was used by her *mother*, even though Lilith knew that just touching it could be fatal. Besides, Lilith—or do you prefer Echidna?"

"I do, though I'm no longer in the habit of answering to it," she answered with a smile. "Bellar wouldn't allow it. He much preferred me to use Lilith because that name didn't say divinity, and Lilith is normally known as someone not to be trusted."

He nodded and turned back to the Hunter. "Echidna is a goddess of Earth." He shook his head. "No, Marco, I think they've earned the right to stay here. She's certainly earned the right to return home."

"Fine," Marco said shortly. "But don't think that we're not going to keep an eye on all three of you. If it looks like you've stepped one toe out of line, we'll come after you," he warned the demons.

Wade growled. "Careful, Marco."

Again stepping in to smooth things over, Julian added, "Evane, Echidna, I'd be happy to help you both settle into living here. And I know Wade will help, too. Get you legal identities, a place to live, things like that."

"That would be wonderful. Thank you," Echidna said with a smile. "I don't imagine Sam needs any help in that department," she added, grinning at her daughter, who was still sitting in Wade's lap.

"Nope," Wade agreed, and the thought had his wolf relaxing.

Sam huffed. "Don't I get a choice in this?"

"Nope," he said again, voice curt this time. "Can you guys give us a minute, though?"

"Yes, but when you're done talking to her, I still need to heal you," Suni told him as she walked to Marco. "And we're going to heal you, too, just as soon as we step outside." She helped him to his feet, then slowly guided him out of the room, the others following.

"Is something wrong?" Sam asked when they were alone, her brows furrowed in concern.

"That depends on you, but hopefully not," Wade said, rubbing his cheek against hers before he nuzzled the spot where he'd marked her. A spot that had been healed with her other injuries. That was okay. He'd just get to mark her again, at the earliest possible moment.

"Well, what is it? Haven't I had enough excitement for one day?" she grumbled.

He chucked and kissed her lightly. "You don't want to go back to Olarid, right?"

"Of course not. Why would I want to go back? Other than to get Keen, anyway. Assuming that's where he is, anyway."

"Good. Then marry me, Sam."

Stunned, Sam stared at him. "You want me to marry you?" It wasn't something she'd expected to ever hear directed to her, but then, she had also expected to die killing Bellar.

He nodded and used his thumb to rub a streak of blood from her cheek. "I told you I loved you, and I meant it. And wolves mate for life, baby. I know we won't have long together since shifters aren't as long-lived as demons, but it'd be a few centuries, and I want those centuries with you," he said, more serious than she'd ever seen him.

To his shock, she laughed softly. For a moment, he could only stare at her, stunned and hurt. "You...think this is funny?" he asked, a growl creeping back into his voice.

She shook her head and lifted her arms to wrap them around his neck. "Not the proposal, no, and not that you love me. They're amazing and wonderful, but not funny."

"Then why in the hell are you laughing?"

"Because you only think we'll have a couple hundred years together."

He leaned back, his face a mask of confusion. "What do you mean? I'm almost three hundred years old. All I've got left is a few centuries. Okay, so hopefully close to seven hundred years, but still, just centuries."

"Without me, perhaps." She smiled and kissed him. "It amazes me sometimes how little self-professed demon hunters know about demons. You know how to kill us, yes, even how to track us or what some of our powers are, but you don't know the important things."

"Such as?"

"That we're not all the same. That being born a demon doesn't make us inherently evil." She smiled. "Or such as the power our blood can have."

"Your blood?"

"My blood. If I were to give you a little of my blood, you'd share in my longevity and you'd probably even get a hint of my powers," she explained, her hand moving up and down his arm. After nearly dying, she found she didn't want to stop touching him, as though the contact was anchoring her to the world of the living.

He frowned. "Would I become a demon? Is that how it'd work?"

She shook her head. "Not for a small amount, no. You'd still be a wolf, you'd just live longer and be able to do more than you can now. If you kept drinking it, then yes, you would eventually become a demon, or at least turn demonic." She glanced at the door the others had gone through and smiled sadly. It made him wonder just how Lilith—Echidna—had turned into a demon, but she went on. "But a few sips, once in your life? No, you'd still be you. I promise."

"Well damn. You guys have kept that secret really close to the chest, haven't you?" Wade said, absolutely shocked.

"Of course. We can't have people hunting us down and keeping us caged so they can drink us to death. Not to mention the fact that most demons are really stingy with their blood and power. They don't share, they take. Hell, in my whole lifetime, I've only heard of two other demons willingly giving their blood to another, and one was ridiculed when it came out."

He glanced at the door as well. "I get that you want to keep this between us, though your mom and brother are going figure it out, I assume. But Julian and Red will need to know, too."

She frowned and cocked her head. "Why?"

He grinned. "Because they're immortal, too, and I don't want to spend eternity hiding from my best friends."

Her fingers absently stroked the back of his neck while she considered. She wanted to know how a couple of witches had gained immortality, but it wasn't important in the moment. "Julian seems very trustworthy, so if you say he'll keep it to himself, then I'll believe you. The same goes for...Red?"

"Her name's Paige, but she's got red hair, so I call her Red. She's like a little sister, and I never had a sibling growing up, so I kind of adopted her."

She smiled. "Then yes, we'll tell them both. But I think before this happens, we should rest up and recover a bit. It can take a lot out of a person."

"We also have to take the spear back to the mound," he reminded her.

"I'd forgotten about that. We should wait until that's done. It wouldn't let me in, remember? If you have my blood in your veins, it may bar you from entering, too."

"Huh. Good point. Okay, rest, recover, return spear, get hitched." He grinned wolfishly. "We could always get hitched here and do the blood thing later. Vegas is known for the many quickie wedding chapels," he teased as he gently eased her off his lap and got to his feet. "Though if you want a big, flashy wedding, we can do that, too."

She laughed and shook her head as he helped her rise. "No, not right now, but here sounds good to me. This city will always be special to me, but not today. We can come back after we've dealt with everything else. And when neither of us are exhausted. I want to thoroughly enjoy my wedding."

He chuckled. "Fair enough." He took her hand and picked up the spear before they left to join the others.

CHAPTER 39

While Sam and Wade were busy talking, the Hunters were busy. As it turned out, four of the people who'd been fighting for Bellar actually lived in the house he'd been using. It made things a little simpler, though it meant that Hunters needed to watch them until the house was cleaned of all signs of the fight.

Julian teleported home and brought Paige back to help deal with the rest of the now confused people. She was a little pale at the sight of all the blood and injuries, but one by one she helped the Hunters modify memories until no one remembered the supernatural events or things they'd seen. It left her exhausted, but looking pleased. And yet, even when the Hunters escorted the humans home and left themselves, she refused to return to England.

When Wade and Sam came downstairs, hand in hand, Julian motioned them over to where he sat with Paige.

Wade grinned and quickened his pace. "Red! Julian didn't say that he was bringing you," he said as he swept Paige up in a hug. "Though you're a little pale. Do I need to kick Julian's ass and tell him to treat you right?" he teased.

She laughed and shook her head. "No, I'm just tired. I helped wipe the memories of the humans. I'll be fine tomorrow, I promise." She drew back and looked at Sam, who stood back a few paces. "Is this Samara?"

"Sam, and yeah, it is," he said proudly as he moved to Sam's side and drew her in close. "Sam, this is Red."

Sam smirked up at him. "I figured when you yelled her name and Julian looked like he wanted to punch you for touching her. It's nice to meet you, but do you prefer Paige or Red?"

"It might be odd having someone other than Wade calling me Red, so Paige, please," the redhead decided. "And it's good to meet you, too."

Wade looked around until he spotted Evane and Echidna, then waved them over. "This is Sam's mom, Lilith—sorry, Echidna—and brother, Evane," he told Paige.

"Echidna? That's an unusual name. I haven't met anyone who's named after her."

Wade grinned wolfishly. "You still haven't. She *is* Echidna."

Paige goggled, though Echidna wasn't the first deity she'd met. But she wasn't given much time to process before Wade went on.

"And this is Julian's wife, Paige." Before anyone could even begin a greeting, he hurried on. "I'm glad you brought Red, actually. I've got something to tell you guys." Paige started to smile and Wade wagged a finger at her. "That's cheating. You know it's dangerous in my head."

Her lips twitched. "I won't say a word," she promised. "Carry on."

Sam was almost as amused as Paige, and tried to hide her laughter against Wade's shoulder, but she couldn't conceal the subtle shaking of her shoulders.

"I see how it is," Wade grumbled, but he grinned only a second later. "Sam's agreed to marry me."

All four started to offer their congratulations, though Echidna seemed happiest for them and gave them both a hug. "I hoped this would happen," she whispered to Wade before she smiled up at him.

Knowing that Echidna was a seer, he cocked his head. "Did you see this exactly?"

She shook her head. "I saw a shadow of it. The future isn't set in stone, but the possibility was there, and I did all I could to make it a reality," she confirmed with a smile.

"Then thank you. I owe you big time."

Still smiling, she shook her head. "No, you don't. You make her happy, and that's all I wanted."

After the well wishing had died down, Wade added, "I tried to talk her into a Vegas wedding since we're here, but she wants to wait a bit. So how do you guys feel about coming back to Vegas in a month or two to see us get married?"

Paige looked surprised. "You want to get married in Las Vegas?"

"I do," Sam confirmed. "From what Wade said, I know it isn't considered the classiest of places, but Vegas is important to me. I got my mom back here, and my dad's evil ended here. It's also where Wade asked me to marry him. Though I want a wedding that's going to last longer than a quickie," she warned him, bumping her hip against his.

"I think that can be arranged," he told her, kissing her temple. "How about you guys still hang around for a day or two anyway? I think we've all earned a short vacation."

"I don't think we're going anywhere for few days," Evane said with a shrug. "Especially not if my mom and sister are going to be here."

Echidna smiled. "It has been too long since we were able to spend time as a family. I'll stay as long as my children are here."

Julian cleared his throat quietly. "I know I mentioned it before, but since you're staying here, I really would like to speak to you at some point. I'm a demonologist, and I'll confess that I've read about you—both as Lilith and Echidna—but from what Sam has said, it's not accurate."

She hesitated before slowly nodding. "I can't promise that I'll tell you everything about my past, but I'll tell you some."

"That's all I'm asking. I don't like to pry into people's lives, and I'm discreet."

"He is," Wade confirmed. "You can trust him as far as that goes."

She smiled. "I'll keep that in mind. Now, I'd very much like to go somewhere to clean up," she said, plucking at her blood-soaked shirt.

"I think I can take care of that," Julian said, stepping in the middle of their loose circle and extending his arm. "How do you feel about a trip to England instead of spending a few days in a hotel room?"

"Since I left some clothes there last time, I'm game," Wade said, and the others all agreed, so Wade yelled to Marco that they were leaving before Julian took them all to Mooreton.

Five people was a lot to teleport at once, but soon enough, they all stood in the study of his home. "Make yourselves at home. Wade, you can have your usual room. Echidna, Evane, I'll show you to your rooms."

"Sounds good. See you all in the morning," Wade said before he lightly tossed Sam over his shoulder and grinned. "Maybe tomorrow afternoon," he added as Sam gave a surprised shriek.

"Put me down, wolf!" she said as she hung upside down, though she was laughing.

"In a minute," he said before he hurried up the stairs to the room that had unofficially become his.

Behind him, he heard Julian say, "I think I should put you two on the opposite side of the house from them..."

Wade didn't stop until he'd closed the door and carefully dropped Sam on the edge of the bed.

She instantly bounded up to her feet, but before she could get a word out, he was kissing her. Wild and passionate, it instantly heated her blood and made her head spin. But he wasn't content just to kiss her. What remained of her halter was literally ripped off her before he started to work on her pants.

Though she seemed to always want him, this display of how badly he needed her made her body come alive and she forgot all about playfully chiding him for carrying her off in favor of getting him naked as quickly as she could. They had both come so close to dying, and now that the adrenaline of the fight was fading, she discovered she desperately needed him, too.

As her pants were pushed down, her hands dove beneath his shirt and skimmed low over his belly, making him growl. She shoved his shirt up until he had to break the kiss so she could get it off him, but the second it was gone his mouth was on hers again and he yanked her close, so her breasts were crushed against his chest.

He kicked his boots off as she got his pants undone and yanked them over his hips. Already hard, he sprung free and pressed against her belly. The feel of her against him drew another growl from his lips, and his hold on her shifted so he could scoop her up. Except, understanding he was about to throw her on the bed, Sam wiggled free of his grip and sank down to her knees. His hands tangled in her hair.

"Sam...you don't have to...I don't know if I have the patience tonight," he warned her. Once again he'd come so close to losing her, and he needed to prove to himself that she was well and whole and his, which made his control thin now that they were alone.

She rubbed her cheek against his thigh. "I want to do this, so try," she murmured, and his cock jerked at the wash of warm breath over him. When she kissed along his length, he groaned and had to close his eyes. If he had to watch, this would be over before she'd even begun, and he wasn't going to stop until he'd joined his body with hers. As it was, when he felt her hot mouth close around the head of his shaft, he nearly lost it.

Testingly, she slid her lips over him, and his hands tightened in her hair. His whole body shook with the effort not to spill on her tongue. And still he wasn't able to stand it for more than a few moments before he gently tugged her off him. It took an act of intense will to manage it, because it felt so damn good, but there was something that would feel so much better.

"Anymore of that and I'll be useless to you." Wade drew her to her feet, then backed her up against the bed. An arm wrapped around her hips and he lifted her up and onto the comforter. Her legs spread for him and he settled between them. When he brushed against her damp folds, he almost shouted in relief to find her ready for him. Without another word, he slid slowly into her, not stopping until she'd taken him completely. She gasped and rocked up to meet him as her head fell back.

He ground against her. "You'd better hold on to me."

"Always." Sam wrapped her arms around him and he started to move. There wasn't any control tonight, not after everything. Both were mindless for one another, eager, desperate to sate their bodies while reassuring their hearts. He slammed into her over and over as he stared down into her eyes. Nails dug into his back, while only spurred him to move faster, harder, until she was writhing beneath him.

"Come for me, baby," he growled, as he slid a hand between them. His thumb found her clit and rubbed, which made her cry his name as her nails scored down his back.

Between one stroke and the next, she splintered beneath him. Her legs lifted and clamped around his hips, pulling him flush against her and joining them completely. Though he couldn't move in her grip, the feel of her clutching him so tightly broke the last of his restraint. He captured her mouth again as they fell together, holding each other like they'd never let the other go.

As the high slowly dwindled, the kiss gentled, as did her hold on him, until they lay entwined and sated, adoring each other.

He propped himself up on an elbow but made no effort to move off her. "I thought I was going to lose you earlier," he murmured, brushing a strand of hair back from her face.

She stroked her hands up and down his back, loving the feel of his hard, hot body beneath her fingers. "I know," she responded quietly. "I thought the same about you. I was willing to do anything to keep Bellar from killing you."

"Don't. Save yourself, if we're ever in a situation like that again," he said, shaking his head as his arms tightened around her. "I'd never been more scared than when I thought you might die."

"Hey, he's dead. Yes, there are other bastards out there, but I doubt there are any as bad as he was." She smiled and lifted her head to kiss him. "And we're both strong, both tough, and we're not alone. We've got friends, we've got family. And in a pinch, we've got the Hunters."

"I know, but I don't want to feel that kind of fear again, so do your best not to be in that kind of danger again. Please."

"I'll do my best, as long as you do the same," she promised.

"I will. And thank you. Now, we need a shower," he said, kissing the tip of her nose, "because you stink."

"Hey!" she cried out in mock outrage and shoved at his shoulder until he rolled off of her.

He kept going, rolling off the bed and onto his feet, grinning at her.

She chased him into the shower, and he showed her again just how much he loved her.

EPILOGUE

Keen appeared at Julian's home only hours after they did, and he was relieved to hear that Bellar was gone and they'd no longer be going back to Olarid. He was a little concerned until Wade and Sam both made it clear that he could live with them if he wanted. That thrilled him, especially after Wade promised that he had access to hundreds of movies.

Who knew the way to an imp's heart was through cartoons? He made a note to stock up on more movies soon.

A week later, Julian had returned Wade, Sam, and her family back to the United States. Echidna and Evane got a two-bedroom house not far from Wade's cabin after they decided to stay close for a while. No one could blame them, not after Bellar had kept them from being a family for so long.

Marco had one of the Hunters return Wade's car to him, so the SUV was sitting in front of Wade's cabin when they got back, all their things inside.

Julian helped Wade and Sam out by offering the use of his plane to get down to Louisiana, since they couldn't get the spear on a commercial flight and had both had enough of road trips for a while. They rented a car once on the ground and drove back to the mound where they'd found the spear. This time, they found the location more easily and had no problem opening the lock. They each cut the palm of their hand and smeared the blood on the stone.

As they walked around to the hollow tree, Sam took his free hand. "I wish I could go in with you. I'd love to meet this ghost that's protecting the spear."

"I know. I wish you could, too. I've seen ghosts before, but never one who was quite so lucid. Not to mention one who could actually touch something so easily," Wade said, giving her hand a squeeze.

"I wonder how he's going to feel about the spear being used by a demon, on a demon."

"Not sure, but I can't keep it from him," he said, shrugging. "For all I know, it affected the magic of the spear. But your mom being part goddess might help. Either way, it's done, so we can't exactly do anything about it at this point."

Sam frowned. "I hadn't thought about that. I hope not. A weapon like that is too important to ruin, even if it did mean that it saved the Earth from corruption by Bellar."

He stopped in front of the tree and kissed her. "Whatever happens, we'll get through it. Don't worry about it too much. Just think about how when we get home, we'll make sure that we get that forever we want."

She grinned. "That's a much better thought. Now hurry, take the spear back to the ghost so we can go home and make this forever."

He returned the grin and stepped through the tree. More confident on this second trip into the mound, he made it quickly to the main chamber. The shaft of light was still extinguished, and the chamber empty until the ghost materialized.

"Is it done? Is the evil dead?" he asked.

Wade nodded. "He is. The spear worked even better than I could have hoped. Thank you for allowing me to use it."

Something must have shown on Wade's face, because the ghost cocked his head. "What is it? Did something happen?" He stepped closer, examined the weapon in Wade's hand. "The spear looks intact."

"It is, but...it wasn't my hand that used it against Bellar. Another demon picked it up and used it," he confessed.

He hadn't known a ghost could look so surprised, but this one did. "And this second demon...was it the one outside now, or did that demon perish as well?"

Wade shook his head. "No, it wasn't Sam. It was her mother, and she survived. It did hurt her and leave her exceptionally drained, but she lived."

"That is...remarkable. I truly didn't believe any demon could use it and survive."

"She isn't fully demonic. She began life as a goddess. We think that's what saved her."

The ghost beckoned Wade forward then held out his hands for the spear. When it was given to him, he wrapped his fingers around the shaft and closed his eyes. "The magic remains, though it's changed. It's subtle, so the spear should work as intended on any other demons it's used against."

Wade let out a relieved breath. "I'm glad to hear it. I didn't want to mess up the spear, but we probably would have all died if Lilith—Echidna—hadn't used the spear on Bellar."

The ghost moved to where the light had been and held the spear out before releasing it. It began to hover, just as Wade had first seen it, and the glow returned, bathing the weapon. "I understand. And it was better to potentially destroy it to save the world than to save it for a future threat that may never surface. Thank you for keeping your word and returning it here to me."

"No thanks needed." He hesitated, unsure if he should offer something more to the ghost. To visit and break up the monotony of the passing years, perhaps.

The ghost smiled. "You can go without guilt. I don't feel the weight of time like you probably imagine. I sleep when the mound is empty, so it only feels like minutes since you were last here, rather than however long it has truly been."

"Oh. Well, good. I'll check in now and again, though, or send someone to check in. Just to make sure no one's stolen the spear or anything and to say hi."

"I'd appreciate that. Now go, your woman waits."

Wade grinned. "She's impatient, too. Be safe," he said before leaving the mound.

"What'd he say?" Sam asked the moment she saw him.

"The spear's changed a little, but not bad. It should be fine. Now let's go home. I want to claim you as mine so we can hurry up and get married," Wade said, and picked her up in a fireman's carry again.

She laughed and landed a playful smack to his butt. "You love doing this way too much."

It took longer than Wade would have liked to make it back to his Montana cabin. Sam made noises about stopping in to see her mom and Evane, but Wade pointed out that they'd still be there tomorrow.

They walked into the cabin and Sam headed for the fridge, grabbing a bottle of water.

"So how's this work? Is it a full on vampire exchange, with the neck biting and blood sucking? Or more, just make a cut somewhere and I drink it?" Wade asked, leaning a hip against the counter.

"Well, I don't think your teeth are really good for puncturing, so I'm voting no on the neck biting." Sam paused, then smiled. "Not for that, anyway. Some nibbling in bed, though, now that I enjoy. Especially when you mark me."

He gave her a toothy grin. "So noted."

"Easiest is just to make a cut just deep enough to bleed. It tends to be less messy than other methods, and I can choose a place that won't be too painful." She took a drink while watching him, concern and love both showing in her black eyes. "You ready for this? There'll be a physical sensation at the very least, and since we're not sure which of my powers you'll get—if any—I can't tell you how that'll manifest. Though it is doubtful you'll get my main Fury abilities since they only go to women."

He walked over to her. "I don't want to leave you in a few centuries, so I'm ready. I don't care if I just get the crappy side effects of your power, or if my fur turns to feathers. That's not the reason why I'm doing this. I'm doing this to be with you."

She laughed. "A feathered wolf? I'm kind of hoping for that, now." She set the water aside and drew her knife. He gave a sympathetic wince when she drew the point of the blade along the fleshy part of her hand beneath her thumb. Blood welled up and she offered it to him. "You don't have to take much. Just a few swallows is enough. Anything more than that and you risk turning more demonic than you'd like."

He nodded and cradled her hand in his. Before he even touched the blood, he kissed her wrist then the middle of her palm, making her shiver. Only then did his mouth cover the cut and he watched her as he swallowed once, twice, drawing his mouth back at her nod.

Sam watched him with a worried expression. "How do you feel?"

Wade mentally assessed his body. "Fine, I guess. I don't feel any—" A surge of energy rushed through him, filling every cell of his body. "Oh wow, that was almost as good as sex," he said breathlessly. But the effects of the blood weren't finished with him yet.

A sharp pain shot through his back and he hissed in a breath as his body bowed.

"What is it?" Sam asked in a rush, laying a hand on his cheek and studying his face intently.

"My back." The pain surged higher, before a new kind of agony presented itself. It didn't feel like any part of his body that could identify, and his shirt was suddenly tight enough he heard a seam rip.

She stepped around him and gasped. "Quick, take your shirt off," she said, even as she drew the blade through the material, cutting it in half.

Instantly, he felt better and relaxed fractionally. "What is it? What happened?"

Slowly, she answered with, "You know how you joked about having feathers instead of fur?"

"Yeah." It clicked. "No way. I've got wings?" he asked excitedly, trying to twist around to see them. Unfortunately, they moved as he did, so he couldn't get more than a glimpse.

"You've got wings," she confirmed and gently extended one of them so he could see the feathers that were identical to hers. "I'll admit, this is a new one. I didn't know you could get something physical beyond the longevity," she admitted, but she was smiling with delight as she released his wing, then drew her fingers across the feathers. "You should be able to hide them at will like I do. Just think of pulling them into your body."

He focused for a moment and they hid themselves within his back. Another few seconds, and they were back out. It was basically like shifting into his wolf form, which meant it was easy for him. "This is amazing! I wonder if I'll have them in wolf form, too. Imagine how badass a flying wolf would be."

She laughed and stroked her fingers over his wings, which made him shiver. "I'm just happy that we'll be able to fly together. You'll love it."

"Let's go try now. And later we can fly over to see your mom and Evane. And I promise to hide the wings at the wedding."

She grinned as she freed her wings and walked outside with him. "You'd better, since we'll be around humans. But when it's just me? I kind of like seeing my wings on you."

Hand in hand, they spent the rest of the night practicing flying, and the early hours of the morning in bed, loving each other.

Two weeks later, when they did the same thing, they did it as husband and wife.

COMING SOON

The Last Lemurian

Releasing July 25, 2023

No one expects to discover a slumbering woman in a long-sealed tomb.

When treasure hunter Seth Montgomery does just that, he inadvertently signs up for the craziest and most dangerous month of his life.

As the last member of a forgotten race, Tempest finds herself the target of gods and mortals alike. Having slept for thousands of years, she has no choice but to trust in strangers.

Learning what happened to her people will require a great deal of luck, because someone is willing to kill to prevent the truth of the Lemurians from ever surfacing again.

ABOUT AUTHOR

Meg M. Robinson is a fantasy author who lives in north Georgia with her husband, a teenager, and a small menagerie of animals. She's goofy and a little dorky, which greatly amuses her family.

She's obsessed with crows, sea turtles, and houseplants. And, of course, books. When she's not focused on either reading or writing a book, she enjoys playing video games, archery, and baking.

www.megmrobinson.com

9 781960 218018